Thomas Arnold, Arthur P. Stanley

The Life and Correspondence of Thomas Arnold, D.D.

Volume 1

Thomas Arnold, Arthur P. Stanley

The Life and Correspondence of Thomas Arnold, D.D.
Volume 1

ISBN/EAN: 9783337399726

Printed in Europe, USA, Canada, Australia, Japan

Cover: Foto ©Andreas Hilbeck / pixelio.de

More available books at **www.hansebooks.com**

THE
LIFE AND CORRESPONDENCE

OF

THOMAS ARNOLD, D.D.,

LATE HEAD-MASTER OF RUGBY SCHOOL, AND REGIUS PROFESSOR OF MODERN HISTORY IN THE UNIVERSITY OF OXFORD.

By ARTHUR PENRHYN STANLEY, D.D.,

DEAN OF WESTMINSTER.

IN TWO VOLUMES.—VOL. I.

TENTH EDITION.

London:
JOHN MURRAY, ALBEMARLE STREET.
1877.

PREFACE

THE sources from which this work has been drawn have necessarily been exceedingly various. It was in fact originally intended that the several parts should have been supplied by different writers, as in the instance of the valuable contribution which, in addition to his kind assistance throughout, has been furnished to the earlier part by Mr. Justice Coleridge; and although, in its present shape, the responsibility of arranging and executing it has fallen upon one person, yet it should still be clearly understood how largely I have availed myself of the aid of others, in order to supply the defects of my own personal knowledge of Dr. Arnold's life and character, which was confined to the intercourse I enjoyed with him, first as his pupil at Rugby, from 1829 to 1834, and thenceforward, on more familiar terms, to the end of his life.

To his family, I feel that the fewest words will best express my sense, both of the confidence which they reposed in me by entrusting to my care so precious a charge, and of the manifold kindness with which they have assisted me, as none others could. To the many attached friends of his earlier years, the occurrence of whose names in the following pages makes it unnecessary to mention them more particularly here, I would also take, this opportunity of expressing my deep obligations, not only for the readiness with which they have given me access to all letters and information that I could require, but still more for the active interest which they have taken in lightening my responsibility and labour, and for the careful and most valuable criticism to which some of them have allowed me to subject the whole or the greater part of this work. Lastly, his pupils will perceive the unsparing use I have made of their numerous contributions. I had at one time thought of indicating the various distinct authorities from which the chapter on his "School Life at Rugby" has been compiled, but I found that this would be impracticable. The names of some of those who have most aided me will be found in the Correspondence. To those many others, who are not there mentioned—and may I here be allowed more especially to name my younger schoolfellows, with whom I have become acquainted chiefly through the means of this work, and whose recollections, as being the most recent and the most lively, have been amongst the most valuable that I have received—I would here express my warmest thanks for the more than assistance which they have rendered me. Great as has been the anxiety and difficulty of this undertaking, it has been relieved by nothing so much as the assurance which I have received through their co-operation, that I was not mistaken in the estimate I had formed of our common friend and master, and that the influence of his teaching and example continues and will continue to produce the fruits which he would most have desired to see.

The Correspondence has been selected from the mass of letters preserved, in many cases, in almost unbroken series from first to last. One large class—those to the parents of his pupils—I have been unable to procure, and possibly they could not have been made available for the present work. Another numerous body of letters—those which were addressed to scientific or literary men on questions connected with his edition of Thucydides or his History,—I have omitted, partly as thinking them too minute to occupy space wanted for subjects of more general importance; partly because their substance or their results have for the most part been incorporated into his published works. To those which appear in the present collection, something of a fragmentary character has been imparted by the necessary omission, wherever it was possible, of repetitions, such as must necessarily occur in letters written to different persons at the same time, —of allusions which would have been painful to living individuals,—of domestic details, which, however characteristic, could not have been published without a greater infringement on privacy than is yet possible,— of passages which, without further explanation than could be given, would certainly have been misunderstood. Still, enough remains to give in his own words, and in his own manner, what he thought and felt on the subjects of most interest to him. And though the mode of expression must be judged by the relation in which he stood to those whom he addressed, and with the usual and just allowance for the familiarity and unreservedness of epistolary intercourse, yet, on the whole, the Letters represent (except where they correct themselves) what those who knew him best believe to have been his deliberate convictions and his habitual feelings.

The object of the Narrative has been to state so much as would enable the reader to enter upon the Letters with a correct understanding of their writer in his different periods of life, and his different spheres of action. In all cases where it was possible, his opinions and plans have been given in his own words, and in no case, whether in speaking of what he did or intended to do, from mere conjecture of my own or of any one else. Wherever the Narrative has gone into greater detail, as in the chapter on his "School Life at Rugby," it has been where the Letters were comparatively silent, and where details alone would give to those who were most concerned a true representation of his views and actions.

In conclusion, it will be obvious that to have mixed up any judgment of my own, either of praise or censure, with the facts or the statements contained in this work would have been wholly irrelevant. The only question which I have allowed myself to ask in each particular act or opinion that has come before me, has been not whether I approved or disapproved of it, but whether it was characteristic of him. To have assumed the office of a judge, in addition to that of a narrator or editor, would have increased the responsibility, already great, a hundredfold; and in the present case, the vast importance of many of the questions discussed—the insufficient time and knowledge which I had at command—the almost filial relation in which I stood towards him—would have rendered it absolutely impossible, even had it not been effectually precluded by the nature of the work itself. For similar reasons, I have abstained from giving any formal account of his general character. He was one of a class whose whole being, intellectual, moral, and spiritual, is like the cloud of the poet,

> Which moveth altogether, if it move at all,

and whose character, therefore, is far better expressed by their own words and deeds, than by the representation of others. Lastly, I would also hope that the plan, which I have thus endeavoured to follow, will in some measure compensate for the many deficiencies, which I have vainly endeavoured to remedy in the execution of the task which I have undertaken. Some, indeed, there must be, who will painfully feel the contrast, which probably always exists in the case of any remarkable man, between the image of his inner life, as it was known to those nearest and dearest to him, and the outward image of a written biography, which can rarely be more than a faint shadow of what they cherish in their own recollections—the one representing what he was—the other only what he thought and did ; the one formed in the atmosphere which he had himself created,—the other necessarily accommodating itself to the public opinion to which it is mainly addressed. But even to these — and much more to readers in general—it is my satisfaction to reflect that any untrue or imperfect impression of his thoughts and feelings which may be gathered from my account of them will be sufficiently corrected by his own representation of them in his Letters, and that the attention will not be diverted by any extraneous comments or inferences from the lessons which will be best learned from the mere record itself of his life and teaching.

May 14th, 1844.
University College, Oxford.

The additions contained in this and the previous editions, subsequent to the first, are contained in a Supplement.

CONTENTS OF VOL. I.

CHAPTER I.

EARLY LIFE AND EDUCATION.

CHAPTER II.

LIFE AT LALEHAM.

LETTERS.

CHAPTER III.

SCHOOL LIFE AT RUGBY.

State of opinion on English Public Schools—His qualifications for
the situation of Head-master of Rugby—Difficulties—Changes—
Fixed principles of education—His relation to the public—To
the trustees—To the assistant-masters—To the school—His

CHAPTER IV.

GENERAL LIFE AT RUGBY.

CHAPTER V.

LIFE AND CORRESPONDENCE, AUGUST 1828 TO AUGUST 1830.

LETTERS.

CHAPTER VI.

LIFE AND CORRESPONDENCE, SEPTEMBER 1830 TO DECEMBER 1832.

Alarm at the social condition of the lower orders in England—Wish
    to rouse the Clergy—Attempts to influence the Useful Know-
    ledge Society—Establishment of the *Englishman's Register*—
    Thirteen letters in the Sheffield *Courant*—Want of Sympathy
    —Evangelical party—Wish for Commentary on Old Testament—
    Second Volume of Sermons, with Essays on Interpretation of
    Scripture   241

LETTERS.

CHAPTER VII.

LIFE AND CORRESPONDENCE, JANUARY 1833 TO SEPTEMBER 1835.

Fears for the Church Establishment—Pamphlet on the " Principles
of Church Reform "—Outcry occasioned by it—Settlement of his
own views—Preface to the third volume of Thucydides—Fragments on " the State and the Church "—Third Volume of Sermons—Purchase of Fox How—Return to Roman History—
Influence over his Scholars 286

LETTERS.

The names of his former Rugby pupils, where not otherwise specified, are marked with an *.

The names of his Laleham pupils are marked by a †.

The letters of the alphabet affixed are merely for the sake of distinguishing between the several pupils.

THE LIFE

OF

THOMAS ARNOLD, D.D.

CHAPTER I.

EARLY LIFE AND EDUCATION.

THOMAS ARNOLD, seventh child and youngest son of William and Martha Arnold, was born on June 13th, 1795, at West Cowes, in the Isle of Wight, where his family had been settled for two generations, their original residence having been at Lowestoff, in Suffolk.

His father, who was collector of the Customs at Cowes, died suddenly of spasm in the heart, on March 3rd, 1801. His two elder brothers, William and Matthew, died, the first in 1806, the second in 1820. His sisters all survived him, with the exception of the third, Susannah, who, after a lingering complaint in the spine, died at Laleham in 1832.

His early education was confided by his mother to her sister, Miss Delafield, who took an affectionate pride in her charge, and directed all his studies as a child. In 1803 he was sent to Warminster school, in Wiltshire, under Dr. Griffiths, with whose assistant master, Mr. Lawes, he kept up his intercourse long after they had parted. In 1807 he was removed to Winchester, where, having entered as a commoner, and afterwards become a scholar of the college, he remained till 1811. In after life he always cherished a strong Wykehamist feeling, and, during his head-mastership at Rugby, often recurred to his knowledge, there first acquired, of the peculiar constitution of a public school, and to his recollections of the tact in managing boys shown by Dr. Goddard, and the skill in imparting scholarship which distinguished Dr. Gabell ;—both, during his stay there, successively head-masters of Winchester.

He was then, as always, of a shy and retiring disposition, but his manner as a child, and till his entrance at Oxford, was marked by a stiffness and formality the very reverse of the joyousness and simplicity of his later years ; his family and schoolfellows both remember him as unlike those of his own age, and with peculiar pursuits of his own ; and the tone and style of his early letters, which have been for the most part preserved, are such as might naturally have been produced by living chiefly in the company of his elders, and reading, or hearing read to him before he could read himself, books suited to a more advanced age. His boyish friendships were strong and numerous. It is needless here to enumerate the names of those Winchester schoolfellows of whose after years it was the pride and delight to watch the course of their companion through life ; but the fond recollections, which were long cherished on both sides, of his intercourse with his earliest friend at Warminster, of whom he saw and heard nothing from that time till he was called upon in 1829 to write his epitaph, are worth recording,* as a remarkable instance of strong impressions of nobleness of character, early conceived and long retained.

* See Letter on the death of George Evelyn, in 1829.

Both as a boy and a young man he was remarkable for a difficulty in early rising, amounting almost to a constitutional infirmity; and though his after life will show how completely this was overcome by habit, yet he often said that early rising was a daily effort to him, and that in this instance he never found the truth of the usual rule, that all things are made easy by custom. With this, however, was always united great occasional energy; and one of his schoolfellows gives it as his impression of him that "he was stiff in his opinions, and utterly immovable by force or fraud, when he had made up his mind, whether right or wrong."

It is curious to trace the beginnings of some of his later interests in his earliest amusements and occupations. He never lost the recollection of the impression produced upon him by the excitement of naval and military affairs, of which he naturally saw and heard much by living at the Isle of Wight in the time of the war; and the sports in which he took most pleasure, with the few playmates of his childhood, were in sailing rival fleets in his father's garden, or acting the battles of the Homeric heroes with whatever implements he could use as spear and shield, and reciting their several speeches from Pope's translation of the Iliad. He was from his earliest years extremely fond of ballad poetry, which his Winchester schoolfellows used to learn from his repetition before they had seen it in print; and his own compositions as a boy all ran in the same direction. A play of this kind, in which his schoolfellows were introduced as the dramatis personæ, and a long poem of " Simon de Montfort," in imitation of Scott's Marmion, procured for him at school, by way of distinction from another boy of the same name, the appellation of Poet Arnold. And the earliest specimen of his composition which has been preserved is a little tragedy, written before he was seven years old, on "Piercy, Earl of Northumberland," suggested apparently by Home's play of Douglas; which, however, contains nothing worthy of notice, except, perhaps, the accuracy of orthography, language, and blank verse metre, in which it is written, and the precise arrangement of the different acts and scenes.

He was, however, most remarked for his forwardness in history and geography. It was on these subjects that he chiefly gave early indications of that strong power of memory which, though in later years it depended mainly on association, used to show itself in very minute details, extending to the exact state of the weather on particular days, or the exact words and position of passages which he had not seen for twenty years. One of the few recollections which he retained of his father was, that he received from him, at three years old, a present of Smollett's History of England, as a reward for the accuracy with which he had gone through the stories connected with the portraits and pictures of the successive reigns; and at the same age he used to sit at his aunt's table arranging his geographical cards, and recognising by their shape at a glance the different counties of the dissected map of England.

He long retained a grateful remembrance of the miscellaneous books to which he had access in the school library at Warminster, and when, in his Professorial chair at Oxford, he quoted Dr. Priestley's Lectures on History, it was from his recollection of what he had there read when he was eight years old. At Winchester he was a diligent student of Russell's Modern Europe; Gibbon and Mitford he had read twice over before he left school; and amongst the comments on his reading and the bursts of political enthusiasm on the events of the day in which he indulged in his Winchester letters, it is curious, as connected with his later labours, to read his indignation, when fourteen years old, "at the numerous boasts which are everywhere to be met with in the Latin writers." "I verily believe," he adds, "that half at least of the Roman history is, if not totally false, at least scandalously exaggerated: how far different are the modest, unaffected, and impartial narrations of Herodotus, Thucydides, and Xenophon."

The period both of his home and school education was too short to exercise much influence upon his after life. But he always looked back upon it with a marked tenderness. The keen sense which he entertained of the bond of relationship and of early association,—not the less from the blank in his own domestic recollections, occasioned by his father's death and his own subsequent removal from the Isle of Wight,—invested with a peculiar interest the scenes and companions of his childhood. His strong domestic affections had acted as an important safeguard to him when he was thrown at so early an age into the new sphere of an Oxford life; and when, in later years, he was left the head of the family, he delighted in gathering round him the remains of his father's household, and in treasuring up every particular relating to his birthplace and parentage, even to the graves of the older generations of the family in the parish church at Lowestoff, and the great willow tree in his father's grounds at Slattwoods, from which he transplanted shoots successively to Laleham, to Rugby, and to Fox How. Every date in the family history, with the alteration of hereditary names, and the changes of their residence, was carefully preserved for his children in his own handwriting, and when in after years he fixed on the abode of his old age in Westmoreland, it was his great delight to regard it as a continuation of his own early home in the Isle of Wight. And when, as was his wont, he used to look back from time to time over the whole of this period, it was with the solemn feeling which is expressed in one of his later journals, written on a visit to the place of his earliest school education, in the interval between the close of his life at Laleham, and the beginning of his work at Rugby. "Warminster, January 5th [1828]. I have not written this date for more than twenty years, and how little could I foresee, when I wrote it last, what would happen to me in the interval. And now to look forward twenty years—how little can I guess of that also. Only may He in whose hands are time and eternity, keep me evermore His own; that whether I live, I may live unto Him; or whether I die, I may die unto him; may He guide me with his counsel, and after that receive me to glory through Jesus Christ our Saviour."

In 1811, in his 16th year, he was elected as a scholar at Corpus Christi College, Oxford; in 1814, his name was placed in the first class in Litteræ Humaniores; in the next year he was elected Fellow of Oriel College; and he gained the Chancellor's prize for the two University Essays, Latin and English, for the years 1815 and 1817. Those who know the influence which his college friendships exercised over his after life, and the deep affection which he always bore to Oxford, as the scene of the happiest recollections of his youth, and the sphere which he hoped to occupy with the employments of his old age, will rejoice in the possession of the following record of his under-graduate life by that true and early friend, to whose timely advice, protection, and example, at the critical period when he was thrown with all the spirits and the inexperience of boyhood on the temptations of the University, he always said and felt, that "he had owed more than to any other man in the world."

LETTER FROM MR. JUSTICE COLERIDGE.

Heath's Court, September, 1843.

MY DEAR STANLEY,

When you informed me of Mrs. Arnold's wish that I would contribute to your memoir of our dear friend, Dr. Arnold, such recollections as I had of his career as an under-graduate at Oxford, with the intimation that they were intended to fill up that chapter in his life, my only hesitation in complying with her wish, arose from my doubts, whether my impressions were so fresh and true, or my powers of expression such as to enable me to do justice to the subject. A true and lively picture of him at that time would be, I am sure, interesting in itself; and I feel certain also that his Oxford residence contributed essentially to the formation of his character in after life. My doubts remain; but I have not thought them important enough to prevent my endeavouring at least to comply with her request; nor will I deny that I promise myself much pleasure, melancholy though it may be, in this attempt to recall those days. They had their troubles, I dare say, but in retrospect they always appear to me among the brightest and least chequered, if not the most useful, which have ever been vouchsafed to me.

Arnold and I, as you know, were under-graduates of Corpus Christi, a college very small in its numbers, and humble in its buildings, but to which we and our fellow-students formed an attachment never weakened in the after course of our lives. At the time I speak of, 1809, and thenceforward for some few years, it was under the presidency, mild and inert, rather than paternal, of Dr. Cooke. His nephew, Dr. Williams, was the vice-president and medical fellow, the only lay fellow permitted by the statutes. Retired he was in his habits, and not forward to interfere with the pursuits or studies of the young men. But I am bound to record not only his learning and good taste, but the kindness of his heart, and his readiness to assist them by advice and criticism in their compositions. When I wrote for the Latin verse prize, in 1810, I was much indebted to him for advice in matters of taste and Latinity, and for the pointing out many faults in my rough verses.

Our tutors were the present Sedleian Professor, the Rev. G. L. Cooke, and the lately deceased President, the Rev. T. Bridges. Of the former, because he is alive, I will only say that I believe no one ever attended his lectures without learning to admire his unwearied industry, patience, and good temper, and that few, if any, quitted his pupil room without retaining a kindly feeling towards him. The recent death of Dr. Bridges would have affected Arnold as it has me: he was a most amiable man; the affectionate earnestness of his manner, and his high tone of feeling, fitted him especially to deal with young men; he made us always desirous of pleasing him; perhaps his fault was that he was too easily pleased; I am sure that he will be long and deeply regretted in the University.

It was not, however, so much by the authorities of the college that Arnold's character was affected, as by its constitution and system, and by the residents whom it was his fortune to associate with familiarly there. I shall hardly do justice to my subject, unless I state a few particulars as to the former, and what I am at liberty to mention as to the latter. Corpus is a very small establishment—twenty fellows, and twenty scholars, with four exhibitioners form the foundation.   No independent members were admitted except gentlemen commoners, and they were limited to six.   Of the scholars several were bachelors, and the whole number of students actually under college tuition seldom exceeded twenty.   But the scholarships, though not entirely open, were yet enough so to admit of much competition ; their value, and still more, the creditable strictness and impartiality with which the examinations were conducted (qualities at that time more rare in college elections than now) insured a number of good candidates for each vacancy, and we boasted a more than proportionate share of successful competitors for university honours.   It had been generally understood (I know not whether the statutes prescribe the practice) that in the examinations a large allowance was made for youth ! certain it was that we had many very young candidates, and that of these, many remarkable for early proficiency succeeded.   We were then a small society, the members rather under the usual age, and with more than the ordinary proportion of ability and scholarship ; our mode of tuition was in harmony with these circumstances ; not by private lectures, but in classes of such a size as excited emulation, and made us careful in the exact and neat rendering of the original, yet not so numerous as to prevent individual attention on the tutor's part, and familiar knowledge of each pupil's turn and talents.   In addition to the books read in lecture, the tutor at the beginning of the term settled with each student upon some book to be read by himself in private, and prepared for the public examination at the end of the term in Hall ; and with this book something on paper, either analysis of it, or remarks upon it, was expected to be produced, which insured that the book should have really been read.   It has often struck me since, that this whole plan, which is now I believe in common use in the University, was well devised for the tuition of young men of our age. We were not entirely set free from the leading-strings of the school; accuracy was cared for; we were accustomed to *viva voce* rendering, and *viva voce* question and answer in our lecture-room, before an audience of fellow-students, whom we sufficiently respected; at the same time the additional reading, trusted to ourselves alone, prepared us for accurate private study, and for our final exhibition in the schools.

One result of all these circumstances was, that we lived on the most familiar terms with each other : we might be, indeed we were, somewhat boyish in manner, and in the liberties we took with each other ; but our interest in literature, ancient and modern, and in all the stirring matters of that stirring time, was not boyish ; we debated the classic and romantic question ; we discussed poetry and history, logic and philosophy : or we fought over the Peninsular battles and the Continental campaigns with the energy of disputants personally concerned in them. Our habits were inexpensive and temperate : one break-up party was held in the junior common room at the end of each term, in which we indulged our genius more freely and our merriment, to say the truth, was somewhat exuberant and noisy; but the authorities wisely forebore too strict an inquiry into this.

It was one of the happy peculiarities of Corpus that the bachelor scholars were compelled to residence. This regulation, seemingly inconvenient, but most wholesome as I cannot but think for themselves, and now unwisely relaxed, operated very beneficially on the under-graduates; with the best and the most advanced of these they associated very usefully : I speak here with grateful and affectionate remembrances of the privileges which I enjoyed in this way.

You will see that a society thus circumstanced was

exactly one most likely to influence strongly the character
of such a lad as Arnold was at his election. He came
to us in Lent Term, in 1811, from Winchester, winning
his election against several respectable candidates. He
was a mere boy in appearance as well as in age; but we
saw in a very short time that he was quite equal to take
his part in the arguments of the common room; and he
was, I rather think, admitted by Mr. Cooke at once into
his senior class. As he was equal, so was he ready to take
part in our discussions; he was fond of conversation on
serious matters, and vehement in argument; fearless too
in advancing his opinions—which, to say the truth, often
startled us a good deal; but he was ingenuous and candid,
and though the fearlessness with which, so young as he
was, he advanced his opinions might have seemed to be-
token presumption, yet the good temper with which he
bore retort or rebuke, relieved him from that imputation;
he was bold and warm, because so far as his knowledge
went he saw very clearly, and he was an ardent lover of
truth, but I never saw in him even then a grain of vanity
or conceit. I have said that some of his opinions startled
us a good deal; we were indeed for the most part Tories
in Church and State, great respecters of things as they
were, and not very tolerant of the disposition which he
brought with him to question their wisdom. Many and
long were the conflicts we had, and with unequal numbers. I think I have seen all the leaders of the common
room engaged with him at once, with little order or consideration, as may be supposed, and not always with great
scrupulosity as to the fairness of our arguments. This
was attended by no loss of regard, and scarcely ever, or
seldom, by even momentary loss of temper. We did not
always convince him—perhaps we ought not always to
have done so—yet in the end a considerable modification
of his opinions was produced; in one of his letters to me,

written at a much later period, he mentions this change. In truth, there were those among us calculated to produce an impression on his affectionate heart and ardent ingenuous mind; and the rather because the more we saw of him, and the more we battled with him, the more manifestly did we respect and love him. The feeling with which we argued gave additional power to our arguments over a disposition such as his: and thus he became attached to young men of the most different tastes and intellects; his love for each taking a different colour, more or less blended with respect, fondness, or even humour, according to those differences; and in return they all uniting in love and respect for him.

There will be some few to whom these remembrances will speak with touching truth; they will remember his single-hearted and devout schoolfellow, who early gave up his native land, and devoted himself to the missionary cause in India; the high-souled and imaginative, though somewhat indolent lad, who came to us from Westminster —one bachelor, whose father's connection with the House of Commons, and residence in Palace Yard, made him a great authority with us as to the world without, and the statesmen whose speeches he sometimes heard, but we discussed much as if they had been personages in history; and whose remarkable love for historical and geographical research, and his proficiency in it, with his clear judgment, quiet humour, and mildness in communicating information made him peculiarly attractive to Arnold— and above all, our senior among the under-graduates, though my junior in years, the author of the Christian Year, who came fresh from the single teaching of his venerable father, and achieved the highest honours of the University at an age when others frequently are but on her threshold. Arnold clung to all these with equal fidelity, but regarded each with different feelings; each produced on him a salutary, but different effect. His love for all without exception I know, if I know anything of another man's heart, continued to his life's end; it survived (how can the mournful facts be concealed in any complete and truth-telling narrative of his life?) separation, suspension of intercourse, and entire disagreement of opinion, with the last of these, on points believed by them both to be of essential importance. These two held their opinions with a zeal and tenacity proportionate to their importance; each believed the other in error pernicious to the faith and dangerous to himself; and what they believed sincerely, each thought himself bound to state, and stated it openly, it may be with too much of warmth; and unguarded expressions were unnecessarily, I think inaccurately, reported. Such disagreements in opinion between the wise and good are incident to our imperfect state; and even the good qualities of the heart, earnestness, want of suspicion, may lay us open to them; but in the case before me the affectionate interest with which each regarded the other never ceased. I had the good fortune to retain the intimate friendship and correspondence of both, and I can testify with authority that the elder spoke and wrote of the younger as an elder brother might of a younger whom he tenderly loved, though he disapproved of his course; while it was not in Arnold's nature to forget how much he had owed to Keble: he bitterly lamented, what he laboured to avert, the suspension of their intimate intercourse; he was at all times anxious to renew it; and although, where the disagreement turned on points so vital between men who held each to his own so conscientiously, this may have been too much to expect, yet it is a most gratifying thought to their common friends that they would probably have met at Fox How under Arnold's roof, but a few weeks after he was called away to that state in which the doubts and controversies of this life will receive their clear resolution.

I return from my digression—Arnold came to us of course not a formed scholar, nor, I think, did he leave the college with scholarship proportioned to his great abilities and opportunities. And this arose in part from the decided preference which he gave to the philosophers and historians of antiquity over the poets, coupled with the distinction which he then made, erroneous as I think, and certainly extreme in degree, between words and things, as he termed it. His correspondence with me will show how much he modified this too in after life; but at that time he was led by it to undervalue those niceties of language, the intimate acquaintance with which he did not then perceive to be absolutely necessary to a precise knowledge of the meaning of the author. His compositions, therefore, at this time, though full of matter, did not give promise of that clear and spirited style which he afterwards mastered; he gained no verse prize, but was an unsuccessful competitor for the Latin verse in the year 1812, when Henry Latham succeeded, the third brother of that house who had done so; and though this is the only occasion on which I have any memorandum of his writing, I do not doubt that he made other attempts. Among us were several who were fond of writing English verse; Keble was even then raising among us those expectations which he has since so fully justified, and Arnold was not slow to follow the example. I have several poems of his written about this time, neat and pointed in expression, and just in thought, but not remarkable for fancy or imagination. I remember some years after his telling me that he continued the practice "on principle;" he thought it a useful and humanizing exercise.

But, though not a poet himself, he was not insensible of the beauties of poetry—far from it. I reflect with some pleasure, that I first introduced him to what has been somewhat unreasonably called the Lake Poetry: my near relation to one, and connection with another of the poets, whose works were so called, were the occasion of this; and my uncle having sent me the Lyrical Ballads, and the first edition of Mr. Wordsworth's poems, they became familiar among us. We were proof, I am glad to think, against the criticism, if so it might be called, of the "Edinburgh Review;" we felt their truth and beauty, and became zealous disciples of Wordsworth's philosophy. This was of peculiar advantage to Arnold, whose leaning was too direct for the practical and evidently useful—it brought out in him that feeling for the lofty and imaginative which appeared in all his intimate conversation, and may be seen spiritualizing those even of his writings, in which, from their subject, it might seem to have less place. You know in later life how much he thought his beloved Fox How enhanced in value by its neighbourhood to Rydal Mount, and what store he set on the privilege of frequent and friendly converse with the venerable genius of that sweet spot.

But his passion at the time I am treating of was for Aristotle and Thucydides; and however he became some few years after more sensible of the importance of the poets in classic literature, this passion he retained to the last; those who knew him intimately or corresponded with him, will bear me witness how deeply he was imbued with the language and ideas of the former; how in earnest and unreserved conversation, or in writing, his train of thoughts was affected by the Ethics and Rhetoric; how he cited the maxims of the Stagyrite as oracles, and how his language was quaintly and racily pointed with phrases from him. I never knew a man who made such familiar, even fond, use of an author: it is scarcely too much to say, that he spoke of him as of one intimately and affectionately known and valued by him ; and when he was selecting his son's University, with much leaning for Cambridge, and many things which at the time made him incline against Oxford, dearly as he loved her, Aristotle turned the scale ; "I could not consent," said he, "to send my son to a University where he would lose the study of him altogether." "You may believe," he said with regard to the London University, "that I have not forgotten the dear old Stagyrite in our examinations, and I hope that he will be construed and discussed in Somerset House as well as in the schools." His fondness for Thucydides first prompted a Lexicon Thucydideum, in which he made some progress at Laleham in 1821 and 1822, and ended as you know in his valuable edition of that author.

Next to these he loved Herodotus. I have said that he was not, while I knew him at Oxford, a formed scholar, and that he composed stiffly and with difficulty, but to this there was a seeming exception ; he had so imbued himself with the style of Herodotus and Thucydides, that he could write narratives in the style of either at pleasure with wonderful readiness, and as we thought with the greatest accuracy. I remember, too, an account by him of a Vacation Tour in the Isle of Wight, after the manner of the Anabasis.

Arnold's bodily recreations were walking and bathing. It was a particular delight to him, with two or three companions, to make what he called a skirmish across the country; on these occasions we deserted the road, crossed fences, and leaped ditches, or fell into them : he enjoyed the country round Oxford, and while out in this way his spirits would rise and his mirth overflowed. Though delicate in appearance, and not giving promise of great muscular strength, yet his form was light, and he was capable of going long distances and bearing much fatigue.

You know that to the last moment of health he had the same predilections; indeed he was, as much as any I ever knew, one whose days were

"Bound each to each by natural piety."

His manner had all the tastes and feelings of his youth, only more developed and better regulated. The same passion for the sea and shipping, and his favourite Isle of Wight; the same love for external nature, the same readiness in viewing the characteristic features of a country and its marked positions, or the most beautiful points of a prospect, for all which he was remarkable in after life, we noticed in him then. When Professor Buckland, then one of our Fellows, began his career in that science, to the advancement of which he has contributed so much, Arnold became one of his most earnest and intelligent pupils, and you know how familiarly and practically he applied geological facts in all his later years.

In June, 1812, I was elected Fellow of Exeter College, and determined to pursue the law as my profession: my residence at Oxford was thenceforward only occasional; but the friendship which had grown up between us suffered no diminution. Something, I forget now the particular circumstance, led to an interchange of letters, which ripened into a correspondence, continued with rather unusual regularity, when our respective occupations are considered, to within a few days of his death. It may show the opinion which I even then entertained of him, that I carefully preserved from the beginning every letter which I ever received from him: you have had an opportunity of judging of the value of the collection.

After I had ceased to reside, a small debating society called the Attic Society was formed in Oxford,* which held its meetings in the rooms of the members by turns. Arnold was among the earliest members, and was, I believe, an embarrassed speaker. This I should have expected; for, however he might appear a confident advancer of his own opinions, he was in truth bashful, and at the same time had so acute a perception of what was ill-seasoned or irrelevant, that he would want that freedom from restraint which is essential at least to young speakers. This society was the germ of the Union, but I believe he never belonged to it.

In our days the religious controversies had not begun, by which the minds of young men at Oxford are, I fear, now prematurely and too much occupied; the routine theological studies of the University were, I admit, deplorably low, but the earnest ones amongst us were diligent readers of Barrow, Hooker, and Taylor. Arnold was among these, but I have no recollection of anything at that time distinctive in his religious opinions. What occurred afterwards does not properly fall within my chapter, yet it is not unconnected with it, and I believe I can sum up all that need be said on such a subject, as shortly and as accurately, from the sources of information in my hands, as any other person can. His was an anxiously inquisitive mind, a scrupulously conscientious heart; his inquiries, previously to his taking orders, led him on to distressing doubts on certain points in the Articles; these were not low nor rationalistic in their tendency, according to the bad sense of that term; there was no indisposition in him to believe merely because

---

* In this society he formed or confirmed his acquaintance with a new circle of friends, chiefly of other colleges, whose names will appear in the ensuing correspondence by the side of those of an earlier date from Corpus, and of a somewhat later date from Oriel, Mr. Lowe, Mr. Hull, Mr. Randall, Mr. Blackstone, and Mr. Hare, and through him with his Cambridge brother, now Archdeacon Hare.

the article transcended his reason; he doubted the proof
and the interpretation of the textual authority. His state
was very painful, and I think morbid; for I remarked
that the two occasions on which I was privy to his distress were precisely those in which to doubt was against
his dearest schemes of worldly happiness; and the consciousness of this seemed to make him distrustful of the
arguments which were intended to lead his mind to acquiescence. Upon the first occasion to which I allude
he was a Fellow of Oriel, and in close intercourse with
one of the friends I have before mentioned, then also a
Fellow of the same college: to him as well as to me he
opened his mind, and from him he received the wisest
advice, which he had the wisdom to act upon; he was
bid to pause in his inquiries, to pray earnestly for help
and light from above, and turn himself more strongly
than ever to the practical duties of a holy life; he did
so, and through severe trials was finally blessed with
perfect peace of mind, and a settled conviction. If there
be any so unwise as to rejoice that Arnold in his youth
had doubts on important doctrines, let him be sobered
with the conclusion of those doubts, when Arnold's mind
had not become weaker, nor his pursuit of truth less
honest or ardent, but when his abilities were matured,
his knowledge greater, his judgment more sober; if there
be any who, in youth, are suffering the same distress
which befell him, let his conduct be their example, and
the blessing which was vouchsafed to him, their hope
and consolation. In a letter from that friend to myself,
of the date of February 14, 1819, I find the following
extract, which gives so true and considerate an account
of this passage in Arnold's life, that you may be pleased
to insert it.

"I have not talked with Arnold lately on the distressing thoughts which he wrote to you about, but I am

fearful, from his manner at times, that he has by no means got rid of them, though I feel quite confident that all will be well in the end. The subject of them is that most awful one, on which all *very* inquisitive reasoning minds are, I believe, most liable to such temptations —I mean the doctrine of the blessed Trinity. Do not start, my dear Coleridge ; I do not believe that Arnold has any serious scruples of the *understanding* about it, but it is a defect of his mind that he cannot get rid of a certain feeling of objections—and particularly when, as he fancies, the bias is so strong upon him to decide one way from interest ; he scruples doing what I advise him, which is, to put down the objections by main force, whenever they arise in his mind, fearful that in so doing he shall be violating his conscience for a maintenance' sake. I am still inclined to think with you that the wisest thing he could do would be to take John M. (a young pupil whom I was desirous of placing under his care) and a curacy somewhere or other, and cure himself not by physic, *i.e.*, reading and controversy, but by diet and regimen, *i.e.*, holy living. In the meantime what an excellent fellow he is. I do think that one might safely say, as someone did of some other, ' One had better have Arnold's doubts than most men's certainties.' "*

I believe I have exhausted my recollections ; and if I have accomplished as I ought, what I proposed to myself, it will be hardly necessary for me to sum up formally his character as an Oxford under-graduate. At the commencement a boy—and at the close retaining, not ungracefully, much of boyish spirits, frolic, and simplicity ; in mind vigorous, active, clear-sighted, industrious, and daily accumulating and assimilating treasures of knowledge ; not averse to poetry, but delighting rather in dialectics, philosophy, and history, with less of ima-

---

* On this subject see further, the note in Chapter IX.

gination than reasoning power; in argument bold almost to presumptive and vehement; in temper easily roused to indignation, yet more easily appeased, and entirely free from bitterness; fired, indeed, by what he deemed ungenerous or unjust to others, rather than by any sense of personal wrong; somewhat too little deferential to authority; yet without any real inconsistency loving what was good and great in antiquity the more ardently and reverently because it was ancient; a casual or unkind observer might have pronounced him somewhat too pugnacious in conversation and too positive. I have given, I believe, the true explanation; scarcely anything would have pained him more than to be convinced that he had been guilty of want of modesty, or of deference where it was justly due; no one thought these virtues of more sacred obligation. In heart, if I can speak with confidence of any of the friends of my youth, I can of his, that it was devout and pure, simple, sincere, affectionate, and faithful.

It is time that I should close; already, I fear, I have dwelt with something like an old man's prolixity on passages of my youth, forgetting that no one can take the same interest in them which I do myself: that deep personal interest must, however, be my excuse. Whoever sets a right value on the events of his life for good or for evil, will agree that next in importance to the rectitude of his own course and the selection of his partner for life, and far beyond all the wealth or honours which may reward his labour, far even beyond the unspeakable gift of bodily health, are the friendships which he forms in youth. That is the season when natures soft and pliant grow together, each becoming part of the other, and coloured by it; thus to become one in heart with the good, and generous, and devout, is, by God's grace, to become, in measure, good, and generous, and devout.

Arnold's friendship has been one of the many blessings of my life. I cherish the memory of it with mournful gratitude, and I cannot but dwell with lingering fondness on the scene and the period which first brought us together. Within the peaceful walls of Corpus I made friends, of whom all are spared me but Arnold—he has fallen asleep—but the bond there formed, which the lapse of years and our different walks in life did not unloosen, and which strong opposition of opinions only rendered more intimate; though interrupted in time, I feel not to be broken — may I venture, without unseasonable solemnity, to express the firm trust, that it will endure for ever in eternity.

Believe me, my dear Stanley,

Very truly yours,

J. T. C.

CHAPTER II.

THE society of the Fellows of Oriel College then, as for some time afterwards, numbered amongst its members some of the most rising men in the University, and it is curious to observe the list which, when the youthful scholar of Corpus was added to it, contained the names of Copleston, Davison, Whately, Keble, Hawkins, and Hampden, and shortly after he left it, those of Newman and Pusey, the former of whom was elected into his. vacant Fellowship. Amongst the friends with whom he thus became acquainted for the first time, may chiefly be mentioned Dr. Hawkins, since Provost of Oriel, to whom in the last year of his life he dedicated his Lectures on Modern History, and Dr. Whately, afterwards Principal of St. Alban's Hall, and now Archbishop of Dublin, towards whom his regard was enhanced by the domestic intercourse which was constantly interchanged in later years between their respective families, and to whose writings and conversations he took an early opportunity of expressing his obligations in the Preface to his first volume of Sermons, in speaking of the various points on which the communication of his friend's views had " extended or confirmed his own." For the next four years he remained at Oxford taking private pupils, and reading extensively in the Oxford libraries, an advantage which he never ceased to remember gratefully himself, and to impress upon others, and of which the immediate results remain in a great number of MSS., both in the form of abstracts of other works, and of original sketches on history and theology. They are remarkable rather as proofs of industry than of power, and the style of all his compositions, both at this time and for some years later, is cramped by a stiffness and formality alien alike to the homeliness of his first published works and the vigour of his later ones, and strikingly recalling his favourite lines—

> " The old man clogs our earliest years,
> And simple childhood comes at last."

But already in the examination of the Oriel Fellowships, Dr. Whately had pointed out to the other electors the great capability of "growth" which he believed to be involved in the crudities of the youthful candidate's exercises, and which, even in points where he was inferior to his competitors, indicated an approaching superiority. And widely different as were his juvenile compositions in many points from those of his after life, yet it is interesting to observe in them the materials which those who knew the pressure of his numerous avocations used to wonder when he could have acquired, and to trace amidst the strangest contrast of his general thoughts and style occasional remarks of a higher strain, which are in striking, though in some instances perhaps accidental, coincidence with some of his later views. He endeavoured in his historical reading to follow the plan which he afterwards recommended in his Lectures, of making himself thoroughly master of some one period—the 15th century, with Philip de Comines as his text-book, seems to have

been the chief sphere of his studies—and the first book
after his election which appears in the Oriel library as
taken out in his name, is Rymer's Fœdera. Many of
the judgments in his maturer years on Gibbon, Livy, and
Thucydides are to be found in a MS. of 1815, in which,
under the name of " Thoughts on History," he went
through the characteristics of the chief ancient and modern
historians. And it is almost startling, in the midst of a
rhetorical burst of his youthful Toryism in a journal of
1815, to meet with expressions of real feeling about the
social state of England such as might have been written
in his latest years ; or amidst the commonplace remarks
which accompany an analysis of St. Paul's Epistles and
Chrysostom's Homilies, in 1818, to stumble on a statement complete as far as it goes, of his subsequent doctrine
of the identity of Church and State.

Meanwhile he had been gradually led to fix upon
his future course in life. In December, 1818, he was
ordained deacon at Oxford ; and on August 11th, 1820,
he married Mary, youngest daughter of the Rev. John
Penrose, Rector of Fledborough, in Nottinghamshire,
and sister of one of his earliest school and college friends,
Trevenen Penrose ; having previously settled in 1819 at
Laleham, near Staines, with his mother, aunt, and sister,
where he remained for the next nine years, taking seven
or eight young men as private pupils in preparation for the
Universities, for a short time in a joint establishment with
his brother-in-law, Mr. Buckland, and afterwards independently by himself. Here were born six out of his
nine children. The three youngest, besides one, which
died in infancy in 1832, were born at Rugby.

In the interval which had elapsed between the end of
his under-graduate career at Oxford, and his entrance
upon life, had taken place the great change from boyhood
to manhood, and with it a corresponding change or

growth of character, more marked and more important than at any subsequent period of his life. There was indeed another great step to be taken before his mind reached that later stage of development which was coincident with his transition from Laleham to Rugby. The prosaic and matter of fact element which has been described in his early Oxford life still retained its predominance, and to a certain extent dwarfed and narrowed his sphere of thought ; the various principles of political and theological science which contained in germ all that was to grow out of them, had not yet assumed their proper harmony and proportions ; his feelings of veneration, if less confined than in later years, were also less intense ; his hopes and views, if more practicable and more easily restrained by the advice of others, were also less wide in their range, and less lofty in their conception.

But, however great were the modifications which his character subsequently underwent, it is the change of tone at this time between the earlier letters of this period (such as the one or two first of the ensuing series) and those which immediately succeed them, that marks the difference between the high spirit and warm feelings of his youth and the fixed earnestness and devotion which henceforth took possession of his whole heart and will. Whatever may have been the outward circumstances which contributed to this—the choice of a profession— the impression left upon him by the sudden loss of his elder brother—the new and to him elevating influences of married life—the responsibility of having to act as the guide and teacher of others—it was now for the first time that the principles, which before he had followed rather as a matter of course, and as held and taught by those around him, became emphatically part of his own convictions, to be embraced and carried out for life and for death.

From this time forward such defects as were peculiar to his boyhood and early youth entirely disappear; the indolent habits—the morbid restlessness and occasional weariness of duty—the indulgence of vague schemes without definite purpose—the intellectual doubts which beset the first opening of his mind to the realities of religious belief, when he shared at least in part the state of perplexity which in his later sermons he feelingly describes as the severest of earthly trials, and which so endeared to him throughout life the story of the confession of the Apostle Thomas—all seem to have vanished away and never again to have diverted him from the decisive choice and energetic pursuit of what he set before him as his end and duty. From this time forward no careful observer can fail to trace that deep consciousness of the invisible world, and that power of bringing it before him in the midst and through the means of his most active engagements which constituted the peculiarity of his religious life, and the moving spring of his whole life.

It was not that he frequently introduced sacred names in writing or in conversation, or that he often dwelt on divine interpositions; where many would have done so without scruple, he would shrink from it, and in speaking of his own religious feelings, or in appealing to the religious feelings of others, he was, except to those most intimate with him, exceedingly reserved. But what was true generally of the thorough interpenetration of the several parts of his character, was peculiarly true of it in its religious aspect: his natural faculties were not unclothed, but clothed upon; they were at once coloured by, and gave a colour to, the belief which they received. It was in his common acts of life, whether public or private, that the depth of his religious convictions most visibly appeared; it was in his manner of dwelling on religious subjects that the characteristic tendencies of his mind chiefly displayed themselves.

Accordingly, whilst it is impossible, for this reason, to understand his religious belief except through the knowledge of his actual life and his writings on ordinary subjects, it is impossible, on the other hand, to understand his life and writings without bearing in mind how vivid was his realisation of those truths of the Christian Revelation on which he most habitually dwelt. It was this which enabled him to undertake labours which without such a power must have crushed or enfeebled the spiritual growth which in him they seemed only to foster. It was the keen sense of thankfulness consciously awakened by every distinct instance of his many blessings, which more than anything else explained his close union of joyousness with seriousness. In his even tenor of life it was difficult for anyone who knew him not to imagine "the golden chain of heavenward thoughts and humble prayers by which, whether standing or sitting, in the intervals of work or amusement," he "linked together" his "more special and solemn devotions" (Serm. vol. iii. p. 227), or not to trace something of the consciousness of an invisible presence in the collectedness with which, at the call of his common duties, he rose at once from his various occupations: or in the calm repose which, in the midst of his most active labours, took all the disturbing accidents of life as a matter of course, and made toil so real a pleasure, and relaxation so real a refreshment to him. And in his solemn and emphatic expressions on subjects expressly religious; in his manner of awful reverence when in speaking of God or of the Scriptures; in his power of realising the operation of something more than human, whether in his abhorrence of evil or in his admiration of goodness;—the impression on those who heard him was often as though he knew what others only believed, as though he had seen what others only talked about. "No one could know him even a little," says one who was himself not amongst his most intimate friends, "and not be struck by his absolute wrestling with evil, so that like St. Paul he seemed to be battling with the wicked one, and yet with the feeling of God's help on his side, scorning as well as hating him."

Above all it was necessary for a right understanding, not only of his religious opinions, but of his whole character, to enter into the peculiar feeling of love and adoration which he entertained towards our Lord Jesus Christ,—peculiar in the distinctness and intensity which, as it characterised almost all his common impressions, so in this case gave additional strength and meaning to those feelings with which he regarded not only His work of Redemption but Himself, as a living Friend and Master. "In that unknown world in which our thoughts become instantly lost," it was his real support and delight to remember that "still there is one subject on which our thoughts and imaginations may fasten, no less than our affections; that amidst the light, dark from excess of brilliance, which surrounds the throne of God, we may yet discern the gracious form of the Son of Man." (Serm. vol. iii. p. 90.) In that consciousness which pressed upon him at times even heavily, of the difficulty of considering God in his own nature, believing as he did that "Providence, the Supreme Being, the Deity, and other such terms repel us to an infinite distance," and that the revelation of the Father, in Himself unapproachable, is to be looked upon rather as the promise of another life, than as the support of this life, it was to him a thought of perhaps more than usual comfort to feel that "our God" is "Jesus Christ our Lord, the image of the invisible God," and that "in Him is represented all the fulness of the Godhead, until we know even as we are known" (vol. v. p. 222).   And with this full conviction both of his conscience and understanding, that He of whom he spoke was "still the very selfsame Jesus in all human affections and divine excellencies ; " there was a vividness and tenderness in his conception of Him, on which, if one may so say, all his feelings of human friendship and affection seemed to fasten as on their natural object, "bringing before him His actions, imaging to himself his very voice and look :" there was to him (so to speak) a greatness in the image thus formed of Him, on which all his natural instincts of reverence, all his range of historical interest, all his admiration of truth and goodness at once centered. " Where can we find a name so holy as that we may surrender our whole souls to it, before which obedience, reverence without measure, intense humility, most unreserved adoration may be all duly rendered ?" was the earnest inquiry of his whole nature intellectual and moral, no less than religious. And the answer to it in like manner expressed what he endeavoured to make the rule of his own personal conduct, and the centre of all his moral and religious convictions: One name there is, and one alone, one alone in heaven and earth—not truth, not justice, not benevolence, not Christ's mother, not His holiest servants, not His blessed sacraments, nor His very mystical body the Church, but Himself only who died for us and rose again, Jesus Christ, both God and Man." (Serm. vol. iv. p. 210.)

These were the feelings which, though more fully developed with the advance of years, now for the first time took thorough possession of his mind ; and which struck upon his moral nature at this period, with the same kind of force (if one may use the comparison) as the new views which he acquired from time to time of persons and principles in historical or philosophical speculations, impressed themselves upon his intellectual nature. There is naturally but little to interrupt the retirement of his life at Laleham, which was only broken by the short tours in England or on the Continent, in which then, as afterwards, he employed his vacations. Still it is not without interest to dwell on these years, the profound peace of which is contrasted so strongly with the almost incessant agitations of his subsequent life, and "to remain awhile" (thus applying his own words on another subject) "on the high ground where the waters which are hereafter to form the separate streams" of his various social and theological views, "lie as yet undistinguished in their common parent lake."

Whatever may have been the exact notions of his future course which presented themselves to him, it is evident that he was not insensible to the attraction of visions of extensive influence, and almost to his latest hour he seems to have been conscious of the existence of the temptation within him, and of the necessity of contending against it. "I believe," he said, many years afterwards, in speaking of these early struggles to a Rugby pupil who was consulting him on the choice of a profession—"I believe that, naturally, I am one of the most ambitious men alive," and "the three great objects of human ambition," he added, to which alone he could look as deserving the name, were "to be the prime minister of a great kingdom, the governor of a great empire, or the writer of works which should live in every age and in every country." But in some respects the loftiness of his aims made it a matter of less difficulty to confine himself at once to a sphere in which, whilst he felt himself well and usefully employed, he felt also that the practical business of his daily duties acted as a check upon his own inclinations and speculations. Accordingly, when he entered upon his work at Laleham, he seems to have regarded it as his work for life. "I have always thought," he writes in 1823, "with regard to ambition, that I should like to be aut Cæsar aut nullus, and as it is pretty well settled for me that I shall not be Cæsar, I am quite content to live in peace as nullus."

It was a period, indeed, on which he used himself to look back, even from the wider usefulness of his later years, almost with a fond regret, as to the happiest time of his life. "Seek ye first the kingdom of God and his righteousness, and then all other things shall be added to you," was a passage to which now, more than any other time, he was in the habit of recurring, as one of peculiar truth and comfort. His situation supplied him exactly with that union of retirement and work which more than any other condition suited his natural inclinations, and enabled him to keep up more uninterrupted than was ever again in his power the communication which he so much cherished with his friends and relations. Without undertaking any directly parochial charge, he was in the habit of rendering constant assistance to Mr. Hearn, the curate of the place, both in the parish church and workhouse, and in visiting the villagers—thus uniting with his ordinary occupations greater means than he was afterwards able to command, of familiar intercourse with his poorer neighbours, which he always so highly valued. Bound as he was to Laleham by all these ties, he long loved to look upon it as his final home ;—and the first reception of the tidings of his election at Rugby was overclouded with deep sorrow at leaving the scene of so much happiness. Years after he had left it, he still retained his early affection for it, and till he had purchased his house in Westmoreland, he entertained a lingering hope that he might return to it in his old age, when he should have retired from Rugby. Often he would revisit it, and delighted in renewing his acquaintance with all the families of the poor whom he had known during his residence; in showing to his children his former haunts; in looking once again on his favourite views of the great plain of Middlesex—the lonely walks along the quiet banks of the Thames—the retired garden, with its "Campus Martius," and the "wilderness of trees," which lay behind his house, and which had been the scene of so many sportive games and serious conversations—the churchyard of Laleham, then doubly dear to him, as containing the graves of his infant child, whom he buried there in 1832, and of his mother, his aunt, and his sister Susannah, who had long formed almost a part of his own domestic circle, and whom he lost within a few years after his departure to Rugby.

His general view of his work as a private tutor is best given in his own words in 1831 to a friend who was about to engage in a similar occupation.

"I know it has a bad name, but my wife and I always happened to be fond of it, and if I were to leave Rugby for no demerit of my own, I would take to it again with all the pleasure in life. I enjoyed, and do enjoy, the society of youths of seventeen or eighteen, for they are all alive in limbs and spirits at least, if not in mind, while in older persons the body and spirits often become lazy and languid without the mind gaining any vigour to compensate for it. Do not take your work as a dose, and I do not think you will find it nauseous. I am sure you will not, if your wife does not, and if she is a sensible woman, she will not either if you do not. The misery of private tuition seems to me to consist in this, that men enter upon it as a means to some further end; are always impatient for the time when they may lay it aside; whereas if you enter upon it heartily as your life's business, as a man enters upon any other profession, you are not then in danger of grudging every hour you give to it, and thinking of how much privacy, and how much society it is robbing you; but you take to it as a matter of course, making it your material occupation, and devote your time to it, and then you find that it is in itself full of interest, and keeps life's current fresh and wholesome by bringing you in such perpetual contact with all the spring of youthful liveliness. I should say, have your pupils a good deal with you, and be as familiar with them as you possibly can. I did this continually more and more before I left Laleham, going to bathe with them, leaping, and all other gymnastic exercises within my capacity, and sometimes sailing or rowing with them. They I believe always liked it, and I enjoyed it myself like a boy, and found myself constantly the better for it."

In many respects his method at Laleham resembled the plan which he pursued on a larger scale at Rugby. Then, as afterwards, he had a strong sense of the duty of protecting his charge, at whatever risk to himself, from the presence of companions who were capable only of exercising an evil influence over their associates; and, young as he was, he persisted in carrying out this principle, and in declining to take any additional pupils as long as he had under him any of such a character, whom yet he did not feel himself justified in removing at once. And in answer to the request of his friends that he would raise his terms, "I am confirmed in my resolution not to do so," he writes in 1827, "lest I should get the sons of very great people as my pupils whom it is almost impossible to *sophronize*." In reply to a friend in 1821, who had asked his advice in a difficult case of dealing with a pupil—

"I have no doubt," he answers, "that you have acted perfectly right; for lenity is seldom to be repented of; and besides, if you should find that it has been ill bestowed, you can have recourse to expulsion after all. But it is clearly right to try your chance of making an impression; and if you can make any at all, it is at once your justification and encouragement to proceed. It is very often like kicking a football up hill; you kick it onwards twenty yards, and it rolls back nineteen; still you have gained one yard, and thus in a good many kicks you make some progress. This, however, is on the supposition that the pupil's fault is ἀκρασία and not κακία; for if he laughs behind your back at what you say to him, he will corrupt others, and then there is no help for it, but he must go. This is to me all the difference: I would be as patient as I possibly could with irresolution, unsteadiness, and fits of idleness; but if a pupil has set his mind to do nothing, but considers all the work as so much fudge, which he will evade if he can, I have made up my resolution that I will send him away without scruple; for not to speak of the heartless trouble that such an animal would give to myself, he is a living principle of mischief in the house, being ready at all times to pervert his companions: and this determination I have expressed publicly, and if I know myself I will act upon it, and I advise you most heartily to do the same. Thus, then, with Mr. ——, when he appeared penitent and made professions of amendment, you were clearly right to give him a longer trial. If he be sincere, however unsteady and backsliding, he will not hurt the principles of your other pupils; for he will not glory in his own misconduct, which I suppose is the danger; but if you have reason to think that the impression you made on him was only temporary, and that it has since entirely gone away, and his own evil principles as well as evil practices are in vigour, then I would advise you to send him off without delay; for then taking the mischief he will do to others into the account, the football rolls down twenty-five yards to your kick of twenty, and that is a losing game."

"*"Εχθιστη ὀδύνη πολλὰ φρονέοντά πὲς μηδένος κρατέειν,*" he writes, "must be the feeling of many a working tutor who cannot open the eyes of his pupils to see what knowledge is,—I do not mean human knowledge only, but 'wisdom.'"

"You could scarcely conceive the rare instances of ignorance that I have met with amongst them. One had no notion of what was meant by an angel; another could not tell how many Gospels there are, nor could he, after due deliberation, recollect any other names than Matthew, Mark, and Luke; and a third holds the first concord in utter contempt, and makes the infinitive mood supply the place of the principal verb in the sentence without the least suspicion of any impropriety. My labour, therefore, is more irksome that I have ever known it; but none of my pupils give me any uneasiness on the most serious points, and five of them staid the sacrament when it was last administered. I ought constantly to impress upon my mind how light an evil is the greatest ignorance or dulness when compared with habits of profligacy, or even of wilful irregularity and riotousness."

"I regret in your son," he says (in writing to a parent), "a carelessness which does not allow him to think seriously of what he is living for, and to do what is right not merely as a matter of regularity, but because it is a duty. I trust you will not think that I am meaning anything more than my words convey, or that what I am regretting in your son is not to be found in nineteen out of twenty young men of his age; but I conceive that you would wish me to form my desire of what your son should be, not according to the common standard, but according to the highest,—to be satisfied with no less in him than I should have been anxious to find in a son of my own. He is capable of doing a great deal; and I have not seen anything in him which has called for reproof since he has been with me. I am only desirous that he should work more heartily,—just, in short, as he would work if he took an interest of himself in his own improvement. On this, of course, all distinction in Oxford must depend: but much more than distinction depends on it; for the difference between a useful education, and one which does not affect the future life, rests mainly on the greater or less activity which it has communicated to the pupil's mind, whether he has learned to think, or to act, and to gain knowledge by himself, or whether he has merely followed passively as long as there was some one to draw him."

It is needless to anticipate the far more extended influence which he exercised over his Rugby scholars, by describing in detail the impression produced upon his pupils at Laleham. Yet the mere difference of the relation in which he stood towards them in itself gave a peculiar character to his earlier sphere of education, and as such may best be described in the words of one amongst those whom he most esteemed, Mr. Price, who afterwards became one of his assistant-masters at Rugby.*

* I cannot allow Mr. Price's name to appear in these pages without expressing how much I am indebted to him for the assistance which, amidst his many pressing duties, he has rendered to this work, not only here, but throughout, and which in many cases, from his long knowledge and complete understanding of Dr. Arnold's views and character, he alone could have rendered. Nothing, indeed, but the very fact of the perpetual recurrence of instances in which I have availed myself not only of his suggestions, but of his words, would have prevented me from more frequently acknowledging obligations for which I here wish to return my thanks, however inadequately, once for all.

"Nearly eighteen years have passed away since I resided at Laleham, and I had the misfortune of being but two months as a pupil there. I am unable, therefore, to give you a complete picture of the Laleham life of my late revered tutor; I can only impart to you such impressions as my brief sojourn there has indelibly fixed in my recollection.

"The most remarkable thing which struck me at once on joining the Laleham circle was, the wonderful healthiness of tone and feeling which prevailed in it. Everything about me I immediately found to be most real; it was a place where a new comer at once felt that a great and earnest work was going forward. Dr. Arnold's great power as a private tutor resided in this, that he gave such an intense earnestness to life. Every pupil was made to feel that there was a work for him to do—that his happiness as well as his duty lay in doing that work well. Hence an indescribable zest was communicated to a young man's feeling about life; a strange joy came over him on discovering that he had the means of being useful, and thus of being happy; and a deep respect and ardent attachment sprang up towards him who had taught him thus to value life and his own self, and his work and mission in this world. All this was founded on the breadth and comprehensiveness of Arnold's character, as well as its striking truth and reality; on the unfeigned regard he had for work of all kinds, and the sense he had of its value both for the complex aggregate of society and the growth and perfection of the individual. Thus, pupils of the most different natures were keenly stimulated; none felt that he was left out, or that, because he was not endowed with large powers of mind, there was no sphere open to him in the honourable pursuit of usefulness. This wonderful power of making all his pupils respect themselves, and of awakening in them a consciousness of the duties that God assigned to them personally, and of the consequent reward each should have of his labours, was one of Arnold's most characteristic features as a trainer of youth; he possessed it eminently at Rugby; but, if I may trust my own vivid recollections, he had it quite as remarkably at Laleham. His hold over all his pupils I know perfectly astonished me. It was not so much an enthusiastic admiration for his genius, or learning, or eloquence which stirred within them; it was a sympathetic thrill, caught from a spirit that was earnestly at work in the world—whose work was healthy, sustained, and constantly carried forward in the fear of God—a work that was founded on a deep sense of its duty and its value; and was coupled with such a true humility, such an unaffected simplicity, that others could not help being invigorated by the same feeling, and with the belief that they too in their measure could go and do likewise.

" In all this there was no excitement, no predilection for one class of work above another; no enthusiasm for any one-sided object; but an humble, profound, and most religious consciousness that work is the appointed calling of man on earth, the end for which his various faculties were given, the element in which his nature is ordained to develope itself, and in which his progressive advance towards heaven is to lie. Hence, each pupil felt assured of Arnold's sympathy in his own particular growth and character of talent; in striving to cultivate his own gifts, in whatever direction they might lead him, he invariably found Arnold not only approving, but positively and sincerely valuing for themselves the results he had arrived at; and that approbation and esteem gave a dignity and a worth both to himself and his labour.

" His humility was very deeply seated; his respect for all knowledge sincere. A strange feeling passed over the pupil's mind when he found great, and often undue, credit given him for knowledge of which his tutor was ignorant. But this generated no conceit: the example before his eyes daily reminded him that it was only as a means of usefulness, as an improvement of talents for his own good and that of others, that knowledge was valued. He could not find comfort, in the presence of such reality, in any shallow knowledge.

" There was then, as afterwards, great simplicity in his religious character. It was no isolated part of his nature, it was a bright and genial light shining on every branch of his life. He took very great pains with the Divinity lessons of his pupils: and his lectures were admirable, and, I distinctly remember, very highly prized for their depth and originality. Neither generally in ordinary conversation, nor in his walks with his pupils, was his style of speaking directly or mainly religious; but he was ever very ready to discuss any religious question; whilst the depth and truth of his nature, and the earnestness of his religious convictions and feelings, were ever bursting forth, so as to make it strongly felt that his life, both outward and inward, was rooted in God.

" In the details of daily business, the quantity of time that he devoted to his pupils was very remarkable. Lessons began at seven, and with the interval of breakfast lasted till nearly three; then he would walk with his pupils, and dine at half-past five. At seven he usually had some lesson on hand; and it was only when we all were gathered up in the drawing-room after tea, amidst young men on all sides of him, that he would commence work for himself, in writing his sermons or Roman History.

"Who that ever had the happiness of being at Laleham, does not remember the lightness and joyousness of heart, with which he would romp and play in the garden, or plunge with a boy's delight into the Thames; or the merry fun with which he would battle with spears with his pupils? Which of them does not recollect how the Tutor entered into his amusements with scarcely less glee than himself?

"But I must conclude : I do not pretend to touch on every point. I have told you what struck me most, and I have tried to keep away all remembrance of what he was when I knew him better. I have confined myself to the impression Laleham left upon me.

"B. PRICE."

The studies which most occupied his spare time at Laleham were philology and history, and he employed himself chiefly on a Lexicon of Thucydides. and also on an edition of that author with Latin notes, subsequently exchanged for English ones, a short History of Greece, never finished or published, and on articles on Roman History from the times of the Gracchi to that of Trajan, written for the Encyclopædia Metropolitana, between 1821 and 1827.

It was in 1825 that, through the recommendation of Archdeacon Hare, he first became acquainted with Niebuhr's History of Rome. In the study of this work, which was the first German book he ever read, and for the sake of reading which he had learned that language, a new intellectual world dawned upon him, not only in the subject to which it related, but in the disclosure to him of the depth and research of German literature, which from that moment he learned more and more to appreciate, and as far as his own occupations would allow him, to emulate.

On his view of Roman History its effect was immediate: " It is a work (he writes on first perusing it) of such extraordinary ability and learning, that it opened wide before my eyes the extent of my own ignorance;" and he at once resolved to delay any independent work of his own till he had more completely studied the new field of inquiry suggested to him, in addition to the doubts he had himself already expressed as to the authenticity of much of the early Roman history in one of his first articles in the Encyclopædia Metropolitana.   In an article in the Quarterly Review of 1825, he was (to use Niebuhr's own words of thanks to him in the second edition of his first volume, Note 1053, i. p. 451, Eng. Transl.) " the scholar who introduced the first edition of this history to the English public;" and the feeling which had dictated this friendly notice of it grew with years.   The reluctance which he had at first entertained to admit the whole of Niebuhr's conclusions, and which remained even to 1832, when in regard to his views of ancient history he was inclined to " charge him with a tendency to excessive scepticism," (Pref. to 1st ed. of 2nd vol. of Thucyd. p. xiv.,) settled by degrees into a determination " never to differ from him without a full consciousness of the probability that further inquiry might prove him to be right ;" (Pref. to Hist. of Rome, vol. i. p. x.;) and with this increasing adhesion to his views, increased also a sentiment of something like personal veneration, which made him, as he used to say, " at once emulous and hopeless," rendering him jealous for Niebuhr's reputation, as if for his own, and anxious, amidst the pressure of his other occupations, to undertake, or at least superintend, the translation of the third volume when it was

given up by Hare and Thirlwall,. from a "desire to have
his name connected with the translation of that great
work, which no one had studied more or admired more
entirely." But yet more than by this mere reading, all
these feelings towards Niebuhr, towards Germany, and
towards Roman history, were strengthened by his visit to
Rome in 1827, and by the friendship which he there
formed with Chevalier Bunsen, successor to Niebuhr as
minister at the Papal court. He was at Rome only
thirteen days, but the sight of the city and of the neighbourhood to which he devoted himself to the almost
entire exclusion of the works of art, gave him a living
interest in Rome which he had before wanted and which
he never lost. The Chevalier Bunsen he saw no more
till 1838; but the conversation which he had there
enjoyed with him formed the ground of an unbroken
intercourse by letters between .them : by his encouragement he was principally induced in later years to resume
the History of Rome, which he eventually dedicated to
him ; whilst dwelling on the many points of resemblance
between their peculiar pursuits and general views, he used
to turn with enthusiastic delight to seek for his sympathy
from the isolation in which he often seemed to be placed
in his own country.

But now, as afterwards, he found himself most attracted
towards the interpretation of Scripture and the more practical aspect of Theology; and he was only restrained from
entering upon the study of them more directly, partly by
diffidence in his own powers, partly by a sense that more
time was needed for their investigation than he had at
his command. His early intimacy with the leading men
of the then Oriel School, remarkable as it was for exhibiting a union of religious earnestness with intellectual
activity, and distinct from any existing party amongst the
English clergy, contributed to foster the independence

which characterised his theological and ecclesiastical views from the first time that he took any real interest in serious matters. And he used to look back to a visit to Dr. Whately, then residing on his cure in Suffolk, as a marked era in the formation of his views, especially as opening to his mind, or impressing upon it more strongly, some of the opinions on which he afterwards laid so much stress with regard to the Christian Priesthood.

But although in the way of modification or confirmation his thoughts owed much to the influence of others, there was always, even at this less stirring period of his mind, an original spring within. The words, "He that judgeth me is the Lord," as they stand at the head of one of the most characteristic sermons of this period*, are a true expression of his general views at this time of his life. The distinctness and force with which the words and acts recorded in the Gospel history came before him, seemed to have impressed him early with a conviction that there was something in them very different from what was implied in the common mode of talking and acting on religious subjects. The recollections of his conversations which have been preserved from this period abound with expressions of his strong sense of the "want of Christian principle in the literature of the day," and an anxious foreboding of the possible results which might thence ensue in the case of any change in existing notions and circumstances. "I fear," he said, "the approach of a greater struggle between good and evil than the world has yet seen, in which there may well happen the greatest trial to the faith of good men that can be imagined, if the greatest talent and ability are decidedly on the side of their adversaries, and they will have nothing but faith and holiness to oppose to it." "Something of this kind," he said, "may have been the meaning or part of the

* Serm. vol. i. p. 229.

meaning of the words, 'that by signs and wonders they should deceive even the elect.' What I should be afraid of would be, that good men, taking alarm at the prevailing spirit, would fear to yield even points they could not maintain, instead of wisely giving them up, and holding on where they could." Hence one object of his early attempts at his Roman History was the hope, as he said, that its tone might be such "that the strictest of what is called the Evangelical party would not object to putting it into the hands of their children." Hence again he earnestly desired to see some leading periodical taking a decidedly religious tone, unconnected with any party feeling :—

"It would be a most happy event," he writes in 1822, "if a work which has so great a sale, and contains so much curious information, and has so much the tone of men of the world, [as the Quarterly Review,] could be disciplined to a uniformly Christian spirit, and appear to uphold good principles for their own sake, not merely as tending to the maintenance of things as they are. It would be delightful to see a work sincerely Christian, which should be neither High Church, nor what is called Evangelical."

Out of this general sense of the extreme contrast between the high standard of the Christian religion and the evils of the existing state of Christendom, especially in his own age and country, arose one by one those views which, when afterwards formed into a collected whole, became the animating principle of his public life, but which it is not necessary to anticipate here, except by indicating how rapidly they were in the process of formation in his own mind.

It was now that his political views began to free themselves alike from the more childish Jacobinism of his boyhood, and from the hardly less stable Toryism which he had imbibed from the influence of his early Oxford friends—a change which is best to be seen in his own words, in a letter to Mr. Justice Coleridge many years afterwards (Jan. 26, 1840). And though his interest in public affairs was much less keen at this period than in the subsequent stages of his life, his letters contain, especially after 1826, indications of the same lively sense of social evils, founded on his knowledge of history, which became more and more part of his habitual thoughts.

"I think daily," he said, in speaking of the disturbances in 1819, "of Thucydides, and the Corcyrean sedition, and of the story of the French Revolution, and of the Cassandra-like fate of history, whose lessons are read in vain even to the very next generation."

"I cannot tell you," he writes in 1826, "how the present state of the country occupies my mind, and what a restless desire I feel that it were in my power to do any good. My chief fear is that when the actual suffering is a little abated, people will go on as usual, and not probing to the bottom the deep disease which is to my mind ensuring no ordinary share of misery in the country before many years are over. But we know that it is our own fault if our greatest trials do not turn out to be our greatest advantages."

In ecclesiastical matters in like manner he had already begun to conceive the necessity of great alterations in the Church Establishment, a feeling which at this period, when most persons seemed to acquiesce in its existing state, was naturally stronger than in the later years of his life, when the attacks to which it was exposed from without and from within, appeared at times to endanger its existence.

"I hope to be allowed before I die, to accomplish something on Education, and also with regard to the Church," he writes in 1826; "the last indeed even more than the other, were not the task, humanly speaking, so hopeless. But the more I think of the matter, and the more I read of the Scriptures themselves, and of the history of the Church, the more intense is my wonder at the language of admiration with which some men speak of the Church of England, which certainly retains the foundation sure as all other Christian societies do, except the Unitarians, but has overlaid it with a very sufficient quantity of hay and stubble, which I devoutly hope to see burnt one day in the fire. I know that other churches have their faults also, but what have I to do with them? It is idle to speculate in *alienâ republicâ*, but to reform one's own is a business which nearly concerns us."

His lively appreciation of the high standard of practical and social excellence, enjoined in the Christian dispensation, was also guiding him to those principles of interpretation of Scripture, which he applied so extensively in his later works.

"The tendency," he writes to Dr. Hawkins in 1827, " which so many Christians have had and still have, to fancy that the goodness of the old Patriarchs was absolute rather than relative, and that men who are spoken of as having had personal communication with God, must have had as great knowledge of a future state as ourselves, is expressed in one of G. Herbert's poems, in which he seems to look upon the revelations of the patriarchal Church almost with envy, as if they had nearer communion with God than Christians have. All which seems to me to arise out of a forgetfulness or misapprehension of the privileges of Christians in their communion with the Holy Spirit—and to originate partly in the tritheistic notions of the Trinity, which make men involuntarily consider the *Third* Person as inferior in some degree to those who are called the First and Second, whereas the Third relation of the Deity to man is rather the most perfect of all ; as it is that in which God communes with man, not 'as a man talketh with his friend,' but us a Spirit holding discourse invisibly and incomprehensibly, but more effectually than by any outward address —with the *spirits* only of his creatures. And therefore it was expedient for the disciples that God should be with their hearts as the Spirit, rather than speaking to their ears as the Son. This will give you the clue to my view of the Old Testament, which I never can look upon as addressed to men having a Faith in Christ such as Christians have, or looking forward to eternal life with any settled and uniform hope."

Lastly, the following extracts give his approaches to his subsequent views on Church and State.

"What say you," he writes in 1827, to Dr. Whately, "to a work on πολιτικὴ, in the old Greek sense of the word, in which I should try to apply the principles of the Gospel to the legislation and administration of a state? It would begin with a simple statement of the τέλος of man according to Christianity, and then would go on to show how the knowledge of this τέλος would affect all our views of national wealth, and the whole question of political economy; and also our practice with regard to wars, oaths, and various other relics of the στοιχεῖα τοῦ κόσμου."

And to Mr. Blackstone in the same year:—

"I have long had in my mind a work on Christian Politics, or the application of the Gospel to the state of man as a citizen, in which the whole question of a religious establishment and of the education proper for Christian members of a Christian Commonwealth would naturally find a place. It would embrace also an historical sketch of the pretended conversion of the kingdoms of the world to the kingdom of Christ in the fourth and fifth centuries, which I look upon as one of the greatest *tours d'adresse* that Satan ever played, except his invention of popery. I mean that by inducing kings and nations to conform nominally to Christianity, and thus to get into their hands the direction of Christian society, he has in a great measure succeeded in keeping out the peculiar principles of that society from any extended sphere of operation, and in ensuring the ascendancy of his own. One real conversion there seems to have been, that of the Anglo-Saxons; but that he soon succeeded in corrupting; and at the Norman Conquest we had little I suppose to lose even from the more direct introduction of popery and worldly religion which came in with the Conqueror."

All these floating visions, which were not realised till long afterwards, are best represented in the first volume of his Sermons, which were preached in the parish church at Laleham, and form by far the most characteristic record of this period.

"My object," he said in his Preface, "has been to bring

the great principles of the Gospel home to the hearts and practices of my own countrymen in my own time—and particularly to those of my own station in society, with whose sentiments and language I am naturally most familiar, and for this purpose, I have tried to write in such a style as might be used in real life, in serious conversation with our friends, or with those who asked our advice ; in the language, in short, of common life, and applied to the cases of common life ; but ennobled and strengthened by those principles and feelings which are to be found only in the Gospel."

This volume is, not only in the time of its appearance, but also in its style and substance, the best introduction to all his later works; the very absence of any application to particular classes or states of opinion, such as gives more interest to his subsequent sermons, is the more fitted to exhibit his fundamental views, often not developed in his own mind, in their naked simplicity. And it is in itself worthy of notice, as being the first or nearly the first attempt, since followed in many other quarters, at ·breaking through the conventional phraseology with which· English preaching had been so long encumbered, and at uniting the language of reality and practical sense with names and words which, in the minds of so many of the educated classes, had become closely associated with notions of sectarianism or extravagance.

It was published in 1828, immediately after his removal to Rugby, and had a rapid circulation. Many, both then and long afterwards, who most differed from some of his more peculiar opinions, rejoiced in the possession of a volume which contained so much in which they agreed, and so little from which they differed. The objections to its style or substance may best be gathered from the following extracts of his own letters.

1. "If the sermons are read, I do not care one farthing if the readers think me the most unclassical writer in the English language. It will only remove me to a greater distance from the men of elegant minds with whom I shall most loathe

to be associated. But, however, I have looked at the sermons again, with a view to correcting the baldness which you complain of, and in some places I have endeavoured to correct it. And I again assure you, that I will not knowingly leave unaltered anything violent, harsh, or dogmatical. I am not conscious of the ex-cathedrâ tone of my sermons—at least not beyond what appears to me proper in the pulpit, where one does in a manner speak ex-cathedrâ. But I think my decided tone is generally employed in putting forward sentiments of Scripture, not in drawing my own conclusions from it."

2. In answer to a complaint that " they carry the standard so high as to unchristianize half the community," he says, " I do not see how the standard can be carried higher than Christ or his Apostles carry it, and I do not think that we ought to put it lower. I am sure that the habitually fixing it so much lower, especially in all our institutions and public practice, has been most mischievous."

3. " I am very much gratified by what you say of my sermons ; yet pained to find that their tone is generally felt to be so hard and severe. I believe the reason is, that I mostly thought of my pupils in preaching, and almost always of the higher classes, who I cannot but think have commonly very little of the 'bruised reed' about them. You must remember that I never had the regular care of a parish, and therefore have seen comparatively little of those cases of a troubled spirit, and of a fearful and anxious conscience, which require comfort far more than warning. But still, after all, I fear that the intense mercy of the Gospel has not been so prominently represented as it should have been, while I have been labouring to express its purity."

Meanwhile his friends had frequently represented to him the desirableness of a situation which would secure a more certain provision, and a greater sphere of usefulness than that which he occupied at Laleham ; and he had been urged, more than once, to stand for the Mastership at Winchester, which he had declined first from a distrust of his own fitness or inclination for the office, and afterwards from more generous reasons. But the expense of the neighbourhood of Laleham had already determined him to leave it, and he was framing plans for a change

of life, when, in August, 1827, the head-mastership of
Rugby became vacant by the resignation of Dr. Wooll,
who had held it for twenty-one years. It was not till late
in the contest for the situation that he finally resolved to
offer himself as a candidate. When, therefore, his testimonials were sent in to the twelve trustees, noblemen and
gentlemen of Warwickshire, in whom the appointment
rests, the canvass for the office had advanced so far as to
leave him, in the opinion of himself and many of his
friends, but little hope of success. On the day of the
decision, the testimonials of the several candidates were
read over in the order in which they had been sent in ;
his own were therefore among the last; and whilst none
of the trustees were personally acquainted with him, few,
if any of them owing to the lateness of his appearance,
had heard his name before. His testimonials were few
in number, and most of them couched in general language, but all speaking strongly of his qualifications.
Amongst them was a letter from Dr. Hawkins, now
Provost of Oriel, in which it was predicted that if Mr.
Arnold were elected to the head-mastership of Rugby, he
would change the face of education all through the public
schools of England. The trustees had determined to be
guided entirely by the merits of the candidates, and the
impression produced upon them by this letter, and by the
general confidence in him expressed in all the testimonials, was such, that he was elected at once, in December,
1827. In June, 1828, he received Priest's orders from
Dr. Howley, then Bishop of London ; in April and
November of the same year took his degree of B.D. and
D.D. ; and in August entered on his new office.

The following letters and extracts have been selected,
not so much as important in themselves, but rather as
illustrating the course of his thoughts and general views
at this period.

LETTERS FROM 1817 TO 1828.

I.   TO J. T. COLERIDGE, ESQ.

Oxford, May 28, 1817.

. . . . . I thank you very heartily for the kindness which all your letter displays, and I cannot better show my sense of it than by telling you without reserve my feelings and arguments on both sides of the question. The study of the law in many respects I think I should like, and certainly it holds out better encouragement to any ambitious particles which I may have in my nature than the Church does. But I do not think, if I know myself, which is perhaps begging an important question, that my sober inclinations would lead me to the law so much as to the Church. I am sure the Church would be the best for me, for as I hope never to enter it with light views, so the forming my mind to a proper sense of the clerical duties and then an occasion and call for the practice of them immediately succeeding, would I trust be most beneficial to me. To effect this, I have great advantages in the advice and example of many of my friends here in Oxford, and whether I know myself or not is another question, but I most sincerely feel that I could with most pleasure devote myself to the employments of a clergyman ; and that I never should for a moment put any prospects of ambition or worldly honour in competition with the safe happiness which I think a clergyman's life would grant me. Seriously, I am afraid of the law ; I know how much even here I am led away by various occupations from those studies and feelings which are essential to every man ; and I dare not risk the consequences of such a necessary diversion of mind from all religious subjects, as would be caused by my attending to a study so engrossing as that of law. To this I am sure in your eyes nothing need be added ; but besides I doubt whether my health would support so much reading and confinement to the house ; and after all, knowing who are at this moment contending for the prizes of the law, it would, I think, be folly to stake much on the chance of my success. Again, my present way of life enables me to be a great deal at home with my mother, aunt, and sister, who are so circumstanced that I should not think myself justified in lightly choosing any occupation that would separate me greatly from them. On the other hand, if I find that I cannot conscientiously subscribe to the articles of the Church, be assured I never will go into orders, but even then I should doubt whether I could support either the expense or labour of the law. I hope you have overrated my "ambitious, disputatious, and democratical" propensities; if, indeed, I have not more of the two first than of the last, I think I should not hesitate about my fitness for the Church, as far as they are concerned. I think you have not quite a correct notion of my political faith; perhaps I have not myself, but I do not think I am democratically inclined, and God forbid I should ever be such a clergyman as Horne Tooke.

II.   TO REV. GEORGE CORNISH.

Laleham, September 20, 1819.

. . . . . Poor dear old Oxford ! if I live till I am eighty, and were to enjoy all the happiness that the warmest wish could desire, I should never forget, or cease to look back with something of a painful feeling on the years we were together there, and on all the delights that we have lost ; and I look forward with extreme delight to my intended journey, down to the audit in October, when I shall take a long and last farewell of my old haunts, and will, if I possibly can, yet take one more look at Bagley Wood, and the pretty field, and the wild stream that flows down between Bullington and Cowley Marsh, not forgetting even your old friend, "the Lower London Road." Well, I must endeavour to get some such associations to combine with Laleham and its neighbourhood ; but at present all is harsh and ruffled, like woods in a high wind, only I am beginning to love my own little study, where I have a sofa full of books as of old, and the two verse books lying about on it, and a volume of Herodotus ; and where I sit up and read or write till twelve or one o'clock.

III.　TO REV. F. C. BLACKSTONE.

(On a proposal of a Mastership at Winchester.)

Laleham, October 28, 1819.

I might defer any discussion of the prospects which you recommend to me till we meet, were it a subject on which I could feel any hesitation in making up my mind. But thanking you as I do very sincerely for the kindness of your suggestion, the situation which you advised me to try for, is one which nothing but the most positive call of duty would ever induce me to accept, were it even offered to me. It is one which, in the first place, I know myself very ill qualified to fill; and it would besides completely upset every scheme which I have formed for my future comfort in life. I know that success in my present undertaking is of course doubtful; still my chance is, I think, tolerably fair, not indeed of making my fortune, but of earning such an income as shall enable me to live with economy as a married man; and, as far as I can now foresee, I should wish to continue many years at Laleham, and the house, which I have got on a long lease, is one which I already feel very well inclined to regard as my settled and permanent home in this world. My present way of life I have tried, and am perfectly contented with it; and I know pretty well what the life of a master of Winchester would be, and feel equally certain that it would be to me excessively disagreeable. I do not think you could say anything to shake me for an instant on this head; still believe me that I am very much obliged to you for the friendliness of your recommendation, which I decline for reasons that in all probability many people would think very empty and ridiculous.

IV.　TO REV. JOHN TUCKER.

Laleham, November 20, 1819.

This day eight years, about this time, we were assembled in the Junior Common Room, to celebrate the first foundation of the room, and had been amused by hearing Bartholomew's song about "Musical George," and "Political Tommy," and now, of the party then assembled, you are the only one still left in Oxford, and the rest of us are scattered

over the face of the earth to our several abodes.   There is a
"souvenir intéressant" for you, as a Frenchman would say,
and one full well fitted for a November evening.   But do you
know that I am half disposed to quarrel with you instead of
giving you "Souvenirs"—for did you not covenant to write
to me first? . . . . Indeed, in the pictures that I have to
form of my future life, my friends have always held a part;
and it has been a great delight to me to think, that M. will
feel doubly and naturally bound to so many of them, that
she will have little trouble in learning to love them, and the
benefits which I have received from my Oxford friendships
have been so invaluable, as relating to points of the very
highest importance, that it is impossible for me ever to forget
them, or to cease to look on them as the greatest blessings I
have ever yet enjoyed in life, and for which I have the deepest
reason to be most thankful.   Being then separated from you
all, I am most anxious that absence should not be allowed
to weaken the regard we bear each other; and besides, I
cannot forego that advice and assistance which I have so long
been accustomed to rely on, and with which I cannot as yet
at least safely dispense ; for the management of my own mind
is a thing so difficult, and brings me into contact with much
that is so strangely mysterious, that I stand at times quite
bewildered, in a chaos where I can see no light either before
or behind.   How much of all this is constitutional and physical, I cannot tell ; perhaps a great deal of it; yet it is surely
dangerous to look upon all the struggles of the mind as
arising from the state of the body or the weather, and so
resolve to bestow no attention upon them.   Indeed I think
I have far more reason to be annoyed at the extraordinary
apathy and abstraction from everything good, which the
routine of the world's business brings with it ; there are
whole days in which all the feelings or principles of belief or
of religion altogether, are in utter abeyance ; when one goes
on very comfortably, pleased with external and worldly comforts, and yet would find it difficult, if told to inquire, to find a
particle of Christian principle in one's whole mind.   It seems
all quite moved out bodily, and one retains no consciousness
of a belief in any one religious truth, but is living a life of
virtual Atheism.   I suppose these things are equalised some-
how, but I am often inclined to wonder at and to envy those
who seem never to know what mental trouble is, and who seem
to have nothing else to disturb them than the common petty

annoyances of life, and when these let them alone, then they are εὐ εὐπαθείῃσι.　But I would compound for all this, if I could but find that I had any liking for what I ought to like ; but there is the Sunday School here, for instance, which I never visit without the strongest reluctance, and really the thought of having this to do makes me quite dread the return of the Sunday.　I have got it now entirely into my own hands, so attend it I *must* and *will*, if I can answer for my perseverance, but it goes sadly against me.

V.　TO J. T. COLERIDGE, ESQ.

Lalcham, November 29, 1819.

At last I am going to redeem the promise which I made so long ago, and give you some account of our *summa rerum*. I have had lately the additional work of a sermon every week to write, and this has interfered very much with my correspondence ; and I fear I have not yet acquired that careful economy of time which men in your profession often so well practice, and do not make the most of all the odd five and ten minutes' spaces which I get in the course of the day.　However, I have at last begun my letter, and will first tell you that I still like my business very well, and what is very comfortable, I feel far more confidence in myself than I did at first, and should not now dread having the sole management of pupils, which at one time I should have shrunk from.　(After giving an account of the joint arrangement of the school and the pupils with his brother-in-law ;)　Buckland is naturally fonder of the school, and is inclined to give it the greatest part of his attention ; and I, from my Oxford habits, as naturally like the other part of the business best ; and thus I have extended my time of reading with our four pupils in the morning before breakfast, from one hour to two.　Not that I dislike being in the school, but quite the contrary ; still, however, I have not the experience in that sort of work, nor the perfect familiarity with my grammar requisite to make a good master, and I cannot teach Homer as well as my friends Herodotus and Livy, whom I am now reading, I suppose, for about the fiftieth time.

Nov. 30th.—I was interrupted last night in the middle of my letter, and as the evening is the only time for such occupations, it cannot now go till to-morrow. You shall derive this benefit, however, from the interruption, that I will trouble you with no more details about the *trade*; a subject which I find growing upon me daily, from the retired life we are leading, and from my being so much engrossed by it. There are some very pleasant families settled in this place besides ourselves; they have been very civil to us, and in the holidays I daresay we shall see much of them, but at present I do not feel I have sufficient time to make an acquaintance, and cannot readily submit to the needful sacrifice of formal visits, &c., which must be the prelude to a more familiar knowledge of any one. As it is, my garden claims a good portion of my spare time in the middle of the day, when I am not engaged at home or taking a walk; there is always something to interest me even in the very sight of the weeds and litter, for then I think how much improved the place will be when they are removed; and it is very delightful to watch the progress of any work of this sort, and observe the gradual change from disorder and neglect to neatness and finish. In the course of the autumn I have done much in planting and altering, but these labours are now over, and I have now only to hope for a mild winter as far as the shrubs are concerned that they may not all be dead when the spring comes. Of the country about us, especially on the Surrey side, I have explored much; but not nearly so much as I could wish. It is very beautiful, and some of the scenes at the junction of the heath country with the rich valley of the Thames are very striking. Or if I do not venture so far from home, I have always a resource at hand in the bank of the river up to Staines; which, though it be perfectly flat, has yet a great charm from its entire loneliness, there being not a house anywhere near it; and the river here has none of that stir of boats and barges upon it, which makes it in many places as public as the high road. . . . . . Of what is going on in the world, or anywhere indeed out of Laleham, I know little or nothing. I can get no letters from Oxford, the common complaint I think of all who leave it; and if Penrose did not bring us sometimes a little news from Eton, and Hull from London, I should really, when the holidays begin, find myself six months behind the rest of the world. . . . . .

Don Juan has been with me for some weeks, but I am determined not to read it, for I was so annoyed by some specimens that I saw in glancing over the leaves, that I will not worry myself with any more of it. I have read enough of the debates since parliament has met to make me marvel at the nonsense talked on both sides, though I am afraid the opposition have the palm out and out. The folly or the mischievous obstinacy with which they persist in palliating the excesses of the Jacobins is really scandalous, though I own I do not wish to see Carlton House trimming up the constitution as if it were an hussar's uniform. . . . . . I feel, however, growing less and less political.

VI.   TO REV. GEORGE CORNISH.

Fledborough, January 3, 1820.

. . . . . I conclude that Tucker is with you, so I will begin by sending you both my heartiest wishes for a happy new year ; and for you and yours, that you may long go on as you have begun, and enjoy every succeeding New Year's Day better and better, and have more solid grounds for the enjoyment of it : and for Tucker, that he may taste equal happiness even if it should not be precisely in the same way. Well, here we are, almost at the extremities of the kingdom ; Tucker and you at Sidmouth, and Trevenen and I at Fledborough. . . . . We are snowed up all round, and shall be drowned with the flood when it begins to thaw ; and as for cold, at nine A.M. on Saturday the thermometer stood at o. Alas! for my fingers. Good night "to both on ye," as the poor crazy man used to say in Oxford. . . . . I saw Coleridge when I passed through town on the 22nd, and also his little girl, one of the nicest little children I ever saw. It would have formed a strange contrast with past times, to have seen us standing together in his drawing-room, he nursing the baby in his arms, and dangling it very skilfully, and the little animal in high spirits playing with my hair and clawing me, and laughing very amusingly.

I found them all very well, and quite alone ; and since that time I have not stirred beyond these parishes, and except on Sundays have hardly gone further than the garden and the great meadows on the Trent banks. These vast meadows were flooded and frozen before the snow came, and being now covered with snow, afford a very exact picture of those snowy regions which Thalaba passed over on his way to consult the great Simorg at Kaf. I never before saw so uninterrupted and level a space covered with snow, and the effect of it, when the sun is playing over it, is something remarkably beautiful.   The river, too, as I saw it in the intense frost of Saturday morning, was uncommonly striking.   It had subsided to its natural bed before the snow came ; but the frost had set in so rapidly, that the water had been arrested in the willows and thick bushes that overhang the stream, and was forming on them icicles, and as it were fruits of crystal innumerable on every spray, while the snow formed besides a wintry foliage exactly in character with such wintry fruit.   The river itself rolled dark and black between these glittering banks, full of floating masses of ice, which from time to time dashed against each other, and as you looked up it in the direction of the sun, it smoked like a furnace.   So much for description !   Well, now, I will tell you a marvel.   I wanted to bring down some presents for each of the sisters here ; and for M—— I brought no other than George Herbert's Divine Songs, which I really bought out of my own head, which " I like very much," which I endeavour to interpret —no easy matter in the hard parts—and which I mean to get for myself.   Now do you not think I shall become quite a right-thinking sort of person in good time ?   You need not despair of hearing that I am a violent admirer of Mr. Addison and Mr. Pope, and have given up " the Lord Protector."

. . . . . I owe Tucker many thanks for his letter altogether, and congratulate him on the Water-Eaton altar-piece, as I condole with him on his abandonment of his ancient walks. He ought to bind himself by vow to visit once a term each of our old haunts, in mournful pilgrimage ; and as the spring comes on, if the combined influence of wood-anemones, and souvenirs, and nightingales, does not draw him to Bagley Wood, I think the case must be desperate.   I know I shall myself cry once or twice in the course of the next half year, *"O ubi Campi."*

VII.   TO REV. GEORGE CORNISH.

Laleham, February 23, 1820.

. . . . . You must know that you are one of three persons in the world to whom I hold it wrong to write short letters ; that is to say, you are one of three on whom I can find it in my heart to bestow all my tediousness ; and therefore though February 23rd stands at the top of the page, I do not expect that this sheet will be finished for some time to come.   The first thing I must say is to congratulate you on Charles's appointment. If this letter reaches you amid the pain of parting, congratulation will indeed seem a strange word; yet it is, I think, a matter of real joy after all; it is just what Charles seems best fitted for; his principles and character you may fully depend on, and India is of all fields of honourable ambition that this world offers, to my mind the fairest. You know I always had a sort of hankering after it myself, and but that I prefer teaching Greek to learning Hindustanee, and fear there is no immediate hope of the conquest of China, I should have liked to have seen the Ganges well. To your family India must seem natural ground; and for the separation, painful as it must be, yet do we not all in reality part almost as decisively with our friends when we once settle in life, even though the ocean should not divide us? How little intercourse may I dare to anticipate in after days with those who for so many years have been almost my constant companions; and how little have I seen for several years past of my own brother! But this is prosing. If Charles be still with you, give him my kindest remembrances, with every wish for his future happiness; it already seems a dream to look back on the time when he used to come to my rooms to read Herodotus. Tell him I retain some of his scribbling on the pages of my Hederic's Lexicon, which may many a time remind me of him, when he is skirmishing perhaps with Mahrattas or Chinese, and I am still going over the old ground of $\iota\sigma\tau o\rho\iota\eta s$ $\dot{a}\pi\acute{o}\delta\epsilon\xi\iota s$ $\mathring{\eta}\delta\grave{\epsilon}$. You talk to me of "cutting blocks with a razor;" indeed, it does me no good to lead my mind to such notions; for to tell you a secret, I am quite inclined enough of myself to feel above my work, which is very wrong and very foolish. I believe I am usefully employed, and I am sure I am employed more safely for myself than if I had more time for higher studies; it does my mind a marvellous deal of good, or ought to do, to be kept upon bread and water. But be this as it may, and be the price that I am paying much or little, I cannot forget for what I am paying it. (After speaking of his future prospects.) Here, indeed, I sympathise with you in the fear that this earthly happiness may interest me too deeply. The hold which a man's affections have on him is the more dangerous because the less suspected; and one may become an idolater almost before one feels the least sense of danger. Then comes the fear of losing the treasure, which one may love too fondly; and that fear is indeed terrible. The thought of the instability of one's happiness comes in well to interrupt its full indulgence; and if often entertained must make a man either an Epicurean or a Christian in good earnest. Thank eleven o'clock for stopping my prosing! Good night and God bless you!

VIII.   TO THE SAME.

(On the Death of his Brother.)

Laleham, December 6, 1820.

It is really quite an alarming time since I wrote to you in February; for I cannot count as anything the two brief letters that passed between us at the time of my marriage. I had intended, however, to have written to you a good long one, so soon as the holidays came; but hearing from ——, a few days ago, that you had been expressing a wish to hear from me, I thought I would try to anticipate my intention, and despatch an epistle to you forthwith. It has been an eventful period for me in many ways, since February last,—more so, both for good and for evil, than I ever remember before. The loss which we all sustained in May, was the first great affliction that ever befell me; and it has been indeed a heavy one. At first it came so suddenly that I could not feel it so keenly; and I had other thoughts besides upon me, which would not then allow me to dwell so much upon it. But time has rather made the loss more painful than less so; and now that I am married, and living here calmly and quietly, I often think how he would have enjoyed to have come to Laleham; and all the circumstances of his death occur to me like a frightful dream. It is very extraordinary how often I dream that he is alive, and always with the consciousness that he is alive, after having been supposed dead; and this sometimes has gone so far, that I have in my dream questioned the reality of his being alive, and doubted whether it were not a dream, and have been convinced that it was not, so strongly, that I could hardly shake off the impression on waking. I have, since that, lost another relation, my uncle Delafield, who died quite suddenly at Hastings, in September; his death fell less severely on my mother and aunt, from following so near upon a loss still more distressing to them; but there was in both the same circumstance, which for the time made the shock tenfold greater, that my mother was expecting to see both my brother and my uncle within a few days at Laleham, when she heard of their respective deaths. I attended my uncle's funeral at Kensington, and never did I see greater affliction than that of his children, who were all present. I ought not, however, to dwell only on the painful events that have befallen us, when I have so much of a different kind to be thankful for. My mother is settled, with my aunt, and Susannah, in a more comfortable situation than they have ever been in since we left the Isle of Wight. My mother has got a very good garden, which is an amusement to her in many ways, but chiefly as it enables her to send little presents, &c., to her children; and Susannah's crib lying in a room opening to the garden, she too can enjoy it; and she has been buying some flowering shrubs this autumn, and planting them where they will show themselves to her to the best advantage. My aunt is better, I think, than she commonly is; and she too enjoys her new dwelling, and amuses herself in showing Martha pictures and telling her stories just as she used to do to me. Going on from my mother's house to Buckland's, you will find Frances with two children more than you are acquainted with. . . . From about a quarter before nine till ten o'clock every evening, I am at liberty, and enjoy my wife's company fully: during this time I read out to her (I am now reading to her Herodotus, translating it as I go on), or write my Sermons, when it is my fortnight to preach; or write letters, as I am doing at this moment. And though the space of time that I can thus enjoy be but short, yet perhaps I relish it more keenly even on this very account; and when I am engaged, I ought to think how very many situations in life might have separated me from my wife's society, not for hours only, but for months, or even years; whereas now I have not slept from home once since I have been married; nor am I likely for the greatest part of the year to do so. The garden is a constant source of amusement to us both; there are always some little alterations to be made, some few spots where an additional shrub or two would be ornamental, something coming into blossom, or some crop for the more vulgar use of the table coming into season; so that I can always delight to go round and see how things are going on. Our snowdrops are now just thrusting their heads out of the ground, and I to-day gathered a pink primrose. Trevenen comes over generally about twice a week to see us, and often stays to dine with us; Whately and Blackstone have also at different times paid us visits, and Mary was very much pleased with them both. . . . We set off for Fledborough so soon as the holidays begin, which will be next Wednesday week, and think of staying there almost to the end of them ; only allowing time for a visit to dear old Oxford, when I will try hard to get Mary to Bagley Wood, and show her the tree where you and Tucker and I were once perched all together. . . . I am now far better off than I formerly was in point of lectures ; for I have one in Thucydides, and another in Aristotle's Ethics ; if you dive in the former of these, as I suppose you do, it will be worth your while to get Poppo's " Observationes Criticæ in Thucydidem," a small pamphlet published at Leipzig, in 1815, and by far the best thing—indeed one may say the only good one—that has ever yet been written on the subject. I have been very highly delighted with it, and so I think would any one be, who has as much interest in Thucydides as we have, who have been acquainted with him so long. Another point concerning my trade has puzzled me a good deal. It has been my wish to avoid giving my pupils any Greek to do on a Sunday, so that we do Greek Testament on other days ; but on the Sunday always do some English book ; and they read so much, and then I ask them questions in it. But I find it almost impossible to make them read a mere English book with sufficient attention to be able to answer questions out of it ; or if they do cram themselves for the time, they are sure to forget it directly after. I have been thinking, therefore, of making them take notes of the sermon, after our Oriel fashion, but this does not quite satisfy me ; and as you are a man of experience, I should like to know what your plan is, and whether you have found the same difficulty which I complain of. I have a great deal to hear about you all, and I shall be very glad to have tidings of you, and especially to know how Charles is going on, if you have yet heard from him ; and also how Hubert is faring, to whom I beg you will give my love. It is idle to lay schemes for a time six months distant, —but I do hope to see you in Devonshire in the summer, if you are at home, as we have something of a plan for going into Cornwall to see my innumerable relations there. I heard from Tucker about a week since—perhaps his last letter from Oxford ; it quite disturbs me to think of it. And so he will set up at Malling after all, and by-and-by perhaps we shall see the problem solved, whether he has lost his heart or no. I cannot make out when we are all to see one another, if we all take pupils, and all leave home in the vacations. I think we must fix some inn on some great road, as the place where we may meet en passant once a year. How goes on poetry? With me it is gone, I suppose for ever, and prose too, as far as writing is concerned ; for I do nothing now in that way, save sermons and letters. But this matters little. ·Have you seen or heard of Cramer's book about Hannibal's passage of the Alps? It is, I think, exceedingly good, and I rejoice for the little club's sake. I have been this day to Egham, to sign my name to a loyal address to the king from the gentlemen and householders of this neighbourhood, expressing our confidence in the wisdom and vigour of the constituted authorities. I hope this would please Dyson. I must now leave off scribbling. Adieu, my dear Cornish : Mary begs to join me in all kind wishes and regards to you and yours ; and so would all at the other two houses, if they were at hand.

IX.   TO J. T. COLERIDGE, ESQ.

(In answer to criticisms on a review of Poppo's Observationes Criticæ.)

Laleham Garden, April 25, 1821.

. . . . . Now for your remarks on my Poppo. All clumsiness in the sentences, and want of connexion between the parts, I will do my best to amend ; and the censure on verbal criticism I will either soften or scratch out entirely, for J. Keble objected to the same part. The translations also I will try to improve, and indeed I am aware of their baldness. The additions which you propose I can make readily : but as to the general plainness of the style, I do not think I clearly see the fault which you allude to, and to say the truth, the plainness, *i.e.* the absence of ornament and long words, is the result of deliberate intention. At any rate, in my own case, I am sure an attempt at ornament would make my style so absurd that you would yourself laugh at it. I could not do it naturally, for I have now so habituated myself to that unambitious and plain way of writing, and absence of Latin words as much as possible, that I could not write otherwise without manifest affectation. Of course I do not mean to justify awkwardnesses and clumsy sentences, of which I am afraid my writings are too full, and all of which I will do my best to alter wherever you have marked them ; but anything like puff, or verbal ornament,

I cannot bring myself to. Richness of style I admire heartily, but this I cannot attain to for lack of power. All I could do would be to produce a bad imitation of it, which seems to me very ridiculous. For the same reason I know not how to make the review more striking; I cannot make it so by its own real weight and eloquence, and therefore I think I should only make it offensive by trying to make it fine. Do consider what you recommend is ἁπλῶς ἄριστον, but I must do what is ἄριστον ἐ μοὶ. You know you always told me I should never be a poet, and in like manner I never could be really eloquent, for I have not the imagination or fulness of mind needful to make me so.

X. TO REV. JOHN TUCKER.

Laleham, October 21, 1822.

. . . . . I have not much to say in the way of news; so I will notice that part of your letter which speaks of my not employing myself on something theological. You must remember that what I am doing in Greek and Roman History is only my amusement during the single hour of the day that I can employ on any occupation of my own, namely, between nine and ten in the evening. With such limited time, it would be ridiculous to attempt any work which required much labour, and which could not be promoted by my common occupations with my pupils. The Grecian History is just one of the things I can do most easily; my knowledge of it beforehand is pretty full, and my lectures are continually keeping the subject before my mind; so that to write about it is really my recreation; and the Roman History is the same to me, though in a less degree. I could not name any other subject equally familiar, or which, in my present circumstances, would be practicable, and certainly if I can complete plain and popular histories of Greece and Rome. of a moderate size, cleared of nonsense and unchristian principles, I do not think I shall be *amusing* myself ill; for as I now am, I could not do anything besides my proper work that was not an amusement. For the last fortnight, during which I have had two sermons to write, I have not been able to do a word of my History; and it will be the same this week, if I write some letters which I wish to write : so that you see I am in no condition to undertake anything of real labour. Be assured there is nothing I would so gladly do as set about a complete Ecclesiastical History; and I love to fancy myself so engaged at some future time, if I live; but to begin such a thing now would be utterly desperate. The want of books alone, and my inability to consult libraries, would be a sufficient hindrance. I have read a new book lately, which is rather an event for me, Jowett's Christian Researches in the Mediterranean. You know it of course, and I doubt not like it as much as I do, which is very much indeed. It is a very wonderful and a very beautiful thing to see the efforts made on so large a scale, and with motives so pure, to diffuse all good both temporal and spiritual; and I suppose that the world is gradually dividing more and more into two divided parties of good and evil; the lukewarm and the formal Christians are, I imagine, daily becoming less numerous. I am puzzled beyond measure what to think about Ireland. What good can be done permanently with a people who literally do make man's life as cheap as beasts'; and who are content to multiply in idleness and in such beggary that the first failure of a crop brings them to starvation? I would venture to say that luxury never did half so much harm as the total indifference to comfort is doing in Ireland, by leading to a propagation of the human species in a state of brutality. I should think that no country in the world needs missionaries so much, and in none would their success be so desperate.

XI.   TO J. T. COLERIDGE, ESQ.

Laleham, March 3, 1823.

. . . . . . I do not know whether you have ever seen John Keble's Hymns. He has written a great number for most of the holidays and several of the Sundays in the year, and I believe intends to complete the series. I live in hopes that he will be induced to publish them; and it is my firm opinion that nothing equal to them exists in our language: the wonderful knowledge of Scripture, the purity of heart, and the richness of poetry which they exhibit, I never saw paralleled. If they are not published, it will be a great neglect of doing good. I wish you could see them; the contemplation of them would be a delightful employment for your walks between Hadlow Street and the Temple. . . . . . Have you heard anything more about ———'s Roman History? I am really anxious to know what sort of a man he is, and whether he will write like a

Christian or no ; if he will, I have not a wish to interfere with him ; if not, I would labour very hard indeed to anticipate him, and prevent an additional disgrace from being heaped upon the historical part of our literature.

XII. TO REV. JOHN TUCKER.

Laleham, February 22, 1824.

. . . . . My pupils all come up into the drawing-room a little before tea, and stay for some time, some reading, others talking, playing chess or backgammon, looking at pictures, &c. —a great improvement if it lasts ; and if this fair beginning continues, I care not a straw for the labour of the half-year, for it is not labour but vexation which hurts a man, and I find my comfort depends more and more on their good and bad conduct. They are an awful charge, but still to me a very interesting one, and one which I could cheerfully pursue till my health or faculties fail me. Moreover I have now taken up the care of the workhouse, *i.e.* as far as going there once a week to read prayers and give a sort of lecture upon some part of the Bible. I wanted to see more of the poor people, and I found that unless I devoted a regular time to it, I should never do it, for the hunger for exercise on the part of myself and my horses, used to send me out riding as soon as my work was done ; whereas now I give up Thursday to the village, and it will be my own fault if it does not do me more good than the exercise would. You have heard I suppose of Trevenen's tour with me to Scotland. Independent of the bodily good which it did me, and which I really wanted, I have derived from it the benefit of getting rid of some prejudices, for I find myself often thinking of Edinburgh quite affectionately, so great was the kindness which we met with there, and so pleasant and friendly were most of the people with whom we became acquainted. As to the scenery it far surpassed all my expectations : I shall never forget the effect of the setting sun on the whole line of the Grampians, covered with snow, as we saw them from the steamboat on the Forth between Alloa and Stirling. It was so delightful also to renew my acquaintance with the English lakes and with Wordsworth. . . . . . I could lubricate largely *de omni scibili*, but paper happily runs short. I am very much delighted with the aspect of the Session of Parliament, and see with hearty gratitude the real reforms and the purer spirit of government which this happy rest from war is every year I trust gradually encouraging. The West India question is thorny : but I suppose the government may entrench upon individual property for a great national benefit, giving a fair compensation to the parties, just as is done in every Canal Bill. Nay, I cannot see why the rights of the planters are more sacred than those of the old despotic kings and feudal aristocracies who were made to part with many good things which they had inherited from their ancestors because the original tenure was founded on wrong : and so is all slavery, all West Indian slavery at least, most certainly.

XIII.   TO W. W. HULL, ESQ.

Laleham, September 30, 1824.

. . . . . . I am now working at German in good earnest, and have got a master who comes down here to me once a week. I have read a good deal of Julius Hare's friend Niebuhr, and have found it abundantly overpay the labour of learning a new language, to say nothing of some other very valuable German books with which I am becoming acquainted, all preparatory to my Roman History. I am going to set to work at the " Coke upon Littleton " of Roman law—to make myself acquainted, if possible, with the tenure of property ; and I think I shall apply to you for the loan of some of your books touching the civil law, and especially Justinian's Institutes. As my knowledge increases, I only get a clearer insight into my ignorance ; and this excites me to do my best to remove it before I descend to the Avernus of the press. But I am twice the man for labour that I have been lately, for the last year or two, because the pupils, I thank God, are going on well ; I have at this moment the pleasure of seeing three of them sitting at the round table in the drawing-room, all busily engaged about their themes ; and the general good effect of their sitting with us all the evening is really very surprising.

XIV.   TO REV. JOHN TUCKER.

Laleham, April 5, 1825.

. . . . . . I am getting pretty well to understand the history of the Roman kings, and to be ready to commence writing.

One of my most useful books is dear old Tottle's [Aristotle's] Politics ; which give one so full a notion of the state of society and opinions in old times, that by their aid one can pick out the wheat from the chaff in Livy with great success. Mr. Penrose has lately mentioned a work by a Mr. Cooper, in which he applies the prophecies in the eleventh chapter of Daniel to Buonaparte.—Have you read the work yourself? My own notion is, that people try to make out from prophecy too much of a detailed history, and thus I have never seen a single commentator who has not perverted the truth of history to make it fit the prophecy. I think that, with the exception of those prophecies which relate to our Lord, the object of prophecy is rather to delineate principles and states of opinion which shall come, than external events. I grant that Daniel seems to furnish an exception, and I do not know how Mr. Cooper has done his work ; but in general, commentaries or expositions of the prophecies give me a painful sense of unfairness in their authors, in straining the facts to agree with the imagined prediction of them. Have you seen Cobbett's " History of the Protestant Reformation," which he is publishing monthly in threepenny numbers ? It is a queer compound of wickedness and ignorance with strong sense, and the mention of divers truths which have been too much disguised or kept in the background, but which ought to be generally known. Its object is to represent the Reformation in England as a great national evil, accomplished by all kinds of robbery and cruelty, and tending to the impoverishment and misery of the poor, and to the introduction of a careless clergy and a spirit of ignorance and covetousness amongst every body. It made me groan, while reading it, to think that the real history and effects of the Reformation are so little known, and the evils of the worldly policy of Somerset's and Elizabeth's government so little appreciated. As it is, Cobbett's book can do nothing but harm, so bad is its spirit, and so evident its unfairness.

XV.   TO REV. GEORGE CORNISH.

Florence, July 15, 1825.

I wish I could tell you something about the people—but how is it possible, travelling at the rate that we are obliged to do ? We see, of course, the very worst specimens—innkeepers, postillions, and beggars ; and one is thus in danger of getting an unfavourable impression of the inhabitants in spite of one's judgment.   A matter of more serious thought, and on which I am vainly trying to procure information, is the condition of the lower orders.   I have long had a suspicion that Cobbett's complaints of the degradation and sufferings of the poor in England contained much truth, though uttered by him in the worst possible spirit.   It is certain that the peasantry here are much more generally proprietors of their own land than with us ; and I should believe them to be much more independent and in easier circumstances.   This is, I believe, the grand reason why so many of the attempts at revolution have failed in these countries.   A revolution would benefit the lawyers, the savants, the merchants, bankers, and shopkeepers, but I do not see what the labouring classes would gain by it.   For them the work has been done already, in the destruction of the feudal tyranny of the nobility and great men ; and, in my opinion, this blessing is enough to compensate the evils of the French Revolution ; for the good endures, while the effects of the massacres and devastations are fast passing away.   It is my delight everywhere to see the feudal castles in ruins, never, I trust, to be rebuilt or reoccupied; and in this respect the watchword " Guerre aux châteaux, Paix aux Chaumières," was prophetic of the actual result of the French Revolution.   I am sure that we have too much of the oligarchical spirit in England, both in church and state ; and I think that those one-eyed men, the political economists, encourage this by their language about national wealth, &c.   Toutefois, there is much good in the oligarchical spirit as it exists in England. . . . . . .

———

XVI. TO REV. J. TUCKER.

Laleham, August 22, 1825.

. . . . . . I got no books of any consequence, nor did I learn anything except that general notion of the climate, scenery, and manners of the country, which can only be gained by actual observation.   We crossed the Tiber a little beyond Perugia, where it was a most miserable ditch with hardly water enough to turn a mill ; indeed, most of the streams which flow from the Apennines were altogether dried up, and the dry and thirsty appearance of everything was truly oriental.   The flowers were a great delight to me, and it was very beautiful to see the hedges full of the pomegranate in full flower: the bright scarlet blossom is so exceedingly ornamental, to say nothing of one's associations with the fruit. What we call the Spanish broom of our gardens is the common wild broom of the Apennines, but I do not think it so beautiful as our own. The fig trees were most luxuriant, but not more so than in the Isle of Wight, and I got tired of the continual occurrence of fruit trees, chiefly olives, instead of large forest trees. The vale of Florence looks quite poor and dull in comparison of our rich valleys, from the total want of timber; and in Florence itself there is not a tree. How miserably inferior to Oxford is Florence altogether, both within and as seen from a distance; in short, I never was so disappointed in any place in my life. My favourite towns were Genoa, Milan, and Verona. The situation of the latter just at the foot of the Alps, and almost encircled, like Durham, by a full and rapid river, the Adige, was very delightful. Tell me any news you can think of, remembering that two months in the summer are a gap in my knowledge, as I never saw a single newspaper during my absence. Specially send me a full account of yourself and your sisters, and the Kebles if you know aught of them. How pure and beautiful was J. Keble's article on Sacred Poetry in the Quarterly, and how glad I am that he was prevailed on to write it. It seemed to me to sanctify in a manner the whole Number. Mine on the early Roman History was slightly altered by Coleridge here and there, so that I am not quite responsible for all of it.

XVII. TO REV. G. CORNISH.

Laleham, October 18, 1825.

. . . . . . I have also seen some sermons, preached before the University of Cambridge, by a Mr. Rose, directed against the German theologians, in the advertisement to which he attacks my article in the Quarterly with great vehemence. . . . . . He is apparently a good man, and his book is likely, I think, to do good; but it does grieve me to find persons of his stamp quarrelling with their friends when there are more than enough of enemies in the world for every Christian to strive against. I met five Englishmen at the public table at our inn at Milan, who gave me great matter for cogitation.

One was a clergyman, and just returned from Egypt; the rest were young men, *i.e.* between twenty-five and thirty, and apparently of no profession. I may safely say, that since I was an undergraduate, I never heard any conversation so profligate as that which they all indulged in, the clergyman particularly; indeed, it was not merely gross, but avowed principles of wickedness, such as I do not remember ever to have heard in Oxford. But what struck me most was, that with this sensuality there was united some intellectual activity,— they were not ignorant, but seemed bent on gaining a great variety of solid information from their travels. Now this union of vice and intellectual power and knowledge seems to me rather a sign of the age; and if it goes on, it threatens to produce one of the most fearful forms of Antichrist which has yet appeared. I am sure that the great prevalence of travelling fosters this spirit, not that men learn mischief from the French or Italians, but because they are removed from the check of public opinion, and are, in fact, self-constituted outlaws, neither belonging to the society which they have left, nor taking a place in that of the countries where they are travelling. What I saw also of the Pope's religion in his own territories excited my attention a good deal. Monkery seems flourishing there in great force, and the abominations of their systematic falsehoods seem as gross as ever. In France, on the contrary, the Catholics seemed to me to be Christians, and daily becoming more and more so. In Italy they seem to me to have no more title to the name than if the statues of Venus and Juno occupied the place of those of the Virgin. It is just the old Heathenism, and, as I should think, with a worse system of deceit.

XVIII.　TO REV. J. TUCKER.

Laleham, 1826.

. . . . . . It delighted me to hear —— speak decidedly of the great need of reform in the Church, and from what I have heard in other quarters, I am in hopes that these sentiments are gaining ground. But the difficulty will always be practically, who is to reform it? For the clergy have a horror of the House of Commons, and Parliament and the country will never trust the matter to the clergy. If we had our General Assembly, there might be some chance; but as it is, I know no more hopeless prospect, and every year I live, this is to me more painful. If half the energy and resources which have been turned to Bible societies and missions, had steadily been applied to the reform of our own institutions, and the enforcing the principles of the Gospel among ourselves, I cannot but think that we should have been fulfilling a higher duty, and with the blessing of God might have produced more satisfactory fruit. " These things ought ye to have done, and not to have left the other undone."*   Of the German divines, if Mr. Rose is to be trusted, there can be but one opinion : they exemplify the evils of knowledge without a Christian watchfulness over the heart and practice ; but I greatly fear that there are some here who would abuse this example to the discouragement of impartial investigation and independent thought ; as if ignorance and blind following the opinions of others were the habits that best become Christians. "He that is spiritual judgeth all things,"—if cleared from fanaticism and presumption, and taken in connexion with "But yet I show unto you a more excellent way,"—is at once, I think, our privilege and our duty.

<hr>

XIX.   TO REV. JOHN TUCKER.

Laleham, March 4, 1827.

I meant to have written almost immediately upon my return home from Kent ; for delightful as is the recollection of my short visit to you on every other ground, I was, and have been ever since, a good deal annoyed by some part of our conversation, *i.e.* by observing the impression produced on your mind by some of the opinions which I expressed. It is to me personally a very great pain that I should have excited feelings of disapprobation in the mind of a man whom I so entirely approve and love, and yet that I cannot feel the disapprobation ‹to be deserved, and therefore cannot remove the cause of it. And on more general grounds it makes me fear, that those engaged in the same great cause will never heartily sink their little differences of opinion, when I find that you, who have known me so long, cannot hear them without thinking them not merely erroneous, but morally wrong, and such, therefore, as give you pain when uttered.

* The words of the English version are here substituted for the quotations from the Greek.

I am not in the least going to renew the argument; it is very likely that I was wrong in it; and I am sure it would not annoy me that you should think me so, just as I may think you wrong in any point, or as I think J. Keble wrong in half an hundred, yet without being grieved that he should hold them, that is, grieved as at a fault. You may say that a great many erroneous opinions imply no moral fault at all, but that mine did, namely, the fault of an unsubmissive understanding. But it seems to me that, of all faults, this is the most difficult to define or to discern : for who shall say where the understanding ought to submit itself, unless where it is inclined to advocate anything immoral ? We know that what in one age has been called the spirit of rebellious reason, has in another been allowed by all good men to have been nothing but a sound judgment exempt from superstition. We know that the Catholics look with as great horror on the consequences of denying the infallibility of the Church as you can do on those of denying the entire inspiration of the Scriptures ; and that, to come nearer to the point, the inspiration of the Scriptures in points of physical science was once insisted on as stoutly as it is now maintained with regard to matter of history. Now it may be correct to deny their inspiration in one and not in the other ; but I think it is hard to ascribe the one opinion to anything morally faulty more than the other. I am far from thinking myself so good a man by many degrees as you are. I am not so advanced a Christian. But I am sure that my love for the Gospel is as sincere, and my desire to bring every thought into the obedience of Christ is one which I think I do not deceive myself in believing that I honestly feel. It is very painful, therefore, to be suspected of paying them only a divided homage, or to be deficient in reference to Him whom every year that I live my whole soul and spirit own with a more entire certainty and love. Let me again say, that I am neither defending the truth of the particular opinions which I expressed to you, nor yet disavowing them. I only think that it is a pity that they should shock you ; as I think we ought to know one another's principles well enough by this time, not certainly to make us acquiesce in all each other's opinions, but to be satisfied that they may be entertained innocently, and that, therefore, we may differ from each other without pain. But enough of this ; only it has annoyed me a great deal, and has made me doubt where I can find a person to whom I may speak freely if I cannot do so even to you.

LETTERS RELATING TO THE ELECTION AT RUGBY.

XX. TO REV. E. HAWKINS.

Laleham, October 21, 1827.

I feel most sincerely obliged to you and my other friends in Oxford for the kind interest which you show in my behalf, in wishing to procure for me the head-mastership at Rugby. Of its being a great deal more lucrative than my present employment I have no doubt; nor of its being in itself a situation of more extensive usefulness; but I do doubt whether it would be so in my hands, and how far I am fitted for the place of head-master of a large school. . . . I confess that I should very much object to undertake a charge in which I was not invested with pretty full discretion. According to my notions of what large schools are, founded on all I know and all I have ever heard of them, expulsion should be practised much oftener than it is. Now, I know that trustees, in general, are averse to this plan, because it has a tendency to lessen the numbers of the school, and they regard quantity more than quality. In fact, my opinions on this point might, perhaps, generally be considered as disqualifying me for the situation of master of a great school; yet I could not consent to tolerate much that I know is tolerated generally, and, therefore, I should not like to enter on an office which I could not discharge according to my own views of what is right. I do not believe myself, that my system would be, in fact, a cruel or a harsh one, and I believe that with much care on the part of the masters, it would be seldom necessary to proceed to the *ratio ultima*; only I would have it clearly understood, that I would most unscrupulously resort to it, at whatever inconvenience, where there was a perseverance in any habit inconsistent with a boy's duties.

XXI. TO REV. GEORGE CORNISH.

Laleham, November 30, 1827.

You have often wanted me to be master at Winchester, so I think you will be glad to hear that I am actually a candidate for Rugby. I was strongly urged to stand, and money tempted me, but I cannot in my heart be sorry to stay where both M. and myself are so entirely happy. If I do get it, I feel as if I could set to work very heartily, and, with God's blessing, I should like to try whether my notions of Christian education are really impracticable, whether our system of public schools has not in it some elements which, under the blessing of the Spirit of all holiness and wisdom, might produce fruit even to life eternal. When I think about it thus, I really long to take rod in hand; but when I think of the πρὸς τὸ τέλος, the perfect vileness which I must daily contemplate, the certainty that this can at best be only partially remedied, the irksomeness of "fortemque Gyan fortemque Cloanthum," and the greater form and publicity of the life which we should there lead, when I could no more bathe daily in the clear Thames, nor wear old coats and Russia duck trousers, nor hang on a gallows,* nor climb a pole, I grieve to think of the possibility of a change; but as there are about thirty candidates, and I only applied very late, I think I need not disquiet myself. I send you this brief notice, because you ought to hear my plans from myself rather than from others; but I have no time to write more. Thucydides prospers.

XXII. TO REV. J. TUCKER.

December 28, 1827.

Our united warmest thanks to you and to your sisters for the joy you have felt about Rugby. For the labour I care nothing, if God gives me health and strength as he has for the last eight years. But whether I shall be able to make the school what I wish to make it,—I do not mean wholly or perfectly, but in some degree,—that is, an instrument of God's glory, and of the everlasting good of those who come to it,— that indeed is an awful anxiety.

XXIII. TO REV. E. HAWKINS.

Laleham, December 28, 1827.

Your kind little note ought not to have remained thus long unanswered, especially as you have a most particular claim on

----

* His gymnastic exercises.

my thanks for your active kindness in the whole business, and for your character of me to Sir H. Halford, that I was likely to improve generally the system of public education, a statement which Sir H. Halford told me had weighed most strongly in my favour. You would not, I am sure, have recommended me, if you had supposed that I should alter things violently, or for the pleasure of altering; but as I have at different times expressed in conversation my disapprobation of much of the existing system, I find that some people expect that I am going to sweep away root and branch, quod absit! I need not tell you how wholly unexpected this result has been to us, and I hope I need not say what a solemn and almost overwhelming responsibility I feel is imposed on me. I would hope to have the prayers of my friends, together with my own, for a supply of that true wisdom which is required for such a business. To be sure, how small in comparison is the importance of my teaching the boys to read Greek, and how light would be a school-master's duty if that were all of it. Yet, if my health and strength continue as they have been for the last eight years, I do not fear the labour, and really enjoy the prospect of it. I am so glad that we are likely to meet soon in Oxford.

XXIV. TO REV. JOHN TUCKER.

Laleham, March 2.

With regard to reforms at Rugby, give me credit, I must beg of you, for a most sincere desire to make it a place of Christian education. At the same time my object will be, if possible, to form Christian men, for Christian boys I can scarcely hope to make; I mean that, from the natural imperfect state of boyhood, they are not susceptible of Christian principles in their full development upon their practice, and I suspect that a low standard of morality in many respects must be tolerated amongst them, as it was on a larger scale in what I consider the boyhood of the human race.* But I believe that a great deal may be done, and I should be most unwilling to undertake the business, if I did not trust that much might be done. Our impressions of the exterior of everything that

---

* See Sermons, vol. ii. p. 440. His later sermons and letters seem to indicate that subsequently this opinion would not have been expressed quite so strongly.

we saw during our visit to Dr. Wooll in January, were very favourable ; at the same time that I anticipate a great many difficulties in the management of affairs, before they can be brought into good train. But both M. and myself, I think, are well inclined to commence our work, and if my health and strength be spared me, I certainly feel that in no situation could I have the prospect of employment so congenial to my taste and qualifications ; that is, supposing always that I find that I can manage the change from older pupils to a school. Your account of yourself was most delightful : my life for some years has been one of great happiness, but I fear not of happiness so safe and permitted. I am hurried on too fast in the round of duties and of domestic enjoyments, and I greatly feel the need, and shall do so even more at Rugby, unless I take heed in time, of stopping to consider my ways, and to recognise my own infinite weakness and unworthiness. I have read the "Letters on the Church," and reviewed them in the Edinburgh Review for September, 1826, if you care to know what I think of them. I think that any discussion on church matters must do good, if it is likely to lead to any reform ; for any change, such as is within any human calculation, would be an improvement. What might not ———— do, if he would set himself to work in the House of Lords, not to patch up this hole or that, but to recast the whole corrupt system, which in many points stands just as it did in the worst times of popery, only reading "King" or "Aristocracy," in the place of "Pope."

XXV.   TO REV. F. C. BLACKSTONE.

Laleham, March 14, 1828.

...... We are resigning private pupils, I imagine, with very different feelings ; you looking forward to a life of less distraction, and I to one of far greater, insomuch that all here seems quietness itself in comparison with what I shall meet with at Rugby. There will be a great deal to do, I suspect, in every way, when I first enter on my situation ; but still, if my health continues, I do not at all dread it, but on the contrary look forward to it with much pleasure. I have long since looked upon education as my business in life ; and just before I stood for Rugby, I had offered myself as a candidate for the historical professorship at the London University ; and had indulged in various dreams of attaching myself to that institution, and trying as far as possible to influence it. In Rugby there is a fairer field, because I start with greater advantages. You know that I never ran down public schools in the lump, but grieved that their exceeding capabilities were not turned to better account; and if I find myself unable in time to mend what I consider faulty in them, it will at any rate be a practical lesson to teach me to judge charitably of others who do not reform public institutions as much as is desirable. I suppose that you have not regarded all the public events of the last few months without some interest. My views of things certainly become daily more *reforming*; and what I above all other things wish to see is, a close union between Christian reformers and those who are often, as I think, falsely charged with being enemies of Christianity. It is a part of the perfection of the Gospel that it is attractive to all those who love truth and goodness, as soon as it is known in its true. nature, whilst it tends to clear away those erroneous ways and evil passions with which philanthropy and philosophy, so long as they stand aloof from it, are ever in some degree corrupted. My feeling towards men whom I believe to be sincere lovers of truth and the happiness of their fellow-creatures, while they seek these ends otherwise than through the medium of the Gospel, is rather that they are not far from the kingdom of God, and might be brought into it altogether, than that they are enemies whose views are directly opposed to our own. That they are not brought into it is, I think, to a considerable degree, charge-able upon the professors of Christianity; the High Church party seeming to think that the establishment in Church and State is all in all, and that the Gospel principles must be accommodated to our existing institutions, instead of offering a pattern by which those institutions should be purified; and the Evangelicals by their ignorance and narrow-mindedness, and their seeming wish to keep the world and the Church ever dis-tinct, instead of labouring to destroy the one by increasing the influence of the other, and making the kingdoms of the world indeed the kingdoms of Christ.

XXVI. TO AUGUSTUS HARE, ESQ.

Lalcham, March 7, 1828.

. . . . . I trust that you have recovered your accident at Perugia, and that you are enabled to enjoy your stay at that glorious Rome.   I think that I have never written to you since my return from it last spring, when I was so completely over-powered with admiration and delight at the matchless beauty and solemnity of Rome and its neighbourhood.   But I think my greatest delight after all was in the society of Bunsen, the Prussian minister at Rome. . . . . He reminded me continually of you more than of any other man whom I know, and chiefly by his entire and enthusiastic admiration of everything great and excellent and beautiful, not stopping to see or care for minute faults ; and though I cannot rid myself of that critical propensity, yet I can heartily admire and almost envy those who are without it. . . . . I have derived great benefit from sources of information, that your brother has at different times recommended to me, and the perusal of some of his articles in the "Guesses at Truth" has made me exceedingly desirous of becoming better acquainted with him, as I am sure that his conversation would be really profitable to me in the highest sense of the word, as well as delightful.   And I have a double pleasure in saying this, because I did not do him justice for-merly in my estimate of him, and am anxious to do myself justice now by saying that I have learnt to judge more truly. You will have heard of my changed prospects in consequence of my election at Rugby.   It will be a severe pang to me to leave Laleham ; but otherwise I rejoice in my appointment, and hope to be useful if life and health are spared me. . . . . I think of going to Leipsic, Dresden, and Prague, to worship the Elbe and the country of John Huss and Ziska.   All here unite in kindest remembrances to you, and I wish you could convey to the very stones and air of Rome the expression of my fond recollection for them.

XXVII.   TO. REV. JOHN TUCKER.

Laleham, May 25, 1828.

(After speaking of Mr. Tucker's proposed intention of going as a missionary to India.)   If you should go to India before we have an opportunity of meeting again, I would earnestly beg of you not to go away with the notion, which I sometimes fear that my oldest friends are getting of me, that I am become a hard man, given up to literary and scholastic pursuits, and full of worldly and political views of things.   It has given me very great pain to think that some of those whom I most love, and with whom I would most fain be one in spirit, regard my views of things as jarring with their own, and are losing towards me that feeling of Christian brotherhood which I think they once entertained.   I am not in the slightest degree speaking of any offence given or received, or any personal decay of regard, but I fancy they look upon me as not quite one with themselves, and as having my affections fixed upon lower objects. Assuredly I have no right to regret that I should be thought deficient in points in which I know I am deficient; but I would most earnestly protest against being thought wilfully and contentedly deficient in them, and not caring to be otherwise. And I cannot help fearing that my conversation with you last winter twelvemonth led you to something, at least, of a similar impression.

XXVIII.   TO J. T. COLERIDGE, ESQ.

Laleham, April 24, 1828.

It seems an age since I have seen you or written to you; and I hear that you are now again returned to London, and that your eldest boy, I am grieved to find, is not so well and strong as you could wish.   I could really be half romantic, yet I do not know that I ought to use any such equivocal epithet. When I think how little intercourse I hold with my most valued friends, it is almost awful to feel the tendencies of life to pare down one's affections and feelings to the minimum compatible with anything like humanity.   There is one's trade and one's family, and beyond it seems as if the great demon of worldly-mindedness would hardly allow one to bestow a thought or care.

But, if it please God, I will not sink into this state without some struggles, at least, against it.   I saw Dyson the other day in Oxford, where I went to take my degree of B.D., and he and his wife were enough to freshen one's spirit for some time to come.   I wish that you and I could meet oftener, and instead of that, I fear that when I am at Rugby, we shall meet even seldomer; but I trust that we shall meet sometimes still.   You know, perhaps,—and yet how should you ?—that my sixth child, and fourth son, was born on the 7th of April, and that his dear mother has been again preserved to me. All the rest of my children are quite well, and they are also tolerably well at the other houses, though the coming parting is a sad cloud both to them and to us. Still, without any affectation, I believe that John Keble is right, and that it is good for us to leave Laleham, because I feel that we are daily getting to regard it as too much of a home. I cannot tell you how we both love it, and its perfect peace seems at times an appalling contrast to the publicity of Rugby. I am sure that nothing could stifle this regret, were it not for my full consciousness that I have nothing to do with rest here, but with labour ; and then I can and do look forward to the labour with nothing but satisfaction, if my health and faculties be still spared to me.

I went down to Rugby, a fortnight since, to meet the trustees. The terms of the school, which were far too low, have been raised on my representation ; and there is some possibility of my being put into the situation of the head-masters of Eton and Westminster, that is, to have nothing to do with any boarders.. . . . . . I have got six maps for Thucydides, all entirely original, and I have nearly finished half of the last book ; so that I hope I may almost say "Italiam ! Italiam !"

XXIX.   TO REV. F. C. BLACKSTONE.

Laleham, July 11, 1828.

. . . . . It would be foolish to talk of the deep love that I bear to Laleham, and the wrench which it will be to part from it ; but this is quite consistent with a lively interest in Rugby, and when I strolled with —— in the meadows there, during our visit of last week, I thought that I already began to feel it as my home. . . . . . There will be enough to do, I imagine, without any addition ; though I really feel very sanguine as to my own relish for the work, and think that it will come more naturally to me than I at first imagined. May God grant that I may labour with an entire confidence in Him, and with none in myself without Him.

XXX.   TO W. W. HULL, ESQ.

Laleham, July 29, 1828.

. . . . . . I never would publish* without a considerable

---

* In allusion to the first volume of his Sermons, which was now in the process of publication.

revision of them. I well know their incompleteness, and suspect much worse faults in them. Do not imagine that I neglect your remarks; far from it: I would attend to them earnestly, and would soften gladly anything that was too harsh, or that might give offence, and would alter the mere inadvertencies of my hasty writing in point of style. But certainly the character of the style I could not alter, because no other would be natural to me; and though I am far from wishing other people to write as I do, yet for myself I hold it best to follow my own fashion. . . . . . .

I owe it to Rugby not to excite needless scandal by an isolated and uncalled-for publication. I shall never be Mr. Dean, nor do I wish it; but having undertaken the office of Dr. Wooll, with double *l* or single *l*, as best suits your fancy, I do wish to do my utmost in it, and not to throw difficulties in my own way by any imprudence. This, of course, would apply either to minor points, or to those on which I distrusted my own competent knowledge. Where I am fully decided on a matter of consequence, I would speak out as plainly and boldly as your heart could wish.

We are all in the midst of confusion; the books all packed, and half the furniture; and on Tuesday, if God will, we shall leave this dear place, this nine years' home of such exceeding happiness. But it boots not to look backwards. Forwards, forwards, forwards,—should be one's motto. I trust you will see us in our new dwelling ere long; I shall want to see my old friends there to wear off the gloss of its newness.

XXXI. TO REV. JOHN TUCKER.

Laleham, August, 1828.

I am inclined to write to you once again before we leave Laleham, as a sort of farewell from this dear place; and you shall answer it with a welcome to Rugby. You fancy us already at Rugby, and so does J. Keble, from whom I received a very kind letter some time since, directed to me there. But we do not move till Tuesday, when we go, fourteen souls, to Oxford, having taken the whole coach; and on Wednesday we hope to reach Rugby, having in like manner secured the whole Leicester coach from Oxford to Rugby. Our goods and chattels, under convoy of our gardener, are at this time somewhere on the Grand Junction Canal, and will reach Rugby I hope this evening. The poor house here is sadly desolate; all the carpets up, half the furniture gone, and signs of removal everywhere visible. And so ends the first act of my life since I arrived at manhood. For the last eight years it has been a period of as unruffled happiness as I should think could ever be experienced by man. M——'s illness, in 1821, is almost its only dark spot;—and how was that softened and comforted ! It is almost a fearful consideration ; and yet that is a superstitious notion, and an unbelieving one, too, which cannot receive God's mercies as his free gift, but will always be looking out for something wherewith to purchase them. An humbling consideration much rather it is and ought to be ; yet all life is humbling, if we think upon it, and our greatest mercies, which we sometimes least think of, are the most humbling of all . . . The Rugby prospect I contemplate with a very strong interest: the work I am not afraid of if I can get my proper exercise ; but I want absolute play, like a boy, and neither riding nor walking will make up for my leaping-pole and gallows, and bathing, when the youths used to go with me, and I felt completely for the time a boy as they were. It is this entire relaxation, I think, at intervals, such again as my foreign tours have afforded, that gives me so keen an appetite for my work at other times, and has enabled me to go through it not only with no fatigue, but with a sense of absolute pleasure. I believe that I am going to publish a volume of Sermons. You will think me crazed perhaps ; but I have two reasons for it ; chiefly, the repeated exhortations of several individuals for the last three or four years ; but these would not alone have urged me to do it, did I not wish to state for my own sake what my opinions really are, on points where I know they have been grievously misrepresented. Whilst I lived here in Laleham my opinions mattered to nobody; but I know that while I was a candidate for Rugby, it was said in Oxford that I did not preach the Gospel, nor even touch upon the great doctrines of Christianity in my sermons, and if this same impression be prevalent now, it will be mischievous to the school in a high degree. Now, if what I really do preach be to any man's notions not the Gospel, I cannot help it, and must be content to abide by the consequences of his opinion ; but I do not want to be misunderstood and accused of omitting things which I do not omit.

XXXII.   TO REV. GEORGE CORNISH.

Rugby, August 16, 1828.

. . . . . If I can do my work as I ought to do it, we shall have every reason to be thankful for the change. I must not, it is true, think of dear old Laleham, and all that we have left there, or the perfect peace of our eight years of wedded life passed there together. It is odd that both you and I should now for the first time in our lives be moving from our parents' neighbourhood ; but in this respect our happiness was very uncommon, and to me altogether Laleham was so like a place of premature rest, that I believe I ought to be sincerely thankful that I am called to a scene of harder and more anxious labour. . . . . . The boys come back next Saturday week. So here begins the second act of our lives. May God bless it to us, and make it help forward the great end of all.

CHAPTER III.

SCHOOL LIFE AT RUGBY.

IT would be useless to give any chronological details of
a life so necessarily monotonous as that of the head-
master of a public school ; and it is accordingly only
intended to describe the general system which Dr. Arnold
pursued during the fourteen years he was at Rugby.
Yet some apology may seem to be due for the length of
a chapter, which to the general reader must be comparatively deficient in interest. Something must, indeed,
be forgiven to the natural inclination to dwell on those
recollections of his life, which to his pupils are the most
lively and the most recent—something to the almost
unconscious tendency to magnify those scenes which are
most nearly connected with what is endeared to oneself.
But independently of any local or personal considerations, it has been felt that if any part of Dr. Arnold's
work deserved special mention, it was his work at Rugby ;
and that if it was to be of any use to those of his own
profession who would take any interest in it, it could only
be made so by a full and minute account.

Those who look back upon the state of English education in the year 1827, must remember how the feeling
of dissatisfaction with existing institutions which had

begun in many quarters to display itself, had already
directed considerable attention to the condition of public
schools.   The range of classical reading, in itself confined, and with no admixture of other information, had
been subject to vehement attacks from the liberal party
generally, on the ground of its alleged narrowness and
inutility.   And the more undoubted evil of the absence
of systematic attempts to give a more directly Christian
character to what constituted the education of the whole
English gentry, was becoming more and more a scandal
in the eyes of religious men, who at the close of the last
century and the beginning of this—Wilberforce, for
example, and Bowdler—had lifted up their voices against
it.   A complete reformation, or a complete destruction
of the whole system, seemed to many persons sooner or
later to be inevitable.   The difficulty, however, of making
the first step, where the alleged objection to alteration
was its impracticability, was not to be easily surmounted.
The mere resistance to change which clings to old
institutions, was in itself a considerable obstacle, and, in
the case of some of the public schools, from the nature
of their constitution, in the first instance almost insuperable ; and whether amongst those who were engaged in
the existing system, or those who were most vehemently
opposed to it, for opposite but obvious reasons, it must
have been extremely difficult to find a man who would
attempt, or if he attempted, carry through any extensive
improvement.

It was at this juncture that Dr. Arnold was elected
head-master of a school which, whilst it presented a fair
average specimen of the public schools at that time, yet
by its constitution imposed fewer shackles on its head,
and offered a more open field for alteration than was the
case at least with Eton or Winchester.   The post itself,
in spite of the publicity, and to a certain degree

formality, which it entailed upon him, was in many respects remarkably suited to his natural tastes;—to his love of tuition, which had now grown so strongly upon him, that he declared sometimes that he could hardly live without such employment; to the vigour and spirits which fitted him rather to deal with the young than the old; to the desire of carrying out his favourite ideas of uniting things secular with things spiritual, and of introducing the highest principles of action into regions comparatively uncongenial to their reception.

Even his general interest in public matters was not without its use in his new station. Many, indeed, both of his admirers and of his opponents, used to lament that a man with such views and pursuits should be placed in such a situation. " What a pity," it was said on the one hand, " that a man fit to be a statesman should be employed in teaching school-boys." "What a shame," it was said on the other hand, "that the head-master of Rugby should be employed in writing essays and pamphlets." But, even had there been no connexion between the two spheres of his interest, and had the inconvenience resulting from his public prominence been far greater than it was, it would have been the necessary price of having him at all in that place. He would not have been himself, had he not felt and written as he did; and he could not have endured to live under the grievance of remaining silent on subjects, on which he believed it to be his most sacred duty to speak what he thought.

As it was, however, the one sphere played into the other. Whatever labour he bestowed on his literary works was only part of that constant progress of self-education which he thought essential to the right discharge of his duties as a teacher. Whatever interest he felt in the struggles of the political and ecclesiastical

world, reacted on his interest in the school, and invested
it in his eyes with a new importance.   When he thought
of the social evils of the country, it awakened a corresponding desire to check the thoughtless waste and selfishness of school-boys ; a corresponding sense of the
aggravation of those evils by the insolence and want of
sympathy too frequently shown by the children of the
wealthier classes towards the lower orders ; a corresponding desire that they should there imbibe the first
principles of reverence to law and regard for the poor
which the spirit of the age seemed to him so little to
encourage.   When he thought of the evils of the Church,
he would "turn from the thought of the general temple
in ruins, and see whether they could not, within the walls
of their own little particular congregation," endeavour to
realise what he believed to be its true idea ; "what use
they could make of the vestiges of it still left amongst
themselves—common reading of the Scriptures, common
prayer, and the communion."   (Serm. vol. iv. pp. 266,
316.)   Thus, "whatever of striking good or evil, happened in any part of the wide range of English do-
minion "—brought to his thoughts "on what important
scenes some of his own scholars might be called upon to
enter ;" "whatever new and important things took place
in the world of thought," suggested the hope "that they,
when they went forth amidst the strifes of tongues and
of minds, might be endowed with the spirit of wisdom
and power."   (Serm. vol. v. p. 405.)   And even in the
details of the school, it would be curious to trace how he
recognised in the peculiar vices of boys the same evils
which, when full grown, became the source of so much
social mischief : how he governed the school precisely on
the same principles as he would have governed a great
empire ; how constantly, to his own mind or to his
scholars, he exemplified the highest truths of theology

and philosophy in the simplest relations of the boys towards each other, or towards him.

In entering upon his office he met with difficulties, many of which have since passed away, but which must be borne in mind, if points are here dwelt upon that have now ceased to be important, but were by no means insignificant or obvious when he came to Rugby. Nor did his system at once attain its full maturity. He was a long time feeling his way amongst the various institutions which he formed or invented :—he was constantly striving after an ideal standard of perfection, which he was conscious that he had never attained ; to the improvements which, in a short time, began to take place in other schools—to those at Harrow, under his friend Dr. Longley, and to those at Winchester, under Dr. Moberly, to which he alluded in one of his later sermons (vol. v. p. 150), he often looked as models for himself ;—to suggestions from persons very much younger than himself, not unfrequently from his former pupils, with regard to the course of reading, or to alterations in his manner of preaching, or to points of discipline, he would often listen with the greatest deference. His own mind was constantly devising new measures for carrying out his several views. "The school," he said, on first coming, "is quite enough to employ any man's love of reform ; and it is much pleasanter to think of evils, which you may yourself hope to relieve, than those with regard to which you can give nothing but vain wishes and opinions." "There is enough of Toryism in my nature," he said, on evils being mentioned to him in the place, "to make me very apt to sleep contentedly over things as they are, and therefore I hold it to be most true kindness when anyone directs my attention to points in the school which are alleged to be going on ill."

The perpetual succession of changes which resulted

from this was by many objected to as excessive, and calculated to endanger the stability of his whole system. "He awakes every morning," it was said of him, "with the impression that everything is an open question." But rapid as might be the alterations to which the details of his system were subjected, the general principles remained fixed. The unwillingness which he had, even in common life, to act in any individual case without some general law to which he might refer it, ran through everything, and at times it would almost seem as if he invented universal rules with the express object of meeting particular cases. Still, if in smaller matters this gave an occasional impression of fancifulness or inconsistency, it was, in greater matters, one chief cause of the confidence which he inspired. Amidst all the plans that came before him, he felt, and he made others feel, that whatever might be the merits of the particular question at issue, there were principles behind which lay far more deeply seated than any mere question of school government, which he was ready to carry through at whatever cost, and from which no argument or menace could move him.

Of the mere external administration of the school, little need here be said. Many difficulties which he encountered were alike provoked and subdued by the peculiarities of his own character. The vehemence with which he threw himself into a contest against evil, and the confidence with which he assailed it, though it carried him through perplexities to which a more cautious man would have yielded, led him to disregard interests and opinions which a less earnest or a less sanguine reformer would have treated with greater consideration. His consciousness of his own integrity, and his contempt for worldly advantage, sometimes led him to require from others more than might be reasonably expected from them, and to adopt measures which the world at large was sure to misinterpret; yet these very qualities, in proportion as they became more appreciated, ultimately secured for him a confidence beyond what could have been gained by the most deliberate circumspection. But whatever were the temporary exasperations and excitements thus produced in his dealings with others, they were gradually removed by the increasing control over himself and his work which he acquired in later years. The readiness which he showed to acknowledge a fault when once convinced of it, as well as to persevere in kindness even when he thought himself injured, succeeded in healing breaches which, with a less forgiving or less honest temper, would have been irreparable. His union of firmness with tenderness had the same effect in the settlement of some of the perplexities of his office, which in others would have resulted from art and management; and even his work as a schoolmaster cannot be properly appreciated without remembering how, in the end of his career, he rallied round him the public feeling, which in its beginning and middle, as will appear further on, had been so widely estranged from them.

With regard to the trustees of the school, entirely amicable as were his usual relations with them, and grateful as he felt to them for their active support and personal friendliness, he from the first maintained that in the actual working of the school he must be completely independent, and that their remedy, if they were dissatisfied, was not interference, but dismissal. On this condition he took the post, and any attempt to control either his administration of the school, or his own private occupations, he felt bound to resist, "as a duty," he said on one occasion, " not only to himself, but to the master of every foundation-school in England."

Of his intercourse with the assistant-masters it is for obvious reasons impossible to speak with that detail which the subject deserves. But though the co-operation of his colleagues was necessarily thrown into the shade by the activity and vigour of his own character, it must not be lost sight of in the following account, whether it be regarded as one of his most characteristic means of administration, or as an instance of the powerful influence he exercised over those with whom he was brought into close contact. It was one of his main objects to increase in all possible ways their importance and their interest in the place. "Nothing delights me more," he said, in speaking of the reputation enjoyed by one of his colleagues, "than to think that boys are sent here for his sake rather than for mine." In matters of school discipline he seldom or never acted without consulting them. Every three weeks a council was held, in which all school matters were discussed, and in which every one was free to express his opinion, or propose any measure not in contradiction to any fundamental principle of school administration, and in which it would not unfrequently happen, that he himself was opposed and outvoted. He was anxious that they, like himself, should have time to read for their own improvement, and he was also glad to encourage any occasional help that they might render to the neighbouring clergy. But from the first he maintained that the school business was to occupy their main and undivided interest. The practice which owing to their lower salaries had before prevailed, of uniting some parochial cure with their school duties, was entirely abolished, and the boarding-houses, as they respectively became vacant, he placed exclusively under their care. The connexion thus established between the masters and the boys in the several houses he laboured to strengthen by opening in various ways means for friendly communication between them;—every house was thus to be as it were an epitome of the whole school.   On the one hand, every master was to have, as he used to say, " each a horse of his own to ride," independent of the "mere phantasmagoria of boys" passing successively through their respective forms; and, on the other hand, the boys would thus have some one at hand to consult in difficulties, to explain their case if they got into trouble with the head-master, or the other masters, to send a report[*] of their characters home, to prepare them for confirmation, and in general to stand to them in the relation of a pastor to his flock. " No parochial ministry," he would say to them, "can be more properly a cure of souls than yours;" and though, where it might happen that the masters were laymen, no difference was made between their duties to their boys and those of others, yet he was anxious, as a general rule, that they should be ordained as soon as possible, and procured from the bishop of the diocese a recognition of their situations as titles for orders. Whatever, in short, he was in his own department, he wished them to be in theirs;—whatever he felt about his superintendence of the whole school, he wished them to feel about that part of it especially committed to them.   It was an increasing delight to him to inspire them with general views of education and of life, by which he was himself so fully possessed; and the bond, thus gradually formed, especially when in his later time several of those who had been his pupils became his colleagues, grew deeper and stronger with each successive year that they passed in the place.   Out of his own family there was no circle of which he was so completely the animating

---

[*] This practice, which he first introduced at the end of each half-year, afterwards became monthly. He himself used latterly to write besides every half-year to the parents of every boy in his own form;—shortly, if the boy's character was good—at considerable length if he had cause of complaint.

principle, as amongst those who co-operated with him in the great practical work of his life ; none in which his loss was more keenly felt to be irreparable, or his example more instinctively regarded as a living spring of action, and a source of solemn responsibility, than amongst those who were called to continue their labours in the sphere and on the scene which had been ennobled to them by his counsels and his presence.*

But whatever interest attaches to the more external circumstances of his administration, and to his relations with others, who were concerned in it, is of course centred in his own personal government of the boys.

---

* His views will perhaps be best explained by the two following letters :

LETTER OF INQUIRY FOR A MASTER.

. . . . . . What I want is a man who is a Christian and a gentleman, an active man, and one who has common sense, and understands boys. I do not so much care about scholarship, as he will have immediately under him the lowest forms in the school ; but yet, on second thoughts, I do care about it very much, because his pupils may be in the highest forms ; and besides, I think that even the elements are best taught by a man who has a thorough knowledge of the matter. However, if one must give way, I prefer activity of mind and an interest in his work, to high scholarship: for the one may be acquired far more easily than the other. I should wish it also to be understood that the new master may be called upon to take boarders in his house, it being my intention for the future to require this of all masters as I see occasion, that so in time the boarding-houses may die a natural death . . . . . . With this to offer, I think I have a right to look rather high for the man whom I fix upon, and it is my great object to get here a society of intelligent, gentlemanly, and active men, who may permanently keep up the character of the school, and make it

"vile damnum," if I were to break my neck to-morrow. . . . .

LETTER TO A MASTER ON HIS APPOINTMENT.

. . . . . . The qualifications which I deem essential to the due performance of a master's duties here, may in brief be expressed as the spirit of a Christian and a gentleman,—that a man should enter upon his business not $\dot{\epsilon}\mu$ $\pi\alpha\rho\acute{\epsilon}\rho\gamma\text{ov}$ but as a substantive and most important duty ; that he should devote himself to it as the especial branch of the ministerial calling which he has chosen to follow —that belonging to a great public institution, and standing in a public and conspicuous situation, he should study things "lovely and of good report ;" that is, that he should be public-spirited, liberal, and entering heartily into the interest, honour, and general respectability and distinction of the society which he has joined ; and that he should have sufficient vigour of mind and thirst for knowledge to persist in adding to his own stores without neglecting the full improvement of those whom he is teaching. I think our masterships here offer a noble field of duty, and I would not bestow them on any one whom I thought would undertake them without entering into the spirit of our system heart and hand.

The natural effect of his concentration of interest on what he used to call "our great self," the school, was that the separate existence of the school was in return almost merged in him. This was not indeed his own intention, but it was precisely because he thought so much of the institution and so little of himself, that in spite of his efforts to make it work independently of any personal influence of his own, it became so thoroughly dependent upon him, and so thoroughly penetrated with his spirit. From one end of it to the other, whatever defects it had were his defects; whatever excellences it had were his excellences. It was not the master who was beloved or disliked for the sake of the school, but the school was beloved or disliked for the sake of the master. Whatever peculiarity of character was impressed on the scholars whom it sent forth, was derived not from the genius of the place, but from the genius of the man. Throughout, whether in the school itself, or in its after effects, the one image that we have before us is not Rugby, but ARNOLD.

What was his great object has already appeared from his letters; namely, the hope of making the school a place of really Christian education. These words in his mouth meant something very different from the general professions which every good teacher must be supposed to make, and which no teacher even in the worst times of English education could have openly ventured to disclaim; but it is exceedingly difficult so to explain them, as that they shall not seem to exceed or fall short of the truth. It was not an attempt merely to give more theological instruction, or to introduce sacred words into school admonitions; there may have been some occasions for religious advice that might have been turned to more advantage, some religious practices which might have been more constantly or effectually encouraged. His design arose out of the very nature of his office : the relation of an instructor to his pupils was to him, like all the other relations of human life, only in a healthy state, when subordinate to their common relation to God.   The idea of a Christian school, again, was to him the natural result, so to speak, of the very idea of a school in itself ; exactly as the idea of a Christian State seemed to him to be involved in the very idea of a State itself.   The intellectual training was not for a moment underrated, and the machinery of the school was left to have its own way.   But he looked upon the whole as bearing on the advancement of the one end of all instruction and education ; the boys were still treated as school-boys, but as school-boys who must grow up to be Christian men ; whose age did not prevent their faults from being sins, or their excellences from being noble and Christian virtues ; whose situation did not of itself make the application of Christian principles to their daily lives an impracticable vision.

His education, in short, it was once observed amidst the vehement outcry by which he used to be assailed, " was not (according to the popular phrase) based upon religion, but was itself *religious.*"   It was this chiefly which gave a oneness to his work amidst a great variety of means and occupations, and a steadiness to the general system amidst its almost unceasing change.   It was this which makes it difficult to separate one part of his work from another, and which often made it impossible for his pupils to say in after life, of much that had influenced them, whether they had derived it from what was spoken in school, in the pulpit, or in private.   And, therefore, when either in direct religious teaching, or on particular occasions, Christian principles were expressly introduced by him, they had not the appearance of a rhetorical flourish or of a temporary appeal to the feelings ; they were looked upon as the natural expression of what was constantly implied : it was felt that he had the power, in which so many teachers have been deficient, of saying what he did mean, and of not saying what he did not mean,—the power of doing what was right, and speaking what was true, and thinking what was good, independently of any professional or conventional notions that so to act, speak, or think, was becoming or expedient.

It was not merely an abstract school, but an English public school, which he looked upon as the sphere in which this was to be effected. There was something to him at the very outset full of interest in a great place of national education, such as he considered a public school to be.

" There is," he said, " or there ought to be, something very ennobling in being connected with an establishment at once ancient and magnificent, where all about us, and all the associations belonging to the objects around us, should be great, splendid, and elevating. What an individual ought and often does derive from the feeling that he is born of an old and illustrious race, from being familiar from his childhood with the walls and trees which speak of the past no less than of the present, and make both full of images of greatness ; this, in an inferior degree, belongs to every member of an ancient and celebrated place of education. In this respect every one of us has a responsibility imposed upon him, which I wish that we more considered." (Serm. vol. iii. p. 210.)*

---

* It was one of his most cherished wishes at Rugby, to be enabled to leave to the school some permanent rank or dignity, which should in some measure compensate for its total barrenness of all historical associations, which he always felt painfully in contrast with his own early school, Winchester. Thus amongst other schemes, he exerted himself to procure a medal or some similar favour from the Crown. "I can truly say," he wrote in 1840, "that nothing which could have been given me in the way of preferment, would have been so gratifying to me as to have been the means in any degree of obtaining what I think would be not more an honour than a real and lasting benefit to the school." The general grounds on which he thought this desirable, may best be stated in his own words : "I think that it would be well on public grounds to confer what may be considered as analogous to a peerage conferred on some of the wealthiest

This feeling of itself dictated the preservation of the old school constitution as far as it was possible, and he was very careful not to break through any customs which connected the institution, however slightly, with the past. But in this constitution there were peculiarities of far greater importance in his eyes for good or evil, than any mere imaginative associations ; the peculiarities which distinguish the English public-school system from almost every other system of education in Europe, and which are all founded on the fact that a large number of boys are left for a large portion of their time to form an independent society of their own, in which the influence that they exercise over each other is far greater than can possibly be exercised by the masters, even if multiplied greatly beyond their present number.

How keenly he felt the evils resulting from this system, and the difficulty of communicating to it a really Christian character, will be evident to any one who knows the twelfth Sermon in his second volume, in which he unfolded, at the beginning of his career, the causes which had led good men to declare that " public schools are the seats and nurseries of vice ; " or the three Sermons on " Christian Schools," in his fifth volume, in which, with the added experience of ten years, he analyzed the six evils by which he " supposed that great schools were likely to be corrupted, and to be changed from the likeness of God's temple to that of a den of thieves." (Vol. v. p. 74.)

Sometimes he would be led to doubt whether it

commoners, or to a silk gown bestowed on distinguished lawyers, that is, that when schools had risen from a very humble origin to a considerable place in the country, and had continued so for some time, some royal gift, however small, should be bestowed upon them, merely as a sort of recognition or confirmation on the part of the Crown, of the courtesy rank which they had acquired already. I have always believed that one of the simplest and most effectual means of improving the foundation-schools throughout the country would be to hold out the hope of some mark of encouragement from the Crown, as they might happen to deserve it."

were really compatible with the highest principles of education; sometimes he would seem to have an earnest and almost impatient desire to free himself from it. Still, on the whole, it was always on a reformation, not on an overthrow, of the existing constitution of the school that he endeavoured to act. "Another system," he said, "may be better in itself, but I am placed in this system, and am bound to try what I can make of it."

With his usual undoubting confidence in what he believed to be a general law of Providence, he based his whole management of the school on his early-formed and yearly-increasing conviction that what he had to look for, both intellectually and morally, was not performance but promise; that the very freedom and independence of school life, which in itself he thought so dangerous, might be made the best preparation for Christian manhood; and he did not hesitate to apply to his scholars the principle which seemed to him to have been adopted in the training of the childhood of the human race itself.* He shrunk from pressing on the conscience of boys rules of action which he felt they were not yet able to bear, and from enforcing actions which, though right in themselves, would in boys be performed from wrong motives. Keenly as he felt the risk and fatal consequences of the failure of this trial, still it was his great, sometimes his only support to believe that "the character is braced amid such scenes to a greater beauty and firmness than it ever can attain without enduring and witnessing them. Our work here would be absolutely unendurable if we did not bear in mind that we should look forward as well as backward— if we did not remember that the victory of fallen man lies not in innocence but in tried virtue." (Serm. vol. iv. p. 7.) "I hold fast," he said, "to the great truth, that

---

* Sermons, vol. ii. p. 440.

'blessed is he that overcometh;'" and he writes in 1837: "Of all the painful things connected with my employment, nothing is equal to the grief of seeing a boy come to school innocent and promising, and tracing the corruption of his character from the influence of the temptations around him, in the very place which ought to have strengthened and improved it. But in most cases those who come with a character of positive good are benefited; it is the neutral and indecisive characters which are apt to be decided for evil by schools, as they would be in fact by any other temptation."

But this very feeling led him with the greater eagerness to catch at every means, by which the trial might be shortened or alleviated. "Can the change from child-hood to manhood be hastened, without prematurely exhausting the faculties of body or mind?" (Serm. vol. iv. p. 19) was one of the chief questions on which his mind was constantly at work, and which in the judgment of some he was disposed to answer too readily in the affirmative. It was with the elder boys, of course, that he chiefly acted on this principle, but with all above the very young ones he trusted to it more or less. Firmly as he believed that *a* time of trial was inevitable, he believed no less firmly that it might be passed at public schools sooner than under other circumstances; and, in proportion as he disliked the assumption of a false manliness in boys, was his desire to cultivate in them true manliness, as the only step to something higher, and to dwell on earnest principle and moral thoughtfulness, as the great and distinguishing mark between good and evil.* Hence his wish that as much as possible should be done *by* the boys, and nothing *for* them; hence arose his practice, in which his own delicacy of feeling and uprightness of purpose powerfully assisted

* See Sermons, vol. iv. p. 99.

him, of treating the boys as gentlemen and reasonable beings, of making them respect themselves by the mere respect he showed to them ; of showing that he appealed and trusted to their own common sense and conscience. Lying, for example, to the masters, he made a great moral offence: placing implicit confidence in a boy's assertion, and then, if a falsehood was discovered, punishing it severely,—in the upper part of the school, when persisted in, with expulsion. Even with the lower forms he never seemed to be on the watch for boys ; and in the higher forms any attempt at further proof of an assertion was immediately checked :—"If you say so, that is quite enough—*of course* I believe your word ;" and there grew up in consequence a general feeling that "it was a shame to tell Arnold a lie—he always believes one."

Perhaps the liveliest representation of this general spirit, as distinguished from its exemplification in particular parts of the discipline and instruction, would be formed by recalling his manner, as he appeared in the great school, where the boys used to meet when the whole school was assembled collectively, and not in its different forms or classes. Then, whether on his usual entrance every morning to prayers before the first lesson, or on the more special emergencies which might require his presence, he seemed to stand before them, not merely as the head-master, but as the representative of the school. There he spoke to them as members together with himself of the same great institution, whose character and reputation they had to sustain as well as he. He would dwell on the satisfaction he had in being head of a society, where noble and honourable feelings were encouraged, or on the disgrace which he felt in hearing of acts of disorder or violence, such as in the humbler ranks of life would render them amenable to

the laws of their country ; or again, on the trust which
he placed on their honour as gentlemen, and the baseness
of any instance in which it was abused.   "Is this a
Christian school?" he indignantly asked at the end of
one of those addresses, in which he had spoken of an
extensive display of bad feeling amongst the boys ; and
then added,—" I cannot remain here if all is to be carried
on by constraint and force ; if I am to be here as a gaoler,
I will resign my office at once."   And few scenes can be
recorded more characteristic of him than on one of these
occasions, when, in consequence of a disturbance, he had
been obliged to send away several boys, and when in the
midst of the general spirit of discontent which this
excited, he stood in his place before the assembled
school, and said, " It is *not* necessary that this should be
a school of three hundred, or one hundred, or of fifty
boys ; but it *is* necessary that it should be a school of
Christian gentlemen."

The means of carrying out these principles were of
course various ; they may, however, for the sake of convenience, be viewed under the divisions of the general
discipline of the school, the system of instruction, the
chapel services, and his own personal intercourse and
influence.

I. In considering his general management of the discipline of the school, it will only be possible to touch on
its leading features.

1. He at once made a great alteration in the whole
system of punishments in the higher part of the school,
"keeping it as much as possible in the background, and
by kindness and encouragement attracting the good and
noble feelings of those with whom he had to deal."*
As this appears more distinctly elsewhere, it is needless
to enlarge upon it here ; but a few words may be neces-

* Serm. vol. iv. p. 106.   The whole sermon is a full exposition of his view.

sary to explain the view with which, for the younger part of the school, he made a point of maintaining, to a certain extent, the old discipline of public schools.

" The beau-ideal of school discipline with regard to young boys would seem to be this, that, whilst corporal punishment was retained on principle as fitly answering to and marking the naturally inferior state of boyhood, and therefore as conveying no peculiar degradation to persons in such a state, we should cherish and encourage to the utmost all attempts made by the several boys, as individuals, to escape from the natural punishment of their age by rising above its naturally low tone of principle."

Flogging, therefore, for the younger part, he retained, but it was confined to moral offences, such as lying, drinking, and habitual idleness, while his aversion to inflicting it rendered it still less frequent in practice than it would have been according to the rule he had laid down for it. But in answer to the argument used in a liberal journal, that it was even for these offences and for this age degrading, he replied with characteristic emphasis—

"I know well of what feeling this is the expression; it originates in that proud notion of personal independence which is neither reasonable nor Christian—but essentially barbarian. It visited Europe with all the curses of the age of chivalry, and is threatening us now with those of Jacobinism. . . . . At an age when it is almost impossible to find a true manly sense of the degradation of guilt or faults, where is the wisdom of encouraging a fantastic sense of the degradation of personal correction? What can be more false, or more adverse to the simplicity, sobriety, and humbleness of mind, which are the best ornament of youth, and the best promise of a noble manhood?"*

2. But his object was of course far higher than to check particular vices. "What I want to see in the school," he said, "and what I cannot find, is an abhor-

* Miscellaneous Works, p. 365.

rence of evil: I always think of the Psalm, 'Neither
doth he abhor anything that is evil.'"   Amongst all the
causes, which in his judgment contributed to the absence
of this feeling, and to the moral childishness, which he
considered the great curse of public schools, the chief
seem to him to lie in the spirit which was there encouraged of combination, of companionship, of excessive
deference to the public opinion prevalent in the school.
Peculiarly repugnant as this spirit was at once to his own
reverence for lawful authority, and to his dislike of ser-
vile submission to unlawful authority ; fatal as he
deemed it to all approach to sympathy between himself
and his scholars—to all free and manly feeling in
individual boys—to all real and permanent improvement
of the institution itself—it gave him more pain when
brought prominently before him, than any other evil in
the school.   At the very sight of a knot of vicious or
careless boys gathered together round the great school-
house fire, " It makes me think," he would say, "that I
see the Devil in the midst of them."   From first to last
it was the great subject to which all his anxiety con-
verged.   No half-year ever passed without his preaching
upon it—he turned it over and over in every possible
point of view—he dwelt on it as the one master-fault of
all.   " If the spirit of Elijah were to stand in the midst
of us, and we were to ask him, ' What shall we do then ?'
his answer would be, ' Fear not, nor heed one another's
voices, but fear and heed the voice of God only.'"
(MS. Serm. on Luke iii. 10.   1833.)

Against this evil he felt that no efforts of good individual example, or of personal sympathy with individual
masters, could act effectually, unless there were something to counteract it constantly amongst the boys
themselves.

" He, therefore, who wishes " (to use his own words) " really to improve public education, would do well to direct his attention to this point, and to consider how there can be infused into a society of boys such elements as, without being too dissimilar to coalesce thoroughly with the rest, shall yet be so superior as to raise the character of the whole. It would be absurd to say that any school has as yet fully solved this problem. I am convinced, however, that in the peculiar relation of the highest form to the rest of the boys, such as it exists in our great public schools, there is to be found the best means of answering it. This relation requires in many respects to be improved in its character ; some of its features should be softened, others elevated ; but here, and here only, is the engine which can effect the end desired." (Journ. Ed. p. 292.)

In other words, he determined to use, and to improve to the utmost, the existing machinery of the Sixth Form, and of fagging ; understanding, by the Sixth Form, the thirty boys who composed the highest class—" those who, having risen to the highest form in the school, will probably be at once the oldest and the strongest, and the cleverest ; and if the school be well ordered, the most respectable in application and general character : " and by fagging, "the power given by the supreme authorities of the school to the Sixth Form, to be exercised by them over the lower boys, for the sake of securing a regular government amongst the boys themselves, and avoiding the evils of anarchy ; in other words, of the lawless tyranny of physical strength." (Journ. Ed. pp. 286, 287.)*

In many points he took the institution as he found it, and as he remembered it at Winchester. The responsibility of checking bad practices without the intervention of the masters, the occasional settlement of

---

* It has not been thought necessary here to enter at length into his defence of the general system of fagging, especially as it may be seen by those who are interested in the subject in the article in the ninth volume of the Quarterly Journal of Education, from which the above extracts have been taken, and which is now inserted at length in the volume of his Miscellaneous Works.

difficult cases of school-government, the subjection of
brute force to some kind of order, involved in the maintenance of such an authority, had been more or less
produced under the old system both at Rugby and
elsewhere. But his zeal in its defence, and his confident
reliance upon it as the keystone of his whole government,
were eminently characteristic of himself. It was a point
moreover on which the spirit of the age set strongly and
increasingly against him, on which there was a general
tendency to yield to the popular outcry, and on which
the clamour, that at one time assailed him, was ready to
fasten, as a subject where all parties could concur in
their condemnation.   But he was immovable : and
though, on his first coming, he had felt himself called
upon rather to restrain the authority of the Sixth Form
from abuses, than to guard it from encroachments, yet
now that the whole system was denounced as cruel and
absurd, he delighted to stand forth as its champion.
The power, which was most strongly condemned, of
personal chastisement vested in the Præpostors over
those who resisted their authority, he firmly maintained
as essential to the general support of the good order of
the place ; and there was no obloquy which he would
not undergo in the protection of a boy, who had by due
exercise of this discipline made himself obnoxious to the
school, the parents, or the public.

But the importance which he attached to it arose
from his regarding it not only as an efficient engine of
discipline, but as the chief means of creating a respect
for moral and intellectual excellence, and of diffusing
his own influence through the mass of the school. Whilst
he made the Præpostors rely upon his support in all just
use of their authority, as well as on his severe judgment
of all abuse of it, he endeavoured also to make them
feel that they were actually fellow-workers with him

for the highest good of the school, upon the highest principles and motives—that they had, with him, a moral responsibility and a deep interest in the real welfare of the place. Occasionally during his whole stay, and regularly at the beginning or end of every half-year during his later years, he used to make short addresses to them on their duties, or on the general state of the school, one of which, as an illustration of his general mode of speaking and acting with them, it has been thought worth while to give, as nearly as his pupils could remember it, in the very words he used. After making a few remarks to them on their work in the lessons: "I will now," he proceeded, "say a few words to you as I promised. Speaking to you, as to young men who can enter into what I say, I wish you to feel that you have another duty to perform, holding the situation that you do in the school; of the importance of this I wish you all to feel sensible, and of the enormous influence you possess, in ways in which we cannot, for good or for evil, on all below you; and I wish you to see fully how many and great are the opportunities offered to you here of doing good—good, too, of lasting benefit to yourselves as well as to others; there is no place where you will find better opportunities for some time to come, and you will then have reason to look back to your life here with the greatest pleasure. You will soon find, when you change your life here for that at the Universities, how very few in comparison they are there, however willing you may then be,—at any rate during the first part of your life there. That there is good, working in the school, I most fully believe, and we cannot feel too thankful for it; in many individual instances, in different parts of the school, I have seen the change from evil to good—to mention instances would of course be wrong. The state of the school is a subject of congratulation to us all, but only so far as to encourage us to increased exertions ; and I am sure we ought all to feel it a subject of most sincere thankfulness to God ; but we must not stop here ; we must exert ourselves with earnest prayer to God for its continuance. And what I have often said before I repeat now : what we must look for here is, 1st, religious and moral principle ; 2ndly, gentlemanly conduct ; 3rdly, intellectual ability."

Nothing, accordingly, so shook his hopes of doing good, as weakness or misconduct in the Sixth. "You should feel," he said, "like officers in the army or navy, whose want of moral courage would, indeed, be thought cowardice." "When I have confidence in the Sixth," was the end of one of his farewell addresses, "there is no post in England which I would exchange for this ; but if they do not support me, I must go."

It may well be imagined how important this was as an instrument of education, independently of the weight of his own personal qualities. Exactly at the age when boys begin to acquire some degree of self-respect, and some desire for the respect of others, they were treated with confidence by one whose confidence they could not but regard as worth having ; and found themselves in a station where their own dignity could not be maintained, except by consistent good conduct. And exactly at a time when manly aspirations begin to expand, they found themselves invested with functions of government, great beyond their age, yet naturally growing out of their position ; whilst the ground of solemn responsibility, on which they were constantly taught that their authority rested, had a general, though of course not universal, tendency to counteract any notions of mere personal self-importance.

"I cannot deny that you have an anxious duty—a duty which some might suppose was too heavy for your years.

But it seems to me, the nobler as well as the truer way of stating the case to say, that it is the great privilege of this and other such institutions, to anticipate the common time of manhood ; that by their whole training they fit the character for manly duties at an age when, under another system, such duties would be impracticable ; that there is not imposed upon you too heavy a burden ; but that you are capable of bearing, without injury, what to others might be a burden, and therefore to diminish your duties and lessen your responsibility would be no kindness, but a degradation—an affront to you and to the school." (Serm. vol. v. p. 59.)

3. Whilst he looked to the Sixth Form, as the ordinary corrective for the ordinary evils of a public school, he still felt that these evils from time to time developed themselves in a shape which demanded peculiar methods to meet them, and which may best be explained by one of his letters.

" My own school experience has taught me the monstrous evil of a state of low principle prevailing amongst those who set the tone to the rest. I can neither theoretically nor practically defend our public-school system, where the boys are left so very much alone to form a distinct society of their own, unless you assume that the upper class shall be capable of being in a manner μεσῖται between the masters and the mass of the boys, that is, shall be capable of receiving and transmitting to the rest, through their example and influence, right principles of conduct, instead of those extremely low ones which are natural to a society of boys left wholly to form their own standard of right and wrong. Now, when I get any in this part of the school who are not to be influenced—who have neither the will nor the power to influence others—not from being intentionally bad, but from very low wit, and extreme childishness or coarseness of character—the evil is so great, not only negatively but positively, (for their low and false views are greedily caught up by those below them,) that I know not how to proceed, or how to hinder the school from becoming a place of education for evil rather than for good, except by getting rid of such persons. And then comes the difficulty, that the parents who see their sons only at home—that is just where the points of character, which are so injurious here, are not called into action—can scarcely be brought to understand why they should remove them ; and having, as most people have, only the most vague ideas as to the real nature of a public school, they cannot understand what harm they are receiving or doing to others, if they do not get into some palpable scrape, which very likely they never would do. More puzzling still is it, when you have many boys of this description, so that the evil influence is really very great, and yet there is not one of the set whom you would set down as a really bad fellow if taken alone ; but most of them would really do very well if they were not together and in a situation where, unluckily, their age and size leads them, unavoidably, to form the laws and guide the opinion of their society ; whereas, they are wholly unfit to lead others, and are so slow at receiving good influences themselves, that they want to be almost exclusively with older persons, instead of being principally with younger ones."

The evil undoubtedly was great, and the difficulty, which he describes in the way of its removal, tended to aggravate the evil. When first he entered on his post at Rugby, there was a general feeling in the country, that so long as a boy kept himself from offences sufficiently enormous to justify expulsion, he had a kind of right to remain in a public school ; that the worse and more troublesome to parents were their sons, the more did a public school seem the precise remedy for them ; that the great end of a public school, in short, was to flog their vices out of bad boys. Hence much indignation was excited when boys were sent away for lesser offences : an unfailing supply of vicious sons was secured, and scrupulous parents were naturally reluctant to expose their boys to the influence of such associates.

His own determination had been fixed long before he came to Rugby, and it was only after ascertaining that his power in this respect would be absolute, that he consented to become a candidate for the post.* The reten-

---

* See Letter to Dr. Hawkins, in 1827.

tion of boys who were clearly incapable of deriving good from the system, or whose influence on others was decidedly and extensively pernicious, seemed to him not a necessary part of the trials of school, but an inexcusable and intolerable aggravation of them. " Till a man learns that the first, second, and third duty of a schoolmaster is to get rid of unpromising subjects, a great public school," he said, "will never be what it might be, and what it ought to be." The remonstrances which he encountered both on public and private grounds were vehement and numerous. But on these terms alone had he taken his office ; and he solemnly and repeatedly declared, that on no other terms could he hold it, or justify the existence of the public-school system in a Christian country.

The cases which fell under this rule included all shades of character from the hopelessly bad up to the really good, who yet from their peculiar circumstances might be receiving great injury from the system of a public school ; grave moral offences frequently repeated; boys banded together in sets to the great harm of individuals or of the school at large ; overgrown boys, whose age and size gave them influence over others, and made them unfit subjects for corporal punishment, whilst the low place which, either from idleness or dulness, they held in the school, encouraged all the childish and low habits to which they were naturally tempted.* He would retain boys after offences, which considered in themselves would seem to many almost deserving of expulsion ; he would request the removal of others for offences which to many would seem venial. In short, he was decided by the ultimate result on the whole character of the individual, or on the general state of the school.

* The admission of very young boys, *e.g.* under the age of ten, he earnestly deprecated, as considering them incapable of profiting by the discipline of the place.

It was on every account essential to the carrying out of his principle, that he should mark in every way the broad distinction between this kind of removal, and what in the strict sense of the word used to be called expulsion. The latter was intended by him as a punishment and lasting disgrace, was inflicted publicly and with extreme solemnity, was of very rare occurrence, and only for gross and overt offences. But he took pains to show that removal, such as is here spoken of, whether temporary or final, was not disgraceful or penal, but intended chiefly, if not solely, for a protection of the boy himself or his schoolfellows. Often it would be wholly unknown who were thus dismissed or why ; latterly he generally allowed such cases to remain to the end of the half-year, that their removal might pass altogether unnoticed : the subjoined letters also to the head of a college and a private tutor, introducing such boys to their attention, are samples of the spirit in which he acted on these occasions.*

* 1. To the Head of a College.— "With regard to ——, if you had asked me about him half a year ago, I should have spoken of him in the highest terms in point of conduct and steady attention to his work ; there has been nothing in all that has passed beyond a great deal of party and school-boy feeling, wrong, as I think, and exceedingly mischievous to a school, but from its peculiar character not likely to recur at college or in after life, and not reflecting permanently on a boy's principles or disposition. I think you will have in ——- a steady and gentlemanly man, who will read fairly and give no disturbance, and one who would well repay any interest taken in him by his tutor to direct him either in his work or conduct. He was one of those who would do a great deal better at college than at school ; and of this sort there are many ; as long as they are among boys, and with no closer personal intercourse with older persons than a public school affords, they are often wrong-headed and troublesome ; but older society, and the habits of more advanced life, set them to rights again."

2. . . . . . "Their conduct till they went away was as good as possible, and I feel bound to speak strongly in their favour with regard to their prospects at college ; for there was more of foolishness than of vice in the whole matter, and it was their peculiar situation in the school, and the peculiar danger of their fault among us, that made us wish them to be removed, —— was very much improved in his work, and did some of his business very well ; since he left us he, has been with a private tutor, and I shall be disappointed if he has not behaved there so as to obtain from him a very favourable character."

·3. . . . . . . "—— was not a bad fellow at all, but had overgrown school in his body before he had over-

This system was not pursued without difficulty; the inconvenience attendant upon such removals was occasionally very great; sometimes the character of the boy may have been mistaken, the difficulty of explaining the true nature of the transaction to parents was considerable; an exaggerated notion was entertained of the extent to which this view was carried.

To administer such a system required higher qualifications in a head-master than mere scholarship or mere zeal. What enabled him to do so successfully was, the force of his character; his determination to carry out his principles through a host of particular obstacles; his largeness of view, which endeavoured to catch the distinctive features of every case; the consciousness which he felt, and made others feel, of the uprightness and purity of his intentions. The predictions that boys who failed at school would turn out well with private tutors, were often acknowledged to be verified in cases where the removal had been most complained of; the diminution of corporal punishment in the school was necessarily much facilitated; a salutary effect was produced on the boys by impressing upon them, that even slight offences which came under the head-master's eye, were swelling the sum of misconduct which might end in removal; whilst many parents were displeased by the system, others were induced to send " as many boys," he said, " and more than

grown it in wit; he was therefore the hero of the younger boys for his strength and prowess; and this sort of distinction was doing him harm, so that I advised his father to take him away, and to get him entered at the University as soon as possible."

4. To a private tutor.—" I am glad that you continue to like ———, nor am I surprised at it, for I always thought that school brought out the bad in his character, and repressed the good. There are some others' in the same way whom you would find, I think, very satisfactory pupils, but who are not improving here."

5. " It is a good thing, I have no doubt, that ——— has left us; his is just one of those characters which cannot bear a public school, and may be saved and turned to great good by the humanities of private tuition."

" Ah !" he would say of a case of this kind, " if the Peninsular war were going on now, one would know what to do with him—a few years' hardship would bring a very nice fellow out of him."

he sent away;" lastly, he succeeded in shaking the old notion of the conditions under which boys must be allowed to remain at school, and in impressing on others the standard of moral progress which he endeavoured himself to enforce.

The following letter to one of the assistant-masters expresses his mode of meeting the attacks to which he was exposed on the two subjects last mentioned.

"I do not choose to discuss the thickness of Præpostors' sticks, or the greater or less blackness of a boy's bruises, for the amusement of all the readers of the newspapers; nor do I care in the slightest degree about the attacks, if the masters themselves treat them with indifference. If they appear to mind them, or to fear their effect on the school, the apprehension in this, as in many other instances, will be likely to verify itself. For my own part, I confess that I will not condescend to justify the school against attacks, when I believe that it is going on not only not ill, but positively well. Were it really otherwise, I think I should be as sensitive as any one, and very soon give up the concern. But these attacks are merely what I bargained for, so far as they relate to my conduct in the school, because they are directed against points on which my 'ideas' were fixed before I came to Rugby, and are only more fixed now; *e.g.* that the authority of the Sixth Form is essential to the good of the school, and is to be upheld through all obstacles from within and from without, and that sending away boys is a necessary and regular part of a good system, not as a punishment to one, but as a protection to others. Undoubtedly it would be a better system if there was no evil; but evil being unavoidable we are not a jail to keep it in, but a place of education where we must cast it out, to prevent its taint from spreading. Meanwhile let us mind our own work, and try to perfect the execution of our own 'ideas,' and we shall have enough to do, and enough always to hinder us from being satisfied with ourselves; but when we are attacked we have some right to answer with Scipio, who, scorning to reply to a charge of corruption, said, 'Hoc die cum Hannibale benè et feliciter pugnavi:'—we have done enough good and undone enough evil, to allow us to hold our assailants cheap."

II. The spirit in which he entered on the instruction

of the school, constituting as it did the main business of the place, may perhaps best be understood from a particular exemplification of it in the circumstances under which he introduced a prayer before the first lesson in the Sixth Form, over and above the general prayers read before the whole school. On the morning on which he first used it he said that he had been much troubled to find that the change from attendance on the death-bed of one of the boys in his house to his school-work had been very great : he thought that there ought not to be such a contrast, and that it was probably owing to the school-work not being sufficiently sanctified to God's glory; that if it was made really a *religious* work, the transition to it from a death-bed would be slight : he therefore intended for the future to offer a prayer before the first lesson, that the day's work might be undertaken and carried on solely to the glory of God and their improvement,—that he might be the better enabled to do his work.*

Under this feeling, all the lessons, in his eyes, and not only those which were more distinctly religious, were invested with a moral character ; and his desire to raise the general standard of knowledge and application in the school was as great, as if it had been his sole object.

He introduced, with this view, a variety of new regulations ; contributed liberally himself to the foundation of prizes and scholarships, as incentives to study, and gave up much of his leisure to the extra labour of new examinations for the various forms, and of a yearly examination for the whole school. The spirit of industry which· his method excited in his better scholars, and more or less in the school at large, was considerable ; and it was often complained that their minds and constitutions were overworked by premature exertion.

* See Appendix A.

Whether this was the case more at Rugby than in other schools, since the greater exertions generally required in all parts of education, it is difficult to determine. He himself would never allow the truth of it, though maintaining that it would be a very great evil if it were so. The Greek union of the ἀρετὴ γυμναστικὴ with the ἀρετὴ μουσικὴ, he thought invaluable in education, and he held that the freedom of the sports of public schools was particularly favourable to it; and whenever he saw that boys were reading too much, he always remonstrated with them, relaxed their work, and if they were in the upper part of the school, would invite them to his house in the half-year or the holidays to refresh them.

He had a strong belief in the general union of moral and intellectual excellence. "I have now had some years' experience," he once said in preaching at Rugby, "I have known but too many of those who in their utter folly have said in their heart, there was no God; but the sad sight—for assuredly none can be more sad—of a powerful, an earnest, and an inquiring mind seeking truth, yet not finding it—the horrible sight of good deliberately rejected, and evil deliberately chosen—the grievous wreck of earthly wisdom united with spiritual folly—I believe that it has been, that it is, that it may be —Scripture speaks of it, the experience of others has witnessed it; but I thank God that in my own experience I have never witnessed it yet; I have still found that folly and thoughtlessness have gone to evil; that thought and manliness have been united with faith and goodness." And in the case of boys his experience led him, to use his words in a letter to a friend, "more and more to believe in this connexion, for which divers reasons may be given. One, and a very important one, is, that ability puts a boy in sympathy with his teachers in the matter of his work, and in their delight in the works

of great minds ; whereas a dull boy has much more sympathy with the uneducated and others to whom animal
enjoyments are all in all."   "I am sure," he used to say,
"that in the case of boys the temptations of intellect
are not comparable to the temptations of dulness ; and
he often dwelt on "the fruit which he above all things
longed for,—moral thoughtfulness,—the inquiring love
of truth going along with the devoted love of goodness."

But for mere cleverness, whether in boys or men, he
had no regard. "Mere intellectual acuteness," he used
to say, in speaking (for example) of lawyers, "divested
as it is, in too many cases, of all that is comprehensive
and great and good, is to me more revolting than the
most helpless imbecility, seeming to me almost like the
spirit of Mephistopheles." Often when seen in union
with moral depravity, he would be inclined to deny its
existence altogether ; the generation of his scholars, to
which he looked back with the greatest pleasure, was
not that which contained most instances of individual
talent, but that which had altogether worked steadily ·
and industriously. The university honours which his
pupils obtained were very considerable, and at one time
unrivalled by any school in England, and he was un-
feignedly delighted whenever they occurred. But he
never laid any stress upon them, and strongly deprecated any system which would encourage the notion of
their being the chief end to be answered by school education. He would often dwell on the curious alternations
of cleverness or dulness in school generations, which
seemed to baffle all human calculation or exertion.
"What we ought to do is to send up boys who will not
be plucked." A mere plodding boy was above all others
encouraged by him. At Laleham he had once got out
of patience, and spoken sharply to a pupil of this kind,
when the pupil looked up in his face and said, "Why do

you speak angrily, sir ?—indeed I am doing the best that I can." Years afterwards he used to tell the story to his children, and said, "I never felt so much ashamed in my life—that look and that speech I have never forgotten." And though it would of course happen that clever boys, from a greater sympathy with his understanding, would be brought into closer intercourse with him, this did not affect his feeling, not only of respect, but of reverence to those who, without ability, were distinguished for high principle and industry. "If there be one thing on earth which is truly admirable, it is to see God's wisdom blessing an inferiority of natural powers, where they have been honestly, truly, and zealously cultivated." In speaking of a pupil of this character, he once said, "I would stand to that man *hat in hand*;" and it was this feeling after the departure of such an one that drew from him the most personal, perhaps the only personal praise which he ever bestowed on any boy in his Sermons. (See Sermons, vol. iii. pp. 352, 353.)*

---

* The subjoined letters will best show the feeling with which he regarded the academical successes or failures of his pupils :—

1. To a pupil who had failed in his examination at the University :—

. . . . . . " I hardly know whether you would like my writing to you ; yet I feel strongly disposed so far to presume on the old relation which existed between us, as to express my earnest hope that you will not attach too much importance to your disappointment, whatever it may have been, at the recent examination. I believe that I attach quite as much value as is reasonable to university distinctions ; but it would be a grievous evil if the good of a man's reading for three years were all to depend on the result of a single examination, affected as that result must ever in some degree be by causes independent of a man's intellectual excellence. I am saying nothing but what you know quite well already ; still the momentary feeling of disappointment may tempt a man to do himself great injustice, and to think that his efforts have been attended by no proportionate fruit. I can only say, for one, that as far as the real honour of Rugby is concerned, it is the effort, an hundred times more than the issue of the effort, that is in my judgment a credit to the school ; inasmuch as it shows that the men who go from here to the University do their duty there ; and that is the real point, which alone to my mind reflects honour either on individuals or on societies ; and if such a fruit is in any way traceable to the influence of Rugby, then I am proud and thankful to have had such a man as my pupil. I am almost afraid that you will think me impertinent in writing to you ; but I must be allowed to feel more than a passing interest in those whom I have known and valued here ; and in your case this interest was renewed by having had the pleasure of seeing you

This being his general view, it remains to unfold his ideas of school-instruction in detail.

1. That classical studies should be the basis of intellectual teaching, he maintained from the first. "The study of language," he said, "seems to me as if it was given for the very purpose of forming the human mind in youth; and the Greek and Latin languages, in themselves so perfect, and at the same time freed from the insuperable difficulty which must attend any attempt to teach boys philology through the medium of their own spoken language, seem the very instruments, by which this is to be effected." But a comparison of his earlier and later letters will show how much this opinion was strengthened in later years, and how, in some respects,

in Westmoreland more lately. I should be extremely glad if you can find an opportunity of paying us a visit ere long at Rugby."

2. To a pupil just before his examination at Oxford:—

"I have no other object in writing to you than merely to assure you of my hearty interest about you at this time when I suppose that the prospect of your examination is rising up closely before you. Yet I hope that you know me better than to think that my interest arises merely from the credit which the school may gain from your success, or that I should be in a manner personally disappointed if our men were not to gain what they are trying for. On this score I am very hard, and I know too well the uncertainties of examinations to be much surprised at any result. I am much more anxious, however, that you should not overwork yourself, nor unnerve your mind for after exertion. And I wish to say that if you would like change of air or scene for a single day, I should urge you to come down here, and if I can be of any use to you, when here, in examining you, that you may not think that you would be utterly losing your time in leaving Oxford, I shall be very glad to do it. I am a great believer in the

virtues of a journey for fifty miles, for giving tone to the system where it has been overworked."

3. To a pupil who had been unsuccessful in an examination for the Ireland scholarship:—

"I am more than satisfied with what you have done in the Ireland; as to getting it, I certainly never should have got it myself, so I have no right to be surprised if my pupils do not."

4. To a pupil who had gained a first class at Oxford:—

"Your letter has given all your friends here great joy, and most heartily do I congratulate you upon it. Depend upon it, it is a gift of God, not to be gloried in, but deeply and thankfully to be prized, for it may be made to minister to His glory and to the good of His Church, which never more needed the aid of the Spirit of wisdom, as well as of the Spirit of love."

5. To another, on the same:—

"I must write you in one line my heartiest congratulations, for I should not like not to write on an occasion which I verily believe is to no one more welcome than it is to me. You, I know, will look onwards and upwards—and will feel that God's gifts and blessings bind us more closely to His service."

he returned to parts of the old system, which on his first arrival at Rugby he had altered or discarded. To the use of Latin verse, which he had been accustomed to regard as "one of the most contemptible prettinesses of the understanding," "I am becoming," he said, "in my old age more and more a convert." Greek and Latin grammars in English, which he introduced soon after he came, he found were attended with a disadvantage, because the rules which in Latin fixed themselves in the boys' memories, when learned in English, were forgotten. The changes in his views resulted on the whole from his increasing conviction, that "it was not knowledge, but the means of gaining knowledge which he had to teach;" as well as by his increasing sense of the value of ancient authors, as belonging really to a period of modern civilization like our own: the feeling that in them, "with a perfect abstraction from those particular names and associations, which are for ever biassing our judgment in modern and domestic instances, the great principles of all political questions, whether civil or ecclesiastical, are perfectly discussed and illustrated with entire freedom, with most attractive eloquence, and with profoundest wisdom." (Serm. vol. iii. Pref. p. 13.)

From time to time, therefore, as in the Journal of Education (vol. vii. p. 240), where his reasons are stated at length,* he raised his voice against the popular outcry, by which classical instruction was at that time assailed. And it was, perhaps, not without a share in producing the subsequent reaction in its favour, that the one head-master, who, from his political connexions and opinions, would have been supposed most likely to yield to the clamour, was the one who made the most deliberate and decided protest against it.

---

* This Essay also is inserted in the volume of his Miscellaneous Works, p. 348.

2. But what was true of his union of new with old elements in the moral government of the school, applies no less to its intellectual management. He was the first Englishman who drew attention in our public schools to the historical, political, and philosophical value of philology and of the ancient writers, as distinguished from the mere verbal criticism and elegant scholarship of the last century. And besides the general impulse which he gave to miscellaneous reading, both in the regular examinations and by encouraging the tastes of particular boys for geology or other like pursuits, he incorporated the Study of Modern History, Modern Languages, and Mathematics into the work of the school, which attempt, as it was the first of its kind, so it was at one time the chief topic of blame and praise in his system of instruction. The reading of a considerable portion of modern history was effected without difficulty ; but the endeavour to teach mathematics and modern languages, especially the latter, not as an optional appendage, but as a regular part of the school business, was beset with obstacles, which rendered his plan less successful than he had anticipated ; though his wishes, especially for boys who were unable to reap the full advantage of classical studies, were, to a great extent, answered.*

---

* The instruction in modern languages passed through various stages, of which the final result was that the several forms were taught by their regular masters, French and German in the three higher forms, and French in the forms below. How fully he was himself awake to the objections to this plan will appear from the subjoined letter in 1840 ; but still he felt that it yet remained to be shown how, for a continuance, *all* the boys of a large public school can be taught modern languages, except by English masters, and those the masters of their respective classical forms."

Extract from a Letter to the Earl of Denbigh, Chairman of the Trustees of the School :—

" I assume it certainly, as the foundation of all my view of the case, that boys at a public school never will learn to speak or pronounce French well under any circumstances. But to most of our boys, to read it will be of far more use than to speak it ; and if they learn it grammatically as a dead language, I am sure that whenever they have any occasion to speak it, as in going abroad for instance, they will be able to do it very rapidly. I think that if we can enable the boys to read

What has been said, relates rather to his system of instruction, than to the instruction itself. His personal share in the teaching of the younger boys was confined to the general examinations, in which he took an active part, and to two lessons which he devoted in every week to the hearing in succession every form in the school. These visits were too transient for the boys to become familiar with him ; but great interest was always excited, and though the chief impression was of extreme fear, they were also struck by the way in which his examinations elicited from them whatever they knew, as well as by the instruction which they received merely from hearing his questions, or from seeing the effect produced upon him by their answers. But the chief source of his intellectual as of his moral influence over the school, was through the Sixth Form. To the rest of the boys he appeared almost exclusively as a master, to them he appeared almost exclusively as an instructor. The library tower, which stands over the great gateway of the school-buildings, and in which he heard the lessons of his own form, is the place to which his pupils will revert as the scene of their first real ac-

French with facility, and to know the Grammar well, we shall do as much as can be done at a public school, and should teach the boys something valuable. And, in point of fact, I have heard men, who have left Rugby, speak with gratitude of what they have learnt with us in French and German.

"It is very true that our general practice here, as in other matters, does not come up to our theory ; and I know too well that most of the boys would pass a very poor examination even in French grammar. But so it is with their mathematics ; and so it will be with any branch of knowledge that is taught but seldom, and is felt to be quite subordinate to the boy's main study. Only I am quite sure that if the boy's regular masters fail in this, a foreigner, be he who he may, would fail much more.

"I do not therefore see any way out of the difficulties of the question, and I believe sincerely that our present plan is the *least bad*, I will not say *the best*, that can be adopted ; discipline is not injured as it is with foreign masters, and I think that something is taught, though but little. With regard to German, I can speak more confidently ; and I am sure that there we do facilitate a boy's after study of the language considerably, and enable him, with much less trouble, to read those many German books, which are essential to his classical studies at the University."

quaintance with his powers of teaching, and with himself.

It has been attempted hitherto to represent his principles of education as distinct from himself; but in proportion as we approach his individual teaching, this becomes impracticable—the system is lost in the man—the recollections of the head-master of Rugby are inseparable from the recollections of the personal guide and friend of his scholars. They will at once recall those little traits, which however minute in themselves, will to them suggest, a lively image of his whole manner. They will remember the glance, with which he looked round in the few moments of silence before the lesson began, and which seemed to speak his sense of his own position and of theirs also, as the heads of a great school ; the attitude in which he stood, turning over the pages of Facciolati's Lexicon, or Pole's synopsis, with his eye fixed upon the boy who was pausing to give an answer ; the well-known changes of his voice and manner, so faithfully representing the feeling within. They will recollect the pleased look and the cheerful " Thank you," which followed upon a successful answer or translation ; the fall of his countenance with its deepening severity, the stern elevation of the eyebrows, the sudden " Sit down " which followed upon the reverse ; the courtesy and almost deference to the boys, as to his equals in society, so long as there was nothing to disturb the friendliness of their relation ; the startling earnestness with which he would check in a moment the slightest approach to levity or impertinence; the confidence with which he addressed them in his half-yearly exhortations ; the expressions of delight with which, when they had been doing well, he would say that it was a constant pleasure to him to come into the library.

His whole method was founded on the principle of

awakening the intellect of every individual boy.   Hence it was his practice to teach by questioning. As a general rule, he never gave information, except as a kind of reward for an answer, and often withheld it altogether, or checked himself in the very act of uttering it, from a sense that those whom he was addressing had not sufficient interest or sympathy to entitle them to receive it. His explanations were as short as possible—enough to dispose of the difficulty and no more ; and his questions were of a kind to call the attention of the boys to the real point of every subject and to disclose to them the exact boundaries of what they knew or did not know. With regard to younger boys, he said, " It is a great mistake to think that they should *understand* all they learn ; for God has ordered that in youth the memory should act vigorously, independent of the understanding —whereas a man cannot usually recollect a thing unless he understands it."   But in proportion to their advance in the school he tried to cultivate in them a habit not only of collecting facts, but of expressing themselves with facility, and of understanding the principles on which their facts rested. " You come here," he said, " not to read, but to learn how to read ;" and thus the greater part of his instructions were interwoven with the process of their own minds ; there was a continual reference to their thoughts, an acknowledgment that, so far as their information and power of reasoning could take them, they ought to have an opinion of their own. He was evidently working not for, but with the form, as if they were equally interested with himself in making out the meaning of the passage before them.   His object was to set them right, not by correcting them at once, but either by gradually helping them on to a true answer, or by making the answers of the more advanced part of the form serve as a medium, through which his instructions

might be communicated to the less advanced.   Such a
system he thought valuable alike to both classes of boys.
To those who by natural quickness or greater experience
of his teaching were able to follow his instructions, it
confirmed the sense of the responsible position which
they held in the school, intellectually as well as morally.
To a boy less ready or less accustomed to it, it gave precisely what he conceived that such a character required.
" He wants this," to use his own words, "and he wants it
daily—not only to interest and excite him, but to dispel
what is very apt to grow around a lonely reader not
constantly questioned—a haze of indistinctness as to a
consciousness of his own knowledge or ignorance ; he
takes a vague impression for a definite one, an imperfect
notion for one that is full and complete, and in this way
he is continually deceiving himself." ·

Hence, also, he not only laid great stress on original
compositions, but endeavoured so to choose the subjects
of exercises as to oblige them to read and lead them to
think for themselves.   He dealt at once a death-blow to
themes (as he expressed it) on " Virtus est bona res,"
and gave instead historical or geographical descriptions,
imaginary speeches or letters, etymological accounts of
words, or criticisms of books, or put religious and moral
subjects in such a form as awakened a new and real interest in them ;* as, for example, not simply " carpe
diem," or "procrastination is the thief of time ;" but
"carpere diem jubent Epicurei, jubet hoc idem Christus."
So again, in selecting passages for translation from
English into Greek or Latin, instead of taking them at
random from the Spectator or other such works, he made
a point of giving extracts, remarkable in themselves,
from such English and foreign authors as he most admired, so as indelibly to impress on the minds of his

* See Appendix B.

pupils some of the most striking names and passages in modern literature. "Ha, very good!" was his well-known exclamation of pleasure when he met with some original thought; "is that entirely your own, or do you remember anything in your reading that suggested it to you?" Style, knowledge, correctness or incorrectness of statement or expression, he always disregarded in comparison with indication or promise of real thought. "I call that the best theme," he said, "which shows that the boy has read and thought for himself; that, the next best, which shows that he has read several books, and digested what he has read; and that the *worst*, which shows that he has followed but one book, and followed that without reflection."

The interest in their work which this method excited in the boys was considerably enhanced by the respect which, even without regard to his general character, was inspired by the qualities brought out prominently in the ordinary course of lessons. They were conscious of (what was indeed implied in his method itself) the absence of display, which made it clear that what he said was to instruct them, not to exhibit his own powers; they could not but be struck by his never concealing difficulties and always confessing ignorance; acknowledging mistakes in his edition of Thucydides, and on Latin verses, mathematics, or foreign languages, appealing for help or information to boys whom he thought better qualified than himself to give it. Even as an example, it was not without its use, to witness daily the power of combination and concentration on his favourite subjects which had marked him even from a boy; and which especially appeared in his illustrations of ancient by modern, and modern by ancient history. The wide discursiveness with which he brought the several parts of their work to bear on each other; the readiness with which he referred them to the sources and authorities of information, when himself ignorant of it; the eagerness with which he tracked them out when unknown—taught them how wide the field of knowledge really was. In poetry it was almost impossible not to catch something of the delight and almost fervour, with which, as he came to any striking passage, he would hang over it, reading it over and over again, and dwelling upon it for the mere pleasure which every word seemed to give him. In history or philosophy, events, sayings, and authors, would, from the mere fact that he had quoted them, become fixed in the memory of his pupils, and give birth to thoughts and inquiries long afterwards, which, had they been derived through another medium, would have been forgotten or remained unfruitful. The very scantiness with which he occasionally dealt out his knowledge, when not satisfied that the boys could enter into it, whilst it often provoked a half-angry feeling of disappointment in those who eagerly treasured up all that he uttered, left an impression that the source from which they drew was unexhausted and unfathomed, and to all that he did say gave a double value.

Intellectually as well as morally, he felt that the teacher ought himself to be perpetually learning, and so constantly above the level of his scholars. "I am sure," he said, speaking of his pupils at Laleham, "that I do not judge of them or expect of them, as I should, if I were not taking pains to improve my own mind." For this reason, he maintained that no schoolmaster ought to remain at his post much more than fourteen or fifteen years, lest, by that time, he should have fallen behind the scholarship of the age; and by his own reading and literary works he endeavoured constantly to act upon this principle himself. "For nineteen out of twenty boys," he said once to Archbishop Whately, in speaking of the importance not only of information, but real ability in assistant-masters (and his remark of course applied still more to the station which he occupied himself), "ordinary men may be quite sufficient, but the twentieth, the boy of real talents, who is more important than the others, is liable to suffer injury from not being early placed under the training of one whom he can, on close inspection, look up to as his superior in something besides mere knowledge. The dangers," he observed, "were of various kinds. One boy may acquire a contempt for the information itself, which he sees possessed by a man whom he feels nevertheless to be far below him. Another will fancy himself as much above nearly all the world as he feels he is above his own tutor; and will become self-sufficient and scornful. A third will believe it to be his duty, as a point of humility, to bring himself down intellectually to a level with one whom he feels bound to reverence; and thus there have been instances where the veneration of a young man of ability for a teacher of small powers has been like a millstone round the neck of an eagle."

His practical talent as a scholar consisted in his insight into the general structure of sentences and the general principles of language, and in his determination to discard all those unmeaning phrases and forms of expression, by which so many writers of the last generation and boys of all generations endeavour to conceal their ignorance. In Greek and Latin composition his exceeding indifference to mere excellence of style, when unattended by anything better, made it difficult for him to bestow that praise, which was necessary to its due encouragement as a part of the school work, and he never was able to overcome the deficiency, which he always felt in composing or correcting verse exercises, even after his increased conviction of their use as a mental discipline. But to prose composition in both languages he had from the first attached considerable importance, not only as the best means of acquiring a sound knowledge of the ancient authors, but of attaining a mastery over the English language also, by the readiness and accuracy of expression which it imparted. He retained to himself that happy facility for imitating the style of the Greek historians and philosophers, for which he was remarkable in youth, whilst his Latin prose was peculiar for combining the force of common Latinity with the vigour and simplicity of his own style—perfectly correct and idiomatic, yet not the language of Cicero or Livy, but of himself.

In the common lessons, his scholarship was chiefly displayed in his power of extempore translation into English. This he had possessed in a remarkable degree from the time that he was a boy at Winchester, where the practice of reading the whole passage from Greek or Latin into good English, without construing each particular sentence word by word, had been much encouraged by Dr. Gabell, and in his youthful vacations during his Oxford course he used to enliven the sick-bed of his sister Susannah by the readiness with which in the evenings he would sit by her side, and translate book after book of the history of Herodotus. So essential did he consider this method to a sound study of the classics, that he published an elaborate defence of it in the Quarterly Journal of Education, and, when delivering his Modern History lectures at Oxford, where he much lamented the prevalence of the opposite system, he could not resist the temptation of protesting against it, with no other excuse for introducing the subject, than the mention of the Latin style of the middle-age historians. In itself, he looked upon it as the only means of really entering into the spirit of the ancient authors; and, requiring as he did besides, that the translation should be made into idiomatic English, and if possible, into that style of English which most corresponded to the period or the subject of the Greek or Latin writer in question, he considered it further as an excellent exercise in the principles of taste and in the knowledge and use of the English language, no less than of those of Greece and Rome. No one must suppose that these translations in the least resembled the paraphrases in his notes to Thucydides, which are avowedly not translations, but explanations ; he was constantly on the watch for any inadequacy or redundancy of expression—the version was to represent, and no more than represent, the exact words of the original ; and those who, either as his colleagues or his pupils, were present at his lessons or examinations, well know the accuracy with which every shade of meaning would be reproduced in a different shape, and the rapidity with which he would pounce on any mistake of grammar or construction, however dexterously concealed in the folds of a free translation.

In the subject of the lessons it was not only the language, but the author and the age which rose before him ; it was not merely a lesson to be got through and explained, but a work which was to be understood, to be condemned or to be admired. It was an old opinion of his, which, though much modified, was never altogether abandoned, that the mass of boys had not a sufficient appreciation of poetry, to make it worth while for them to read so much of the ancient poets, in proportion to prose writers, as was usual when he came to Rugby. But for some of them he had besides a personal distaste. The Greek tragedians, though reading them constantly, and portions of them with the liveliest admiration, he thought on the whole greatly overrated ; and still more, the second-rate Latin poets, but whom he seldom used :

and some, such as Tibullus and Propertius, never. "I do really think," he said, speaking of these last as late as 1842, "that any examiners incur a serious responsibility who require or encourage the reading of these books for scholarships ; of all useless reading, surely the reading of indifferent poets is most useless." And to some of them he had a yet deeper feeling of aversion. It was not till 1835 that he himself read the plays of Aristophanes, and though he was then much struck with the "Clouds," and ultimately introduced the partial use of his Comedies in the school, yet his strong moral disapprobation always interfered with his sense of the genius both of that poet and Juvenal.

But of the classical lessons generally his enjoyment was complete. When asked once whether he did not find the repetition of the same lessons irksome to him, "No," he said, "there is a constant freshness in them : I find something new in them every time that I go over them." The best proof of the pleasure which he took in them is the distinct impression which his scholars retained of the feeling, often rather implied than expressed, with which he entered into the several works ; the enthusiasm with which, both in the public and private orations of Demosthenes, he would contemplate piece by piece "the luminous clearness" of the sentences ; the affectionate familiarity which he used to show towards Thucydides, knowing as he did the substance of every single chapter by itself ; the revival of youthful interest with which he would recur to portions of the works of Aristotle ; the keen sense of a new world opening before him, with which in later years, with ever-increasing pleasure, he entered into the works of Plato ;—above all, his childlike enjoyment of Herodotus, and that "fountain of beauty and delight which no man," he said, "can ever drain dry," the poetry of Homer. The simple language of that early age was exactly what he was most able to reproduce in his own simple and touching translations; and his eyes would fill with tears, when he came to the story which told how Cleobis and Bito, as a reward for their filial piety, lay down in the temple, and fell asleep and died.

To his pupils, perhaps, of ordinary lessons, the most attractive were the weekly ones on Modern History. He had always a difficulty in finding any work which he could use with satisfaction as a text-book. "Gibbon, which in many respects would answer the purpose so well, I dare not use." Accordingly, the work, whatever it might be, was made the groundwork of his own observations, and of other reading from such books as the school library contained. Russell's Modern Europe, for example, which he estimated very low, though perhaps from his own early acquaintance with it at Winchester, with less dislike than might have been expected, served this purpose for several years. On a chapter of this he would engraft, or cause the boys to engraft, additional information from Hallam, Guizot, or any other historian who happened to treat of the same period, whilst he himself, with that familiar interest which belonged to his favourite study of history and of geography, which he always maintained could only be taught in connexion with it, would by his searching and significant questions gather the thoughts of his scholars round the peculiar characteristics of the age or the country on which he wished to fix their attention. Thus, for example, in the Seven Years' War, he would illustrate the general connexion of military history with geography, by the simple instance of the order of Hannibal's successive victories; and then, chalking roughly on a board the chief points in the physical conformation of Germany, apply the same principle to the more complicated campaigns of

Frederick the Great. Or, again, in a more general examination, he would ask for the chief events which occurred, for instance, in the year 15 of two or three successive centuries, and, by making the boys contrast or compare them together, bring before their minds the differences and resemblances in the state of Europe in each of the periods in question.

Before entering on his instructions in theology, which both for himself and his scholars had most peculiar interest, it is right to notice the religious character which more or less pervaded the rest of the lessons. When his pupils heard him in preaching recommend them " to note in any common work that they read, such judgments of men and things, and such a tone in speaking of them as are manifestly at variance with the Spirit of Christ," (Serm. vol. iii. p. 116,) or when they heard him ask " whether the Christian ever feels more keenly awake to the purity of the spirit of the Gospel, than when he reads the history of crimes related with no true sense of their evil ?" (Serm. vol. ii. p. 223,) instances would immediately occur to them from his own practice, to prove how truly he felt what he said. No direct instruction could leave on their minds a livelier image of his disgust at moral evil, than the black cloud of indignation which passed over his face when speaking of the crimes of Napoleon, or of Cæsar, and the dead pause which followed, as if the acts had just been committed in his very presence. No expression of his reverence for a high standard of Christian excellence could have been more striking than the almost involuntary expressions of admiration which broke from him whenever mention was made of St. Louis of France. No general teaching of the providential government of the world could have left a deeper impression, than the casual allusions to it, which occurred as they came to any of the critical moments in the history of

Greece and Rome. No more forcible contrast could have been drawn between the value of Christianity and of heathenism, than the manner with which, for example, after reading in the earlier part of the lesson one of the Scripture descriptions of the Gentile world, " Now," he said, as he opened the Satires of Horace, " we shall see what it was."

Still it was in the Scripture* lessons that this found most scope. In the lower forms it was rather that more prominence was given to them, and that they were placed under better regulations than that they were increased in amount. In the Sixth Form, besides the lectures on Sunday, he introduced two lectures on the Old or New Testament in the course of the week, so that a boy who remained there three years would often have read through a great part of the New Testament, much of the Old Testament, and especially of the Psalms in the Septuagint version, and also committed much of them to memory ; whilst at times he would deliver lectures on the history of the early Church, or of the English Reformation. In these lessons on the Scriptures he would insist much on the importance of familiarity with the very words of the sacred writers, and of the exact place where passages occurred ; on a thorough acquaintance with the different parts of the story contained in the several Gospels, that they might be referred to at once ; on the knowledge of the times when, and the persons to whom, the Epistles were written. In translating the New Testament, while he encouraged his pupils to take the language of the authorized version as much as possible, he was very particular in not allowing them to use words which fail to convey the meaning of the original, or which by frequent use have lost all definite meaning of their own—such as "edification," or "the Gospel." What-

---

* For his own feeling about them, see Sermons, vol. iv. pp. 317, 321.

ever dogmatical instruction he gave was conveyed almost
entirely in a practical or exegetical shape; and it was
very rarely indeed that he made any allusion to existing
parties or controversies within the Church of England.
His own peculiar views, which need not be noticed in
this place, transpired more or less throughout; but the
great proportion of his interpretations were such as most
of his pupils, of whatever opinions, eagerly collected and
preserved for their own use in after life.

But more important than any details was the union
of reverence and reality in his whole manner of treating
the Scriptures, which so distinguished these lessons from
such as may in themselves almost as little deserve the
name of religious instruction as many lessons commonly
called secular.   The same searching questions, the same
vividness which marked his historical lessons,—the same
anxiety to bring all that he said home to their own feelings, which made him, in preparing them for confirmation, endeavour to make them say, " Christ died for me,"
instead of the general phrase, "Christ died for us,"—
must often, when applied to the natural vagueness of
boys' notions on religious subjects, have dispelled it for
ever.   "He appeared to me," writes a pupil, whose intercourse with him never extended beyond these lessons,
"to be remarkable for his habit of realizing everything
that we are told in Scripture. You know how frequently
we can ourselves, and how constantly we hear others go
prosing on in a sort of religious cant or slang, which is
as easy to learn as any other technical jargon, without
seeing as it were by that faculty, which all possess, of
picturing to the mind, and acting as if we really saw
things unseen belonging to another world.   Now he
seemed to have the freshest view of our Lord's life and
death that I ever knew a man to possess. His rich mind
filled up the naked outline of the Gospel history; it was

to him the most interesting *fact* that has ever happened —as real, as *exciting* (if I may use the expression) as any recent event in modern history of which the actual effects are visible." And all his comments, from whatever theory of inspiration they were given, were always made in a tone and manner that left an impression that from the book which lay before him he was really seeking to draw his rule of life, and that, whilst he examined it in earnest to find what its meaning was, when he had found it he intended to abide by it.

The effect of these instructions was naturally more permanent (speaking merely in an intellectual point of view) than the lessons themselves, and it was a frequent topic of censure that his pupils were led to take up his opinions before their minds were duly prepared for them. What was true of his method and intention in the simplest matters of instruction, was true of it as applied to the highest matters. Undoubtedly it was his belief that the minds of young men ought to be awakened to the greatness of things around them ; and it was his earnest endeavour to give them what he thought the best means of attaining a firm hold upon truth. But it was always his wish that his pupils should form their opinions for themselves, and not take them on trust from him. To his particular political principles he carefully avoided allusion, and it was rarely that his subjects for school composition touched on any topics that could have involved, even remotely, the disputed points of party politics. In theological matters, partly from the nature of the case, partly from the peculiar aspect under which for the last six years of his life he regarded the Oxford school, he both expressed his thoughts more openly, and was more anxious to impress them upon his pupils ; but this was almost entirely in the comparatively few sermons preached on what could be called controversial topics.

In his intercourse indeed with his pupils after they had left the school, he naturally spoke with greater freedom on political or theological subjects, yet it was usually when invited by them, and, though he often deeply lamented their adoption of what he held to be erroneous views, he much disliked a merely unmeaning echo of his own opinions. "It would be a great mistake," he said, "if I were to try to make myself here into a Pope."

It was, however, an almost inevitable consequence of coming into contact with his teaching, and with the new world which it opened, that his pupils would often, on their very entrance into life, have acquired a familiarity and encountered a conflict with some of the most harassing questions of morals and religion. It would also often happen, that the increasing reverence which they felt for him would not only incline them to receive with implicit trust all that he said in the lessons or in the pulpit, but also to include in their admiration of the man all that they could gather of his general views, either from report or from his published works: whilst they would naturally look with distrust on the opposite notions in religion and politics, brought before them, as would often be the case, in close connexion with vehement attacks on him, which in most cases they could hardly help regarding as unfounded or unfair. Still the greater part of his pupils, while at school, were, after the manner of English boys, altogether unaffected by his political opinions ; and of those who most revered him, none in after life could be found who followed his views implicitly, even on the subjects on which they were most disposed to listen to him. But though no particular school of opinion grew up amongst them, the end of his teaching would be answered far more truly, (and it may suggest to those who know ancient history, similar results of

similar methods in the hands of other eminent teachers,)
if his scholars learned to form an independent judgment
for themselves, and to carry out their opinions to their
legitimate consequences,—to appreciate moral agreement amidst much intellectual difference, not only in
each other or in him, but in the world at large ;—and
to adopt many, if not all, of his principles, whilst differing
widely in their application of them to existing persons
and circumstances.

III. If there is any one place at Rugby more than
another which was especially the scene of Dr. Arnold's
labours, both as a teacher and as a master, it is the
School chapel.   Even its outward forms, from " the very
cross at the top of the building,"* on which he loved to
dwell as a visible symbol of the Christian end of their
education, to the vaults which he caused to be opened
underneath, for those who died in the school, must
always be associated with his name. " I envy Winchester
its antiquity," he said, "and am therefore anxious to do
all that can be done to give us something of a venerable
outside, if we have not the nobleness of old associations
to help us."   The five painted windows in the chapel
were put up in great part at his expense, altogether at
his instigation.   The subject of the first of these, the
great east window, he delighted to regard as " strikingly
appropriate to a place of education," being the " Wise
Men's Offering," and the first time after its erection that
the chapter describing the Adoration of the Magi was
read in the church service he took occasion to preach
upon it one of his most remarkable sermons, that of
" Christian Professions—Offering Christ our best." (Serm.
vol. iii. p. 112.)   And as this is connected with the
energy and vigour of his life, so the subject of the last,
which he chose himself a short time before his death, is

* MS. Sermon.

the confession of St. Thomas, on which he dwelt with deep solemnity in his last hours, as in his life he had dwelt upon it as the great consolation of doubting but faithful hearts, and as the great attestation of what was to him the central truth of Christianity, our Lord's divinity. Lastly, the monuments of those who died in the school during his government, and whose graves were the first ever made in the chapel; above all, his own, the monument and grave of the only head-master of Rugby who is buried within its walls, give a melancholy interest to the words with which he closed a sermon preached on the Founder's day, in 1833, whilst as yet the recently-opened vaults had received no dead within them :—

"This roof, under which we are now assembled, will hold, it is probable, our children, and our children's children; may they be enabled to think, as they shall kneel perhaps over the bones of some of us now here assembled, that they are praying where their fathers prayed; and let them not, if they mock in their day the means of grace here offered to them, encourage themselves with the thought that the place had long ago been profaned with equal guilt; that they are but infected with the spirit of our ungodliness."*

But of him especially it need hardly be said, that his chief interest in that place lay in the three hundred boys who, Sunday after Sunday, were collected, morning and afternoon, within its walls. "The veriest stranger," he said, "who ever attends divine service in this chapel, does well to feel something more than common interest in the sight of the congregation here assembled. But if the sight so interests a mere stranger, what should it be to ourselves, both to you and to me?" (Serm. vol. v. p. 403.) So he spoke within a month of his death, and to him, certainly, the interest was increased rather than lessened by its familiarity. There was the fixed expression of countenance, exhibiting the earnest attention with

* Serm. vol. iii. p. 211.

which, after the service was over, he sat in his place
looking at the boys as they filed out one by one in the
orderly and silent arrangement which succeeded, in the
latter part of his stay, to the public calling over of their
names in the chapel. There was the complete image of
his union of dignity and simplicity, of manliness and
devotion, as he performed the chapel service, especially
when at the communion-table he would read or rather
repeat almost by heart the Gospel and Epistle of the day,
with the impressiveness of one who entered into it equally
with his whole spirit and also with his whole understanding. There was the visible animation with which by force
of long association he joined in the musical parts of the
service, to which he was by nature wholly indifferent, as
in the chanting of the Nicene Creed, which was adopted
in accordance with his conviction that creeds in public
worship (Serm. vol. iii. p. 310) ought to be used as triumphant hymns of thanksgiving ; or still more in the
Te Deum, which he loved so dearly, and when his whole
countenance would be lit up at his favourite verse—
"When Thou hadst overcome the sharpness of death,
Thou didst open the kingdom of Heaven to all believers."
     From his own interest in the service naturally flowed
his anxiety to impart it to his scholars: urging them in
his later sermons, or in his more private addresses, to join
in the responses, at times with such effect, that at least
from all the older part of the school the responses were
very general. The very course of the ecclesiastical year
would often be associated in their minds with their remembrance of the peculiar feeling, with which they saw
that he regarded the greater festivals, and of the almost
invariable connexion of his sermons with the services of
the day. The touching recollections of those amongst
the living or the dead, whom he loved or honoured, which
passed through his mind as he spoke of All Saints' Day,

and, whenever it was possible, of its accompanying feast, now no longer observed, All Souls' Day;—and the solemn thoughts of the advance of human life, and of the progress of the human race, and of the Church, which were awakened by the approach of Advent—might have escaped a careless observer: but it must have been difficult for anyone not to have been struck by the triumphant exultation of his whole manner on the recurrence of Easter Day. Lent was marked during his last three years, by the putting up of boxes in the chapel and the boarding-houses, to receive money for the poor, a practice adopted not so much with the view of relieving any actual want, as of affording the boys an opportunity for self-denial and alms-giving.*

He was anxious to secure the administration of the rite of confirmation, if possible, once every two years; when the boys were prepared by himself and the other masters in their different boarding-houses, who each brought up his own division of pupils on the day of the ceremony; the interest of which was further enhanced, during his earlier years, by the presence of the late Bishop Ryder,† for whom he entertained a great respect,

---

* He feared, however, to introduce more religious services, than he thought the boys would bear without a sense of tedium or formality, on which principle he dropped an existing practice of devoting all the lessons in Passion Week to the New Testament; and always hesitated to have a chapel service on such festivals as did not fall on Sundays, though in the last year of his life he made an exception with regard to Ascension Day.

† The following extract from a sermon preached in consequence of the delay of confirmation may serve to illustrate as well his general feeling on the subject, as his respect for the individual:—

. . . . . . "And while I say this, it is impossible not to remember to what cause this disappointment has been owing, namely, to the long illness and death of the late excellent Bishop of this diocese. This is neither the place nor the congregation for a funeral eulogy on that excellent person; we knew him too little, and were too much removed out of the ordinary sphere of his ministry, to be able to bear the best witness to him. Yet many here, I think, will remember the manner in which he went through the rite of confirmation in this chapel three years ago; the earnestness and kindness of his manner, the manifest interest which he felt in the service in which he was ministering. And though, as I said, we were comparatively strangers to him, yet we had heard enough of him to receive, without one jarring feeling, the full

and latterly by the presence of his intimate friend, Archbishop Whately. The Confirmation Hymn of Dr. Hinds, which was used on these occasions, became so endeared to his recollections, that when travelling abroad late at night, he would have it repeated or sung to him. One of the earliest public addresses to the school was that made before the first confirmation, and published in the second volume of his sermons ; and he always had something of the kind (over and above the Bishop's charge) either before or after the regular Chapel service.

The Communion was celebrated four times a year. At first some of the Sixth Form boys alone were in the habit of attending ; but he took pains to invite to it boys in all parts of the school, who had any serious thoughts, so that the number out of two hundred and ninety or three hundred boys, was occasionally a hundred, and never less than seventy. To individual boys he rarely spoke on the subject, from the fear of its becoming a matter of form or favour ; but in his sermons he dwelt upon it much, and would afterwards speak with deep emotion of the pleasure and hope which a larger attendance than usual would give him. It was impossible

impression of his words and manner; we knew that as these were solemn and touching, so they were consistent and sincere ; they were not put on for the occasion, nor yet, which is a far more common case, did they spring out of the occasion. It was not the mere natural and momentary feeling which might have arisen even in a careless mind, while engaged in a work so peculiarly striking; but it was truly the feeling not of the occasion but of the man. He but showed himself to us as he was, and thus we might and may dwell with pleasure on the recollection, long after the immediate effect was over ; and may think truly that, when he told us how momentous were the interests involved in the promises and prayers of that service, he told us no more than he himself most earnestly believed ; he urged us to no other faith, to no other course of living, than that which by God's grace he had long made his own. It is a great blessing to God's church when they who are called to the higher offices of the ministry in it, thus give to their ministry the weight, not of their words only, but of their lives. Still we must remember that the care of our souls is our own, —that God's means of grace and warnings furnished us by the ministry of his church, are no way dependent upon the personal character of the minister ; that confirmation, with all its opportunities, is still the same point in our lives, by whomsoever it may be administered."

to hear these exhortations or to see him administer
it, without being struck by the strong and manifold
interest which it awakened in him ; and at Rugby it
was of course more than usually touching to him from
its peculiar relation to the school. When he spoke
of it in his sermons, it was evident that amongst all
the feelings which it excited in himself, and which
he wished to impart to others, none was so prominent
as the sense that it was a communion not only with
God but with one another, and that the thoughts thus
roused should act as a direct and especial counterpoise to
that false communion and false companionship, which,
as binding one another not to good but to evil, he
believed to be the great source of mischief in the school
at large. And when,—especially to the very young boys,
who sometimes partook of the communion,—he bent
himself down with looks of fatherly tenderness, and
glistening eyes, and trembling voice, in the administration of the elements, it was felt, perhaps, more distinctly
than at any other time, how great was the sympathy
which he felt with the earliest advances to good in every
individual boy.

That part of the Chapel service, however, which, at
least to the world at large, is most connected with him,
as being the most frequent and most personal of his
ministrations, was his preaching. Sermons had occasionally been preached by the head-master of this and other
public schools to their scholars before his coming to
Rugby; but (in some cases from the peculiar constitution
or arrangement of the school) it had never before been
considered an essential part of the head-master's office.
The first half year he confined himself to delivering short
addresses, of about five minutes' length, to the boys of
his own house. But from the second half year he began
to preach frequently ; and from the autumn of 1831,

when he took the chaplaincy* which had then become vacant, he preached almost every Sunday of the school year to the end of his life.

It may be allowable to dwell for a few moments on a practice which has since been followed, whenever it was practicable, in the other great public schools, and on sermons which, as they were the first of their kind, will also be probably long looked upon as models of their kind, in English preaching. They were preached always in the afternoon, and lasted seldom more than twenty minutes, sometimes less: a new one almost every time. "A man could hardly," he said, "preach on the same subject, without writing a better sermon than he had written a few years before." However much they may have occupied his previous thoughts, they were written almost invariably between the morning and afternoon service; and though often under such stress of time that the ink of the last sentence was hardly dry when the chapel bell ceased to sound, they contain hardly a single erasure, and the manuscript volumes remain as accessible a treasure to their possessors, as if they were printed.

* Extract from a letter to the Trustees, applying for the situation:—" I had no knowledge nor so much as the slightest suspicion of the vacancy," he writes, "till I was informed of it last night. But the importance of the point is so great that I most respectfully crave the indulgence of the Trustees to the request I venture to submit to them, namely, that if they see no objection to it, I may myself be appointed to the chaplaincy, waiving, of course, altogether the salary attached to the office. Whoever is chaplain, I must ever feel myself, as head-master, the real and proper religious instructor of the boys. No one else can feel the same interest in them, and no one else (I am not speaking of myself personally, but merely by virtue of my situation) can speak to them with so much influence. In fact it seems to me the natural and fitting thing, and the great advantage of having a separate chapel for the school—that the master of the boys should be officially as well as really their pastor, and that he should not devolve on another, however well qualified, one of his own most peculiar and solemn duties. This, however, is a general question, which I only venture so far to enter upon, in explaining my motives in urging and requesting, in this present instance, that the Trustees would present me to the Bishop to be licensed, allowing me altogether to decline the salary, because I consider that I am paid for my services already; and that being head-master and clergyman, I am bound to be the religious instructor of my pupils by virtue of my situation."

When he first began to preach, he felt that his chief duty was to lay bare, in the plainest language that he could use, the sources of the evils of schools, and to contrast them with the purity of the moral law of Christianity. "The spirit of Elijah," he said, "must ever precede the spirit of Christ." But as he advanced, there is a marked contrast between the severe tone of his early sermons in the second volume, when all was as yet new to him, except the knowledge of the evil which he had to combat, and the gentler tone which could not but be inspired by his greater familiarity, both with his work and his pupils —between the direct attack on particular faults which marks the course of Lent Sermons in 1830, and the wish to sink the mention of particular faults in the general principle of love to Christ and abhorrence of sin, which marks the summary of his whole school experience in the last sermon which he ever preached. When he became the constant preacher, he made a point of varying the more directly practical addresses with sermons on the interpretation of Scripture, on the general principles and evidences of Christianity, or on the dangers of their after life, applicable chiefly to the elder boys. Amongst these last should be noticed those which contained more or less the expression of his sentiments on the principles to which he conceived his pupils liable hereafter to be exposed at Oxford, and most of which, as being of a more general interest, he selected for publication in the third and fourth volumes. That their proportion to those that are published affords no measure of their proportion to those that are unpublished, may be seen at once by reference to the year's course in the fifth volume, which out of thirty-four, contains only four, which could possibly be included in this class. That it was not his own intention to make them either personal or controversial, appears from an explanation to a friend of a statement, which, in 1839, appeared in the newspapers, that he "had been preaching a course of sermons against the Oxford errors." "The origin of the paragraph was simply this: that I preached two in February, showing that the exercise of our own judgment was not inconsistent with the instruction and authority of the Church, or with individual modesty and humility [viz., the thirty-first and thirty-second in vol. iv.]. They were not in the least controversial, and neither mentioned nor alluded to the Oxford writers. And I have preached only these two which could even be supposed to bear upon their doctrines. Indeed, I should not think it right, except under very different circumstances from present ones, to occupy the boys' time or thoughts with such controversies." The general principles, accordingly, which form the groundwork of all these sermons, are such as are capable of a far wider application than to any particular school of English opinion, and often admit of direct application to the moral condition of the school. But the quick ears of boys no doubt were always ready to give such sermons a more personal character than he had intended, or perhaps had even in his mind at the moment : and at times, when the fear of these opinions was more forcibly impressed upon him, the allusion and even mention of the writers in question is so direct, that no one could mistake it.

But it was of course in their direct practical application to the boys, that the chief novelty and excellence of his sermons consisted. Though he spoke with almost conversational plainness on the peculiar condition of public schools, his language never left an impression of familiarity, rarely of personal allusion. In cases of notorious individual misconduct, he generally shrunk from any pointed mention of them, and on one occasion when he wished to address the boys on an instance of untruthfulness which had deeply grieved him, he had the sermon before the regular service, in order to be alone in the chapel with the boys, without the presence even of the other masters.* Earnest and even impassioned as his appeals were, himself at times almost overcome with emotion, there was yet nothing in them of excitement. In speaking of the occasional deaths in the school, he would dwell on the general solemnity of the event, rather than on any individual or agitating details; and the impression thus produced, instead of belonging to the feeling of the moment, has become part of an habitual rule for the whole conduct of life. Often he would speak with severity and bitter disappointment of the evils of the place; yet there was hardly ever a sermon which did not contain some words of encouragement. " I have never," he said in his last sermon, " wished to speak with exaggeration; it seems to me as unwise as it is wrong to do so. I think that it is quite right to observe what is hopeful in us as well as what is threatening; that general confessions of unmixed evil are deceiving and hardening, rather than arousing; that our evil never looks so really dark as when we contrast it with anything which there may be in us of good." (Serm. vol. v. p. 460.)

Accordingly, even from the first, and much more in after years, there was blended with his sterner tone a strain of affectionate entreaty—an appeal to principles, which could be appreciated only by a few—exhortations to duties, such as self-denial, and visiting the poor, which

---

* On another occasion, the practice of drinking having prevailed to a great extent in the school, he addressed the boys at considerable length from his place in the great school, saying that he should have spoken to them from the pulpit, but that as there were others present in the Chapel, he wished to hide their shame. And then (says one who was present), " in a tone of the deepest feeling, as if it wrung his inmost heart to confess the existence of such an evil amongst us," he dwelt upon the sin and the folly of the habit, even where intoxication was not produced—its evil effects both on body and mind—the folly of fancying it to be manly—its general effect on the school.

some at least might practise, whilst none could deny their obligation. There also appeared most evidently— what indeed pervaded his whole school life—the more than admiration, with which he regarded those who struggled against the stream of school opinion, and the abiding comfort which they afforded him. In them he saw not merely good boys and obedient scholars, but the companions of everything high and excellent, with which his strong historical imagination peopled the past, or which his lively sense of things unseen realized in the invisible world. There were few present in the chapel who were not at least for the moment touched, when, in one of his earliest sermons, he closed one of these earnest appeals with the lines from Milton which always deeply moved him,—the blessing on Abdiel.

But more than either matter or manner of his preaching, was the impression of himself. Even the mere readers of his sermons will derive from them the history of his whole mind, and of his whole management of the school. But to his hearers it was more than this. It was the man himself, there more than in any other place, concentrating all his various faculties and feelings on one sole object, combating face to face the evil, with which directly or indirectly he was elsewhere perpetually struggling. He was not the preacher or the clergyman who had left behind all his usual thoughts and occupations as soon as he had ascended the pulpit. He was still the scholar, the historian, and theologian, basing all that he had said, not indeed ostensibly, but consciously, and often visibly, on the deepest principles of the past and present. He was still the instructor and the schoolmaster, only teaching and educating with increased solemnity and energy. He was still the simple-hearted and earnest man, labouring to win others to share in his own personal feelings of disgust at sin, and love of goodness, and to trust to the same faith, in which he hoped to live and die himself.

It is difficult to describe, without seeming to exaggerate, the attention with which he was heard by all above the very young boys. Years have passed away, and many of his pupils can look back to hardly any greater interest than that with which, for those twenty minutes, Sunday after Sunday, they sat beneath that pulpit, with their eyes fixed upon him, and their attention strained to the utmost to catch every word that he uttered. It is true, that, even to the best, there was much, and to the mass of boys, the greater part of what he said, that must have passed away from them as soon as they had heard it, without any corresponding fruits. But they were struck, as boys naturally would be, by the originality of his thoughts, and what always impressed them as the beauty of his language ; and in the substance of what he said, much that might have seemed useless, because for the most part impracticable to boys, was not without its effect in breaking completely through the corrupt atmosphere of school opinion, and exhibiting before them once every week an image of high principle and feeling, which they felt was not put on for the occasion, but was constantly living amongst them. And to all it must have been an advantage, that, for once in their lives, they had listened to sermons, which none of them could associate with the thought of weariness, formality, or exaggeration. On many there was left an impression to which, though unheeded at the time, they recurred in after life. Even the most careless boys would sometimes, during the course of the week, refer almost involuntarily to the sermon of the past Sunday, as a condemnation of what they were doing. Some, whilst they wonder how it was that so little practical effect was produced upon themselves at the time, yet retain the recollection, (to give the words of one who so describes himself,) that, "I used to listen to them from first to last with a kind of awe, and over and over again could not join my friends at the chapel door, but would walk home to be alone ; and I remember the same effects being produced by them, more or less, on others whom I should have thought as hard as stones, and on whom I should think Arnold looked as some of the worst boys in the school."

IV. Although the chapel was the only place in which, to the school at large, he necessarily appeared in a purely pastoral and personal relation—yet this relation extended in his view to his whole management of his scholars ; and he conceived it to be his duty and that of the other masters to throw themselves, as much as possible, into the way of understanding and entering into the feelings of the boys, not only in their official intercourse, but always. When he was first appointed at Rugby, his friends had feared that the indifference which he felt towards characters and persons, with whom he had no especial sympathy, would have interfered with his usefulness as head-master. But in the case of boys, a sense of duty supplied the want of that interest in character, as such, which, in the case of men, he possessed but little. Much as there was in the peculiar humour of boys which his own impatience of moral thoughtlessness, or of treating serious or important subjects with anything like ridicule or irony, prevented him from fully appreciating, yet he truly felt, that the natural youthfulness and elasticity of his constitution gave him a great advantage in dealing with them.—"When I find that I cannot run up the library stairs," he said, "I shall know that it is time for me to go."

Thus traits and actions of boys, which to a stranger would have told nothing, were to him highly significant.

His quick and far-sighted eye became familiar with the face and manner of every boy in the school. " Do you see," he said to an assistant-master who had recently come, " those two boys walking together ? I never saw them together before ; you should make an especial point of observing the company they keep :—nothing so tells the changes in a boy's character." The insight which he thus acquired into the general characteristics of boyhood, will not be doubted by any reader of his sermons ; and his scholars used sometimes to be startled by the knowledge of their own notions, which his speeches to them implied. " Often and often," says one of them, " have I said to myself, ' If it was one of ourselves who had just spoken, he could not more completely have known and understood our thoughts and ideas.'" And though it might happen that his opinion of boys would, like his opinions of men, be too much influenced by his disposition, to judge of the whole from some one prominent feature, and though his fixed adherence to general rules might sometimes prevent him from making exceptions where the case required it ; yet few can have been long familiar with him, without being struck by the distinctness, the vividness, and, in spite of great occasional mistakes, the very general truth and accuracy of his delineation of their individual characters, or the readiness with which, whilst speaking most severely of a mass of boys, he would make allowances, and speak hopefully in any particular instance that came before him. Often before any other eye had discerned it, he saw the germs of coming good or evil, and pronounced confident decisions, doubted at the time, but subsequently proved to be correct ; so that those who lived with him, described themselves as trusting to his opinions of boys as to divinations, and feeling as if by an unfavourable judgment their fate was sealed.

His relation to the boarders in his own house (called by distinction the School-house, and containing between sixty and seventy boys) naturally afforded more scope for communication than with the rest of the school. Besides the opportunities which he took of showing kindness and attention to them in his own family, in cases of distress or sickness, he also made use of the preparation for confirmation for private conversation with them ; and during the later years of his life was accustomed to devote an hour or more in the evening to seeing each of them alone by turns, and talking on such topics as presented themselves, leading them if possible to more serious subjects. The general management of the house, both from his strong dislike to intruding on the privacy even of the youngest, and from the usual principles of trust on which he proceeded, he left as much as possible to the Præpostors. Still his presence and manner when he appeared officially, either on special calls, or on the stated occasions of calling over their names twice a day, was not without its effect. One of the scenes that most lives in the memory of his school-house pupils is their night muster in the rudely-lighted hall—his tall figure at head of the files of the boys ranged on each side of the long tables, whilst prayers were read by one of the Præpostors, and a portion of Scripture by himself. This last was a practice which he introduced soon after his arrival, when, on one of these occasions, he spoke strongly to the boys on the necessity of each reading some part of the Bible every day, and then added, that as he feared that many would not make the rule for themselves, he should for the future always read a passage every evening at this time. He usually brought in his Greek Testament, and read about half a chapter in English, most frequently from the close of St. John's Gospel ; then from the Old Testament, especially his favourite Psalms, the 19th for example, and the 107th, and the others relating to the beauty of the natural world. He never made any comment; but his manner of reading impressed the boys considerably, and it was observed by some of them, shortly after the practice was commenced, that they had never understood the Psalms before. On Sunday nights he read a prayer of his own, and before he began to preach regularly in the chapel, delivered the short addresses which have been before mentioned, and which he resumed, in addition to his other work on Sundays, during the last year and a half of his life.

With the boys in the Sixth Form his private intercourse was comparatively frequent, whether in the lessons, or in questions of school government, or in the more familiar relation in which they were brought to him in their calls before and after the holidays, their dinners with him during the half-year, and the visits which one or more used by turns to pay him in Westmoreland, during part of the vacation. But with the greater part of the school it was almost entirely confined to such opportunities as arose out of the regular course of school discipline or instruction, and the occasional invitations to his house of such amongst the younger boys as he could find any reason or excuse for asking.

It would thus often happen, in so large a number, that a boy would leave Rugby without any personal communication with him at all; and even in the higher part of the school, those who most respected him would sometimes complain, even with bitterness, that he did not give them greater opportunities of asking his advice, or himself offer more frequently to direct their studies and guide their inquiries. Latterly indeed, he communicated with them more frequently, and expressed himself more freely both in public and private on the highest subjects. But he was always restrained from speaking much or often, both from the extreme difficulty which he felt in saying anything without a real occasion for it, and also from his principle of leaving as much as possible to be filled up by the judgment of the boys themselves, and from his deep conviction that, in the most important matters of all, the movement must come not from without but from within. And it certainly was the case that, whenever he did make exceptions to this rule, and spoke rather as their friend than their master, the simplicity of his words, the rareness of their occurrence, and the stern background of his ordinary administration gave a double force to all that was said.

Such, for example, would be the effect of his speaking of swearing to a boy, not so much in anger or reproof, as assuring him how every year he would learn to see more and more how foolish and disgusting such language was; or again, the distinction he would point out to them between mere amusement and such as encroached on the next day's duties, when, as he said, "it immediately becomes what St. Paul calls *revelling*." Such also would be the impression of his severe rebukes for individual faults, showing by their very shortness and abruptness his loathing and abhorrence of evil. "Nowhere," he said, in speaking to some boys on bad behaviour during prayers at the boarding-house, "nowhere is Satan's work more evidently manifest than in turning holy things to ridicule." Such also were the cases, in which boys, who were tormented while at school with sceptical doubts, took courage at last to unfold them to him, and were almost startled to find the ready sympathy with which, instead of denouncing them as profane, he entered into their difficulties, and applied his whole mind to assuage them. So again, when dealing with the worst class of boys, in whom he saw indications of improvement, he would grant indulgences which on ordinary occasions he would have denied, with a view of encouraging them by signs of his confidence in them ; and at times, on discovering cases of vice, he would, instead of treating them with contempt or extreme severity, tenderly allow the force of the temptation, and urge it upon them as a proof brought home to their own minds, how surely they must look for help out of themselves.

In his preparation of boys for Confirmation he followed the same principle. The printed questions which he issued for them were intended rather as guides to their thoughts than as necessary to be formally answered; and his own interviews with them were very brief. But the few words which he then spoke—the simple repetition, for example, of the promise made to prayer, with his earnest assurance, that if that was not true, nothing was true ; if anything in the Bible could be relied upon, it was that—have become the turning-point of a boy's character, and graven on his memory as a law for life.

But, independently of particular occasions of intercourse, there was a deep undercurrent of sympathy which extended to almost all, and which from time to time broke through the reserve of his outward manner. In cases where it might have been thought that tenderness would have been extinguished by indignation, he was sometimes so deeply affected in pronouncing sentence of punishment on offenders as to be hardly able to speak. " I felt," he said once of some great fault of which he had heard in one of the Sixth Form—and his eyes filled with tears as he spoke, " as if it had been one of my own children, and, till I had ascertained that it was really true, I mentioned it to no one, not even to any of the masters." And this feeling began before he could have had any personal knowledge of them. " If he should turn out ill," he said of a young boy of promise to one of the assistant-masters, and his voice trembled with emotion as he spoke, " I think it would break my heart." Nor were any thoughts so bitter to him, as those suggested by the innocent faces of little boys as they first came from home—nor any expressions of his moral indignation deeper, than when he heard of their being tormented or tempted into evil by their companions. " It is a most touching thing to me," he said once in the hearing of one of his former pupils, on the mention of some new comers, " to receive a new fellow from his father—when I think what an influence there is in this place for evil as well as for good. I do not know anything which affects me more." His pupil, who had, on his own first coming, been impressed chiefly by the severity of his manner, expressed some surprise, adding that he should have expected this to wear away with the succession of fresh arrivals. "No," he said, " if ever I could receive a new boy from his father without emotion, I should think it was high time to be off."

What he felt thus on ordinary occasions, was heightened of course when anything brought strongly before him any evil in the school. " If this goes on," he wrote to a former pupil on some such occasion, " it will end either my life at Rugby, or my life altogether." " How can I go on," he said, " with my Roman History? There all is noble and high-minded, and here I find nothing but the reverse." The following extract from a letter to his friend, Sir T. Pasley, describes this feeling :—

"Since I began this letter, I have had some of the troubles of school-keeping ; and one of those specimens of the evil of boy-nature, which makes me always unwilling to undergo the responsibility of advising any man to send his son to a public school. There has been a system of persecution carried on by the bad against the good, and then, when complaint was made to me, there came fresh persecution on that very account ; and divers instances of boys joining in it out of pure cowardice, both physical and moral, when if left to themselves they would have rather shunned it. And the exceedingly small number of boys, who can be relied on for active and steady good on these occasions, and the way in which the decent and respectable of ordinary life (Carlyle's 'Shams') are sure on these occasions to swim with the stream, and take part with the evil, makes me strongly feel exemplified what the Scriptures say about the straight gate and the wide one—a view of human nature, which, when looking on human life in its full dress of decencies and civilizations, we are apt, I imagine, to find it hard to realize. But here, in the nakedness of boy-nature, one is quite able to understand how there could not be found so many as even ten righteous in a whole city. And how to meet this evil I really do not know : but to find it thus rife after I have been [so many] years fighting against it, is so sickening, that it is very hard not to throw up the cards in despair, and upset the table. But then the stars of nobleness, which I see amidst the darkness, in the case of the few good, are so cheering, that one is inclined to stick to the ship again, and have another good try at getting her about."

V. As, on the one hand, his interest and sympathy with the boys far exceeded any direct manifestation of it towards them, so, on the other hand, the impression which he produced upon them was derived, not so much from any immediate intercourse or conversation with him, as from the general influence of his whole character, displayed consistently whenever he appeared before them. This influence, with its consequent effects, was gradually on the increase during the whole of his stay. From the earliest period, indeed, the boys were conscious of something unlike what they had been taught to imagine of a schoolmaster, and by many, a lasting regard was contracted for him ; but it was not till he had been in his post some years, that there arose that close bond of union which characterized his relation to his elder pupils; and it was, again, not till later still that this feeling extended itself, more or less, through the mass of the school, so that, in the higher forms at least, it became the fashion (so to speak) to think and talk of him with pride and affection.

The liveliness and simplicity of his whole behaviour must always have divested his earnestness of any appearance of moroseness and affectation. "He calls us *fellows*," was the astonished expression of the boys when, soon after his first coming, they heard him speak of them by the familiar name in use amongst themselves ; and in his later years they observed with pleasure the unaffected interest with which, in the long autumn afternoons, he would often stand in the school-field and watch the issue of their favourite games of foot-ball. But his ascendancy was, generally speaking, not gained, at least in the first instance, by the effect of his outward manner. There was a shortness, at times, something of an awkwardness in his address, occasioned partly by his natural shyness, partly by his dislike of wasting words on trivial occasions, which to boys must have been often repulsive rather than conciliating ;' something also of extreme severity in his voice and countenance, beyond what he was himself at all aware of. With the very little boys, indeed, his manner partook of that playful kindness and tenderness, which always marked his intercourse with children ; in examining them in the lower forms, he would sometimes take them on his knee, and go through picture-books of the Bible or of English History, covering the text of the narrative with his hand, and making them explain to him the subject of the several prints. But in those above this early age, and yet below the rank in the school which brought them into closer contact with him, the sternness of his character was the first thing that impressed them. In many, no doubt, this feeling was one of mere dread, which, if not subsequently removed or modified, only served to repel those who felt it to a greater distance from him. But in many, also, this was, even in the earlier part of their stay, mingled with an involuntary and, perhaps, an unconscious respect inspired by the sense of the manliness and straightforwardness of his dealings, and still more by the sense of the general force of his moral character; by the belief (to use the words of different pupils) in "his extraordinary knack, for I can call it nothing else, of showing that his object in punishing or reproving, was not his own good or pleasure, but that of the boy"—in a truthfulness—an εἰλικρίνεια—a sort of moral transparency;" in the fixedness of his purpose, and "the searchingness of his practical insight into boys," by a consciousness, almost amounting to solemnity, that "when his eye was upon you, he looked into your inmost heart;" that there was something in his very tone and outward aspect, before which anything low, or false, or cruel, instinctively quailed and cowered.

And the defect of occasional over-hastiness and vehemence of expression, which during the earlier period of his stay at times involved him in some trouble, did not materially interfere with their general notion of his character. However mistaken it might be in the individual case, it was evident to those who took any thought about it, that that ashy paleness and that awful frown were almost always the expression not of personal resentment, but of deep, ineffable scorn and indignation at the sight of vice and sin: and it was not without its effect to observe, that it was a fault against which he himself was constantly on the watch—and which, in fact, was in later years so nearly subdued, that most of those who had only known him during that time can recall no instance of it during their stay.

But as boys advanced in the school, out of this feeling of fear "grew up a deep admiration, partaking largely of the nature of awe, and this softened into a sort of loyalty, which remained even in the closer and more affectionate sympathy of later years."—"I am sure," writes a pupil who had no personal communications with him whilst at school, and but little afterwards, and who never was in the Sixth Form, " that I do not exaggerate my feelings when I say, that I felt a love and reverence for him as one of quite awful greatness and goodness, for whom I well remember that I used to think I would gladly lay down my life ;" adding, with reference to the thoughtless companions with whom he had associated, " I used to believe that I too had a work to do for him in the school, and I did for his sake labour to raise the tone of the set I lived in, particularly as regarded himself." It was in boys immediately below the highest form that this new feeling would usually rise for the first time, and awaken a strong wish to know more of him.   Then, as they came into personal contact with him, their general sense of his ability became fixed, in the proud belief that they were scholars of a man, who would be not less remarkable to the world than he was to themselves ; and their increasing consciousness of his own sincerity of purpose, and of the interest which he took in them, often awakened, even in the careless and indifferent, an out-ward respect for goodness, and an animation in their work before unknown to them.   And when they left school, they felt that they had been in an atmosphere unlike that of the world about them ; some of those, who lamented not having made more use of his teaching whilst with him, felt that " a better thought than ordinary often reminded them how he first led to it ; and in matters of literature almost invariably found that when any idea of seeming originality occurred to them, that its germ was first suggested by some remark of Arnold " —that " still, to this day in reading the Scriptures, or other things, they could constantly trace back a line of thought that came originally from him, as from a great parent mind." And when they heard of his death, they became conscious—often for the first time—of the large place which he had occupied in their thoughts, if not in their affections.

Such was the case with almost all who were in the Sixth Form with him during the last ten years of his life ; but with some who, from peculiar circumstances of greater sympathy with him, came into more permanent communication with him, there was a yet stronger bond of union. His interest in his elder pupils, unlike a mere professional interest, seemed to increase after they had left the school. No sermons were so full of feeling and instruction, as those which he preached on the eve of their departure for the Universities. It was now that the intercourse which at school had been so broken, and as it were stolen by snatches, was at last enjoyed between them to its full extent. It was sometimes in the few parting words—the earnest blessing which he then bestowed upon them—that they became for the first time conscious of his real care and love for them. The same anxiety for their good which he had felt in their passage through school, he now showed, without the necessity of official caution and reserve, in their passage through life. To any pupil who ever showed any desire to continue his connexion with him, his house was always open, and his advice and sympathy ready. No half-year, after the four first years of his stay at Rugby, passed without a visit from his former scholars : some of them would come three or four times a year ; some would stay in his house for weeks. He would offer to prepare them for the university examinations by previous examinations of his own ; he never shrunk from adding any of them to his already numerous correspondents, encouraging them to write to him in all perplexities. To any who were in narrow circumstances, not in one case, but in several, he would at once offer assistance, sometimes making them large presents of books on their entrance at the University, sometimes tendering them large pecuniary aid, and urging to them that his power of doing so was exactly one of those advantages of his position which he was most bound to use. In writing for the world at large, they were in his thoughts, "in whose welfare," he said, "I naturally have the deepest interest, and in whom old impressions may be supposed to have still so much force, that I may claim from them at least a patient hearing." (Serm. vol. iv. Pref. p. lv.) And when annoyed by distractions from within the school or opposition from without, he turned, he used to say, to their visits, as "to one of the freshest springs of his life."

They on their side now learned to admire those parts of his character which, whilst at school, they had either not known or only imperfectly understood. Pupils with characters most different from each other's, and from his own—often with opinions diverging more and more widely from his as they advanced in life—looked upon him with a love and reverence which made his gratification one of the brightest rewards of their academical studies—his good or evil fame, a constant source of interest and anxiety to them—his approbation and censure, amongst their most practical motives of action —his example, one of their most habitual rules of life. To him they turned for advice in every emergency of life, not so much for the sake of the advice itself, as because they felt that no important step ought to be taken without consulting him. An additional zest was imparted to whatever work they were engaged in by a consciousness of the interest which he felt in the progress of their undertaking, and the importance which he attached to its result. They now felt the privilege of being able to ask him questions on the many points which his school teaching had suggested without fully developing—but yet more, perhaps, they prized the sense of his sympathy and familiar kindness, which made them feel that they were not only his pupils, but his companions. That youthfulness of temperament which has been before noticed in his relation to boys, was still more important in his relation to young men. All the new influences which so strongly divide the students of the nineteenth century from those of the last, had hardly less interest for himself than for them ; and, after the dulness or vexation of business or of controversy, a visit of a few days to Rugby would remind them, (to apply a favourite image of his own,) " how refreshing it is in the depth of winter, when the ground is covered with snow, and all is dead and lifeless, to walk by the sea-shore, and enjoy the eternal freshness and liveliness of ocean." His very presence seemed to create a new spring of health and vigour within them, and to give to life an interest and an elevation which remained with them long after they had left him again, and dwelt so habitually in their thoughts, as a living image, that, when death had taken him away, the bond appeared to be still unbroken, and the sense of separation almost lost in the still deeper sense of a life and an union indestructible.

What were the permanent effects of this system and influence, is a question which cannot yet admit of an adequate answer, least of all from his pupils. The mass of boys are, doubtless, like the mass of men, incapable of receiving a deep and lasting impression from any individual character, however remarkable ; and it must also be borne in mind, that hardly any of his scholars were called by rank or station to take a leading place in English society, where the effect of his teaching and character, whatever it might be in itself, would have been far more conspicuous to the world at large.

He himself, though never concealing from himself the importance of his work, would constantly dwell on the scantiness of its results. " I came to Rugby," he said, "full of plans for school reform; but I soon found that the reform of a public school was a much more difficult thing than I had imagined." And again, " I dread to hear this called a religious school. I know how much there is to be done before it can really be called so."—"With regard to one's work," he said, " be it school or parish, I suppose the desirable feeling to entertain, is always to expect to succeed, and never think that you have succeeded." He hardly ever seems to have indulged in any sense of superiority to the other public schools. Eton, for example, he would often defend against the attacks to which it was exposed, and the invidious comparisons which some persons would draw between that school and Rugby. What were his feelings towards the improvements taking place there and elsewhere, after his coming to Rugby, have been mentioned already; even between the old system and his own, he rarely drew a strong distinction, conscious though he must have been of the totally new elements which he was introducing. The earliest letters from Rugby express an unfeigned pleasure in what he found existing, and there is no one disparaging mention of his predecessor in all the correspondence, published or unpublished, that has been collected for this work.

If, however, the prediction of Dr. Hawkins at his election, has been in any way fulfilled, the result of his work need not depend on the rank, however eminent, to which he raised Rugby School; or the influence, however powerful, which he exercised over his Rugby scholars. And, if there be any truth in the following letter from Dr. Moberly, to whose testimony additional weight is given, as well by his very wide difference of political and ecclesiastical opinion, as by his personal experience, first as a scholar at Winchester, and an under-graduate at Oxford, then as the tutor of the most flourishing college in that University, and lastly, in his present position as head-master of Winchester, it will be felt that, not so much amongst his own pupils, nor in the scene of his actual labours, as in every Public School throughout England, is to be sought the chief and enduring monument of Dr. Arnold's head-mastership at Rugby.

EXTRACT FROM A LETTER OF DR. MOBERLY, HEAD-MASTER OF WINCHESTER.

" Possibly," he writes, after describing his own recollections as a school-boy, " other schools may have been less deep in these delinquencies than Winchester ; I believe that in many respects they were. But I did not find, on going to the University, that I was under disadvantages as compared with those who came from other places ; on the contrary, the tone of young men at the University, whether they came from Winchester, Eton, Rugby, Harrow, or wherever else, was universally irreligious. A religious under-graduate was very rare, very much laughed at when he appeared ; and I think I may confidently say, hardly to be found among public-school men ; or, if this be too strongly said, hardly to be found except in cases where private and domestic training, or good dispositions, had prevailed over the school habits and tendencies. A most singular and striking change has come upon our public schools—a change too great for any person to appreciate adequately, who has not known them in both these times. This change is undoubtedly part of a general improvement of our generation in respect of piety and reverence, but I am sure that to Dr. Arnold's personal earnest simplicity of purpose, strength of character, power of influence, and piety, which none who ever came near him could mistake or question, the carrying of this improvement into our schools is mainly attributable. He was the first. It soon began to be matter of observation to us in the University that his pupils brought quite a different character with them to Oxford than that which we knew elsewhere. I do not speak of opinions ; but his pupils were thoughtful, manly-minded, conscious of duty and obligation, when they first came to college ; we regretted, indeed, that they were often deeply imbued with principles which we disapproved, but we cordially acknowledged the immense improvement in their characters in respect of morality and personal piety, and looked on Dr. Arnold as exercising an influence for good, which (for how many years I know not) had been absolutely unknown to our public schools.

"I knew personally but little of him. You remember the first occasion on which I ever had the pleasure of seeing him : but I have always felt and acknowledged that I owe more to a few casual remarks of his in respect of the government of a public school, than to any advice or example of any other person. If there be improvement in the important points of which I have been speaking, at Winchester (and from the bottom of my heart I testify with great thankfulness that the improvement is real and great), I do declare, in justice, that his example encouraged me to hope that it might be effected, and his hints suggested to me the way of effecting it.

" I fear that the reply, which I have been able to make to your question, will hardly be so satisfactory as you expected, as it proceeds so entirely upon my own observations and inferences. At the same time I have had, perhaps, unusual opportunity for forming an opinion, having been six years at a public school at the time of their being at the lowest,—having then mingled with young men from other schools at the University, having had many pupils from different schools, and among them several of Dr. Arnold's most distinguished ones ; and at last, having had near eight years' experience as the master of a school which has undergone, in great measure, the very alteration which I have been speaking of. Moreover, I have often said the very things, which I have here written, in the hearing of men of all sorts, and have never found anybody disposed to contradict them.

"Believe me, my dear Stanley,

" Yours most faithfully,

" GEORGE MOBERLY."

CHAPTER IV.

GENERAL LIFE AT RUGBY.

IT was natural that with the wider range of duty, and the more commanding position which Dr. Arnold's new station gave him, there should have been a new stage in his character and views, hardly less marked intellectually, than that which accompanied his change from Oxford to Laleham had been morally. The several subjects of thought, which more or less he had already entertained, especially during the two or three preceding years, now fall rapidly one by one into their proper places. Ready as he still was to take the advice of his friends in practice, his opinions now took a more independent course ; and whatever subsequent modification they underwent, came not from without, but from within. Whilst he became more and more careful to reconcile his own views with those whom, in ages past or present, he reverenced as really great men, the circle within which he bestowed his veneration became far more exclusive. The purely practical element sank into greater subordination to the more imaginative and philosophical tendencies of his mind ;— in works of poetical or speculative genius, which at an earlier period he had been inclined to depreciate, he now, looking at them from another point of view, took an increasing delight. Within. the letters of the very first year there is a marked alteration visible even in the mere form of his handwriting, and the mode of addressing his friends. The character which has already been given of his boyish verses at Oxford, becomes less and less applicable to the simple and touching fragments of poetry in which from time to time he expressed the feelings of his later years. The change of style in his published writings from the baldness of his earlier works to the vigorous English of his mature age, indicates the corresponding impulse given to his powers, and the greater freedom and variety of his new range of thought.

With his entrance, therefore, on his work at Rugby, his public life (if it may so be called) no less than his professional life, properly begins. But what was true of the effect of his own character in his sphere as a teacher, is hardly less true of it in his sphere as an author. His works were not merely the inculcations of particular truths, but the expression of his whole mind ; and excited in those who read them a sentiment almost of personal regard or of personal dislike, as the case might be, over and above the approbation or disapprobation of the opinions which they contained. Like himself, they partook at once of a practical and speculative character, which exposed them, like himself, to considerable misapprehension. On the one hand, even the most permanent of them seemed to express the feeling of the hour which dictated them. On the other hand, even the most transitory seemed to express no less the fixed ideas by which his whole life was regulated ; and it may be worth while, therefore, in regard to both these aspects, without descending into the details and circumstances of each particular work, which the ensuing correspondence will of itself sufficiently describe, to offer briefly a few remarks which may serve as a preface to all of them.

I. Greatly as his practical turn of mind was modified in his later years, and averse as he always was to what are technically called "practical men," yet, in the sense of having no views, however high, which he did not labour to bring into practice sooner or later, he remained eminently practical to the end of his life. "I always think," he used to say, "of that magnificent sentence of Bacon, 'In this world, God only and the angels may be spectators.'" "Stand still and see the salvation of God," he observed in allusion to Dr. Pusey's celebrated sermon on that passage, "was true advice to the Israelites on the shores of the Red Sea ; but it was not the advice which is needed in ordinary circumstances ; it would have been false advice when they were to conquer Canaan." "I cannot," he said, "enter fully into these lines of Wordsworth—

> ' To me the meanest flower that breathes can give
> Thoughts that do often lie too deep for tears.'

There is to me something in them of a morbid feeling— life is not long enough to take such intense interest in objects themselves so little." Secluded as he was, both by his occupations and his domestic habits, from contact with the world, even more than most men in his station, yet the interest with which, now more than ever, he entered into public affairs was such as can rarely be felt by men not actually engaged in the government of the country. The life of a nation, he said, was to him almost as distinct as that of an individual ; and whatever might be his habitual subjects of public interest,—the advance of political and social reform,—the questions of peace and war,—the sufferings of the poorer classes,—the growth of those rising commonwealths in the Australian colonies, where, from time to time, he entertained an ardent desire to pass the close of his life, in the hope of influencing, if possible, what he conceived to be the germs of the future destinies of England and of the world,—came before him with a vividness, which seemed to belong rather to a citizen of Greece or Rome, than to the comparative apathy and retirement of the members of modern states.

It was of course only or chiefly through his writings, that he could hope to act on the country at large: and they accordingly, almost all, became inseparably bound up with the course of public events. They were not, in fact, so much words as deeds ; not so much the result of an intention to instruct, as of an incontrollable desire to give vent to the thoughts that were struggling within him. " I have a testimony to deliver," was the motive which dictated almost all of them. " I must write or die," was an expression which he used more than once in times of great public interest, and which was hardly too strong to describe what he felt. If he was editing Thucydides, it was with the thought that he was engaged, " not on an idle inquiry about remote ages and forgotten institutions, but a living picture of things present, fitted not so much for the curiosity of the scholar, as for the instruction of the statesman and the citizen." (Pref. vol. iii. p. xxii.) If he felt himself called upon to write the history of Rome, one chief reason was, because it " could be understood by none so well as by those who have grown up under the laws, who have been engaged in the parties, who are themselves citizens of our kingly commonwealth of England." (Pref. vol. i. p. vii.) If he was anxious to set on foot a Commentary of the Scriptures, it was mostly at times when he was struck by the reluctance or incapacity of the men of his own generation to apply to their own social state the warnings of the Apostles and Prophets. If he was desirous of maintaining against the Oxford school his own views of the

Church, it was that, "when he looked at the social condition of his countrymen," he "could not doubt that here was the work for the Church of Christ to do, that none else could do it, and that with the blessing of her Almighty Head she could."   (Serm. vol. iv. Pref. p. cxv.)

It is not, therefore, to be wondered at, if that impatience of present evil, which belonged alike to his principles and his disposition, appeared in his writings, and imparted to them—often, probably, unknown to himself—something, if not of a polemical aspect, at least of an attitude of opposition and attack, averse though he was himself to controversy, and carefully avoiding it with those whom he knew personally, even when frequently challenged to enter upon it.   " The wisdom of winter is the folly of spring," was a maxim with him, which would often explain changes of feeling and expression that to many might seem inconsistencies.   " If I were living in London," he said, " I should not talk against the evil tendencies of the clergy, any more than if I were living in Oxford I should talk against the evil tendencies of the political economists.   It is my nature always to attack that evil which seems to me most present."   It was thus a favourite topic, in his exposition of Scripture, to remark how the particular sins of the occasion were denounced, the particular forms of Antichrist indicated often without the qualification, which would have been required by the presence of the opposite danger.   " Contrast," he used to say, "the language of the first chapter of Isaiah, when the hierarchy of Judah was in its full pride and power, with the language of the second chapter of Malachi, when it was in a state of decline and neglect."

Connected with this was the peculiar vehemence of language which he often used, in speaking of the subjects and events of the day.   This was indeed partly to be accounted for by his eagerness to speak out whatever

was in his mind, especially when moved by his keen
sense of what he thought evil—partly by the natural
simplicity of his mode of speech, which led him to adopt
phrases in their simplest sense, without stopping to
explain them, or suspecting that they would be misunderstood. But with regard to public principles and
parties, it was often more than this. With every wish to
be impartial, yet his natural temperament, as he used
himself to acknowledge, made it difficult for him to
place himself completely in another's point of view ; and
thus he had a tendency to judge individuals, with whom
he had no personal acquaintance, from his conception
of the party to which they belonged, and to look at both
through the medium of that strong power of association,
which influenced materially his judgment, not only of
events, but of men, and even of places. Living individuals, therefore, and existing principles, became lost to
his view in the long line of images, past and future, in
which they only formed one link. Every political or
ecclesiastical movement suggested to him the recollection of its historical representative in past times—and
yet more, as by an instinct, half religious and half
historical, the thought of what he conceived to be the
prototypes of the various forms of error and wickedness
denounced by the Prophets in the Old Testament, or by
our Lord and his Apostles in the New. And looking
not backwards only, but forwards, to their remotest consequences, and again guiding himself, as he thought, by
the example of the language of St. Paul, who " seemed
to have had his eye fixed in vision rather upon the full-
grown evil of later times, than upon the first imperfect
show—the faint indications of it—in his own time,"
(Serm. vol. v. p. 346,) he saw in them the germs of mischief yet to come—not only the mischief of their actual
triumph, but the mischief of the reaction against them.

There was besides a peculiar importance attaching, in his view, to political questions, with which every reader of his works must be familiar. The life of the Commonwealth is to him the main subject of history— the laws of political science the main lesson of history— "the desire of taking an active share in the great work of government, the highest earthly desire of the ripened mind." And those who read his letters will be startled at times by the interest with which he watches the changes of administration, where to many the real difference would seem to be comparatively trifling. Thus he would speak of a ministry advocating even good measures inconsistently with their position or principles, "as a daily painfulness—a moral east wind, which made him feel uncomfortable, without any particular ailment" —or lament the ascendancy of false political views, as tending "to the sure moral degradation of the whole community, and the ultimate social disorganization of our system," "not from reading the *Morning Chronicle* or the Edinburgh Review, but from reading the Bible and Aristotle, and all history."

Such expressions as these must indeed be taken with the necessary qualifications which belong to all words spoken to intimate friends in a period of great excitement. But they may serve to illustrate at least the occasional strength of feeling which it is the object of these remarks to explain. It arose, no doubt, in part from his tendency to view all things in a practical and concrete form, and in part from his belief of the large power possessed by the supreme governors of society over the social and moral condition of those entrusted to them. But there were also real principles present to his mind whenever he thus spoke, which seemed to him so certain, that "daily experience could hardly remove his wonder at finding that they did not appear so to others."

(Mod. Hist. Lect., p. 391.)   What these principles were
in detail, his own letters will sufficiently show.   But it
must be borne in mind how, whilst he certainly believed
that they were exemplified to a great degree in the
actual state of English politics, the meaning which he
attached to them rose so far above their meaning as
commonly used, that it could hardly be thought that the
same subject was spoken of.   Conservatism in his mouth
was not merely the watchword of an English party, but
the symbol of an evil, against which his whole life, public
and private, was one continued struggle, which he dreaded
in his own heart no less than in the institutions of his
country, and his abhorrence of which will be found to
pervade not only the pamphlets which have been most
condemned, but the sermons which have been most
admired—namely, the spirit of resistance to all change.
Jacobinism, again, in his use of the word, included not
only the extreme movement party in France or England, to which he usually applied it, but all the natural
tendencies of mankind, whether " democratical, priestly,
or chivalrous," to oppose the authority of law, divine and
human, which he regarded with so deep a reverence.
Popular principles and democracy (when he used these
words in a good sense) were not the opposition to an
hereditary monarch or peerage, which he always valued
as precious elements of national life, but were inseparably '
blended with his strong belief in the injustice and want
of sympathy generally shown by the higher to the lower
orders—a belief which he often declared had been first
brought home to him, when, after having as a young
man at Oxford held the opposite view, he first began
seriously to study the language used with regard to it by
St. James and the Old Testament Prophets.   Liberal
principles were not merely the expression of his adherence to a Whig ministry, but of his belief in the

constant necessity of applying those principles of advance and reform, which, in their most perfect development, he conceived to be identical with Christianity itself. Even in their lower exemplifications, and in every age of the world except that before the Fall of man from Paradise, he maintained them to have been, by the very constitution of human society, the representatives of the cause of wisdom and goodness. And this truth, no less certain in his judgment than the ordinary deductions of natural theology, he believed to have been placed on a still firmer basis by the higher standard held out in the Christian religion, and the revelation of a moral law, which no intermixture of races or change of national customs could possibly endanger.

That he was not, in the common sense of the word, a member of any party, is best shown by the readiness with which all parties alike, according to the fashion of the time, claimed or renounced him as an associate. Ecclesiastically, he neither belonged, nor felt himself to belong, to any of the existing sections of the English clergy ; and from the so-called High Church, Low Church, and Evangelical bodies he always stood, not perhaps equally, but yet decidedly aloof. Politically, indeed, he held himself to be a strong Whig ; but as a matter of fact, he found that in cases of practical co-operation with that party, he differed almost as much from them as from their opponents, and would often confess with sorrow, that there were none among them who realized what seemed to him their true principles.* And whilst in later years his feelings and language on

* The interest which in his earlier life he took in the leading questions of political economy, though it was always kept alive by his general sympathy with all subjects relating to the social state of the country, was yet in his later years considerably abated, by growing consciousness of his ignorance of the subject. On some points, however, he always felt and spoke strongly. The corn laws, for example, he always regarded, though not as the chief cause of national distress, yet as a great evil, the removal of which was

these subjects were somewhat modified, he at all times, even when most tenaciously holding to his opinions, maintained the principle, that "political truths are not, like moral truths, to be held as absolutely certain, nor ever wholly identical with the professions or practice of any party or individual." (Pref. to Hist. of Rome, vol. i. p. 11.) There were few warnings to his pupils on the entrance into life more solemn than those against party spirit, against giving to any human party, sect, society, or cause, that undivided sympathy and service which he held to be due only to the one party, and cause of all good men under their Divine Head.* There were few more fervent aspirations for his children than that with which he closes a letter in 1833 : "May God grant to my sons, if they live to manhood, an unshaken love of truth, and a firm resolution to follow it for themselves, with an intense abhorrence of all party ties, save that one tie which binds them to the party of Christ against wickedness."

II. But no temporary interest or excitement was allowed to infringe on the loftiness or the unity of his ultimate ends, to which every particular plan that he took up, and every particular line of thought which he followed, was completely subordinate. However open to objection may have been many of his practical suggestions, it must be remembered, that they were never the result of accidental fancies, but of fixed and ruling ideas. However fertile he might be in supplying details when called for, it was never on them, but on principles, that he rested his claim to be heard ; often and often he

---

imperatively demanded by sound economical principles ; and of the practice of accumulating national debts, he said, in the last year of his life, that he rejoiced in few things more in his professorial lectures at Oxford, than in the protest which he had there made against it. "Woe be to that generation that is living in England," he used to say, "when the coal-mines are exhausted and the national debt not paid off."

* See Sermon on "Who are partakers in our hope?" vol. iii.

declared that if these could be received and acted upon, he cared nothing for the particular applications of them, which he might have proposed, and nothing for the failure of particular schemes, if he could hope that his example would excite others to execute them better.

Striving to fulfil in his measure the definition of man, in which he took especial pleasure, "a being of large discourse, looking before and after," he learned more and more, whilst never losing his hold on the present, to live also habitually in the past and for the future. Vehement as he was in assailing evil, his whole mind was essentially not destructive but constructive ; his love of reform was in exact proportion to his love of the institutions which he wished to reform ; his hatred of shadows in exact proportion to his love of realities. "He was an idoloclast," says Archdeacon Hare, "at once zealous and fearless in demolishing the reigning idols, and at the same time animated with a reverent love for the ideas which those idols carnalize and stifle." Impatient as he was, even to restlessness, of evils which seemed to him capable of remedy, he yet was ready, as some have thought even to excess, to repose with the most undoubting confidence on what he held to be a general law. "Ah," he said, speaking to a friend of the parable of the "earth, of herself, bringing forth first the blade, then the ear, then the full corn in the ear,"—"how much there is in those words : I hope some day to be able to work at them thoroughly." "We walk by faith and not by sight," was a truth on which in its widest sense he endeavoured to dwell alike in his private and public relations,—alike in practice and in speculation. "You know you do what God does," was his answer to an expression of a painful sense of the increase of a child's responsibility by an early Christian education. "We may be content, I think, to share the responsibility with Christ." And on more general subjects, "We must brace our minds," he said, in an unpublished sermon, "We must brace our minds to the full extent of that great truth--that 'no man hath seen God at any time;' still amidst outward darkness and inward,—amidst a world going on, as it seems, its own course, with no other laws than those which God has given to nature;—amidst all the doubts and perplexities of our own hearts—the deepest difficulties sitting hard beside the most blessed truths—still we must seek after the Lord with unabated faith if so be that we may find him." It was not that he was not conscious of difficulties—but that (to apply his own words) "before a confessed and unconquerable difficulty his mind reposed as quietly as in possession of a discovered truth."

His time for reading at Laleham and Rugby was necessarily limited by his constant engagements—but his peculiar habits and turn of mind enabled him to accomplish much, which to others in similar circumstances would have been impossible. He had a remarkable facility for turning to account spare fragments of time— for appropriating what he casually heard, and for mastering the contents of a book by a very rapid perusal. His memory was exceedingly retentive of all subjects in which he took any interest; and the studies of his youth —especially of what he used to call the "golden time" between his degree and his leaving Oxford—were perpetually supplying him with materials for his later labours. The custom which he then began, of referring at once to the sources and original documents of history, as in Rymer, Montfaucon, and the Summa Conciliorum, gave a lasting freshness and solidity to his knowledge; and, instead of merely exchanging his later for his earlier acquisitions, the one seemed to be a natural development of the other.

Whenever a new line of study was opened to him, he fearlessly followed it ; a single question would often cost him much research in books for which he naturally cared but little ; for philological purposes he was endeavouring even in his latest years to acquire a knowledge of the Sanscrit and Sclavonic languages ; he was constantly engaged in correspondence with scientific men or scholars on minute points of history or geography; in theology he had almost always on hand one of the early Christian writers, with a view to the ultimate completion of his great work on Church and State. He had a great respect for learning, though impatient of the pretensions to the name often made by a mere amount of reading ; and the standard of what was required in order to treat of any subject fully, was perpetually rising before him. It would often happen from the necessity of the case, that his works were written in haste, and were therefore sometimes expressed nakedly and abruptly. But it would be wrong to infer from the unblotted, unrevised manuscript, which went to the press as it came from his pen, that it was not the result of much thought and reading ; although he hardly ever corrected what he had once written, yet he often approached the same subject in various forms ; the substance of every paragraph had, as he often said, been in his mind for years, and sometimes had been actually written at greater length or in another shape; his sense of deficient knowledge often deterred him from publishing on subjects of the greatest interest to him ; he always made it a point to read far more than he expressed in writing, and to write much which he never gave to the world.

What he actually achieved in his works falls so far short of what he intended to achieve, that it seems almost like an injustice to judge of his aims and views by them. Yet, even in what he had already published in his lifetime, he was often the first to delineate in outline what others may hereafter fill up ; the first to give expression in England to views which, on the Continent, had been already attained ; the first to propose, amidst obloquy or indifference, measures and principles, which the rapid advance of public opinion has so generally adopted, as almost to obliterate the remembrance of who first gave utterance to them.   And those, who know the intentions which were interrupted by his premature death, will form their notion of what he was as an historian, philosopher, and theologian, not so much from the actual writings which he lived to complete, as from the design of the three great works, to which he looked forward as the labours of his latest years, and which, as belonging not more to one period of his life than another, and as forming, even in his mere conception of them, the centres of all that he thought or wrote on whatever subject, would have furnished the key to all his views—a History of Rome, a Commentary on the New Testament, and, in some sense including both of these within itself, a Treatise on Church and State, or Christian Politics.

1. His early fondness for history grew constantly upon him ; he delighted in it, as feeling it to be "simply a search after truth, where, by daily becoming more familiar with it, truth seems for ever more within your grasp :" the images of the past were habitually in his mind, and haunted him even in sleep with a vividness which would bring before him some of the most striking passages in ancient history—as if present at the assassination of Cæsar, remembering distinctly his conversation with Decimus Brutus, and all the tumult of the scene in the Capitol, or again at the siege of Jerusalem in the army of Titus, or walking round the walls of Syracuse with Alcibiades ; or watching the events of the civil wars of Rome, crowded by the vagaries of a dream into the space

of twenty-four hours, with all their different characters—
Sylla especially with the livid spots upon his face, but yet
with the air and manner of Walter Scott's Claverhouse.
What objects he put before him, as an historian, may best
be judged from his own view of the province of history.
It was, indeed, altogether imperfect, in his judgment,
unless it was " not only a plan but a picture ; " unless it
represented "what men thought, what they hated, and
what they loved;" unless it "pointed the way to that
higher region, within which she herself is not permitted
to enter ; "* and in the details of geographical or military
descriptions he took especial pleasure, and himself remarkably excelled in them.   Still it was in the dramatic
faculty on the one hand, and the metaphysical faculty on
the other hand, that he felt himself deficient ; and it is
accordingly in the political rather than the philosophical
or biographical department of history—in giving a combined view of different states or of different periods—in
analyzing laws, parties, and institutions, that his chief
merit consists.

What were his views of Modern History will appear
in the mention of his Oxford Professorship. But it was
in ancient history that he naturally felt the greatest
delight. " I linger round a subject, which nothing could
tempt me to quit but the consciousness of treating it too
unworthily," were his expressions of regret when he had
finished his edition of Thucydides ; " the subject of what
is miscalled ancient history, the really modern history of
the civilization of Greece and Rome, which has for years
interested me so deeply that it is painful to feel myself,
after all, so unable to paint it fully." His earliest labours
had been devoted not to Roman, but to Greek history ;
and there still remains amongst his MSS. a short sketch
of the rise of the Greek nation, written between 1820

* History of Rome, vol. i. p. 98 ; vol. ii. p. 173.

and 1823, and carried down to the time of the Persian
wars. And in later years, his edition of Thucydides,
undertaken originally with the design of illustrating that
author rather historically than philologically, contains in
its notes and appendices, the most systematic remains of
his studies in this direction, and at one time promised to
embody his thoughts on the most striking periods of
Athenian history. Nor, after he had abandoned this
design, did he ever lose his interest in the subject ; his
real sympathies (if one may venture to say so) were
always with Athens rather than with Rome ; some of the
most characteristic points of his mind were Greek rather
than Roman ; from the vacancy of the early Roman
annals he was for ever turning to the cotemporary
records of the Greek commonwealths to pay "an involuntary tribute of respect and affection to old associations
and immortal names on which we can scarcely dwell too
long or too often ;" the falsehood and emptiness of the
Latin historians were for ever suggesting the contrast of
their Grecian rivals ; the two opposite poles in which
he seemed to realize his ideals of the worst and the
best qualities of an historian with feelings of personal
antipathy and sympathy towards each, were Livy and
Thucydides.

Even these scattered notices of what he had once
hoped to have worked out more fully, will often furnish
the student of Greek history with the means of entering
upon its most remarkable epochs under his guidance.
Those who have carefully read his works, or shared his
instructions, can still enjoy the light which he has thrown
on the rise and progress of the Greek commonwealths,
and their analogy with the States of modern Europe ;
and apply in their manifold relations, the principles
which he has laid down with regard to the peculiar ideas
attached in the Greek world to race, to citizenship, and

to law.   They can still catch the glow of almost passionate enthusiasm, with which he threw himself into the age of Pericles, and the depth of emotion with which he watched, like an eye-witness, the failure of the Syracusan expedition.   They can still trace the almost personal sympathy with which he entered into the great crisis of Greek society when "Socrates, the faithful servant of truth and virtue, fell a victim to the hatred alike of the democratical and aristocratical vulgar;" when "all that audacity can dare, or subtlety contrive, to make the words of 'good' and 'evil' change their meaning, was tried in the days of Plato, and by his eloquence and wisdom, and faith unshaken was put to shame."   They can well imagine the intense admiration with which he would have dwelt, in detail, on what he has now left only in faint outline:—Alexander at Babylon impressed him as one of the most solemn scenes in all history; the vision of Alexander's career, even to the lively image which he entertained of his youthful and godlike beauty, rose constantly before him as the most signal instance of the effects of a good education against the temptations of power;—as being, beyond anything recorded in Roman history, the career of "the greatest man of the ancient world;" and even after the period, when Greece ceased to possess any real interest for him, he loved to hang with a melancholy pleasure over the last decay of Greek genius and wisdom —"the worn-out and cast-off skin, from which the living serpent had gone forth to carry his youth and vigour to other lands."

But, deep as was his interest in Grecian history, and though in some respects no other part of ancient literature derived so great a light from his researches, it was to his History of Rome that he looked as the chief monument of his historical fame.   Led to it partly by

his personal feeling of regard towards Niebuhr and
Chevalier Bunsen, and by the sense of their encouragement, there was, moreover, something in the subject
itself peculiarly attractive to him, whether in the magnifi-
cence of the field which it embraced,—("the History of
Rome," he said, "must be in some sort the History of the
World,")—or in the congenial element which he naturally
found in the character of a people, " whose distinguishing
quality was their love of institutions and order, and their
reverence for law."   Accordingly, after approaching it in
various forms, he at last conceived the design of the work,
of which the three published volumes are the result, but
which he had intended to carry down, in successive
periods, to what seemed to him its natural termination
in the coronation of Charlemagne.   (Pref. vol. i. p. vii.)

The two earlier volumes occupy a place in the
History of Rome, and of the ancient world generally,
which in England had not and has not been otherwise
filled up.   Yet in the subjects of which they treat, his
peculiar talents had hardly a fair field for their exercise.
The want of personal characters and of distinct events,
which Niebuhr was to a certain extent able to supply
from the richness of his learning and the felicity of his
conjectures, was necessarily a disadvantage to an historian whose strength lay in combining what was already '
known, rather than in deciphering what was unknown,
and whose veneration for his predecessor made him distrustful not only of dissenting from his judgment, but
even of seeing or discovering, more, than had been by
him seen or discovered before.   " No man," as he said,
" can step gracefully or boldly when he is groping his
way in the dark," (Hist. Rome, i. p. 133,) and it is with a
melancholy interest that we read his complaint of the
obscurity of the subject :—" I can but encourage myself,
whilst painfully feeling my way in such thick darkness,

with the hope of arriving at last at the light, and enjoying all the freshness and fulness of a detailed cotemporary history." (Hist. Rome, ii. p. 447.)   But the narrative of the second Punic war, which occupies the third and posthumous volume, both as being comparatively unbroken ground, and as affording so full a scope for his talents in military and geographical descriptions, may well be taken as a measure of his historical powers, and has been pronounced by his editor, Archdeacon Hare, to be the first history which "has given anything like an adequate representation of the wonderful genius and noble character of Hannibal."   With this volume the work was broken off; but it is impossible not to dwell for a moment on what it would have been had he lived to complete it.

The outline in his early articles in the Encyclopædia Metropolitana, of the later history of the Civil Wars, "a subject so glorious," he writes in 1824, "that I groan beforehand when I think how certainly I shall fail in doing it justice," provokes of itself the desire to see how he would have gone over the same ground again with his added knowledge and experience—how the characters of the time, which even in this rough sketch stand out more clearly than in any other English work on the same period, would have been reproduced—how he would have represented the pure* character and military genius

---

* It may be necessary (especially since the recent publication of Niebuhr's Lectures, where a very different opinion is advocated), to refer to Dr. Arnold's own estimate of the moral character of Pompey, which, it is believed, he retained unaltered, in the Encyc. Metrop. ii. 252. (Later Roman Commonwealth, vol. i. 542.) The following extract from a letter of General Napier may not be without interest in confirmation of an opinion which he had himself formed independently of it : "Tell Dr. Arnold to beware of falling into the error of Pompey being a bad general ; he was a very great one, perhaps in a purely military sense greater than Cæsar."— At the same time it should be observed, that his admiration of Cæsar's intellectual greatness was always very strong, and it was almost with an indignant animation that, on the starting of an objection that Cæsar's victories were only gained over inferior enemies, he at once denied the inference, and instantly recounted campaign after campaign in refutation.

of his favourite hero, Pompey—or expressed his mingled admiration and abhorrence of the intellectual power and moral degradation of Cæsar ;—how he would have done justice to the coarseness and cruelty of Marius, "the lowest of democrats"—or amidst all his crimes to the views of "the most sincere of aristocrats," Sylla. And in advancing to the further times of the Empire, his scattered hints exhibit his strong desire to reach those events, to which all the intervening volumes seemed to him only a prelude. "I would not overstrain my eyes or my faculties," he writes in 1840, "but whilst eyesight and strength are yet undecayed, I want to get through the earlier Roman History, to come down to the Imperial and Christian times, which form a subject of such deep interest." What his general admiration for Niebuhr was as a practical motive in the earlier part of his work, that his deep aversion to Gibbon as a man, was in the latter part. "My highest ambition," he said, as early as 1826, "and what I hope to do as far as I can, is to make my history the very reverse of Gibbon in this respect,— that whereas the whole spirit of his work, from its low morality, is hostile to religion, without speaking directly against it, so my greatest desire would be, in my History, by its high morals and its general tone, to be of use to the cause without actually bringing it forward."

There would have been the place for his unfolding the rise of the Christian Church, not in a distinct ecclesiastical history, but as he thought it ought to be written in conjunction with the history of the world. "The period from Augustus to Aurelian," he writes as far back as 1824, "I will not willingly give up to any one, because I have a particular object, namely, to blend the civil and religious history together more than has ever yet been done." There he would, on the one hand, have expressed his view of the external influences, which checked the free growth of the early Church—the gradual revival of Judaic principles under a Christian form—the gradual extinction of individual responsibility, under the system of government, Roman and Gentile in its origin, which, according to his latest opinion, took possession of the Church rulers from the time of Cyprian. There, on the other hand, he would have dwelt on the self-denying zeal and devotion to truth which peculiarly endeared to him the very name of *Martyr*, and on the bond of Christian brotherhood, which he delighted to feel with such men as Athanasius and Augustine, discerning, even in what he thought their weaknesses, a signal testimony to the triumph of Christianity, unaided by other means, than its intrinsic excellence and holiness. Lastly, with that analytical method, which he delighted to pursue in his historical researches, he would have traced to their source, "those evil currents of neglect, of uncharitableness, and of ignorance, whose full streams we now find so pestilent," first, " in the social helplessness and intellectual frivolousness" of the close of the Roman empire ; and then, in that event which had attracted his earliest interest, "the nominal conversion of the northern nations to Christianity,—a vast subject, and one of the greatest importance both to the spiritual and temporal advancement of the nations of Europe (Serm. vol. i. p. 88) as explaining the more confirmed separation of clergy and laity in later times, and the incomplete influence which Christianity has exercised upon the institutions even of Christian countries." (Serm. vol. iii. Pref. p. xiv.)

2. Strong as was his natural taste for History, it was to Theology that he looked as the highest sphere of his exertions, and as the province which most needed them. The chief object which he here proposed to himself—in fact, the object which he conceived as the proper end of Theology itself—was the interpretation and application

of the Scriptures. From the time of his early studies at Oxford, when he analyzed and commented on the Epistles of St. Paul, with Chrysostom's Homilies, down to the last year of his life, when he was endeavouring to set on foot a Rugby edition of them, under his own superintendence, he never lost sight of this design. In the scattered notices of it in his sermons, published and unpublished, there is enough to enable us to combine his principles into a distinct whole; and to conceive them, not in the polemical form, which in his later years they sometimes presented in their external aspect, but as the declaration of his positive views of the Scriptures themselves, wholly independent of any temporary controversy; and as the most complete reflex, not only of his capacities as an interpreter, but also, on the one hand, of his powers of historical discernment, on the other, of the reality of his religious feelings.

Impossible as it is to enter here into any detailed exposition of his views, it has been felt that the liveliest image of what he was in this department will be given by presenting their main features, as they were impressed on the mind of the same earlier pupil and later friend, whose name has before occurred in these pages, and whose personal recollections of the sphere in which he most admired him, will probably convey a truer and more distinct conception than would be left by a representation of the same facts in general language, or from a more distant point of view.

MY DEAR STANLEY,

You ask me to describe Dr. Arnold as an Exegetical Divine : I feel myself altogether unequal to such a task; indeed, I have no other excuse for writing at all on such a subject, than the fact that I early appreciated his greatness as a Theologian, and for many years had the happiness of discussing frequently with him his general views on scientific

Divinity. It was one of my earliest convictions respecting him, that, distinguished as he was in many departments of literature and practical philosophy, he was most distinguished as an interpreter of Scripture; and the lapse of years and an intimate knowledge of his mind and character, have but confirmed this conviction. As an expounder of the word of God, Arnold always has seemed to me to be truly and emphatically great. I do not say this on account of the extent and importance of what he actually achieved in this department; for, unfortunately, he never gave himself up fully to it; he never worked at it, as the great business of his literary life. I shall ever deplore his not having done so; and I well remember how sharp was the struggle, when he had to choose between the interpretation of Scripture and the Roman History; and how the choice was determined, not by the consideration of what his peculiar talent was most calculated for performing successfully, but by regard to extrinsic matters,—the prejudice of the clergy against him, the unripeness of England for a free and unfettered discussion of scriptural Exegesis, and the injury which he might be likely to do to his general usefulness. And, as I then did my utmost to determine his labours to the field of Theology, so now I must deeply regret the heavy loss which I cannot but think that the cause of sound interpretation —and, as founded upon it, of doctrinal theology—has sustained in England. The amount, then, of interpretation which he has published to the world, though not inconsiderable, is still small in respect of what there remained to be done by him; but Arnold has furnished a method—has established principles and rules for interpreting Scripture, which, with God's blessing, will be the guide of many a future labourer, and promise to produce fruit of inestimable value. In his writings the student will find a path opened before him—a manner of handling the word of God—a pointing out of the end to be held in view—and a light thrown on the road that leads to it, that will amply repay the deepest meditation on them, and will (if I may say so without presumption) furnish results full of the richest truth, and destined to exercise a commanding influence on the conduct and determination of religious controversy hereafter.

It must be carefully borne in mind, that there are two methods of reading Scripture, perfectly distinct in their objects and nature; the one is practical, the other scientific; the one aims at the edification of the reader, the other at the enlightenment of his understanding ; the one seeks the religious truth of Scripture as bearing on the inquirer's heart and personal feelings, the other the right comprehension of the literary and intellectual portions of the Bible. That Arnold read and meditated on the word of .God as a disciple of Christ for his soul's daily edification ; that it was to him the word of life, the fountain of his deepest feelings, the rule of his life ; that he dwelt in the humblest, most reverential, most prayerful study of its simplest truths, and under the abiding influence of their power, as they were assimilated into his spiritual being by faith ; that Arnold felt and did all this, the whole tenor of his life and every page of your biography amply attest. Those who were most intimate with him will readily recall the mingled feelings of reverence and devotion with which he would, in his lonelier hours, repeat to himself passages from the Gospels. " Nothing," he said, thus speaking of one of them in his earlier life at Laleham, " is more striking to me than our Lord's own ‘description of the judgment. It is so inexpressibly forcible, coming from His very own lips, as descriptive of what He Himself would do." So also the account of the raising of Lazarus, or the close of the eleventh chapter of St. Matthew, "first touching on His greatness, and the incommunicable nature of His union with God ; and then directly the words, ‘ Come unto me,'—as if He must not for a moment depart from the character of the man of sorrows—the Saviour and Mediator." So, too, in his later life at Rugby, it was impossible to forget the deep emotion with which he was agitated, when, on a comparison having been made in his family circle, which seemed to place St. Paul above St. John, the tears rushed to his eyes, and in his own earnest and loving tone, he repeated one of the verses from St. John, and begged that the comparison might never again be made. It would be easy to multiply illustrations of this feeling ; but one more will suffice. Finding that one of his children had been greatly shocked and overcome by the first sight of death, he tenderly endeavoured to remove the feeling which had been awakened, and opening a Bible, pointed to the words, " Then cometh Simon Peter following him, and went into the sepulchre, and seeth the linen clothes lie, and the napkin, that was about his head, not lying with the linen clothes, but wrapped together in a place by itself." Nothing, he said, to his mind, afforded us such comfort, when shrinking from the outward accompaniments of death,—the grave, the grave-clothes, the loneliness,—as the thought that all these had been around our Lord Himself, round Him who died, and is now alive for evermore.

But I am here concerned with the other, and strictly intellectual process ; the scientific exposition of the Scriptures as a collection of ancient books, full of the mightiest intellectual truths ; as the record of God's dealings with man ; and the historical monument of the most wonderful facts in the history of the world. For the office of such an interpreter, Arnold possessed rare and eminent qualifications ; learning, piety, judgment, historical tact, sagacity. The excellence of his method may be considered under two heads :—

I. He had a very remarkable, I should rather say (if I might) wonderful discernment for the divine, as incorporated in the human element of Scripture ; and the recognition of these two separate and most distinct elements,—the careful separation of the two, so that each shall be subject to its own laws, and determined on its own principles,—was the foundation, the grand characteristic principle of his Exegesis. Our Lord's words, that we must " render to Cæsar the things which are Cæsar's, and to God the things which are God's," seemed to him to be of universal application, and nowhere more so, than in the interpretation of Scripture. And his object was not, according to the usual practice, to establish by its means certain religious truths, but to study its contents themselves—to end, in short, instead of beginning with doctrine. Indeed, doctrine in the strict sense, doctrine as pure religious theory, such as it is exhibited in scientific articles and creeds, never was his object. Doctrine, in its practical and religious side, as bearing on religious feeling and character, not doctrine, in the sense of a direct disclosure of spiritual or material essences, as they are in themselves, was all that he endeavoured to find, and all that he believed could be found, in the teaching of Scripture.

First of all he approached the human side of the Bible in the same real historical spirit, with the same methods, rules, and principles as he did Thucydides. He recognised in the writers of the Scriptures the use of a human instrument— language ; and this he would ascertain and fix, as in any other authors, by the same philological rules. Further too, the Bible presents an assemblage of historical events, it announces an historical religion ; and the historical element Arnold judged of historically by the established rules of history, substantiating the general veracity of Scripture even amidst occasional inaccuracies of detail, and proposing to himself, for his special end here, the reproduction, in the language and forms belonging to our own age, and therefore familiar to us, of the exact mode of thinking, feeling, and acting which prevailed in the days gone by.

But was this all? Is the Bible but a common book, recording, indeed, more remarkable occurrences, but in itself possessed of no higher authority than a faithful and trustworthy historian like Thucydides? Nothing could be farther from Dr. Arnold's feeling. In the Bible, he found and acknowledged an oracle of God—a positive and supernatural revelation made to man, an immediate inspiration of the Spirit. No conviction was more deeply seated in his nature ; and this conviction placed an impassable gulf between him and all rationalizing divines. Only it is very important to observe how this fact, in respect of scientific order, presented itself to his mind. He came upon it historically ; he did not start with any preconceived theory of inspiration ; but rather, in studying the writings of those who were commissioned by God to preach His Gospel to the world, he met with the fact, that they claimed to be sent from God, to have a message from Him, to be filled with His Spirit. Any accurate, precise, and sharply-defined theory of inspiration, to the best of my knowledge, Arnold had not; and, if he had been asked to give one, I think he would have answered that the subject did not admit of one. I think he would have been content to realize the feelings of those who heard the Apostles ; he would have been sure, on one side, that there was a voice of God in them ; whilst, on the other, he would have believed that probably no one in the apostolic age could have defined the exact limits of that inspiration. And this I am sure I may affirm with certainty, that never did a student feel his positive faith, his sure confidence that the Bible was the word of God, more indestructible, than in Arnold's hands. He was conscious that, whilst Arnold interpreted Scripture as a scholar, an antiquarian, and an historian, and that in the spirit and with the development of modern science, he had also placed the supernatural inspiration of the sacred writers on an imperishable historical basis, a basis that would be proof against any attack which the most refined modern learning could direct against it. Those only who are fully aware of the importance of harmonizing the progress of knowledge with Christianity, or rather, of asserting, amidst every form of civilization, the objective truths of Christianity and its life-giving power, can duly appreciate the value of the confidence inspired by the firm faith of a man, at once liberal, unprejudiced, and, in the estimation of even the most worldly men, possessed of high historical ability.

II. But I have not yet mentioned the greatest merit of Arnold's Exegesis; it took a still higher range. It was not confined to a mere reproduction of a faithful image of the words and deeds recorded in the Bible, such as they were spoken, done, and understood at the times when they severally occurred. It is a great matter to perceive what Christianity was, such as it was felt and understood to be by the hearers of the Apostles. But the Christian prophet and interpreter had in his eyes a still more exalted office. God's dealings with any particular generation of men are but the application of the eternal truths of His Providence to their particular circumstances, and the form of that application has at different times greatly varied. Here it was that Arnold's most characteristic eminence lay. He seemed to me to possess the true χάρισμα, the very spiritual gift of γνῶσις, having an insight not only into the actual form of the religion of any single age, but into the meaning and substance of God's moral government generally; a vision of the eternal principles by which it is guided; and such a profound understanding of their application, as to be able to set forth God's manifold wisdom, as manifested at divers times, and under circumstances of the most opposite kind; nay, still more, to reconcile with his unchangeable attributes those passages in Holy Writ at which infidels had scoffed, and which pious men had read in reverential silence. Thus, he vindicated God's command to Abraham to sacrifice his son, and to the Jews to exterminate the nations of Canaan, by explaining the principles on which these commands were given, and their reference to the moral state of those to whom they were addressed; thereby educing light out of darkness, unravelling the thread of God's religious education of the human race, from its earliest infancy down to the fulness of times, and holding up God's marvellous counsels to the devout wonder and meditation of the thoughtful believer. As I said at first, Arnold has rather pointed out the path, than followed it out to any extent himself; the student will find in his writings the principles of his method rather than its development. They are scattered, more or less, throughout all his writings, but more especially in the Appendix to vol. ii. of the Sermons, the Preface to the third, the Notes to the fourth, and the Two

Sermons on Prophecy.* These last furnish to the student a very instructive instance of his method; for whilst he will recognise there the double sense of Prophecy, and much besides that was held by the old commentators, he will also perceive how different an import they assume, as treated by Arnold; and how his wide and elevated view could find in Prophecy a firm foundation for a Christian's hope and faith, without their being coupled with that extravagance with which the study of the Prophecies has been so often united. His sermons, also, generally exhibit very striking illustrations of his faculty to discern general truth under particular circumstances, and his power to apply it in a very altered, nay, often opposite form to cases of a different nature; thus making God's word an ever-living oracle, furnishing to every age those precise rules, principles, and laws of conduct which its actual circumstances may require.

I must not forget to add, that his principles of interpretation were of slow and matured growth; he arrived at them gradually, and, in some instances, even reluctantly; and one of the most elaborate of his early sermons, which he had intended to have preached before the University, was in defence of what is called the verbal inspiration of Scripture. But, since I became acquainted with him, I have never known him to maintain anything but what I have here tried to set forth. It is very possible that much of what I have here said may appear to many to be exaggerated; but I know not how else to express adequately my firm confidence that the more the principles which guided Arnold's interpretation of Scripture are studied in his writings, the more will their power to throw light on the depths of God's wisdom be appreciated.—Yours ever,

B. PRICE.

3. Lastly, his letters will have already shown how early he had conceived the idea of the work,† to which he chiefly looked forward, as that of his old age, on Christian Politics, or Church and State. But it is only

---

* To these may be added the posthumous volume of " Sermons, mostly on Interpretation of Scripture."

† This work he approached at four different times: 1. In a sketch drawn up in 1827; 2. In two fragments in 1833, 34; 3. In a series of Letters to Chevalier Bunsen, 1839; 4. In an historical fragment, 1838–1841. These have all been since published in the " Fragment on the Church."

a wider survey of his general views that will show how completely this was the centre round which were gathered not only all his writings, but all his thoughts and actions on social subjects, and which gave him a distinct position amongst English divines, not only of the present, but of almost all preceding generations. We must remember how the Greek science, πολιτικὴ, of which the English word "politics," or even political science, is so inadequate a translation—society in its connexion with the highest welfare of men—exhibited to him the great problem which every educated man was called upon to solve. We must conceive how lofty were the aspirations which he entertained of what Christianity was intended to effect, and what, if rightly applied, it might yet effect, far beyond anything which has yet been seen, or is ordinarily conceived, for the moral and social restoration of the world. We must enter into the keen sense of the startling difficulty which he felt to be presented by its comparative failure. "The influence of Christianity no doubt has made itself felt in all those countries which have professed it ; but ought not its effects," he urged, "to have been far more perceptible than they are, now that nearly eighteen hundred years have elapsed since the kingdom of God was first proclaimed ? Is it, in fact, the kingdom of God in which we are now living ? Are we at this hour living under the law or under grace ?" Everything, in short, which he thought or said on this subject, was in answer to what he used to call "the very question of questions ; " the question which occurs in the earliest of all his works, and which he continued to ask of himself and of others as long as he lived. "Why amongst us in this very country, is the mighty work of raising up God's kingdom stopped ; the work of bringing every thought and word and deed to the obedience of Christ ?"   (Serm. vol. i. p. 115.)

The great cause of this hindrance to the triumph of Christianity, he believed to lie (to adopt his own distinction) in the corruption not of the Religion of Christ, but of the Church of Christ. The former he felt had on the whole done its work—"its truths," he said, "are to be sought in the Scriptures alone, and are the same at all times and in all countries." But "the Church, which is not a revelation concerning the eternal and unchangeable God, but an institution to enable changeable man to apprehend the unchangeable," had, he maintained, been virtually destroyed; and thus, "Christianity being intended to remedy the intensity of the evil of the Fall by its Religion, and the universality of the evil by its Church, has succeeded in the first, because its religion has been retained as God gave it, but has failed in the second, because its Church has been greatly corrupted." (Serm. vol. iv. Pref. p. xliv.)

What he meant by this corruption, and why he thought it fatal to the full development of Christianity will best appear by explaining his idea of the Church, both with regard to its true end, and its true nature. Its end he maintained to be "the putting down of moral evil." "And if this idea," he asks, "seems strange to anyone, let him consider whether he will not find this notion of Christianity everywhere prominent in the Scriptures, and whether the most peculiar ordinances of the Christian Religion are not founded upon it ; or again, if it seem natural to him, let him ask himself whether he has well considered the legitimate consequences of such a definition, and whether, in fact, it is not practically forgotten ?" Its true nature he believed to be not an institution of the clergy, but a living society of all Christians. "When I hear men talk of the Church," he used to say, "I cannot help recalling how Abbé Sièyes replied to the question, 'What is the Tiers État ?' by saying, 'La nation moins la noblesse et la clergé;' and so I, if I were asked, What are the laity? would answer, the Church minus the clergy." "This," he said, "is the view taken of the Church in the New Testament; can it be said that it is the view held amongst ourselves, and if not, is not the difference incalculable?" It was as frustrating the union of all Christians, in accomplishing what he believed to be the true end enjoined by their common Master, that he felt so strongly against the desire for uniformity of opinion or worship, which he used to denounce under the name of sectarianism; it was as annihilating what he believed to be the Apostolical idea of a Church, that he felt so strongly against that principle of separation between the clergy and laity, which he used to denounce under the name of priestcraft. "As far as the principle on which Archbishop Laud and his followers acted went to reactuate the idea of the Church, as a co-ordinate and living power by virtue of Christ's institution and express promise, I go along with them; but I soon discover that by the Church they meant the clergy, the heirarchy exclusively, and there I fly off from them at a tangent. For it is this very interpretation of the Church that, according to my conviction, constituted the first and fundamental apostacy." Such was the motto from Coleridge's. Remains which he selected as the full expression of his own views, and it was as realizing this idea that he turned eagerly to all institutions which seemed likely to impress on all Christians the moral, as distinct from the ceremonial, character of their religion, the equal responsibility and power which they possessed, not "as friends or honorary members" of the Church, but as its most essential parts.

Such (to make intelligible, by a few instances, what in general language must be obscure) was his desire to revive the order of deacons, as a link between the clergy and laity,—his defence of the union of laymen with clerical synods, of clergy with the civil legislature,—his belief that an authoritative permission to administer the Eucharist, as well as Baptism, might be beneficially granted to civil or military officers, in congregations where it was impossible to procure the presence of clergy, —his wish for the restoration of Church discipline, " which never can and never ought to be restored, till the Church puts an end to the usurpation of her powers by the clergy ; and which, though it must be vain when opposed to public opinion, yet, when it is the expression of that opinion, can achieve anything." (Serm. vol. iv. pp. liii. 416.) Such was his suggestion of the revival of many " good practices, which belong to the true Church no less than to the corrupt Church, and would there be purely beneficial ; daily church services, frequent communions, memorials of our Christian calling, presented to our notice in crosses and wayside oratories ; commemorations to holy men of all times and countries ; the doctrine of the communion of saints practically taught ; religious orders, especially of women, of different kinds, and under different rules, delivered only from the snare and sin of perpetual vows." (Serm. vol. iv. Pref. p. lvi.)

A society organized on these principles, and with such or similar institutions, was, in his judgment, the " true sign from heaven " meant to be " the living witness of the reality of Christ's salvation, which should remind us daily of God, and work upon the habits of our life as insensibly as the air we breathe," (Serm. vol. iv. p. 307,) which would not " rest satisfied with the lesser and imperfect good, which strikes thrice and stays," (ibid. Pref. p. liv.) which would be " something truer and deeper than satisfied not only the last century, but the last seventeen centuries." (Ibid. Pref. p. liii.)   .

But it was almost impossible for his speculations to

have stopped short of the most tangible shape which they assumed, viz., his idea not of an alliance or union, but of the absolute identity of the Church with the State. In other words, his belief that the object of the State and the Church was alike the highest welfare of man, and that, as the State could not accomplish this, unless it acted with the wisdom and goodness of the Church, nor the Church, unless it was invested with the sovereign power of the State, the State and the Church in their ideal form were not two societies, but one ; and that it is only in proportion as this identity is realized in each particular country, that man's perfection and God's glory can be established on earth. This theory had, indeed, already been sanctioned by some of the greatest names in English theology and philosophy, by Hooker in his Ecclesiastical Polity, and in later times by Burke, and in part by Coleridge. But (if a negative may be universally asserted on such a subject) it had never before, at least in England, been so completely the expression of a man's whole mind, or the basis of a whole system, political as well as religious, positive as well as negative.

The peculiar line of his historical studies—the admiration which he felt for the Greek and Roman commonwealths—his intensely political and national turn of mind—his reverence for the authority of law—his abhorrence of what he used to consider the anarchical spirit of dissent on the one hand, and the sectarianism of a clerical government on the other—all tended to the same result. His detestation, on the one hand, of what he used to call the secular or Jacobinical notion of a State, as providing only for physical ends,—on the other hand, of what he used to call the superstitious or antichristian view of the Church, as claiming to be ruled not by national laws, but by a divinely-appointed succession of priests or governors,—both combined to make him look to the nation or commonwealth as the fit sphere for the full realization of Christianity ; to the perfect identification of Christian with political society, as the only mode of harmonizing the truths which, in the opposite systems of Archbishop Whately and Mr. Gladstone, he lamented to see " each divorced from its proper mate."

Accordingly, no full development of the Church, no full Christianization of the State, could in his judgment take place, until the Church should have become not a subordinate, but a sovereign society ; not acting indirectly on the world, through inferior instruments, but directly through its own government, the supreme legislature. Then at last all public officers of the State, feeling themselves to be necessarily officers of the Church, would endeavour " each in his vocation and ministry," to serve its great cause " not with a subject's indifference, but with a citizen's zeal." Then the jealousy, with which the clergy and laity at present regard each other's interference, would, as he hoped, be lost in the sense that their spheres were in fact the same ; that nothing was too secular to claim exemption from the enforcement of Christian duty, nothing too spiritual to claim exemption from the control of the government of a Christian State. Then the whole nation, amidst much variety of form, ceremonial, and opinion, would at last feel that the great ends of Christian and national society, now for the first time realized to their view, were a far stronger bond of union between Christians, and a far deeper division from those who were not Christians, than any subordinate principle either of agreement or separation.

It was thus only, that he figured to himself the perfect consummation of earthly things,—the triumph of what he used emphatically to call the *Kingdom* of God.

Other good institutions, indeed, he regarded as so many steps towards this end. The establishment of a parochial clergy, even in its present state, seemed to him one of the highest national blessings,—much more the revival of the Church, as he would have wished to see it revived. Still the work of Christianity itself was not accomplished, so long as political and social institutions were exempt from its influence', so long as the highest power of human society professed to act on other principles than those declared in the Gospel. But, whenever it should come to pass that the strongest earthly bond should be identical with the bond of Christian fellowship,—that the highest earthly power should avowedly minister to the advancement of Christian holiness—that crimes should be regarded as sins—that Christianity should be the acknowledged basis of citizenship—that the region of political and national questions, war and peace, oaths and punishments, economy and education, so long considered by good and bad alike as worldly and profane, should be looked upon as the very sphere to which Christian principles are most applicable,—then he felt that Christianity would at last have gained a position, where it could cope for the first time, front to front, with the power of evil ; that the unfulfilled promises of the older prophecies, so long delayed, would have received their accomplishment ; that the kingdoms of this world would have indeed become the kingdoms of the Lord and of his Christ.

No one felt more keenly than himself how impossible it was to apply this view directly to existing circumstances ; how the whole frame-work of society must be reconstructed before it could be brought into action ; how far in the remote future its accomplishment must necessarily lie. "So deeply," he said, "is the distinction between the Church and the State seated in our laws, our language, and our very notions, that nothing less than a miraculous interposition of God's Providence seems capable within any definite time of eradicating it."*

Still it was not in his nature to postpone, even in thought, the fulfilment of his desires to a remote Millennium or Utopia, such as in the minds of many men acts rather as a reason for acquiescence in the existing order of the world, than as a motive for rising above it. The wisdom of Hesiod's famous paradox, "He is a fool who does not know how much the half is better than the whole," was often in his mouth; in answer to the frequent allegation that because the complete fulfilment of the theory was impracticable, therefore no part of it could be made available. "I cannot answer all your objections fully," he writes to Archbishop Whately, "because if I could, it were to suppose that the hardest of all human questions contained no great difficulties; but I think on the whole, that the objections to my scheme are less than to any other, and that on the positive side it is in theory perfect: and though it never will be wholly realized, yet if men can be brought to look at it as the true theory, the practical approximations to it may in the course of time be indefinitely great."

It was still the thought which animated all his exertions in behalf of his country, where he felt that "the means were still in our hands, which it seems far better to use even at the eleventh hour, than desperately to throw them away."† And, convinced as he was, that the founders of our present constitution in Church and State did "truly consider them to be identical, the Christian nation of England to be the Church of England, the head of that nation to be for that very reason the head of the Church," he asked with an indignant sorrow, "whether it were indeed indifference or latitudinarianism, to wish

* Pref. to Hist. of Rome, vol. i. p. ix.   † Serm. vol. ii. Pref. p. vi.

most devoutly that this noble, this divine theory might be fully and for ever realized."* It was still the vision which closed the vista of all his speculations; the ideal whole, which might be incorporated part by part into the existing order of society; the ideal end which each successive age might approach more closely,—its very remoteness only impressing him more deeply with the conviction of the enormous efforts which must be made to bring all social institutions nearer to that perfection which Christianity designed for them, of the enormous mass of evil which lay undisturbed because so few dared to acknowledge the identity of the cause of reform with the cause of Christianity. It was still, in its more practical form, the great idea of which the several parts of his life were so many distinct exemplifications; his sermons—his teaching—his government of the school—his public acts—his own personal character; and to which all his dreams of wider usefulness instinctively turned, from the first faint outline of his hopes in his earliest letters down to the last evening of his life, when the last thought which he bestowed on the future, was of "that great work, if he might be permitted to take part in it."

The general view of Dr. Arnold's life at Rugby must not be closed, without touching, however briefly and imperfectly, on that aspect of it, which naturally gave the truest view of his mind and character, whilst to those at a distance it was comparatively but little known.

Perhaps the scene which, to those who knew him best, would bring together the recollections of his public and private life in the most lively way, was his study at Rugby. There he sat at his work, with no attempt at

* Church Reform, Postscript, p. 24. Misc. Works, p. 335.

seclusion, conversation going on around him—his children
playing in the room—his frequent guests, whether friends
or former pupils, coming in or out at will—ready at once
to break off his occupations to answer a question, or to
attend to the many interruptions to which he was liable ;
and from these interruptions, or from his regular avocations, at the few odd hours or minutes which he could
command, would he there return and recommence his
writing, as if it had not been broken off. " Instead of
feeling my head exhausted," he would sometimes say
after the day's business was over, " it seems to have
quite an eagerness to set to work." " I feel as if I could
dictate to twenty secretaries at once." " Unhasting,
unresting diligence," was the strong impression which a
one day's visit at Rugby left on one of the keenest
observers amongst English authors—and he was one of
a class, who however engaged, whether in business, in
writing, or in travelling, was emphatically never in a
hurry.

Still he would often wish for something more like
leisure and repose. " We sometimes feel," he said, " as
if we should like to run our heads into a hole—to be
quiet for a little time from the stir of so many human
beings which greets us from morning to evening." And
it was from amidst this chaos of employments that he
turned, with all the delight of which his nature was
capable, to what he often dwelt upon as the rare, the unbroken, the almost awful happiness of his domestic life.
It is impossible adequately to describe the union of the
whole family round him, who was not only the father and
guide, but the elder brother and playfellow of his children ;
the first feelings of enthusiastic love and watchful care,
carried through twenty-two years of wedded life ; the
gentleness and devotion which marked his whole feeling
and manner in the privacy of his domestic intercourse.

Those who had known him only in the school can re-member the kind of surprise with which they first wit-nessed his tenderness and playfulness. Those who had known him only in the bosom of his family, found it difficult to conceive how his pupils or the world at large should have formed to themselves so stern an image of one in himself so loving. Yet both were alike natural to him ; the severity and playfulness expressing each in their turn the earnestness with which he entered into the business of life, and the enjoyment with which he entered into its rest ; whilst the common principle, which linked both together, made every closer approach to him in his private life a means for better understanding him in his public relations.

Enough, however, may perhaps be said to recall some-thing at least of its outward aspect. There were his hours of thorough relaxation, when he would throw off all thoughts of the school and of public matters—his quiet walks by the side of his wife's pony, when he would enter into the full enjoyment of air and exercise, and the outward face of nature, observing with distinct pleasure each symptom of the burst of spring or of the richness of summer—"feeling like a horse pawing the ground, impatient to be off," "as if the very act of existence was an hourly pleasure to him." There was the cheerful voice that used to go sounding through the house in the early morning, as he went round to call his children ; the new spirits which he seemed to gather from the merc glimpses of them in the midst of his occupations—the in-creased merriment of all in any game in which he joined —the happy walks on which he would take them in the fields and hedges, hunting for flowers—the yearly excur-sion to look in the neighbouring clay-pit for the earliest coltsfoot, with the mock siege that followed. Nor, again, was the sense of his authority as a father ever lost

in his playfulness as a companion. His personal superintendence of their ordinary instruction was necessarily
limited by his other engagements, but it was never
wholly laid aside ; in the later years of his life it was his
custom to read the Psalms and Lessons of the day with
his family every morning ; and the common reading of a
chapter in the Bible every Sunday evening, with repetition of hymns or parts of Scripture by every member of
the family—the devotion with which he would himself
repeat his favourite poems from the Christian Year,
or his favourite passages from the Gospels—the same
attitude of deep attention in listening to the questions of
his youngest children, the same reverence in answering
their difficulties that he would have shown to the most
advanced of his friends or his scholars—form a picture
not soon to pass away from the mind of any one who
was ever present. But his teaching in his family was
naturally not confined to any particular occasions ; they
looked to him for information and advice at all times ;
and a word of authority from him was a law not to be
questioned for a moment. And with the tenderness
which seemed to be alive to all their wants and wishes,
there was united that peculiar sense of solemnity, with
which in his eyes the very idea of a family life was
invested. "I do not wonder," he said, "that it was
thought a great misfortune to die childless in old times,
when they had not fuller light—it seems so completely
wiping a man out of existence." The anniversaries of
domestic events—the passing away of successive generations—the entrance of his sons on the several stages of
their education,—struck on the deepest chords of his
nature, and made him blend with every prospect of the
future, the keen sense of the continuance (so to speak)
of his own existence in the good and evil fortunes of his
children, and to unite the thought of them with the

yet more solemn feeling, with which he was at all times wont to regard "the blessing" of "a whole house transplanted entire from earth to heaven without one failure."

In his own domestic happiness he never lost sight of his early friends. "He was attached to his family," it was truly said of him by Archbishop Whately, "as if he had no friends; to his friends, as if he had no family; and," he adds, "to his country, as if he had no friends or relations." Debarred as he was from frequent intercourse with most of them by his or their occupations, he made it part of the regular business of his life to keep up a correspondence with them. "I never do," he said, "and I trust I never shall excuse myself for not writing to old and dear friends, for it is really a duty which it is mere indolence and thoughtlessness to neglect." The very aspect of their several homes lived as distinct images in his mind, and seemed to have an equal claim on his interest. To men of such variety of opinion and character, that the very names of some of them are identified with measures and views the most opposite that good men can entertain, he retained to the end a strong and almost equal affection. The absence of greater mutual sympathy was to him almost the only shadow thrown over his happy life; no difference of opinion ever destroyed his desire for intercourse with them; and where, in spite of his own efforts to continue it, it was so interrupted, the subject was so painful to him that even with those most intimate with him, he could hardly bear to allude to it.

How lively was his interest in the state of England generally, and especially in the lower orders, will appear elsewhere. But the picture of his ordinary life would be incomplete without mention of his intercourse with the poor. He purposely abstained, as will be seen, from mixing much in the affairs of the town and neighbourhood of Rugby. But he was always ready to assist in

matters of local charity and usefulness, giving lectures,
for example, before the Mechanics' Institute at Rugby
and Lutterworth, writing tracts on the appearance of the
cholera in the vicinity, and, after the establishment of the
railway station at half a mile from the town, procuring
the sanction of the Bishop for the performance of a short
service there on Sundays by himself and the assistant-
masters in turn. In preaching to parochial congregations, as he did occasionally at Rugby and at Rydal, he
always, he said, found a difficulty from " the consideration,* not only of what was fit for them to hear, but also
fit for him to say,"—and accordingly they were usually
on " some particular point not of the very deepest character, but yet important and capable of being sufficiently
discussed at one time," such as that on " Christian Conviction," preached at Carfax Church in Oxford, or on
Wills, at Rydal, or again, on some of the great social
questions which concerned the country generally, such
as those published at the close of the second volume,
preached in 1831. At other times, however, both at
Rugby and in Westmoreland, and always at the above-
mentioned service at the railway station, his addresses
were spoken and not written, and rather after the manner
of one talking seriously to his neighbours, or explaining
parts of scripture which occurred in the service, than
would commonly be called preaching. His style seems
to have been too simple to be generally popular amongst
the poorer classes ; but cases often occurred of its having
made a deep impression. A passing traveller, shortly
after his death, was struck with the unfeigned regret
expressed by the men at the railway station for the loss
of his visits to them ; and at Harrow, where he once
spent a Sunday with Dr. Longley, there were found
amongst the few papers of a poor servant maid, who

* Serm. v. 31.

died some time afterwards, notes of a sermon which he preached there in the parish church, and to which she was known to have recurred frequently afterwards.

The poor of the place, as might be expected, shared largely in that liberality which marked both his public and his private dealings, and which, in fact, from the impression it made on the naturally suspicious senses of boys, ought not to be overlooked : even in the management of the school his direct intercourse with the poor was, of course, much more limited than it had been in the village of Laleham; yet with some few, chiefly aged persons in the almshouses of the town, he made a point of keeping up a frequent and familiar acquaintance. In this intercourse, sometimes in conversations with them as he met or overtook them alone on the road, usually in such visits as he could pay to them in his spare moments of relaxation, he assumed less of the character of a teacher than most clergymen would have thought right, reading to them occasionally, but generally talking to them with the manner of a friend and an equal. This resulted partly from the natural reserve and shyness which made him shrink from entering on sacred subjects with comparative strangers, and which, though he latterly somewhat overcame it, almost disqualified him, in his own judgment, from taking charge of a parish. But it was also the effect of his reluctance to address them in a more authoritative or professional tone than he would have used towards persons of his own rank. Feeling keenly what seemed to him at once the wrong and the mischief done by the too wide separation between the higher and lower orders, he wished to visit them "as neighbours, without always seeming bent on relieving or instructing them;"* and could not bear to use language which to anyone in a higher station would have been thought an interference.

* Sermons, vol. ii. p. 411.

With the servants of his household, for the same reasons,
he was in the habit, whether in travelling or in his own
house, of consulting their accommodation and speaking
to them familiarly as to so many members of the domestic
circle.   And in all this, writes one who knew well his
manner to the poor, "there was no affectation of con-
descension, it was a manly address to his fellow-men, as
man addressing man."   "I never knew such a humble
man as the Doctor," said the parish clerk at Laleham,
after he had revisited it from Rugby; "he comes and
shakes us by the hand as if he was one of us."   He used
to come into my house," said an old woman near his
place in Westmoreland, "and talk to me as if I was a
lady."   Often, no doubt, this was not appreciated by the
poor, and might, at times, be embarrassing to himself,
and it is said that he was liable to be imposed upon by
them, and greatly to overrate their proficiency in moral
and religious excellence.   But he felt this intercourse to
be peculiarly needful for one engaged in occupations such
as his ; to the remembrance of the good poor, whom he
visited at Rugby, he often recurred when absent from
them ; and nothing can exceed the regret which they
testify at his loss, and the grateful affection with which
they still speak of him, pointing with delight to the seat
which he used to occupy by their firesides : one of them
especially, an old almswoman, who died a few months
after his own decease, up to the last moment of consciousness never ceasing to think of his visits to her, and of the
hope with which she looked forward now to seeing his
face once more again.

Closely as he was bound to Rugby by these and
similar bonds of social and familiar life, and yet more
closely by the charm with which its mere outward aspect
and localities were invested by his interest in the school,
both as an independent institution and as his own sphere

of duty, yet the place in itself never had the same strong
hold on his affections as Oxford or Laleham, and his
holidays were almost always spent away from Rugby,
either in short tours, or in later years at his Westmoreland home, Fox How, a small estate between Rydal and
Ambleside, which he purchased in 1832, with the view
of providing for himself a retreat, in case of his retirement from the school, or for his family in case of
his death. The monotonous character of the midland
scenery of Warwickshire was to him, with his strong love
of natural beauty and variety, absolutely repulsive; there
was something almost touching in the eagerness with
which, amidst that "endless succession of fields and hedge-
rows," he would make the most of any features of a
higher order; in the pleasure with which he would cherish
the few places where the current of the Avon was perceptible, or where a glimpse of the horizon could be discerned ; in the humorous despair with which he would
gaze on the dull expanse of fields eastward from Rugby.
" It is no wonder we do not like looking that way,
when one considers that there is nothing fine between us
and the Ural mountains. Conceive what you look over,
for you must miss Sweden, and look over Holland, the
north of Germany, and the centre of Russia." With this
absence of local attraction in the place, and with the conviction that his occupations and official station must make
him look for his future home elsewhere, " I feel," he said,
"that I love Middlesex and Westmoreland, but I care
nothing for Warwickshire, and am in it like a plant sunk
in the ground in a pot ; my roots never strike beyond
the pot, and I could be transplanted at any minute without tearing or severing of my fibres. To the pot itself,
which is the school, I could cling very lovingly, were it
not that the laborious nature of the employment makes
me feel that it can only be temporary, and that, if I live

to old age, my age could not be spent in my present situation.

Fox How accordingly became more and more the centre of all his local and domestic affections. " It is with a mixed feeling of solemnity and tenderness," he said, "that I regard our mountain nest, whose surpassing sweetness, I think I may safely say, adds a positive happiness to every one of my waking hours passed in it." When absent from it, it still, he said, "dwelt in his memory as a vision of beauty from one vacation to another," and when present at it he felt that "no hasty or excited admiration of a tourist could be compared with the quiet and hourly delight of having the mountains and streams as familiar objects, connected with all the enjoyments of home, one's family, one's books, and one's friends,"—" associated with our work-day thoughts as well as our gala-day ones."

Then it was that, as he sat working in the midst of his family, " never raising his eyes from the paper to the window without an influx of ever new delights," he found that leisure for writing, which he so much craved at Rugby. Then it was that he enjoyed the entire relaxation, which he so much needed after his school occupations, whether in the journeys of coming and returning, those long journeys, which, before they were shortened by railway travelling, were to him, he used to say, the twelve most restful days of the whole year ;—or in the birthday festivities of his children, and the cheerful evenings when all subjects were discussed, from the gravest to the lightest, and when he would read to them his favourite stories from Herodotus, or his favourite English poets. Most of all, perhaps, was to be observed his delight in those long mountain walks, when they would start with their provisions for the day, himself the guide and life of the party, always on the look-out how best to break the ascent by gentle stages, comforting the little ones in their falls, and helping forward those who were tired, himself always keeping with the laggers, that none might strain their strength by trying to be in front with him—and then, when his assistance was not wanted, the liveliest of all ; his step so light, his eye so quick in finding flowers to take home to those who were not of the party.

Year by year bound him with closer ties to his new home ; not only Fox How itself with each particular tree, the growth of which he had watched, and each particular spot in the grounds, associated by him with the playful names of his nine children ; but also the whole valley in which it lay became consecrated with something of a domestic feeling. Rydal Chapel, with the congregation to which he had so often preached—the new circle of friends and acquaintance with whom he kept up so familiar an intercourse—the gorges and rocky pools which in many instances owed their nomenclature to him, all became part of his habitual thoughts. He delighted to derive his imagery from the hills and lakes of Westmoreland, and to trace in them the likenesses of his favourite scenes in poetry and history ; even their minutest features were of a kind that were most attractive to him ; " the running streams," which were to him " the most beautiful objects in nature ;"—the wild flowers on the mountain sides, which were to him, he said, " his music :" and which, whether in their scarcity at Rugby, or their profusion in Westmoreland, " loving them," as he used to say, " as a child loves them," he could not bear to see removed from their natural places by the wayside, where others might enjoy them as well as himself. The very peacefulness of all the historical and moral associations of the scenery—free alike from the remains of feudal ages in the past, and suggesting comparatively so little of

suffering or of evil in the present,—rendered doubly
grateful to him the refreshment which he there found
from the rough world in the school, or the sad feelings
awakened in his mind by the thoughts of his Church and
country. There he hoped, when the time should have
come for his retreat from Rugby, to spend his declining
years. Other visions, indeed, of a more practical and
laborious life, from time to time passed before him, but
Fox How was the image, which most constantly presented itself to him in all prospects for the future ; there
he intended to have lived in peace, maintaining his connexion with the rising generation by receiving pupils
from the Universities ; there, under the shade of the
trees of his own planting, he hoped in his old age to give
to the world the fruits of his former experience and
labours, by executing those works for which at Rugby
he felt himself able only to prepare the way, or lay the
first foundations, and never again leave his retirement
till (to use his own expression) " his bones should go
to Grasmere churchyard, to lie under the yews which
Wordsworth planted, and to have the Rotha with its
deep and silent pools passing by."

CHAPTER V.

LIFE AND CORRESPONDENCE, AUGUST, 1828, TO AUGUST, 1830.

THE two first years of Dr. Arnold's life at Rugby remarkably exhibit the natural sanguineness of his character, whether in the feeling with which he entered on the business of the school, or in the hopefulness with which he regarded public affairs, and which, more or less, pervaded all that he wrote at this time.

The first volume of sermons, and the first volume of his edition of Thucydides, containing, as they did in many respects, the basis of his theological and historical views, were published in February, 1829, and May, 1830; and little need be added to what has already been said of them. To the latter, indeed, an additional interest is imparted from its being the first attempt in English philology to investigate not merely the phrases and formulæ, but the general principles of the Greek language, and to illustrate, not merely the words, but the history and geography of a Greek historian. And in the Essay on the different periods of national existence appended to this first volume, but, in fact, belonging more to his general views of history and politics than to any particular illustration of Thucydides, is brought out,

more forcibly than in any other of·his writing, his belief
in the progress and inherent excellence of popular principles ; in the distinct stages of civilization through which
nations have to pass ; and in the philosophical divisions
of ancient and modern history, of which he made so
much use in treating of either of them. But the work
which naturally excited most public attention, was a
pamphlet on, "the Christian Duty of Conceding the
Claims of the Roman Catholics," published in February,
1829. To those who knew him in later life, it may appear strange that he should have treated at length of the
question of Ireland, which he was accustomed to shun as
a problem of inextricable difficulty, and on which nothing
but a sense of justice would ever prevail upon him to
enter. But this sense of justice was, at this time, quick-
ened by the deep conviction which, for some years past,
he had entertained of the alarming state of the Irish
nation. "There is more to be done there," he writes in
1828, from Laleham, "than in any corner of the world.
I had, at one time, a notion of going over there and
taking Irish pupils, to try what one man could do towards
civilizing the people, by trying to civilize and Christianize
their gentry." And the particular crisis of the Roman
Catholic Relief Act was exactly one of those occasions
which brought him into direct collision, both with the
tone of the Liberal party, who assumed that, as being a
political measure, it could not be argued on religious
grounds ; and of the·Tory party, who assumed that, as
being a religious question, it was one on which the almost
united authority of the English clergy ought to have
decisive weight; whereas, his own views of course led
him to maintain that, being a great national question of
right and wrong, it must, on the one hand, be argued on
Christian grounds, and yet, on the other hand, that the
clergy would not be the best judges of it, because " the

origin, rights, and successive revolutions of society were subjects which they avowedly neglected to study." The pamphlet was published at so late a stage of the controversy, that it had not time to reach a second edition before the Act was passed. But the grounds of solemn duty on which his vindication of the Relief Act was based, as the best mode of repairing the sin and mischief, never yet effaced, of the original conquest of Ireland, and as a right, which, as being still a distinct national society, the Irish people justly claimed—attracted considerable attention. Other parts, such as that in which he denied the competence of the clergy to pronounce upon historical questions, created an impression against him in the great body of his profession, which, perhaps, was never wholly removed. Its intrinsic interest, independent of the particular controversy, consists in its being his first and most emphatic protest against the divorce of religion and politics, and the most complete statement of his abstract views of political science, as his Appendix to Thucydides furnished his statement of their historical development.

I.   TO J. T. COLERIDGE, ESQ.

Rugby, August 29, 1828.

. . . . . . Here we are actually at Rugby, and the school will open to-morrow. I cannot tell you with what deep regret we left Laleham, where we had been so peaceful and so happy, and left my mother, aunt, and sisters for the first time in my life, except during my school and college absences. It was quite " feror exul in altum," &c., but then we both looked upon Rugby as on our Italy, and entered it, I think, with hope and with thankfulness. . . . . . . But the things which I have had to settle, and the people whom I have had to see on business, have been almost endless ; to me, unused as I was to business, it seemed quite a chaos ; but, thank God, being in high health and spirits, and gaining daily more knowledge of the state of affairs, I got on tolerably well. Next week, however, will be the grand experiment ; and I look to it naturally with great anxiety.   I trust, I feel how great and solemn a duty I have to fulfil, and that I shall be enabled to fulfil it by that help which can alone give the " Spirit of power and love, and of a sound mind ;" the three great requisites, I imagine, in a school-master.

You need not fear my reforming furiously ; there, I think, I can assure you ; but, of my success in introducing a religious principle into education, I must be doubtful ; it is my most earnest wish, and I pray God that it may be my constant labour and prayer ; but to do this would be to succeed beyond all my hopes ; it would be a happiness so great, that, I think, the world would yield me nothing comparable to it.   To do it, however imperfectly, would far more than repay twenty years of labour and anxiety.

Saturday, August 30th.   I have been receiving, this morning, a constant succession of visitors, and now, before I go out to return——.   August 31st.   I was again interrupted, and now, I think that I had better at once finish my letter.   I have entered twenty-nine new boys, and have got four more to enter: and I have to-day commenced my business by calling over names and going into chapel, where I was glad to see that the boys behaved very well.   I cannot tell you how odd it seems to me, recalling, at once, my school-days more vividly than I could have thought possible.

II.   TO REV. F. C. BLACKSTONE.

Rugby, September 28, 1828.

It is, indeed, a long time since I wrote to you, and there has been much of intense interest in the period which has elapsed since I did write.   But it has been quite an engrossing occupation ; and Thucydides and everything else has gone to sleep while I have been attending to it.   Now it is becoming more familiar to me, but still the actual employment of time is very great, and the matters for thought which it affords are almost endless.   Still I get my daily exercise and bathing very happily, so that I have been, and am perfectly well, and equal in strength and spirits to the work. . . . . . For myself, I like it hitherto beyond my expectation, but, of course, a month is a very short time to judge from.   [After speaking of the details of the school, and expressing his generally favourable impression of it.] I am trying to establish something of a friendly intercourse with the Sixth Form, by asking them in succession, in parties of four, to dinner with us, and I have them each separately up into my room to look over their exercises. . . . . . I mean to bring in something like "gatherings"* before it is long, for they understand that I have not done with my alterations, nor probably ever shall have; and I am going to have an Examination for every form in the school, at the end of the short half-year, in all the business of the half-year, Divinity, Greek and Latin, Arithmetic, History, Geography, and Chronology, with first and second classes, and prize books for those who do well. I find that my power is perfectly absolute, so that I have no excuse if I do not try to make the school something like my beau-ideal—it is sure to fall far enough short in reality. There has been no flogging yet, (and I hope that there will be none,) and surprisingly few irregularities. I chastise, at first, by very gentle impositions, which are raised for a repetition of offences—flogging will be only my *ratio ultima*—and *talking* I shall try to the utmost. I believe that boys may be governed a great deal by gentle methods and kindness, and appealing to their better feelings, if you show that you are not afraid of them; I have seen great boys, six feet high, shed tears when I have sent for them up into my room and spoken to them quietly, in private, for not knowing their lesson, and I have found that this treatment produced its effects afterwards, in making them do better. But, of course, deeds must second words when needful, or words will soon be laughed at.

III. TO THE SAME.

Laleham, December 19, 1828.

. . . . . . I should have greatly enjoyed seeing you again and seeing you with your wife, and at your own home, to say nothing of resuming some of the matters we discussed a little in the summer. The constitutional tone of different minds naturally gives a different complexion to their view of things, even when they may agree in the main; and in discussing matters besides, one, or at least *I*, am apt to dwell on my points of difference with a man rather than on my points of

----

* A Winchester phrase for exercises in criticism.

agreement with him, because, in one case, I may get my own opinions modified and modify his—in the other, we only end where we began. I confess that it does pain me when I find my friends *shocked* at the expression of my sentiments, because, if a man had entered on the same particular inquiry himself, although he should have come to a wholly different conclusion at last, still if he gave me credit for sincerity, he ought not to be shocked at my not having as yet come to the same conclusion with himself, and would rather quietly try to bring me there—and if he had not inquired into the subject, then he certainly ought not to be shocked ; as giving me credit for the same fundamental principles with himself, he ought not to think that non-inquiry would lead to truth, and inquiry to error. In your case, I know that your mind is entirely candid ; and that no man will conduct an inquiry with more perfect fairness ; you have, therefore, the less reason for abstaining from inquiry altogether. I can assure you, that I never remember to have held a conversation such as those which we had last summer, without deriving benefit in some way or other from the remarks urged in opposition to my own views ; very often they have modified my opinions, sometimes entirely changed them—and when they have done neither, they have yet led me to consider myself and my own state of mind ; lest even whilst holding the truth, I might have bought the possession of it too dearly (I mean, of course, in lesser matters) by exercising the understanding too much, and the affections too little.

IV. TO MRS. EVELYN.

(On the death of her husband.)

Rugby, February 22, 1829.

I need not, I trust, say how deeply I was shocked and grieved by the intelligence contained in your letter. I was totally ignorant of your most heavy loss, and it was one of the hopes in which I have often fondly indulged, that I might some time or other again meet one who I believe was my earliest friend, and for whom I had never ceased to retain a strong admiration and regard. I heard of him last winter from a common friend who had been indebted to his kindness, and whom I have also lost within the last few months, Mr.

Lawes, of Marlborough ; and since that time I had again lost sight of him, till I received from you the account of his death. He must indeed be an irreparable loss to all his family ; for I well remember the extraordinary promise which he gave as a boy, of mingled nobleness and gentleness of heart, as well as of very great powers of understanding. These were visible to me even at an earlier period of his life than you are perhaps aware of; for it was not at Harrow that I knew him, but at Warminster, when we were both very young, and since the year 1806 I have never seen him ; but the impression of his character has remained strongly marked on my memory ever since, for I never knew so bright a promise in any other boy ; I never knew any spirit at that age so pure and generous, and so free from the ordinary meannesses, coarsenesses, and little-nesses of boyhood. It will give me great pleasure to comply with your wishes with regard to an inscription to his memory, if you will be kind enough to furnish me with some particulars of his life and character in later years ; for mine is but a know-ledge of his boyhood, and I am sure that his manhood must have been even still better worth knowing. You will, however, I am sure, allow me to state in perfect sincerity, that I feel very ill qualified to write anything of this nature, and that it requires a peculiar talent which I feel myself wholly to want. I should give you, I fear, but a very bad inscription ; but if you really wish me to attempt it, I will do the best I can to express at least my sincere regard and respect for the memory of my earliest friend. *

Let me thank you sincerely for all the particulars which you have been kind enough to give me in your letter.

---

* The following was the inscription which he sent :—

TO THE MEMORY OF

GEORGE EVELYN, ESQ.,

ETC. ETC. ETC.

HIS EARLY YEARS GAVE A BEAUTIFUL PROMISE
OF VIGOUR OF UNDERSTANDING, KINDNESS OF HEART,
AND CHRISTIAN NOBLENESS OF PRINCIPLE :
HIS MANHOOD ABUNDANTLY FULFILLED IT.
LIVING AND DYING IN THE FAITH OF CHRIST,
HE HAS LEFT TO HIS FAMILY A HUMBLE BUT LIVELY HOPE,
THAT, AS HE WAS RESPECTED AND LOVED BY MEN,
HE HAS BEEN FORGIVEN AND ACCEPTED BY GOD.

V. TO REV. J. LOWE.

Rugby, March 16, 1829.

I have been feeding the press sheet by sheet with a pamphlet or booklet on the Catholic Question. You will say there was no need; but I wanted to show that to do national injustice is a *sin*, and that the clergy, whilst they urge the continuance of this injustice, are making themselves individually guilty of it. And I have written at any rate very peaceably; though you know you used to say that I was "violent on both sides." I saw Milman at Oxford, (where I went not as you may suppose to vote for Sir R. Inglis,) and I was sorry to hear from him rather an indifferent account of you. But from your own letter since, I am hoping that I may augur more favourably. I do rejoice that you have got Hilton, and that you are thus released from the prospect of pupils. Much as I enjoy the work of education in health, for it is at once ἕξις πρακτικὴ and ἕξις ποιητικὴ, I think it would press heavily upon me if I were not quite well and strong. I should much like to see you in your new quarters, but my difficulty is that, when I can move at all, I like to move so far; and thus, in the summer, if all goes well, I hope to see the Alps, and swim in the Mediterranean once again. Your cousin, little Jackson, is a nice boy, and reminds me much of his poor eldest brother; but I do not and cannot see much individually of the boys in the lower part of the school, although I know pretty nearly how each is going on. Reform is a great and difficult work : I can readily allow of the difficulties, but not of the dishonest spirit which makes when it cannot find them, and exaggerates them when it can. "Where there is a will there is a way," is true I believe politically as well as spiritually, and you know that mine is a commonwealth, or rather one of Aristotle's or Plato's perfect kingdoms, where the king is superior by nature to all his subjects—propter defectum ætatis. But if the king of Prussia was as sincere a lover of liberty as I am, he would give his people a constitution—for my great desire is to teach my boys to govern themselves—a much better thing than to govern them well myself. Only in their case, " propter defectum ætatis," as aforesaid, they never can be quite able to govern themselves, and will need some of my government. You would be amused to see how the gentlemen in this neighbourhood are coming round about the Catholics. The worst part I think of the whole business is the effectual manner in which the clergy generally, and of Oxford especially, have cut their own throats in the judgment of all enlightened public men—an evil more dangerous to their interests than twenty Catholic Emancipation bills, and which, as in France, may extend to more than their worldly interests, for an ignorant and selfish clergy is one of the greatest stumbling-blocks in the way of able and liberal-minded statesmen embracing Christianity thoroughly. They will compliment it generally, but they will not heartily act upon its principles so long as they who are supposed to represent its spirit best, are such unfaithful mirrors of it. I had no conception how much of the worst Puritanism still subsisted, and now stript even of that which once palliated its evils—the love of civil liberty.

VI.   TO REV. JULIUS HARE.

Rugby, March 30, 1829.

. . . . . I am much obliged to you for sending me your Defence of Niebuhr : and still more for the most kind and gratifying manner in which you have mentioned me in it ; there are few things more delightful than to be so spoken of by those whom we entirely respect, and whose good opinion and regard we have wished to gain.

I should not have troubled you with my pamphlet on the Catholic question, had it not involved points beyond the mere question now at issue, and on which I was desirous to offer you some explanation, as I think our opinions respecting them are widely different. From what you say in the Guesses at Truth, and again in your Defence of Niebuhr, you appear to me to look upon the past with feelings of reverence, in which I cannot participate. It is not that I think we are better than our fathers in proportion to our lights, or that our powers are at all greater ; on the contrary, they deserve more admiration, considering the difficulties they had to struggle with ; yet still I cannot but think, that the habit of looking back upon them as models, and more especially in all political institutions, is the surest way to fetter our own progress, and to deprive us of the advantages of our own superior experience, which, it is no boast to say, that we possess, but. rather, a most disgraceful reproach, since we use them so little. The error of the last century appears to me to have been this, that they undervalued their ancestors without duly studying antiquity; thus they naturally did not gain the experience which they ought to have done, and were confident even whilst digging from under their feet the ground on which their confidence might have rested justly. Yet still, even in this respect, the 16th and 17th centuries have little cause, I think, to insult the 18th. The great writers of those times read, indeed, enormously, but surely their critical spirit was in no proportion to their reading—and thus the true experience to be gained from the study of antiquity was not gained, because antiquity was not fully understood. It is not, I believe, that I estimate our actual doings more highly than you do; but, I believe, I estimate those of our fathers less highly; and instead of looking upon them as in any degree a standard, I turn instinctively to that picture of entire perfection which the Gospel holds out, and from which I cannot but think that the state of things in times past was further removed even than ours is now, although our *little* may be more inexcusable than their *less* was in them. And, in particular, I confess, that if I were called upon to name what spirit of evil predominantly deserved the name of Antichrist, I should name the spirit of chivalry*—the more detestable for the very guise of the " Archangel ruined," which has made it so seductive to the most generous spirits—but to me so hateful, because it is in direct opposition to the impartial justice of the Gospel, and its comprehensive feeling of equal brotherhood, and because it so fostered a sense of honour rather than a sense of duty.

VII.   TO REV. DR. HAWKINS.

May 29, 1829.

[After refusing to reprint the pamphlet on the Roman Catholic claims, and expressing his belief that the school has not and will not sustain any injury from what he has

* " Chivalry," or (as he used more frequently to call the element in the middle ages which he thus condemned) " feudality, is especially Keltic and barbarian — incompatible with the highest virtue of which man is capable, and the last at which he arrives —a sense of justice. It sets up the personal allegiance to the chief above allegiance to God and law." And in like manner he maintained that the great excellence of the 18th century was the development of the idea of justice,—even amidst the excesses to which it was carried in some of the notions then prevalent on what was called civil and religious liberty.

done.] I claim a full right to use my own discretion in writing upon any subject I choose, provided I do not neglect my duties as master in order to find time for it. But those who know me will be aware that, to say nothing of duty, my interest in the school far exceeds what I feel in any sort of composition of my own; and that neither here nor at Laleham, have I ever allowed my own writings to encroach upon the time, or on the spirits and vigour of mind and body, which I hold that my pupils have a paramount claim upon.

As to the principles in the pamphlet, it is a matter of unfeigned astonishment to me, that any man calling himself a Christian, should think them bad, or should not recognise in them the very principles of Christianity itself. If my principles are bad, I only wish that those who think them so would state their own in opposition to them. It is all very well to call certain principles mischievous and democratical; but I believe very few of those, who do so call them, would be able to bear the monstrous nature of their own, if they were obliged fully to develop them. I mean that they would then be seen to involve what in their daily language about things of common life their very holders laugh at as absurdity and mischief. For instance, about continual reforms, or the wisdom of our ancestors—I have heard Tories laugh at the farmers in their parish, for opposing the mending of the roads, because, as they said, what had been good enough for their fathers was good enough for them; and yet these farmers were not an atom more silly than the people who laughed at them, but only more consistent. And as to the arrogance of tone in the pamphlet, I do not consider it to be arrogance to assume that I know more of a particular subject, which I have studied eagerly from a child, than those do who notoriously do not study it at all. The very men who think it hard to be taxed with ignorance of modern history, and of the laws and literature of foreign nations, are men who, till this question came on, never pretended to know anything about them; and, in the case of the Evangelicals, professed to shun such studies as profane. I should consider no man arrogant, who, if I were to talk about some mathematical or scientific question which he had studied habitually, and on which all scientific men were agreed, should tell me that I did not and could not understand the subject, because I had never liked mathematics, and had never pretended to work at them. Those only who have studied history with that fondness that I have done all my life can fully appreciate the pain which it gives me to see the most mischievous principles supported, as they have been on this question, with an ignorance truly audacious. I will only instance Mr. C.'s appeal to English History in proof that God's judgments will visit us if we grant any favour to the Catholics. . . . . . On the point of Episcopacy, I can only say that my notions, whether right or wrong, have been drawn solely from the New Testament itself, according to what appears to me its true meaning and spirit. I do not know that I ever read any Low Church or No Church argument in my life. But I should like to develop my notions on this point more fully hereafter. I have some thoughts of publishing a volume of essays on various points connected with Christian doctrine and practice : I do not mean now—but if I live, and can work out some points, on which I have not yet got far enough to authorize me to address others, yet I think I see my way to some useful truths. Meantime I trust I shall not give just cause of offence to any good and wise man—or of personal offence to any man.

VIII. TO A PARENT HOLDING UNITARIAN OPINIONS.

Rugby, June 15, 1829.

I had occasion to speak to your son this evening on the subject of the approaching confirmation ; and, as I had understood that his friends were not members of the Established Church, my object was not so much to persuade him to be confirmed, as to avail myself of the opportunity thus afforded me to speak with him generally on the subject of his state as a Christian, and the peculiar temptations to which he was now peculiarly exposed, and the nature of that hope and faith which he would require as his best defence. But, on inquiring to what persuasion his friends belonged, I found that they were Unitarians. I felt myself therefore unable to proceed, because, as nothing would be more repugnant to my notions of fair dealing, than to avail myself indirectly of my opportunities of influencing a boy's mind contrary to the religious belief of his parents, without giving them the fullest notice, so, on the other hand, when the differences of belief are so great and so many, I feel that I could not at all enter into the subject, without enforcing principles wholly contrary to those in which your son has been brought up. This difficulty will increase with every half-year that he remains at the school, as he will be gradually coming more and more under my immediate care ; and I can neither suffer any of those boys with whom I am more immediately connected, to be left without religious instruction, nor can I give it in his case, without unavoidably imparting views, wholly different from those entertained by the persons whom he is naturally most disposed to love and honour. Under these circumstances, I think it fair to state to you, what line I shall feel bound to follow, after the knowledge which I have gained of your son's religious belief. In everything I should say to him on the subject, I should use every possible pains and delicacy to avoid hurting his feelings with regard to his relations ; but at the same time, I cannot avoid labouring to impress on him, what is my belief on the most valuable truths in Christianity, and which, I fear, must be sadly at variance with the tenets in which he has been brought up. I should not do this controversially, and in the case of any other form of dissent from the Establishment, I would avoid dwelling on the differences between us, because I could teach all that I conceive to be essential in Christianity, without at all touching upon them. But in this instance, it is impossible to avoid interfering with the very points most at issue. I have a very good opinion of your son, both as to his conduct and abilities, and I should be very sorry to lose him from the school. I think, also, that any one who knows me, would give you ample assurance that I have not the slightest feeling against Dissenters as such, or any desire, but rather very much the contrary, to make this school exclusive. My difficulty with your son is not one which I feel as a Churchman, but as a Christian ; and goes only on this simple principle, that I feel bound to teach the essentials of Christianity to all those committed to my care—and with these the tenets of the Unitarians alone, among all the Dissenters in the kingdom, are in my judgment irreconcileable. I trust that you will forgive me for having troubled you thus at length on this subject.

IX.   TO REV. GEORGE CORNISH.

(After the death of his father-in-law.)

Rugby, September 2, 1829.

I, too, had been meditating a letter to you for some time past, when the sight of yours roused me to make a vigorous

effort, and here I have regularly begun a sheet of paper to you.
You will perhaps have heard already that all our anxiety for
Mr. Penrose was speedily and mercifully terminated, by as
blessed a death as I suppose ever was witnessed. Although
we were naturally anxious about him, because his attacks,
though very slight and transient, had rather increased in fre-
quency, yet he was perfectly able to perform all his usual
duties, and enjoy his usual comforts in his family, and even his ·
amusements in attending to his garden. On the Thursday
before his death he was standing on his ladder, and pruning
his vine for some time, and he went to bed perfectly well. The
next morning he was seized with a more violent attack, but
still without pain, or without affecting his senses, and all he
said indicated perfect Christian peace. A second attack the
same morning made him speechless, and he soon sank into a
lethargic slumber, in which he remained till Sunday night,
when he expired in the arms of his children without a struggle.
We arrived in time to see him alive, although he was then
insensible, and M. followed him to his grave on the Thursday
following, with her aunts, brothers, and sisters, and John Keble
to read the funeral service. . . . . When I dwell on the entire
happiness that we are tasting day after day and year after year,
it really seems startling ; and the sense of so much and such
continued temporal mercy, is even more than humbling,—it is
at times even fearful to me when I look within, and know how
little truly grateful I am for it. All the children are well,
and all, I trust, improving in character—thanks to their dear
mother's care for them, who, under God, has been their constant corrector and guide. As for myself, I think of Wordsworth's lines,

> Yes ; they can make who fail to find
> Brief leisure e'en in busiest days, &c.

and I know how much need I have to make such moments of
leisure ; for else one goes on still employed, till all makes progress, except our spiritual life, and that, I fear, goes backward.
The very dealing, as I do, with beings in the highest state of
bodily health and spirits, is apt to give a corresponding carelessness to my own mind. I must be all alive and vigorous to
manage them, and to do my work ; very different from the
contemplations of sickness and sorrow, which so often present
themselves to a man who has the care of a parish. And,
indeed, my spirits in themselves are a great blessing, for with-

out them the work would weigh me down, whereas now I seem to throw it off like the fleas from a dog's back when he shakes himself.　May I only learn daily and hourly σωφρονεῖν.

I am very much delighted with what you say of my pamphlet [on the Roman Catholic claims].　I know it gave —— pain, and I fear it has ——, and others of my friends.　Yet, I know that I did not write it with one atom of unkindness or violence of feeling—nor do I think that the language or tone is violent; and what I said of the clergy, I said in the very simplicity of my heart, no more imagining that it would give offence, than if I had said that they were unacquainted generally with military tactics or fortification.　The part which you object to was not put in unthinkingly—but I wished very much to bring the matter of schism to an issue; and if any respectable man were to notice that part of the pamphlet, I should like to enter more fully into the subject.　My own notions upon it have grown up wholly out of the New Testament, and because I never have thought, that what people call the Primitive Church, and much less the Ante-Nicene Church more generally, was any better *authority* per se, than the Church of Rome, or the Greek Church.　But I do not know that what I have said in the pamphlet goes at all beyond the fair conclusions to be drawn from our own Article,* which gives to any national Church an authority to manage its own concerns, where God has not laid down any fixed rule; and, besides, what resemblance is there between the government of the most ancient Episcopal Churches, and that of the Church of England, to those who regard resemblances or differences of government to consist in things more than in names?　I think, that what I have said in my pamphlet merely goes so far as to assert, that there is no schism in the Church of England having nothing to do with the Bishop of Rome, or in the Kirk of Scotland having nothing to do with any Archbishops and Bishops at all; but that I have not at all treated of the question of different ecclesiastical societies existing in one and the same civil society like our English Dissenters, whatever my own opinions may be about the matter.　I find people continually misunderstanding the strong distinction which I draw between individuals and societies, insomuch that Faber charges me with saying, that every individual has a right to govern himself, which I have specially disclaimed in divers places;

---

* Article 34.

being, in fact, a firm believer in the duty of absolute passive
obedience, in all cases between an individual and the govern-‐
ment—but not when the individual is acting as a member of
the society, and their concurrence with him tells him that obedience is now a misplaced term—because there is no authority
in a rebellious government—rebellious against society—to
claim obedience. I am sure that my views in this matter are
neither seditious nor turbulent—and I think I stated them
clearly, but it seems they were not clear to everybody.

X.   TO REV. F. C. BLACKSTONE.

Rugby, October 14, 1829.

. . . . . I never felt more strongly the desire of keeping up
my old friendships, and it often grieves me to think how little
I see or hear of many of those for whom I feel the strongest
regard. I do not mean that this is their fault rather than
mine, or that it is a fault at all; but it is a tendency of middle
life and settled occupation, which I think we ought to struggle
against, or else it grows with a fearful rapidity. I am very
anxious to express my repentance of that passage in my pamphlet, which you allude to, "raving about idolatry," &c. I
mean my repentance of its tone and language, for the substance of it I think correct, and that men whose most ignorant,
and worse than ignorant, application of English history had, to
say the truth, made me angry, are likely to do a great deal of
mischief in Ireland. But the expression was unkind, and too
sweeping, and I certainly ought not, nor would I, speak of all
those as "raving about idolatry," whose opinions as to the
guilt of the Romish Church differ from my own. With regard
to the apparent inconsistency between the sermons and the
pamphlet, you will find the term "practically idolatry" applied
to the Roman Catholic system in some countries, even in the
pamphlet. I never wish to mince the matter with their practices, but still, in principle, I cannot call the Romish Church
an idolatrous Church in that strong sense as to warrant Faber's
conclusions, even putting aside the difference of Christian
times from Jewish. I should compare their superstitions to
the worship of the brazen serpent, which Hezekiah did away
with, which appears to have been long in existence, and which,
in many of its worshippers, at any rate, was practically idolatry;

but I should not have called the Jewish Church idolatrous so long as this worship was encouraged, nor applied to it the language of " Come out of her, my people," &c. . . . . .

Of the moral state of the boys, for which of course I care infinitely the most, I can judge the least ; our advantages in that respect are great, at least in the absence of many temptations to gross vice ; but to cultivate a good spirit in the highest sense is a far different thing from shutting out one or two gross evils from want of opportunity.

XI.   TO REV. J. TUCKER.

Rugby, October 26, 1829.

. . . . . If we are alive fifteen years hence, I think I would go with you gladly to Swan River, if they will make me schoolmaster there, and lay my bones in the land of kangaroos and opossums. I laugh about it ; yet if my wife were alive, and able to go, I should think it a very great benefit to the good cause to go out with all my family, and become a Swan River man ; and I should try to get others of our friends to go out with us. My notion is, that no missionaryizing is half so beneficial, as to try to pour sound and healthy blood into a young civilized society ; to make one colony, if possible, like the ancient colonies, or like New England—a living sucker from the mother-country, bearing the same blossoms and the same fruits, not a reproduction of its vilest excrescences, its ignorance, and its wickedness, while all its good elements are left behind in the process. No words can tell the evil of such colonies as we have hitherto planted, where the best parts of the new society have been men too poor to carry with them or to gain much of the higher branches of knowledge ; or else mere official functionaries from England, whose hearts and minds have been always half at home, and who have never identified themselves with the land in which they were working. But if you and your sisters were to go out, with half Southborough after you, — apothecary, lawyers, butchers, bakers, tailors, carpenters, and labourers,—and if we were to join with a similar draught from Rugby and Laleham, I think we should deserve to be ἀναγραπτοὶ εὐεργέται both here and in Swan River. Such are my notions about it ; and I am not clear that I shall not devote my first £1,000 that I make here to the purchase of land in Swan River, that I may have my estate and the school buildings got into due order, before I shut up shop at Rugby.   Meantime, I hope you will not think I ought to shut up shop forthwith, and adjourn to the next asylum for daft people, because I am thus wildly dreaming about Swan River, instead of talking soberly about Rugby. But Rugby is a very nice place all the same, and I wish you would come and form your own judgment of it, or that some of your sisters would, if you cannot or will not.

———

XII.   TO J. T. COLERIDGE, ESQ.

Rugby, November 4, 1829.

What a time it is since I wrote to you !   And how much has occurred and is continually occurring, on which I should like to write to you.   You have heard perhaps of Mr. Penrose's death in September last, when, from the enjoyment of full health and vigour of mind and body, he was called away in three days with no intermediate pain or struggle, but by a gentle lethargic sleep, which lasted uninterrupted to his very last moment.   Coupled with his holy and Christian life, which made him require no long time to go and renew his exhausted oil, his end was a most complete $εὐθανασία$, so rare a blessing, that one dares not hope or pray for a similar mercy in one's own case. . . . .

We are going on comfortably, and I trust, thrivingly, with the school.   We are above 200, and still looking upwards ; but I neither expect, and much less desire, any great addition to our numbers.   The school cannot, I think, regularly expect more than 200 or 250 ; it may ascend higher with a strong flood, but there will be surely a corresponding ebb after it. You may imagine that I ponder over, often enough, the various discussions that I have had with you about education, and verse making, and reading the Poets.   I find the natural leaning of a schoolmaster is so much to your view of the question, that my reason is more than ever led to think my own notions strongly required in the present state of classical education, if it were only on the principle of the bent stick.   There is something so beautiful in good Latin verses, and in hearing fine poetry well construed, and something so attractive altogether in good scholarship, that I do not wonder at masters

directing an undue portion of their attention to a crop so brilliant. I feel it growing in myself daily; and if I feel it, with
prejudices all on the other side, I do not wonder at its being
felt generally. But my deliberate conviction is stronger and
stronger, that all this system is wholly wrong for the greater
number of boys. Those who have talents and natural taste,
and fondness for poetry, find the poetry lessons very useful;
the mass do not feel one tittle about the matter, and, I speak
advisedly, do not, in my belief, benefit from them one grain.
I am not sure that other things would answer better, though I
have very little doubt of it; but at any rate the present plan is
so entire a failure, that nothing can be risked by changing it.
. . . . . . More than half my boys never saw the sea, and
never were in London, and it is surprising how the first of
these disadvantages interferes with their understanding much
of the ancient poetry, while the other keeps the range of their
ideas in an exceedingly narrow compass. Brought up myself
in the Isle of Wight, amidst the bustle of soldiers and sailors,
and familiar from a child with boats and ships, and the flags of
half Europe, which gave me an instinctive acquaintance with
geography, I quite marvel to find in what a state of ignorance
boys are at seventeen or eighteen, who have lived all their
days in inland country parishes, or small country towns. . . . . .
For your comfort, I think I am succeeding in making them
write very fair Latin prose, and to observe and understand
some of the differences between the Latin and English idioms.
On the other hand, what our boys want in one way they get in
another; from the very circumstance of their being the sons of
quieter parents, they have far less ὕβρις and more εὐήθεια, than
the boys of any other school I ever knew. Thus, to say the
least, they have less of a most odious and unchristian quality,
and are thus more open to instruction, and have less repug-
nance to be good, because their master wishes them to be so.
. . . . . . I have almost filled my paper, and can only add that
Thucydides is getting on slowly, but I think it will be a much
less defective book than it was likely to have been had I
remained at Laleham: for though I have still an enormous
deal to learn, yet my scholarship has mended considerably
within the last year at Rugby. I suppose you will think at
any rate that it will be better to publish Thucydides, however
imperfectly, than to write another pamphlet. Poor dear pamphlet ! I seem to feel the greater tenderness for it, because it
has excited so much odium ; and now I hear that it is reported

at Oxford that I wish to suppress it; which is wholly untrue.
I would not print a second edition, because the question was
settled, and controversy about it was become absurd; but I
never have repented of it in any degree, or wished it unwritten,
" pace tuâ dixerim," and I only regret that I did not print a
larger impression.

XIII.   TO REV. H. JENKINS.

Rugby, November 11, 1829.

I thank you heartily for two very kind letters, and am very
anxious to be favoured with some more of your friend's comments [on Thucydides]. . . . . I hope I am not too old or
too lazy or too obstinate to be taught better. . . . . I do
thank you very much for your kindness in taking so much
trouble in my behalf; and I earnestly beg of you to send me
more. . . . . And can you tell me, or, if not, will you ask
Amicus Doct.,—where is to be found a summary of the
opinions of English scholars about ὅπως and ὅπως μή, and the
moods which they require : and further, do you or he hold
their doctrine good for anything?   Dawes, and all men who
endeavour to establish general rules, are of great use in directing one's attention to points which one might otherwise have
neglected; and labour and acuteness often discover a rule,
where indolence and carelessness fancied it was all haphazard.
But larger induction and sounder judgment (which I think
exist in Hermann in an infinite degree beyond any of our English scholars) teach us to distinguish again between a principle
and an usage; the latter may be general, but if it be merely
usage, grounded on no intelligible principle, it seems to me
foolish to insist on its being universal, and to alter texts right
and left, to make them all conformable to the Canon.   Equi-
dem,—both in Greek and in other matters,—I think liberty a
far better thing than uniformity of form merely, where no principle is concerned.   Voilà the cloven foot.

XIV.   TO J. T. COLERIDGE, ESQ.

(In allusion to a libel in the John Bull.)

Rugby, May 11, 1830.

I thank you for another very kind letter.   In a matter of
this sort, I willingly resign my own opinion to that of a man

like yourself, at once my friend and legal adviser. I think, too, that I am almost bound to attend to the opinion of the Bishop of London ; for his judgment of the inexpediency of prosecuting must rest on the scandal which he thinks it will bring upon religion and the Church, and of this he is a far better judge than I am ; nor, to say the truth, should I much like to act in a doubtful manner in opposition to the decided advice of a Bishop in a case that concerned the Church. I say this in sober earnest, in spite of what you call my Whiggery and Radicalism. . . . . .

XV. TO REV. DR. HAWKINS.

Rugby, May 12, 1830.

. . . . . . The authorities which are arrayed against proceeding are quite decisive, and I heartily agree with you that clergymen must not go to law, when lawyers say they should not. Still, as I had no thought of gain or of vengeance, but simply of procuring a public justification of my character—not my opinions—I feel that it would have been no lack of charity to proceed, though I am heartily glad to be spared the necessity of doing so by so many and such powerful representations. But I trust that you and all my friends will give me credit for being perfectly tolerant of all attacks upon my writings or general abuse of my opinions. . . . . Believe me, I am heartily glad of the final result of this discussion, for I had no wish to go to law ; but I thought that my own, or rather my misrepresented opinions on politics, ought to make me particularly anxious to deny any charge respecting religious matters. But I am perfectly willing to take the judgment of my friends and of impartial persons in what rests wholly on opinion, and besides, if the attack or loss to my own character were ever so great, I should quite agree with you that it was better to bear it, than to bring sacred things into discussion in places, and through disputants wholly unfitted for them. But this I at first did not contemplate as the likely result.

XVI. TO F. HARTWELL, ESQ.

Rugby, June 28, 1830.

. . . . . I have just published one volume of Thucydides ; when the others will follow, it is hard to say, for the work here is more and more engrossing continually; but I like it better and better; it has all the interest of a great game of chess, with living creatures for pawns and pieces, and your adversary, in plain English, the Devil: truly he plays a very tough game, and is very hard to beat, if I ever do beat him. It is quite surprising to see the wickedness of young boys; or would be surprising, if I had not my own school experience and a good deal since to enlighten me.

XVII.   TO REV. GEORGE CORNISH.

Rugby, August 24, 1830.

Your letter was a most welcome sight to me the first morning of my arrival at home, amidst the host of strange hand-writings and letters of business which now greet me every morning. It rejoices me to think that we are going to have a cousin of yours at Rugby, and I suppose we shall see him here on Saturday, when the great coach starts. You know that it is licensed to carry not exceeding 260 passengers, besides the foundationers. I agreed with the Pythagoreans that τὸ ἀόριστον was one of the number of κάκα, and so I applied to the Trustees, and got the limit set. We are not near it yet, being not quite 260, including foundationers, and perhaps may never reach it; but that I shall not at all regret, and all I wanted was never to go beyond it. We have got a Cambridge man, a Fellow of Trinity, who was most highly recommended to me, as a new master; and I hope we shall pull hard and all together during the next half-year: there is plenty to be done, I can assure you; but thank God, I continue to enjoy the work, and am now in excellent condition for setting to it. You may see M——'s name and mine amongst the subscribers for the sufferers at Paris. It seems to me a most blessed revolution, spotless beyond all example in history, and the most glorious instance of a royal rebellion against society, promptly and energetically repressed, that the world has yet seen. It magnificently vindicates the cause of knowledge and liberty, showing how humanizing to all classes of society are the spread of thought and information, and improved political institutions; and it lays the crimes of the last revolution just in the right place, the wicked aristocracy, that had so brutalized the people by its long iniquities that they were like slaves broken loose when they first bestirred themselves.

Before all these events took place, on my way out through France, I was reading Guizot's History of the Progress of Civilization in France from the earliest times. You know he is now Minister of the Interior, and one of the ablest writers in France. In his book he gives a history of the Pelagian controversy, a most marvellous contrast with the Liberals of a former day, or with our Westminster Reviewers now. Guizot sides with St. Augustine ; but the whole chapter is most worthy of notice ; the freedom of the will, so far as to leave a consciousness of guilt when we have not done our duty,—the corruption of our nature, which never lets us in fact come up to what we know we ought to do, and the help derived from prayers to God,—are stated as incontrovertible philosophical facts, of which every man's experience may convince him ; and Guizot blames Pelagius for so exaggerating the notion of human freedom as to lose sight of our need of external assistance. And there is another chapter on the unity of the Church no less remarkable. Now Guizot is Professor of History in the University of Paris, and a most eminent Liberal ; and it seems to me worthy of all notice to observe his language with regard to religion. And I saw Niebuhr at Bonn, on my way home, and talked with him for three hours ; and I am satisfied from my own ears, if I had any doubts before, of the grossness of the slander which called him an unbeliever. I was every way delighted with him, and liked very much what I saw of his wife and children. Trevenen and his wife enjoyed the journey exceedingly, and are all the better for it. Amongst other things, I visited the Grand Chartreuse, which is certainly enough to make a man romantic, and the Church of Madonna del Monte ; from whence, or rather from a mountain above it, I counted twelve mountain outlines between me and the horizon, —the last, the ridge of the highest Alps—upon a sky so glowing with the sunset, that instead of looking white from their snow, they were like the teeth of a saw upon a plate of a red hot iron, all deep and black. I was delighted also with Venice ; most of all delighted to see the secret prisons of the old aristocracy converted into lumber rooms, and to see German soldiers exercising authority in that place, which was once the very focus of the moral degradation of the Italian race, the seat of falsehood and ignorance and cruelty. They talk of building a bridge to Venice over the Lagune ; if so, I am glad that I have seen it first. I liked Padua also, more than I thought I could have liked the birthplace of Titus Livius. The influence

of the clergy must be great there, and most beneficially exercised; for a large·institution for the poor of Padua, providing
for those who are out of work, as well as for the old and infirm,
derives its main support from legacies; the clergy never
failing to urge every man who can at all afford it to leave some·
thing at his death for this object.   We came home through the
Tyrol, and through Wurtemburg and Baden, countries apparently as peaceful and prosperous and simple-mannered as I
ever saw; it is quite economical travelling there.   And now,
when shall I travel to Kenwyn?   I hope one of these days;
but whether in the next winter or not it is hard to say; I only
know that there are few things which I should enjoy better.   I
was so sorry to miss old Tucker, who came here for one day
when I was abroad; he was at Leamington with his sister, to
consult our great oracle, Jephson.   Charles, I suppose, is only
coming home upon leave, and will go out again; I should be
very glad to see him, and to show him his marks on my
Hederic's Lexicon when he was at Wyatt's.   I wish I may be
able to do anything for you as to a curate, but I am very much
out of the world in those matters, and I have no regular correspondence with Oxford.   I am afraid I am sadly in disgrace
with all parties, between my Pamphlet and Sermons, and I am
afraid that Thucydides will not mend the matter.   As for the
Pamphlet, that is all natural enough, but I really did not think
there was any cloven foot in the Sermons, nor did I wish to
show any; not, I hope, from time-serving, but because, what
you said about the schism question, I wished to do with that and
divers other points,—*i.e.* reserve them for a separate volume,
which I hope I may be able to publish before I die.   There are
some points on which I feel almost as if I had a testimony to
deliver, which I ought not to withhold.   And Milman's History
of the Jews made me more and more eager to deliver myself of
my conceptions.   But how to do it without interfering with
other and even more pressing duties I cannot tell.   Last half-
year, I preached every Sunday in Lent, and for the last five
Sundays of the half-year also, besides other times; and I had to
write new sermons for all these, for I cannot bear to preach to
the boys anything but what is quite fresh, and suggested by
their particular condition.   I never like preaching anywhere
else so well; for one's boys are even more than a parish, inasmuch as one knows more of them all individually, than can
easily be the case in a parish, and has a double authority over
them, temporal as well as spiritual. . . . . .   Though, to speak

seriously, it is quite awful to watch the strength of evil in such young minds, and how powerless is every effort against it. It would give the vainest man alive a very fair notion of his own insufficiency, to see how little he can do, and how his most earnest addresses are as a cannon-ball on a bolster; thorough careless unimpressibleness beats one all to pieces. And so it is, and so it will be; and, as far as I am concerned, I can quite say that it is much better that it should be so; for it would be too kindling, could one perceive these young minds really led from evil by one's own efforts: one would be sorely tempted to bow down to one's own net. As it is, the net is so palpably ragged, that one sees perforce how sorry an idol it would make. But I must go to bed, and spare your eyes and your patience.

XVIII.   TO REV. DR. HAWKINS.

Rugby, November, 1830.

I am always glad to write to you, but I have now two especial causes for doing so; one to thank you for your Visitation sermon, and another to explain to you why I do not think it right to comply with your wishes touching the tricolour work-bag. For your sermon, I thank you for it; I believe I agree with it almost entirely, waiving some expressions, which I hold one should never cavil about, where one agrees in sub-stance. But have you ever clearly defined to yourself what you mean by " one society," as applied to the whole Christian Church upon earth? It seems to me that most of what I con-sider the errors about " the Church," turn upon an imperfect understanding of this point. In one sense, and that a very important one, all Christians belong to one society; but then it is more like Cicero's sense of " societas," than what we mean by a society. There is a " societas generis humani," and a " societas hominum Christianorum;" but there is not one " respublica " or " civitas " of either, but a great many. The Roman Catholics say there is but one " respublica," and there-fore, with perfect consistency, they say that there must be one central government; our Article, if I mistake not its sense, says, and with great truth, that the Christian Respublica depends on the political Respublica: that is, that there may be at least as many Christian societies as there are political societies, and that there may be, and in our own kingdom are, even more.*

* See Appendix II. (d) to Fragment on the Church.

If there be one Christian society, in the common sense of the
word, there must be one government; whereas, in point of
fact, the Scotch Church, the English Church, and the French
Church, have all separate and perfectly independent govern-
ments; and consequently can only be in an unusual and
peculiar sense " one society;" that is, spiritually one, as having
the same objects and the same principles, and the same sup-
ports, and the same enemies. You therefore seem to be right,
in saying that a Roman Catholic should be addressed in
England as a Dissenter; but all this appears to me to lead
necessarily to this conclusion — that the constitution and
government of every Church is a political institution, and that
conformity and nonconformity are so far matters of civil law,
that, where nonconformity, as in England, is strictly legal, it is
no offence, except in so far as it may be accompanied with
heretical opinions, which is merely κατὰ συμβεβηκὸς. For the
State says that there may be any given number of religious
societies within its jurisdiction—societies, that is, in the common sense of the term, as bodies governing themselves ; and it
is clear that the State may lawfully say this, for, if the Church
were one society, in this sense, by Christ's institution, then the
Romanist doctrine would be true, and, I do not say the Pope,
but certainly a General Council would possess an authority
paramount in ecclesiastical matters, payment of tithes, &c., to
any local and human authority of Kings or Parliaments of
this or that political division of the human race. I have
thought not a little upon all this matter in my time, and I
fancy that I see my own way straight; whether other people
will think so is a different question.

(After explaining a false report about a tricoloured cockade
and work-bag.) It is worse than obnoxious to apply this to
English politics, and if any man seriously considers me to wish
for a revolution here, with my seven children and a good house
to lose (to put it on no other ground,) why he must even continue to think so. But I do admire the Revolution in France
—admire it as heartily and entirely as any event recorded in
history ; and I think that it becomes every individual, still more
every clergyman, and most of all, every clergyman in a public
situation, to express this opinion publicly and decidedly.
I have not forgotten the twenty years' war into which the
English aristocracy and clergy drove Mr. Pitt in 1793, and
which the Quarterly Review and other such writers are now
seeking to repeat. I hold it to be of incalculable importance,

that, while the conduct of France has been beyond all example
pure and heroic, there should be so manifest a display of
sympathy on the part of England, as to lead to a real mutual
confidence and friendship between the two countries. Our
government, I believe, is heartily disposed to do this, and I
will not, for one, shrink from avowing a noble cause and a
noble nation, because a party in England, joined through
timidity by a number of men who have really no sympathy with
it, choose to try to excommunicate all who will not join them.
I have myself heard them expressing hearty approbation of the
French Revolution, and yet shrink from avowing it, lest they
should appear to join the Radicals. And thus they leave the
Radicals in exclusive possession of sentiments which they
themselves join in, just as they would leave the Useful
Knowledge Society to the Benthamites. I quarrel with no
man for disapproving of the revolution, except he does it in
such a manner as to excite national animosities, and so tend to
provoke a war; but in a case so flagrant—a case of as clear
right as the abolition of the slave trade—it is clearly not for
the friends of France to suppress or conceal their sentiments.
About Belgium the case is wholly different: there, the merits
of the quarrel are far more doubtful, and the conduct of the
popular party far less pure; and there I have no sympathy with
the Belgians. But, France, if it were only for the contrast to
the first revolution, deserves, I think, the warmest admiration,
and the most cordial expression of it. I have written now
more upon this subject than I have either written or spoken
upon it before to any one; for indeed I have very little time,
and no inclination for disputes on such matters. But, if I am
questioned about my opinions, and required to conceal them,
as if I were ashamed of them, I think it right then to avow
them plainly, and to explain my reasons for them. There is
not a man in England who is less a party man than I am, for
in fact no party would own me; and, when I was at ——'s in
the summer, he looked upon me to be quite illiberal. But
those who hold their own opinions in a string, will suppose that
their neighbours do the same.

CHAPTER VI.

PERHAPS no more striking instance of his deep interest
in the state of the country could be found, than in the
gloom with which his correspondence is suddenly overcast in the autumn of 1830. The alarming aspect of
English society brought to view in the rural disturbances
in the winter of 1830, and additionally darkened in
1831–32, by the visitation of the Cholera, and the political
agitations of the Reform Bill, little as it came within his
own experience, gave a colour to his whole mind. Of
his state of feeling at this time, no better example can
be given than the five sermons appended to the opening
course of his practical school sermons, in his second
volume, especially the last of them, which was preached
in the chapel on the Sunday when the news of the
arrival of the Cholera in England first reached Rugby.
There are those amongst his pupils who can never forget
the moment when, on that dark November afternoon,
after the simple preface, stating in what sense worldly
thoughts were or were not to be brought into that place,
he at once began with that solemnity which marked his
voice and manner when speaking of what deeply moved

him :—" I need not tell you that this is a marked time—a time such as neither we, nor our fathers for many generations before us, have experienced ; and to those who know what the past has been, it is no doubt awful to think of the change which we are now about to encounter." (Serm. vol. ii. p. 413.) But in him the sight of evil, and the endeavour to remove it, were hardly ever disjoined ; and whilst everything which he felt partook of the despondency with which that sermon opens, everything which he did partakes of that cheerful activity with which the same sermon closes in urging the example of the Apostle's "wise and manly conduct amidst the dangers of storm and shipwreck."

The alarm which he felt was shared by many of the most opposite opinions to his own ; but there could have been few whom it touched at once on so many points. The disturbances of the time were to him the very evils which he had anticipated even as far back as 1819; they struck on some of the most sensitive of his natural feelings—his sense of justice, and his impatience of the sight of suffering : they seemed to him symptoms of a deepseated disease in all the relations of English society—the results of a long series of evils from the neglect of the eighteenth century—of the lawlessness of the feudal system—of the oppressions of the Norman conquest—of the dissoluteness of the Roman empire—of the growth of those social and national sins which the Hebrew Prophets had denounced, and which Christianity in its full practical development was designed to check.*

Hence arose his anxiety to see the clergy take it up, as he had himself endeavoured to do in the sermons already noticed.

" I almost despair," he said, "of anything that any private or local efforts can do. I think that the clergy as a body might

* See Misc. Works, pp. 176, 192, 276. Hist. of Rome, i. 266.

do much, if they were steadily to observe the evils of the times, and preach fearlessly against them. I cannot understand what is the good of a national Church if it be not to Christianize the nation, and introduce the principles of Christianity into men's social and civil relations, and expose the wickedness of that spirit which maintains the game laws, and in agriculture and trade seems to think that there is no such sin as covetousness, and that if a man is not dishonest, he has nothing to do but to make all the profit of his capital that he can."

Hence, again, his anxiety to impart or see imparted to the publications of the Society for the Diffusion of Useful Knowledge, then in the first burst of their reputation, and promising to exercise a really extensive influence on the country at large, something of the religious spirit, in which they seemed to him to be deficient.

"I am not wishing to see the Society's tracts turned into sermons,—far less to see them intermeddle in what are strictly theological controversies;—but I am sure that, with the exception of the Unitarians, all Christians have a common ground in all that is essential in Christianity, and beyond that I never wish to go;—and it does seem to me as forced and unnatural in us now to dismiss the principles of the Gospel and its great motives from our consideration,—as is done habitually, for example, in Miss Edgeworth's books,—as it is to fill our pages with Hebraisms, and to write and speak in the words and style of the Bible. The slightest touches of Christian principle and Christian hope in the Society's biographical and historical articles would be a sort of living salt to the whole;—and would exhibit that union which I never will consent to think unattainable, between goodness and wisdom; —between everything that is manly, sensible, and free, and everything that is pure and self-denying, and humble, and heavenly."

His communications with the Society, made, however, from the nature of the case, rather through individuals than officially, were at one time frequent; and though, from the different view which it took of its proper province, he was finally induced to discontinue them, he felt great reluctance in abandoning his hope of being able to co-operate with a body which he "believed might, with God's blessing, do more good of all kinds, political, intellectual, and spiritual, than any other society in existence."

"There was a show of reason," he said, "in excluding Christianity from the plan of the Society's works, so long as they avowedly confined themselves to science or to intellectual instruction: but in a paper intended to improve its readers *morally*, to make men better and happier, as well as better informed, surely neutrality with regard to Christianity is, virtually, hostility." "For myself," he adds, "I am well aware of my own insignificance, but if there were no other objection to the Penny Magazine assuming a decidedly Christian tone, than mere difficulties of execution, I would most readily offer my best services, such as they are, to the Society, and would endeavour to furnish them regularly with articles of the kind that I desire. My occupations here are so engrossing, that it would be personally very inconvenient to me to do so; and I am not so absurd as to think my offer of any value, except in the single case of a practical difficulty existing as to finding a writer, should the principle itself be approved of. I am fully convinced that if the Penny Magazine were decidedly and avowedly Christian, many of the clergy throughout the kingdom would be most delighted to assist its circulation by every means in their power. For myself, I should think that I could not do too much to contribute to the support of what would then be so great a national blessing; and I should beg to be allowed to offer £50 annually towards it, so long as my remaining in my present situation enabled me to gratify my inclinations to that extent."

The most practical attempt at the realization of these views, was his own endeavours to set up a weekly newspaper, *The Englishman's Register*, which he undertook in 1831, "more to relieve his own conscience than with any sanguine hope of doing good," but "earnestly desiring to speak to the people the words of truth and soberness—to tell them plainly the evils that exist, and lead them, if I can, to their causes and their remedies." He was the proprietor, though not the sole editor, and he contributed the chief articles in it (signed A.), consisting chiefly of explanations of Scripture, and of comments on the political events of the day. It died a natural death in a few weeks, partly from his want of leisure to control it properly, and from the great expenses which it entailed upon him—partly from the want of cordial sympathy in any of the existing parties of the country. Finding, however, that some of his articles had been copied into the Sheffield *Courant*, by its editor, Mr. Platt, he opened a communication with him in July, 1831, which he maintained ever afterwards, and commenced writing a series of Letters in that paper, which, to the number of thirteen, were afterwards published separately, and constitute the best exposition of his views on the main causes of social distress in England.

It was now that, with " the thirst for a lodge in some vast wilderness, which in these times of excitement," he writes to a friend, "is almost irresistible," he began to turn his thoughts to what ultimately became his home in Westmoreland. It was now, also, that as he came more into contact with public affairs, he began to feel the want of sympathy and the opposition which he subsequently experienced on a larger scale. " I have no man like-minded with me," he writes to Archbishop Whately,— "none with whom I can cordially sympathize ; there are many good men to be found, and many clever men, some, too, who are both good and clever ; but yet there is a want of some greatness of mind, or singleness of purpose, or delicacy of feeling, which makes them grate against the edge of one's inner man." This was the period when he felt most keenly his differences with the so-called Evangelical party, to which, on the one hand, he naturally looked for co-operation, as the body which at that time was placed at the head of the religious convictions of the country, but from which, on the other hand, he was constantly repelled by his strong sense of the obstacles which (as he thought) their narrow views and technical phraseology, were for ever opposing to the real and practical application of the Old and New Testament, as the remedy of the great wants of the age, social, moral, and intellectual.*

It was his own conviction of these wants which now more than ever awakened his desire for a commentary on the Scriptures, which should explain their true reference to the present state of England and of the world, as well as remove some of the intellectual difficulties, especially in the Old Testament, to which men's minds seemed to be growing more and more awake. And this, for the time, he endeavoured to accomplish by the statement of some of his general principles of interpretation in the Essay on that subject, which he affixed to his second volume of Sermons published in December, 1831. The objections which this Essay excited at the time, in various quarters were very great, and according to his own belief it exposed him to more misunderstanding than any other of his writings. But he never wavered in the conviction that its publication had been an imperative duty—it was written, as he said, "professionally, from his having had so much to do with young men, and from knowing what they wanted;" even in the last year of his life, he said that he looked upon it as the most

---

* In illustration of this view as represented in the present chapter it may be well to refer to Introd. to Serm. vol. iv. p. xxv., and to give the following extract from a MS. Preface to a volume of Sermons in 1829. "Their peculiarities as a party seem to me to arise simply from these causes—a good Christian, with a low understanding, a bad education, and ignorance of the world, becomes an Evangelical, — whilst, on the other hand, if you were to enlarge the understanding of an Evangelical, if you could remedy the defects of his education, and supply him with abundant knowledge of men and things, he would then become a most complete specimen of a true Christian."

important thing he had ever written. "I thought it
likely," he writes at the time to a friend, "with God's
blessing, to be so beneficial, that I published it at the
end of this volume, rather than wait for another opportunity, because under that sense of the great uncertainty
of human life which the present state of things brings
especially home to my mind, I should be sorry to die
without having circulated what I believe will be to many
most useful and most satisfactory." "I am sure," he
writes, in answer to the objections of another friend,
"that the more the subject is considered, men will find
that they have been afraid of a groundless danger, and
the further I follow up my own views, the more they
appear to me to harmonize with the whole system of
God's revelations, and not only absolutely to do away
with all the difficulties of the Scriptures, but to turn
many of them into valuable instructions."*

XIX.   TO J. T. COLERIDGE, ESQ.

Rugby, November 1, 1830.

It is quite high time that I should write to you, for weeks and
months go by, and it is quite startling to think how little communication I hold with many of those whom I love most dearly.
And yet these are times, when I am least of all disposed to
loosen the links which bind me to my oldest and dearest
friends, for I imagine we shall all want the union of all the good
men we can get together; and the want of sympathy which I
cannot but feel towards so many of those whom I meet with,
makes me think how delightful it would be to have daily intercourse with those with whom I ever feel it thoroughly. What
men do in middle life, without a wife and children to turn to,
I cannot imagine ; for I think the affections must be sadly
checked and chilled, even in the best men, by their intercourse
with people, such as one usually finds them in the world. I

---

* Some of the points touched upon in this Essay are enlarged upon in his Sermons—that on "the Lord's Day," in the third volume, and those on "Phinehas," "Jael," and "the Disobedient Prophet," in the sixth.

do not mean that one does not meet with good and sensible people ; but then their minds are set, and our minds are set, and they will not, in mature age, grow into each other. But with a home filled with those whom we entirely love and sympathize with, and with some old friends, to whom one can open one's heart fully from time to time, the world's society has rather a bracing influence to make one shake off mere dreams of delight. You must not think me bilious or low-spirited ;—I never felt better or more inclined to work ;—but one gets pathetic with thinking of the present and the past, and of the days and the people that you and I have seen together, and of the progress which we have all made towards eternity ; for I, who am nearly the youngest of our old set, have completed half my three score and ten years. Besides, the aspect of the times is really to my mind awful—on one side a party profaning the holiest names by the lowest principles, and the grossest selfishness and ignorance,—on the other a party who seem likely κακὸν κακῷ ἰᾶσθαι, who disclaim and renounce even the very name of that, whose spirit their adversaries have long renounced equally. If I had two necks, I should think that I had a very good chance of being hanged by both sides, as I think I shall now by whichever gets the better, if it really does come to a fight. I read now, with the deepest sympathy, those magnificent lines of your Uncle's, on the departed year, and am myself, in fact, experiencing some portion of the abuse which he met with from the same party ; while, like him, I feel utterly unable to shelter myself in the opposite party, whose hopes and principles are such as I shrink from with abhorrence. So what Thucydides says of τὰ μέσα τῶν πολίτων often rises upon my mind as a promising augury of my future exaltation, ἤ που πρὸ Νεαπύλης αἰωρηθέντος, ἢ ἐμοῦγε πρὸ Ρουγβείας.

November 3rd.—I wrote these two sides in school on Monday, and I hope to finish the rest of my letter this evening, while my boys are translating into Latin from my English that magnificent part in the De Oratore, about the death of Crassus. I see I have given you enough of this discourse on things in general—I will only add one thing more ; that I know there are reports in Oxford of my teaching the boys my politics, and setting revolutionary themes. If you hear these reports, will you contradict them flatly? I never disguise or suppress my opinions, but I have been and am most religiously careful not to influence my boys with them ; and I have just now made them begin Russell's Modern Europe again, because we were come to the period of the French Revolution, and I did not choose to enter upon that subject with them. As to the revolutionary themes, I cannot even imagine the origin of so absurd a falsehood, except it be that one of my subjects last half-year was "the particular evils which civilized society is exposed to, as opposed to savage life," which I gave for the purpose of clearing their notions about luxury, and the old declamations about Scythian simplicity, &c.; but I suppose that I am thought to have a longing for the woods, and an impatience of the restraint of breeches. It is really too great a folly to be talked of as a revolutionist, with a family of seven young children, and a house and income that I should be rather puzzled to match in America, if I were obliged to change my quarters. My quarrel with the anti-liberal party is, that they are going the way to force my children to America, and to deprive me and everyone else of property, station, and all the inestimable benefits of Society in England. There is nothing so revolutionary, because there is nothing so unnatural and so convulsive to society as the strain to keep things fixed, when all the world is by the very law of its creation in eternal progress; and the cause of all the evils of the world may be traced to that natural but most deadly error of human indolence and corruption, that our business is to preserve and not to improve. It is the ruin of us all alike, individuals, schools, and nations.

XX.   TO HIS SISTER SUSANNAH ARNOLD.

Rugby, November, 1830.

The paramount interest of public affairs outweighs with me even the school itself; and I think not unreasonably, for school and all would go to the dogs, if the convulsion which I dread really comes to pass. I must write a pamphlet in the holidays, or I shall burst.

No one seems to me to understand our dangers, or at least to speak them out manfully. One good man, who sent a letter to *The Times* the other day, recommends that the clergy should preach subordination and obedience. I seriously say, God forbid that they should; for if any earthly thing could ruin Christianity in England, it would be this. If they read Isaiah and Jeremiah and Amos and Habakkuk, they will find that the Prophets, in a similar state of society in Judea, did not preach subordination only or chiefly, but they denounced oppression, and amassing overgrown properties, and grinding the labourers to the smallest possible pittance; and they denounced the Jewish high-church party for countenancing all these iniquities, and prophesying smooth things to please the aristocracy. If the clergy would come forward as one man from Cumberland to Cornwall, exhorting peaceableness on the one side, and justice on the other, denouncing the high rents and the game laws, and the carelessness which keeps the poor ignorant and then wonders that they are brutal, I verily believe they might yet save themselves and the state. But the truth is that we are living amongst a population whom we treat with all the haughtiness and indifference that we could treat slaves, whom we allow to be slaves in ignorance, without having them chained and watched to prevent them from hurting us. I only wish you could read Arthur Young's Travels in France in 1789 and 1790, and see what he says of the general outbreak then of the peasantry, when they burnt the chateaux all over France, and ill-used the families of the proprietors, and then compare the orderliness of the French populace now. It speaks volumes for small subdivided properties, general intelligence, and an absence of aristocratical manners and distinctions. We know that, in the first revolution, to be seen in decent clothes was at one time a sure road to the guillotine; so bitter was the hatred engendered in a brute population against those who had gone on in luxury and refinement, leaving their poorer neighbours to remain in the ignorance and wretchedness of savages, and therefore with the ferocity of savages also. The dissolution of the ministry may do something; but the evil exists in every parish in England; and there should be a reform in the ways and manners of every parish to cure it. We have got up a dispensary here, and I am thinking of circulating small tracts *à la* Cobbett in *point of style*, to show the people the real state of things and their causes. Half the truth might be of little use, but ignorance of all the truth is something fearful, and a knowledge of the whole truth would, I am convinced, do nothing but pacify, because the fault of the rich has been a sin of ignorance and thoughtlessness; they have only done what the poor would have done in their places, because few men's morality rises higher than to take care of themselves, abstaining from actual wrong to others. So you have got a long sermon.

—— showed me a copy of *The Record* newspaper, a true specimen of the party, with their infinitely little minds, dis-

puting about anise and cummin, when heaven and earth are
coming together around them ; with much of Christian harm-
lessness, I do not deny, but with nothing of Christian wisdom ;
and these are times when the dove can ill spare the addition of
the serpent.   The state of affairs, therefore, keeps me doubtful
about going from home in the holidays, because, if there is
likely to be any opening for organizing any attempts at general
reform, I should not like to be away from my post.   But the
interest is too intense, and makes me live ten lives in one every
day.   However, I am very well, and perfectly comfortable as
far as regards family and school.

XXI.   TO REV. AUGUSTUS HARE.

December, 24, 1830.

. . . . . . I have longed very much to see you, over and
above my general wish that we could meet oftener, ever since
this fearful state of our poor has announced itself even to the
blindest.   My dread is that when the special Commissions
shall have done their work (necessary and just I most cordially
agree with you that it is) the richer classes will again relapse
into their old callousness, and the seeds be sown of a far more
deadly and irremediable quarrel hereafter.   If you can get
Arthur Young's Travels in France, I think you will be greatly
struck with their applicability to our own times and country.
He shows how deadly was the hatred of the peasantry towards
the lords, and how in 1789 the chateaux were destroyed, and
the families of the gentry insulted, from a common feeling of
hatred to all who had made themselves and the poor *two orders*,
and who were now to pay the penalty of having put asunder
what God had joined.   At this moment Carlisle tells the
poor that they and the rich are enemies, and that to destroy
the property of an enemy, whether by fire or otherwise, is
always lawful in war—A Devil's doctrine, certainly, and devi-
lishly applied ; but unquestionably our aristocratical manners
and habits have made us and the poor two distinct unsym-
pathising bodies ; and from want of sympathy, I fear the transition to enmity is but too easy when distress embitters the
feelings, and the sight of others in luxury makes that distress
still more intolerable. This is the plague spot to my mind in our
whole state of society, which must be removed or the whole

must perish. And under God it is for the clergy to come forward boldly, and begin to combat it. If you read Isaiah, chap. v. iii. xxxii. ; Jeremiah, chap. v. xxii. xxx. ; Amos, iv. ; Habakkuk, ii. ; and the Epistle of St. James, written to the same people a little before the second destruction of Jerusalem, you will be struck, I think, with the close resemblance of our own state to that of the Jews ; while the state of the Greek Churches to whom St. Paul wrote is wholly different, because from their thin population and better political circumstances, poverty among them is hardly noticed, and our duties to the poor are consequently much less prominently brought forward. And unluckily our Evangelicals read St. Paul more than any other part of the Scriptures, and think very little of consulting most those parts of Scriptures which are addressed to persons circumstanced most like ourselves. I want to get up a real Poor Man's Magazine, which should not bolster up abuses and veil iniquities, nor prose to the poor as to children ; but should address them in the *style* of Cobbett, plainly, boldly, and in sincerity, excusing nothing—concealing nothing—and mis-representing nothing—but speaking the very whole truth in love —Cobbett-like in style—but Christian in spirit. Now you are the man I think to join with me in such a work, and most earnestly do I wish that you would think of it. . . . . I should be for putting my name to whatever I wrote of this nature, for I think it is of great importance that our addresses should be those of substantive and tangible persons, not of anonymous shadows.

XXII.   TO REV. F. C. MASSINGBERD.

Rugby, February, 1831.

. . . . . . This is my constant defence of a liberal government. The high wisdom and purity of their principles are overwhelm-ing to their human infirmity, and amidst such a mass of external obstacles ; but what do we gain by getting in exchange men who cannot fall short of their principles only because their principles are zero ? As to the budget, I liked it in its first state, although the Fæx Romuli, *i.e.* the fundholders, made such an outcry about it. What between the landed aristocracy and the moneyed aristocracy, the interests of the productive classes are generally sure to go to the wall ; and this goes on for a time, till at last the squeeze gets intolerable,

and then productive classes put up their backs, and push in
their turn so vigorously, that rank and property get squeezed
in their turn against the wall opposite.   O utinam! that they
would leave each other their fair share of the road; for I
honour aristocracy in its proper place, and in France should
try to raise it with all my might, for there it is now too low,
simply because it was once too high.   Dii omen avertant! and
may the Tories who are hoping to defeat the Ministers on the
Reform question, remember how bitterly the French aristocracy
had cause to repent their triumph over Turgot.   "Flectere si
nequeo superos, Acheronta movebo," is the cry of Reform
when, long ,repulsed and scorned, she is on the point of
changing her visage to that of Revolution.   What you say
about the progress of a people towards liberty, and their unfit-
ness for it at an earlier stage, I fully agree in.   If ever my
Thucydides falls in your way, you will find in the Appendix,
No. 1, a full dissertation on this matter.

———

XXIII.   TO THE ARCHBISHOP OF DUBLIN.

Rugby, March 7, 1831.

   I am most truly obliged to you for all your advice and collected opinions about *The Register*.   Now, certainly, I never
should embark in such a scheme for my own amusement.   I
have enough to do in all reason.   I am not so craving after
the honour of appearing in print, as to wish to turn newspaper
writer on that account.   I should most wish that the thing
were not needed at all; next, that it might be done by some-
body else, without my taking part in it.   But all seem to agree
that it is needed, grievously needed, and will anybody else
undertake it?   That is to my mind the real question.   For if
not, I think there is a great call for much to be risked, and
much to be braved, and the thing done imperfectly is better
than not done at all.   So much for the principle. . . . . The
aid of liberal Tories I should be most thankful for, and I
earnestly crave it; but never will I join with the High Church
party. . . . . It would be exposing myself to the fate of
Amphiareus with a vengeance, for such a co-operation would
sink anything into the earth, or else render it such, that it had
better be sunk. . . . . Most earnestly would I be Conservative; but defend me from the Conservative party—*i.e.* from

those who call themselves so par excellence. Above all, I cannot understand why a failure should be injurious to future efforts. A bad history of any one particular period may doubtless hinder sensible men from writing upon the same period; but I cannot see how a foolish newspaper, dying in 1831, should affect a wise one in 1832; and if the thing is impracticable rei naturâ, then, neither mine, nor any other with the same views, will ever answer. Certainly our failure is very conceivable—very probable if you will; but something must be risked, and I think the experimentum will be made " in corpore vili ;" for all the damage will be the expense which it will cost me, and that of course I shall not stand beyond a certain point. Ergo, I shall try a first number. . . . . In the opinions I have already received, I have been enough reminded of Gaffer Grist, Gaffer's son, and a little jackass, &c., but I have learned this good from it, *i.e.* to follow my own judgment, adopting from the opinions of others just what I approve of, and no more. One thing you may depend on, that nothing shall ever interfere with my attention to the school. Thucydides, *Register* and all, should soon go to the dogs if they were likely to do that. I have got a gallows at last, and am quite happy; it is like getting a new twenty-horse power in my capacities for work. I could laugh like Democritus himself at the notion of my being thought a dangerous person, when I hang happily on my gallows, or make it serve as a target to spear at.

XXIV. TO CHEVALIER BUNSEN.

Rugby, March 20, 1831.

. . . . . . I was reminded of you when I heard of the great loss that all Europe has sustained in the sudden death of Niebuhr. I knew your personal admiration and regard for him, and that you would feel his loss privately as well as publicly. Besides all this, the exceedingly anxious state of public affairs has naturally made me think of you, whose views on those matters I have found to be so entirely in agreement with my own. Our accounts of Italy are very imperfect, but there have been reports of disturbances in Rome itself, which made me wish that you and your family were in a more tranquil country, or at least in one, where, if there were any commotions, you might be able to be of more service than you could be amongst foreigners and Italians.

I was again in Italy this last summer. . . . . We were at
Venice during the Revolution at Paris, and the first intelligence I heard of it was from the postmaster at the little town
of Bludenz in the Vorarlberg. The circumstances under which
I first heard of it, will never, I think, depart from my memory.
We had been enjoying the most delightful summer weather
throughout our tour, and particularly in all the early part of
that very day ; when, just as we arrived at Bludenz, about four
or five in the afternoon, the whole sky was suddenly overcast,
the wind arose violently, and everything announced the
approach of a complete Alpine storm. We were in the very
act of putting up the head of the carriage and preparing for the
coming rain, when the postmaster, in answer to an observation
of mine about the weather when I had passed through France
a few weeks before, seemed to relieve himself by telling me of
all the troubles that were then raging. His expression was,
" Alles ist übel in Frankreich," the mere tumult and violence
of political quarrels seeming to the inhabitant of a Tyrolese
valley, as something shocking, because it was so unpeaceful.
Hearing only indistinct accounts of what was going on, we
resolved not to enter France immediately, but to go round by
the Rhine through Wirtemberg and Baden ; a plan which I shall
now ever think of with pleasure, as otherwise I never should
have seen Niebuhr. I was very glad, too, to see something
more of Germany, only it was rather vexatious to be obliged to
pass on so quickly, for I could not wait at Heidelberg long
enough to see Creuzer, and my stay even at Bonn was only one
afternoon. I had the happiness of sitting three hours with
Niebuhr, and he introduced me to his poor wife and children.
His conversation completely verified the impression which you
had given me of his character, and has left me with no recollections but such as are satisfactory to think of *now*. The
news* of the Duke of Orleans' accession to the French throne
reached Bonn while I was with Niebuhr, and I was struck with
the enthusiastic joy which he displayed on hearing it. I fully
expected that the Revolution in France would lead to one in
Belgium ; and indeed, we passed through Brussels scarcely ten
days before the insurrection broke out. You are so well
acquainted with English politics, that you will take a deep
interest in the fate of the Reform Bill, now before Parliament.
I believe, that, if it passes now, " Felix sæclorum nascitur

---

* See Extracts from Journals, in 1830, in the Appendix.

ordo;" that the aristocracy still retain a strong hold on the respect and regard of England, and if their excessive influence is curtailed, they will be driven to try to gain a more legitimate influence, to be obtained by the exercise of those great and good qualities which so many of them possess. At present this may be done ; but five years hence the democratical spirit may have gained such a height, that the utmost virtue on the part of the aristocracy will be unable to save it. And I think nearly the same with regard to the Church. Reform would now, I fully believe, prevent destruction ; but every year of delayed reform strengthens those who wish not to amend, but to destroy. Meanwhile, the moral state of France is to me most awful ; I sympathized fully with the Revolution in July, but, if this detestable warlike spirit gets head amongst the French people, I hope, and earnestly believe, that we shall see another and more effectual coalition of 1815 to put it down. Nothing can be more opposite than Liberalism and Bonapartism ; and, I fear, the mass of the French people are more thirsting to renew the old career of spoliation and conquest than to establish or promote true liberty ; " for who loves that must first be wise and good." My hope is that, whatever domestic abuses may exist, Germany will never forget the glorious struggle of 1813, and will know that the tread of a Frenchman on the right bank of the Rhine is the worst of all pollutions to her soil. And I trust and think, that the general feeling in England is strong on this point, and that the whole power of the nation would be heartily put forth to strangle in the birth the first symptoms of Napoleonism. I was at a party at —— in the summer at Geneva, where I met Thierry, the historian of " Les Gaulois," and the warlike spirit which I perceived, even then, in the French liberals, made a deep impression on me.

XXV.   TO JOHN WARD, ESQ.

(Co-editor with him of *The Englishman's Register.*)

Rugby, April 27, 1831.

Your own articles I have carefully read over ; and, in style, they more than answer all my expectations. Still, as we are beginning a work which must take its character chiefly from us two, I will fairly say that, considering for whom we are principally writing, I think the spirit too polemical. When I speak of the aristocracy of England bearing hard upon the poor, I always mean the whole class of gentlemen, and not the nobility or great landed and commercial proprietors. I cannot think that you or I suffer from any aristocracy above us, but we ourselves belong to a part of society which has not done its duty to the poor, although with no intention to the contrary, but much the reverse. Again, I regard the Ministerial Reform Bill as a safe and a necessary measure, and I should, above all things, dread its rejection, but I cannot be so sanguine as you are about its good effects; because I think that the people are quite as likely to choose men who will commit blunders and injustice as the boroughmongers are, though not exactly of the same sort. Above all, in writing to the lower people my object is much more to improve them morally than politically; and I would, therefore, carefully avoid exciting political violence in them. . . . . Now so far as *The Register* is concerned, I care comparatively little about the Reform Bill, but I should wish to explain, as you have done most excellently, the baseness of corruption on one hand, and as I think you might do, the mischief of party and popular excitement on the other. I should urge the duty of trying to learn the merits of the case, and that an ignorant vote is little better than a corrupt one, where the ignorance could in any degree be helped. But in such an address I would not assume that the Reform Bill would do all sorts of good, and that every honest man must be in favour of it : because such assertions, addressed to ignorant men, are doing the very thing I deprecate, *i.e.* trying rather to get their vote, than to make that vote, whether it be given for us or against us, really independent and respectable. Again, with the Debt. It is surely a matter of importance to show that the greatest part of our burthens is owing to this, and not to present extravagance. It affords a memorable lesson against foolish and unjust wars, and the selfish carelessness with which they were waged. This you have put very well, and have properly put down the nonsense of the " Debt being no harm." Urge all this as strongly as you will, to prevent any repetition of the loan system for the time to come. But the fundholders are not to blame for the Debt; they lent their money : and if the money was wasted, that was no fault of theirs. Pay the debt off, if you will and can, or make a fair adjustment of the advantages and disadvantages of different sorts of property, with a view of putting them all on equal terms ; but surely the fundholder's dividends are as much his lawful property as a landholder's estate, or a merchant's or manufacturer's capital,. liable justly, like all other property, to the claims of severe national distress ; but only together with other property, and by no means as if it were more just in the nation to lay hands on the fundholder's dividends than on the profits of your law or of my school. Nor can the fundholders be fairly said to be living in idleness at the expense of the nation in any invidious sense, any more than your clients who borrowed my money could say it of me, if they had borrowed £10,000 of me instead of £300, and then chose to go and fool it away in fireworks and illuminations. If they had spent the principal, no doubt they would find it a nuisance to pay the interest, but still, am I to be the loser, or can I fairly be said, if I get my interest duly paid, to be living at their expense? Besides, as a mere matter of policy, we should be ejected at once from most of the quarters where we might otherwise circulate, if we are thought to countenance in any degree the notion of a "sponge."*

The "tea monopoly," as you call it, involves the whole question of the Indian charter, and in fact of the Indian empire. The "timber monopoly" involves far more questions than I can answer, about Canada, and the shipping interest, and whether the economical principle of buying where you can buy cheapest, is always to be acted upon by a nation, merely because it is economically expedient. Even about the Corn Laws, there are difficulties connected with the question, that are not to be despised, and I would rather not cut the knot so abruptly. . . . . . I wish to distinguish *The Register* from all other papers by two things : that politics should hold in it just that place which they should do in a well-regulated mind ; that is, as one field of duty, but by no means the most important one ; and that with respect to this field, our duty should rather be to soothe than to excite, rather to furnish facts and to point out the difficulties of political questions, than to press forward our own conclusions. There are publications enough to excite the people to political reform ; my object is moral and intellectual reform, which will be sure enough to work out political reform in the best way, and my writing on politics would have for its end, not the forwarding any political measure, but the so purifying, enlightening, sobering, and, in one word *Christian-*

---

* The proposal alluded to was the taxation of the funds distinctly from other property, as in the plan proposed by Lord Althorp's first budget.

izing men's notions and feelings on political matters, that from the improved tree may come hereafter a better fruit. With any lower views, or for the sake of furthering any political measures, or advocating a political party, I should think it wrong to engage in *The Register* at all, and certainly would not risk my money in the attempt to set it afloat. . . . . .

XXVI.   TO HIS SISTER SUSANNAH ARNOLD.

Rugby, April, 1831.

. . . . . I should like you to see ——'s letter to me about *The Register*; the letter of a really good man and a thinking one, and a really liberal one. I wrote to him to thank him, and got the kindest of answers in return, in which he concludes by saying that he cannot help taking in *The Register* after all when it does make its appearance. Those are the men whom I would do everything in my power to conciliate, because I honour and esteem them; but for the common Church and King Tories, I never would go one hair's breadth to please them; for their notions, principles they are not, require at all times and at all places to be denounced as founded on ignorance and selfishness, and as having been invariably opposed to truth and goodness from the days of the Jewish aristocracy downwards. It is therefore nothing but what I should most wish, that such opinions and mine should be diametrically opposite. . . . . Not that I anticipate with much confidence any great benefits to result from the Reform Bill; but the truth is, that we are arrived at one of those periods in the progress of society when the Constitution naturally undergoes a change, just as it did two centuries ago. It was impossible then for the king to keep down the higher part of the middle classes; it is impossible now to keep down the middle and lower parts of them. All that resistance to these natural changes can effect is to derange their operation, and make them act violently and mischievously, instead of healthfully or at least harmlessly. The old state of things is gone past recall, and all the efforts of all the Tories cannot save it, but they may by their folly, as they did in France, get us a wild democracy, or a military despotism in the room of it, instead of letting it change quietly into what is merely a new modification of the old state. One would think that people who talk against change were literally as well as metaphorically blind, and really did not see that everything in themselves and around them is changing every hour by the necessary laws of its being.

XXVII. TO W. W. HULL, ESQ.

Rugby, May 2, 1831.

. . . . . Every selfish motive would deter me from *The Register*; it will be a pecuniary loss, it will bring me no credit, but much trouble and probably some abuse, and some of my dearest friends look on it not only coldly, but with aversion. But I *do* think it a most solemn duty to make the attempt. I feel our weakness, and that what I can hope to do is very little, and perhaps will be nothing; but if I can but excite others to follow the same plan, I shall rejoice to be superseded by them if they will do the thing more effectually. I have this morning been over to Coventry to make the required affidavit of Proprietorship, and to sign the bond for the payment of the advertisement duty. And No. 1 will really appear on Saturday with an opening article of mine, and a religious one. The difficulty of the undertaking is indeed most serious; all the Tories turn from me as a Liberal, whilst the strong Reformers think me timid and half corrupt, because I will not go along with them or turn *The Register* into a new *Examiner* or *Ballot.* So that I dare say my fate will be that of τὰ μέσα τῶν πολιτῶν from the days of Thucydides downwards.

I wrote to Parker immediately on the receipt of your letter, proposing to him either to give up [Thucydides] altogether except the Appendices, putting all my materials of every sort into his hands freely to dispose of, or else to share with him all the expenses of the next volume, and to refund at once what I have already received for the first. I have told him often before, and now have told him again, that I cannot do it quickly; and that I never meant or would consent to devote to it every spare moment of my time, so as to leave myself no liberty for any other writing. I have written nothing for two years but Thucydides and Sermons for the boys; but though I will readily give up writing merely for my own amusement, or fame, or profit, I cannot abandon what I think is a positive duty, such as attempting at least *The Register.* Parker wrote immediately a very kind letter, begging me to continue the editorship as at present, and stating in express words "that though advantage might arise from the early completion of the book, no injury whatever has been sustained by him, or is likely to be sustained."

I am proprietor of *The Register*, and will be answerable for it up to a certain point; but I cannot pretend to say that I shall see everything that is inserted in it, or that I should expunge everything with which I did not agree, although I certainly should, if the disagreement were great, or the opinions so differing seemed to me likely to be mischievous. I have no wish to conceal anything about it, and if I cannot control it to my mind, or find the thing to be a failure, I will instantly withdraw it. Sed Dii meliora piis.

XXVIII.   TO THE ARCHBISHOP OF DUBLIN.

Rugby, June 11, 1831.

I confess that your last letter a good deal grieved me, not at all personally, but as it seemed to me to give the death-blow to my hopes of finding co-operators for *The Register*. That very article upon the Tories has been objected to as being too favourable to them, so what is a man to do? You will see by No. 5, that I do not think the Bill perfect, but still I like it as far as it goes, and especially in its disfranchisement clauses. But my great object in *The Register* was to enlighten the poor generally in the best sense of the term; as it is, no one joins me, and of course my nephew and I cannot do it alone. "What is everybody's business is nobody's," is true from the days of the Peloponnesian confederacy downwards. Unless a great change in our prospects takes place, *The Register* will therefore undergo transmigration when the holidays begin; whether into a set of penny papers, or into a monthly magazine I cannot tell. But I cannot sit still without trying to do something for a state of things which often and often, far oftener I believe than any one knows of, comes with a real pang of sorrow to trouble my own private happiness. I know it is good to have these sobering reminders, and it may be my impatience, that I do not take them merely as awakeners and reminders to myself. Still, ought we not to fight against evil, and is not moral ignorance, such as now so sadly prevails, one of the worst kinds of evil?

XXIX. TO W. TOOKE, ESQ.

Rugby, June 18, 1831.

I must take the earliest opportunity of thanking you most heartily for your active kindness towards me, to which I am indebted for the most gratifying offer* announced to me in your letter of yesterday. I feel doubly obliged to you both for your good opinion of me, and for your kind recollection of me. . . . . I trust that you will not think me less grateful to you because I felt that I ought not to avail myself of the Chancellor's offer. Engaged as I am here, I could not reside upon a living, and I would not be satisfied to hold one without residence. I have always strenuously maintained that the clergy engaged in education should have nothing to do with church benefices, and I should be very unwilling to let my own practice contradict what I really believe to be a very wholesome doctrine. But I am sure that I value the offer quite as much, and feel as heartily obliged both to the Chancellor and to you for it, as if I had accepted it.

. . . . . . In this day's number of *The Register* there is a letter on the Cottage Evenings, condemning very decidedly their unchristian tone. It is not written by me, but I confess that I heartily agree with it. You know of old how earnestly I have wished to join your Useful Knowledge Society; and how heartily on many points I sympathize with them. This very work, the Cottage Evenings, might be made everything that I wish, if it were but decidedly Christian. I delight in its plain and sensible tone, and it might be made the channel of all sorts of information, useful and entertaining; but, as it is, so far from co-operating with it, I must feel utterly averse to it. To enter into the deeper matters of conduct and principle, to talk of our main hopes and fears, and yet not to speak of Christ, is absolutely, to my mind, to circulate poison. In such points as this, " He that is not with us is against us."

It has occurred to me that the circumstance of some of the principal members of the Useful Knowledge Society being now in the Government, is in itself a strong reason why the Society should take a more decided tone on matters of religion. Undoubtedly their support of that Society, as it now stands, is a matter of deep grief and disapprobation to a large proportion

---

* *Viz.* of a stall in Bristol Cathe-   offered to him by Lord Brougham.
dral, with a living attached to it—

of the best men in this kingdom, while it encourages the hopes of some of the very worst. And it would be, I do verily think, one of the greatest possible public blessings, if, as they are honest, fearless, and enlightened against political corruption, and, as I hope they will prove, against ecclesiastical abuses also, so they would be no less honest and fearless and truly wise in labouring to Christianize the people, in spite of the sneers and opposition of those who understand full well that, if men do* not worship God, they at once by that very omission worship most surely the power of evil.

You will smile at my earnestness or simplicity ; but it does strongly excite me to see so great an engine as your Society, and one whose efforts I would so gladly co-operate with, and which could effect so easily what I alone am vainly struggling at, to see this engine at the very least neutralizing its power of doing good, and, I fear, doing in some respects absolute evil. On the other side, the Tories would not have my assistance in religious matters, because they so disapprove of my politics ; and in the meantime the people, in this hour of their utmost need, get either the cold deism of the Cottage Evenings, or the folly of the Cottager's Monthly Visitor. Would the Committee accept my assistance for those Cottage Evenings? I would give a larger sum than I should be thought sane to mention, if I might but once see this great point effected.†

XXX. TO MRS. FLETCHER.

(After the death of her Son.)

Rugby, August, 1831.

. . . . . I know that you are rich in friends, and it seems like presumption in me to say it ; but I entreat you earnestly to remember that M—— and myself regard you and yours with such cordial respect and affection, that it would give us real

---

* " There is something to me almost awful," he used to say, speaking of Lord Byron's Cain, "in meeting suddenly in the works of such a man, so great and solemn a truth as is expressed in that speech of Lucifer, ' He who bows not to God hath bowed to me.' "

† From a later letter to the same. —" I cannot tell you how much I was delighted by the conclusion of the article on Mirabeau, in the Penny Magazine of May 12. That article is exactly a specimen of what I wished to see, but done far better than I could do it. I never wanted articles on religious subjects half so much as articles on common subjects written with a decidedly Christian tone. History and Biography are far better vehicles of good, I think, than any direct comments on Scripture, or Essays on Evidences." (The article in question was by Mr. Charles Knight.)

pleasure, if either now or hereafter we can be of any use whatever in any arrangements to be made for your grandchildren. I feel that it would be a delight to me to be of any service to fatherless children, contemplating, as I often do, the possibility of myself or their dear mother being taken away from our own little ones. And I feel it the more, because I confess that I think evil days are threatening, insomuch that, whenever I hear of the death of anyone that is dear to me, there mixes with my sense of my own loss a sort of joy that he is safe from the evil to come. Still more strong is my desire that all Christ's servants who are left should draw nearer every day to him, and to one another, in every feeling and every work of love.

XXXI.   TO REV. DR. HAWKINS.

Skipton, July 11, 1831.

. . . . . . *The Register* is now dead, to revive however in another shape ; but I could not afford at once to pay all, and to write all, and my nephew's own business hindered him from attending to it sufficiently, and it thus devolved on the mere publisher, who put in things of which I utterly disapproved. But the thing has excited attention in some quarters, just as I wished ; all the articles on the labourers were copied at length into one of the Sheffield papers, and, when *The Register* died, the Sheffield proprietor wrote up to our editor, wishing to engage the writer of those articles to continue them for his own paper. By a strange coincidence I happened to walk into the office of this very paper, at Sheffield, to look at the division on the Reform Bill, knowing nothing of the application made to our editor in town. I saw the long quotation from *The Register*, and as the proprietor of the paper happened to be in the shop, I talked to him about it, and finally told him who I was, and what were my objects in *The Register*. He spoke of those articles on the labourers being read with great interest by the mechanics and people of that class, and I have promised to send him a letter or two in continuation.

XXXII.   TO THE ARCHBISHOP OF DUBLIN.

August 12, 1831.

. . . . . . Touching the Magazine, I think it $\delta\epsilon\acute{u}\tau\epsilon\rho\sigma\nu\ \pi\lambda o\hat{u}\nu$ in comparison with a weekly paper ; but $\pi\lambda\acute{\epsilon}o\nu\ \mathring{\eta}\mu\acute{\iota}\sigma\upsilon\ \pi\acute{a}\nu\tau\sigma\varsigma$. I will join in it gladly, and, if required, try to undertake even the editorship, only let something be done. I found all the articles about the labourers in my *Register* had been copied into the Sheffield *Courant*, and the proprietor told me that they had excited some interest. Thus even a little seed may be scattered about, and produce more effect than we might calculate on; by all means let us sow while we can.

What do Mayo and you say to the cholera? Have you read the accounts of the great fifty years' pestilence of the 6th century, or of that of the 14th, both of which seem gradually to have travelled like the cholera? How much we have to learn about the state of the atmosphere and the causes that affect it. It seems to me that there must be a "morbus cœli," which at particular periods favours the spread of disorders, and thus, although the cholera is contagious, yet it also originates in certain constitutions under a certain state of atmosphere, and then is communicated by contagion to many who would not have originated it themselves; while many again are so anti-pathetic to it, that neither contagion nor infection will give it them. Agathias says that the old Persian and Egyptian philo-sophers held that there were certain periodical revolutions of time, fraught with evil to the human race, and others, during which they were exempt from the worst sort of visitations. This is mysticism; yet, from Thucydides downwards, men have remarked that these visitations do not come single; and although the connexion between plague and famine is obvious, yet that between plague and volcanic phenomena is not so; and yet these have been coincident in the most famous instances of long travelling pestilences hitherto on record. Nor is there much natural connexion between the ravages of epidemic disease, and a moral and political crisis, in men's minds, such as we now seem to be witnessing.

XXXIII. TO REV. F. C. BLACKSTONE.

(In answer to a question about Irvingism at Port Glasgow.)

Rugby, October 25, 1831.

..... If the thing be real I should take it merely as a sign of the coming of the day of the Lord,—the only use, as far as I can make out, that ever was derived from the gift of tongues. I do not see that it was ever made a vehicle of instruction, or ever superseded the study of tongues, but that it was merely a sign of the power of God, a man being for the time transformed into a mere instrument to utter sounds which he himself understood not. . . . . However, whether this be a real sign or no, I believe that "the day of the Lord" is coming, *i.e.* the termination of one of the great αἰῶνες of the human race ; whether the final one of all or not, that I believe no created being knows or can know. The termination of the Jewish αἰών in the first century, and of the Roman αἰών in the fifth and sixth, were each marked by the same concurrence of calamities, wars, tumults, pestilences, earthquakes, &c., all marking the time of one of God's peculiar seasons of visitation.* And society in Europe seems going on fast for a similar revolution, out of which Christ's Church will emerge in a new position, purified, I trust, and strengthened by the destruction of various earthly and evil mixtures that have corrupted it. But I have not the slightest expectation of what is commonly meant by the Millennium, and I wonder more and more that any one can so understand Scripture as to look for it. As for the signs of the times in England, I look nowhere with confidence : politically speaking, I respect and admire the present government. The ministry, I sincerely believe, would preserve all our institutions by reforming them ; but still I cannot pretend to say that they would do this on the highest principles, or that they keep their eye on the true polar star, how skilfully soever they may observe their charts, and work their vessel. But even in this I think them far better than the Tories. . . . . We talk, as much as we dare talk of anything two months distant, of going to the Lakes in the winter, that I may get on in peace with Thucydides, and enjoy the mountains besides.

XXXIV.　TO W. W. HULL, ESQ.

Rugby, October 26, 1831.

. . . . . . I spear daily, as the Lydians used to play in the famine, that I may at least steal some portion of the day from

---

* For the same belief in the connexion of physical with moral convulsions, see Niebuhr, Lebens-nachrichten, ii. p. 167. It may be as well to add, that the view above ex-pressed of the apostolical gift of tongues, was founded on a deliberate study of the passages which relate to it, especially 1 Cor. xiv. 13, 14, 21, 28.

thought. My family, the school, and, thank God, the town also, are all full of restful and delightful thoughts and images. All there is but the scene of wholesome and happy labour, and as much to refresh the inward man, with as little to disturb him as this earth, since Paradise, could, I believe, ever present to any one individual. But my sense of the evils of the times, and to what prospects I am bringing up my children, is overwhelmingly bitter. All in the moral and physical world appears so exactly to announce the coming of the "great day of the Lord," *i.e.* a period of fearful visitation to terminate the existing state of things, whether to terminate the whole existence of the human race, neither man nor angel knows,—that no entireness of private happiness can possibly close my mind against the sense of it. Meantime it makes me very anxious to do what work I can, more especially as I think the prospect of the cholera makes life even more than ordinarily uncertain ; and I am inclined to think, from my own peculiar constitution, that I should be very likely to be attacked by it. . . . . .

I believe I told you that I am preparing for the press a new volume of Sermons, and I wish a small book on the Evidences* to accompany them ; not a book to get up like Paley, but taking the real way in which the difficulties present themselves, half moral, half intellectual, to the mind of an intelligent and well-educated young man ; a book which, by God's blessing, may be a real stay in that state of mind when neither an address to the intellect alone, nor one to the moral feelings, is alone most likely to answer. And I wish to make the main point not the truth of Christianity per se, as a theorem to be proved, but the wisdom of our abiding by it, and whether there is anything else for it but the life of beast or of devil. I should like to do this if I could before I die ; for I think that times are coming when the Devil will fight his best in good earnest. I must not write any more, for work rises on every side open mouthed upon me.

XXXV.   TO REV. JULIUS HARE.

November 9, 1831.

(After thanking him for the first number of the Philological Museum, and wishing him success.) For myself, I am afraid

* This he partially accomplished in the 17th Sermon in the second volume, and the 11th and 19th in the third. The work itself was begun, but never finished.

Thucydides will have shown you that I am a very poor philologist, and my knowledge is too superficial on almost every point to enable me to produce anything worth your having ; and to say the truth, every moment of spare time I wish to devote to writing on Religion or πολιτική. I use the Greek word, because "politics" is commonly taken in a much baser sense. I know I can do but little, perhaps nothing, but the " Liberavi animam meam " is a consolation ; and I would fain not see everything good and beautiful sink in ruin without making a single effort to lessen the mischief. Since the death of *The Register*, I am writing constantly in one of the Sheffield papers, the proprietor of which I earnestly believe sincerely wishes to do good.

I heartily sympathize with the feeling of your concluding paragraph—in your note, I mean—but who dare look forward now to anything ?

XXXVI. TO THE ARCHBISHOP OF DUBLIN.

Rugby, November 8, 1831.

You must not go to Ireland without a few lines from me. I cannot yet be reconciled to your being on the other side of St. George's Channel, or to thinking of Oxford as being without you. I do not know where to look for the Mezentius who should "succedat pugnæ," when Turnus is gone away. My great ignorance about Ireland is also very inconvenient to me in thinking about your future operations, as I do not know what most wants mending there, or what is likely to be the disposition to mend it in those with whom you will be surrounded. But you must not go out with words of evil omen ; and, indeed, I do anticipate much happiness for you, seeing that happiness consists, according to our dear old friend, ἐν ἐνεργίᾳ, and of that you are likely to have enough. . . . . .

I am a coward about schools, and yet I have not the satisfaction of being a coward κατὰ προαίρεσιν ; for I am inclined to think that the trials of a school are useful to a boy's after character, and thus I dread not to expose my boys to it ; while, on the other hand, the immediate effect of it is so ugly, that, like washing one's hands with earth, one shrinks from dirting them so grievously in the first stage of the process. . . . . I cannot get over my sense of the fearful state of public affairs : —is it clean hopeless that the Church will come forward and

crave to be allowed to reform itself? . . . . I can have no
confidence in what would be in men like——, but a death-bed
repentance. It can only be done effectually by those who
have not, through many a year of fair weather, turned a deaf
ear to the voice of reform, and will now be thought only to
obey it, because they cannot help it. If I were indeed a
radical, and hated the Church, and longed for a democracy, I
should be jolly enough, and think that all was plain sailing;
but as it is, I verily think that neither my spirits nor my occupation, nor even spearing itself, will enable me to be cheerful
under such an awful prospect of public evils.

XXXVII.   TO W. W. HULL, ESQ.

Knutsford, December 16, 1831.

. . . . . I want to write an Essay on the true use of Scripture; *i.e.* that it is a direct guide so far forth as we are circumstanced exactly like the persons to whom it was originally
addressed; that where the differences are great, there it is a
guide by analogy; *i.e.* if so and so was the duty of men so
circumstanced, ergo, so and so is the duty of men circumstanced thus otherwise; and that thus we shall keep the spirit
of God's revelation even whilst utterly disregarding the letter,
when the circumstances are totally different. *E.g.* the second
commandment is in the letter utterly done away with by the
fact of the Incarnation. To refuse then the benefit which we
might derive from the frequent use of the crucifix, under pre-
tence of the second commandment, is a folly, because God
has sanctioned one conceivable similitude of himself when He
declared himself in the person of Christ. The spirit of the
commandment not to think unworthily of the Divine nature, nor
to lower it, after our own devices, is violated by all unscriptural
notions of God's attributes and dealings with men, such as we
see and hear broached daily, and, though in a less important
degree, by those representations of God the Father which one
sees in Catholic pictures, and by what Whately calls *peristero-
latry*, the foolish way in which people allow themselves to talk
about God the Holy Ghost, as of a dove. The applications of
this principle are very numerous, and embrace, I think, all the
principal errors both of the High Church and of the Evangelical party.

XXXVIII. TO REV. G. CORNISH.

RYDAL ! ! ! December 23, 1831.

We are actually here, and going up Nabb's Scar presently, if the morning holds clear: the said Nabb's Scar being the mountain at whose foot our house stands; but you must not suppose that we are at Rydal Hall; it is only a house by the roadside, just at the corner of the lane that leads up to Wordsworth House, with the road on one side of the garden, and the Rotha on the other, which goes brawling away under our windows with its perpetual music. The higher mountains that bound our view are all snow-capped, but it is all snug, and warm and green in the valley—nowhere on earth have I seen a spot of more perfect and enjoyable beauty, with not a single object out of tune with it, look which way I will. In another cottage, about twenty yards from us, Captain Hamilton, the author of Cyril Thornton, has taken up his abode for the winter; close above us are the Wordsworths; and we are in our own house a party of fifteen souls, so that we are in no danger of being dull. And I think it would be hard to say which of us all enjoys our quarters the most. We arrived here on Monday, and hope to stay here about a month from the present time.

It is indeed a long time since I have written to you, and these are times to furnish ample matter to write or to talk about. How earnestly do I wish that I could see you; it is the only ungratified wish as to earthly happiness of my most happy life, that I am so parted from so many of my dearest friends. . . . . (After speaking of objections which he had heard made to the appointment of Dr. Whately to the Archbishopric of Dublin.) Now I am sure that in point of real essential holiness, so far as man can judge of man, there does not live a truer Christian than Whately; and it does grieve me most deeply to hear people speak of him as of a dangerous and latitudinarian character, because in him the intellectual part of his nature keeps pace with the spiritual—instead of being left, as the Evangelicals leave it, a fallow field for all unsightly weeds to flourish in. He is a truly great man—in the highest sense of the word—and if the safety and welfare of the Protestant Church in Ireland depend in any degree on human instruments, none could be found, I verily believe, in the whole empire, so likely to maintain it. . . . . I am again publishing

Sermons, with an essay at the tail, on the Interpretation of Scripture, embodying things that I have been thinking over for the last six or seven years; and which I hope will be useful to a class whose spiritual wants I am apt to think are badly provided for—young men bringing up for other professions than the Church, who share deeply in the intellectual activity of the day, and require better satisfaction to the working of their minds than I think is commonly given them.

XXXIX. TO THE SAME.

Rugby, February 15, 1832.

A letter from Tucker has this morning informed me of the heavy trial which has fallen upon you. I write because I should wish to hear from you under similar circumstances, and because it is unnatural not to assure you at such a moment how dearly your friends at Rugby love you and your dear wife, and how truly they sympathize with your sorrow. Tucker's letter leaves us anxious both for your wife and for little Robert —especially for the latter; it would be a great comfort to hear favourable accounts of them, if you could give them. I will not add one word more. May God strengthen and support you, my dear friend, and bless all his dispensations towards us both, through Jesus Christ.

XL. TO LADY FRANCES EGERTON.

(On the subject of the conversion of a person with atheistical opinions.)

Rugby, February 15, 1832.

The subject of the letter which I have had the honour of receiving from you has so high a claim upon the best exertions of every Christian, that I can only regret my inability to do it justice. But in cases of moral or intellectual disorder, no less than of bodily, it is difficult to prescribe at a distance; so much must always depend on the particular constitution of the individual, and the peculiarly weak points in his character. Nor am I quite sure whether the case you mention is one of absolute Atheism, or of Epicurism; that is to say, whether it be a denial of God's existence altogether, or only of his moral government, the latter doctrine being, I believe, a favourite resource with those who cannot evade the force of the evidences of design in the works of Creation, and yet cannot bear to entertain that strong and constant sense of personal responsibility, which follows from the notion of God as a moral governor. At any rate, the great thing to ascertain is, what led to his present state of opinions; for the actual arguments by which he would now justify them, are of much less consequence. The proofs of an intelligent and benevolent Creator are given, in my opinion, more clearly in Paley's Natural Theology than in any other book that I know, and the necessity of *faith* arising from the absurdity of scepticism on the one hand, and of dogmatism on the other, is shown with great power and eloquence in the first article of the second part of Pascal's Pensées, a book of which there is an English translation by no means difficult to meet with. In many cases the real origin of a man's irreligion is, I believe, political. He dislikes the actual state of society, hates the Church as connected with it, and, in his notions, supporting its abuses, and then hates Christianity because it is taught by the Church. Another case is, when a man's *religious* practice is degenerated, when he has been less watchful of himself and less constant and earnest in his devotions. The consequence is, that his impression of God's real existence, which is kept up by practical experience, becomes fainter and fainter; and in this state of things it is merely an accident that he remains nominally a Christian; if he happens to fall in with an anti-christian book, he will have nothing in his own experience to set against the difficulties there presented to him, and so he will be apt to yield to them. For it must be always understood that there *are* difficulties in the way of all religion—such, for instance, as the existence of evil—which can never be fairly solved by human powers; all that can be done *intellectually* is to point out the *equal* or greater difficulties of atheism or scepticism; and this is enough to justify a good man's understanding in being a believer. But the real proof is the practical one; that is, let a man live on the hypothesis of its falsehood, the practical result will be bad; that is, a man's besetting and constitutional faults will not be checked; and some of his noblest feelings will be unexercised, so that if he be right in his opinions, truth and goodness are at variance with one another, falsehood is more favourable to our moral perfection than ruth; which seems the most monstrous conclusion which the human mind can possibly arrive at. It follows from this, that if

I were talking with an atheist, I should lay a great deal of stress on *faith* as a necessary condition of our nature, and as a gift of God to be earnestly sought for in the way which God has appointed, that is, by striving to *do his will.* For faith does no violence to our understanding; but the intellectual difficulties being balanced, and it being necessary to act on the one side or the other, faith determines a man to embrace that side which leads to moral and practical perfection ; and unbelief leads him to embrace the opposite, or what I may call the Devil's religion, which is, after all, quite as much beset with intellectual difficulties as God's religion is, and morally is nothing but one mass of difficulties and monstrosities. You may say that the individual in question is a moral man, and you think not unwilling to be convinced of his errors ; that is, he sees the moral truth of Christianity, but cannot be persuaded of it intellectually. I should say that such a state of mind is one of very painful trial, and should be treated as such; that it is a state of mental disease, which like many others is aggravated by talking about it, and that he is in great danger of losing his perception of moral truth as well as of intellectual, of wishing Christianity to be false as well as of being unable to be convinced that it is true. There are thousands of Christians who see the difficulties which he sees quite as clearly as he does, and who long as eagerly as he can do for that time when they shall know, even as they are known. But then they see clearly the difficulties of unbelief, and know that even intellectually they are far greater. And in the meanwhile they are contented to live by faith, and find that in so doing, their course is practically one of perfect light ; the moral result of the experiment is so abundantly satisfactory, that they are sure that they have truth on their side.

I have written a sermon rather than a letter, and perhaps hardly made myself intelligible after all. But the main point is, that we cannot and do not pretend to remove all the intellectual difficulties of religion ; we only contend that even intellectually unbelief is the more unreasonable of the two, and that practically unbelief is folly, and faith is wisdom.

If I can be of any further assistance to you in your charitable labour, I shall be most happy to do my best.

Rugby, March 7, 1832.

I thank you for your last letter, and beg to assure you very sincerely that I shall have great pleasure in placing myself under your directions with regard to this unhappy man; and as he would probably regard me with suspicion, on account of my profession, I think that you would act with the best judgment in alluding to me only in general terms, as you propose to do, without mentioning my name. But I say this merely with a view to the man's own feelings towards the clergy, and not from the slightest wish to have my name kept back from him, if you think that it would be better for him to be made acquainted with it. With respect to your concluding question, I confess that I believe conscientious atheism not to exist. *Weakness of faith* is partly constitutional, and partly the result of education, and other circumstances; and this may go intellectually almost as far as scepticism; that is to say, a man may be perfectly unable to acquire a firm and undoubting belief of the great truths of religion, whether natural or revealed. He may be perplexed with doubts all his days; nay, his fears lest the Gospel should not be true, may be stronger than his hopes that it will. And this is a state of great pain, and of most severe trial, to be pitied heartily, but not to be condemned. I am satisfied that a good man can never get further than this; for his goodness will save him from unbelief, though not from the misery of scanty faith. I call it unbelief, when a man deliberately renounces his obedience to God, and his sense of responsibility to Him: and this never can be without something of an evil heart rebelling against a yoke which it does not like to bear. The man you have been trying to convert stands in this predicament:—he says that he cannot find out God, and that he does not believe in Him; therefore he renounces His service, and chooses to make a god of himself. Now, the idea of God being no other than a combination of all the highest excellencies that we can conceive—it is so delightful to a good and sound mind, that it is misery to part with it; and such a mind, if it cannot discern God clearly, concludes that the fault is in itself—that it cannot yet reach to God, not that God does not exist. You see there must be an assumption in either case, for the thing does not admit of demonstration, and the assumption that God is, or is not, depends on the degree of moral pain which a man feels in relinquishing the idea of God. And here, I think, is the moral fault of unbelief:—that a man can bear to make so great a moral sacrifice, as is implied in renouncing God. He makes the greatest moral sacrifice to obtain partial satisfaction to his intellect: a believer insures the greatest moral perfection, with partial satisfaction to his intellect also; entire satisfaction to the intellect is, and can be, attained by neither. Thus, then, I believe, generally, that he who has rejected God, must be morally faulty, and therefore justly liable to punishment. But of course no man can dare to apply this to any particular case, because our moral faults themselves are so lessened or aggravated by circumstances to be known only by Him who sees the heart, that the judgment of those who see the outward conduct only, must ever be given in ignorance.

XLII.　TO J. T. COLERIDGE, ESQ.

Rugby, April 5, 1832.

. . . . . I could still rave about Rydal—it was a period of five weeks of almost awful happiness, absolutely without a cloud; and we all enjoyed it I think equally—mother, father, and fry. Our intercourse with the Wordsworths was one of the brightest spots of all; nothing could exceed their friendliness—and my almost daily walks with him were things not to be forgotten. Once and once only, we had a good fight about the Reform Bill during a walk up Greenhead Ghyll to see "the unfinished sheepfold" recorded in "Michael." But I am sure that our political disagreement did not at all interfere with our enjoyment of each other's society; for I think that in the great principle of things we agreed very entirely—and only differed as to the τὰ καθ' ἕκαστα. We are thinking of buying or renting a place at Grasmere or Rydal, to spend our holidays at constantly; for not only are the Wordsworths and the scenery a very great attraction, but as I had the chapel at Rydal all the time of our last visit, I got acquainted with the poorer people besides, and you cannot tell what a home-like feeling all of us entertain towards the valley of the Rotha. I found that the newspapers so disturbed me, that we have given them up, and only take one once a week; it only vexes me to read, especially when I cannot do anything in the way of writing. But I cannot understand how you, appreciating so fully the dangers of the times, can blame me for doing the little which I can to counteract the evil. No one feels more than I do the little fruit which I am likely to produce; still I know that the letters have been read and liked by some of the class of men whom I most wish to influence; and, besides, what do I sacrifice, or what do I risk? If things go as we fear, it will make very little difference whether I wrote in the Sheffield *Courant* or no, whereas, if God yet saves us, I may be abused, as I have been long since, by a certain party; but it is a mistake to suppose that either I or the school suffer by that. . . . . I quite think that a great deal will depend on the next three or four years, as to the permanent success of Rugby; we are still living on credit, but of course credit will not last for ever, unless there is something to warrant it. Our general style of composition is still bad, and where the fault is, I cannot say; some of our boys, however, do beautifully; and one copy of Greek verses (Iambics) on Clitumnus, which was sent in to me about a month ago, was one of the most beautiful school copies I ever saw. I should like to show it to you, or even to your brother Edward; for I do not think any of his pupils could write better—τοῦτο δὲ, ὡς εἰκὸς, σπάνιον.

XLIII. TO REV. G. CORNISH.

Rugby, June 9, 1832.

. . . . . We are again, I believe, going to the Lakes in the holidays; to a great house near the head of Winandermere, Brathay Hall; because our dear old house at Rydal is let for a twelvemonth. We all look with delight to our migration, though the half year has gone on very happily as far as the school is concerned, and I am myself perfectly well; but in these times of excitement the thirst for a "lodge in some vast wilderness" is almost irresistible. We are going to have a dinner here for all the town on passing the Reform Bill :—the thing was to be, and I have been labouring to alter its name, and to divest it of everything political, in order that everybody might join in it; but of all difficult offices, that of a peace-maker seems to me to be one of the hardest. What a delightful man we have in Grenfell—so lively and so warm-hearted. I thought of you and of Bagley Wood, and old times, when I

walked with him the other day in the rain to a wood about four
miles from here, dug up orchis roots, and then bathed on our
way home, hanging our clothes on a stick under a tree, to save
them from being wet in the interval. . . . . I do not wonder
at what you say about the civility and compliance of the people
with your instructions, as Rural Dean.   I think it is so still,—
and the game is yet in our hands if we would play it; but I
suppose we shall not play it, and five or ten years hence it will
be no longer ours to play.   120,000 copies of the Penny
Magazine circulate weekly! We join in kindest love and
regards to you all.   Would that we might ever meet, before
perhaps we meet in America or at sea after the Revolution.

<hr>

XLIV.   TO REV. J. E. TYLER.

Rugby, June 10, 1832.

Your letter interested me exceedingly.   I have had some
correspondence with the "Useful Knowledge" people about
their Penny Magazine, and have sent them some things
which I am waiting to see whether they will publish.   I want
to give their Magazine a decidedly Christian character, and
then I think it would suit my notions better than any other;
but of course what I have been doing, or may do for them,
does not hinder me from doing what I can for you.   I only
suspect I should wish to liberalize your Magazine, as I wish to
Christianize theirs; and probably your Committee would recal-
citrate against any such operations, as theirs may do.   The
Christian Knowledge Society has a bad name for the dulness
of its publications; and their contributions to the cause of
general knowledge, and enlightening the people in earnest, may
seem a little tardy and reluctant.   This, however, touches you,
as an individual member of the Society, no more than it does
myself; only the name of the Society is not in good odour.
As for the thing itself, it is one on which I am half wild, and
am not sure that I shall not start one at my own expense down
here, and call it the Warwickshire Magazine; and I believe
that it would answer in the long run, if there were funds to
keep it up for a time; but "experto crede," it is an expensive
work to push an infant journal up hill.   The objection to a
magazine is its desultoriness and vagueness—it is all scraps;

whereas a newspaper has a regular subject, and follows it up
continuously. I would try to do this as much as I could in a
magazine. I would have in every number one portion of the
paper for miscellanies, but I think that in another portion there
should be some subjects followed up regularly : *e.g.* the history
of our present state of society tracked backwards ; the history of
agriculture, including that of inclosures ; the statistics of different countries, &c. &c. I suppose the object is to instruct
those who have few books and little education ; but all instruction must be systematic, and it is this which the people want :
they want to have ἀρχαὶ before them, and comprehensive outlines of what follows from those ἀρχαὶ ; not a parcel of detached
stories about natural history, or this place, or that man,—all entertaining enough, but not instructive to minds wholly destitute of
anything like a frame, in which to arrange miscellaneous information. And I believe, if done spiritedly, that systematic information would be even more attractive than the present hodge-
podge of odds and ends. Above all, be afraid of teaching
nothing : it is vain now to say that questions of religion and
politics are above the understanding of the poorer classes—so
they may be, but they are not above their *misunderstanding*,
and they will think and talk about them, so that they had best
be taught to think, and taught rightly. It is worth while to
look at Owen's paper, *The Crisis*, or at *The Midland Representative*, the great paper of the Birmingham operatives. The
most abstract points are discussed in them, and the very
foundations of all things are daily being probed, as much as by
the sophists, whom it was the labour of Socrates' life to combat.
Phrases which did well enough formerly, now only excite a
sneer ; it does not do to talk to the operatives about our "pure
and apostolical church," and "our glorious constitution ;" they
have no respect for either ; but one must take higher ground,
and show that our object is not to preserve particular institutions, so much as to uphold eternal principles, which are in
great danger of falling into disrepute, because of the vices of
the institutions which profess to exemplify them. The Church,
as it now stands, no human power can save ; my fear is, that,
if we do not mind, we shall come to the American fashion, and
have no provision made for the teaching Christianity at all.
But it is late, and I must go to bed ; and I have prosed to you
enough ; but I am as bad about these things as Don Quixote
with his knight-errantry, and when once I begin, I do not
readily stop.

XLV. TO HIS NEPHEW, J. WARD, ESQ., ON HIS MARRIAGE.

Brathay Hall, July 7, 1832.

. . . . . A man's life in London, while he is single, may be very stirring, and very intellectual, but I imagine that it must have a hardening effect, and that this effect will be more felt every year as the counter tendencies of youth become less powerful. The most certain softeners of a man's moral skin, and sweeteners of his blood, are, I am sure, domestic intercourse in a happy marriage, and intercourse with the poor. It is very hard, I imagine, in our present state of society, to keep up intercourse with God without one or both of these aids to foster it. Romantic and fantastic indolence was the fault of other times and other countries ; here I crave more and more every day to find men unfevered by the constant excitement of the world, whether literary, political, commercial, or fashionable; men who, while they are alive to all that is around them, feel also who is above them. I would give more than I can say, if your Useful Knowledge Society Committee had this last feeling, as strongly as they have the other purely and beneficently. . . . . I care not for one party or the other, but I do care for the country, and for interests more precious than that of the country, which the present disordered state of the human mind seems threatening. But this mixes strangely with your present prospects, and I hope we may both manage to live in peace with our families in the land of our fathers, without crossing the Atlantic.

XLVI. TO THE ARCHBISHOP OF DUBLIN.

Brathay Hall, July 8, 1832.

This place is complete rest, such as I wish you could enjoy after your far more anxious occupations. . . . . As to the state of the country, I find my great concern about it comes by accesses, sometimes weighing upon me heavily, and then again laid aside as if it were nothing. . . . . I wish that your old notion of editing a family Bible could be revived. I do not know anything which more needs to be done, and it would be a very delightful thing if it could be accompanied with really good maps and engravings, which might be done if a large sale could be reckoned upon. It might be published in penny numbers, not beginning with Genesis, but with some of the most important parts of the New Testament, *e.g.* St. John's Gospel or the Epistle to the Romans. Some of the historical books of the Old Testament, I should be inclined to publish last of all, as being the least important, whilst the Psalms and some of the Prophets should appear very early. I am even grand enough to aspire after a new, or rather a corrected translation, for I would only alter manifest faults or obscurities, and even then preserving as closely as possible the style of the old translation. Many could do this for the New Testament, but where is the man, in England at least, who could do it for the Old? . . . . But alas! for your being at Dublin instead of at Canterbury.

XLVII.   TO REV. J. E. TYLER.

Manchester, July 28, 1832.

I am on my way to Laleham from the Lakes, to see my poor sister, whose long illness seems now at last on the point of being happily ended. And whilst waiting here for a coach, I have just bought four of the numbers of the Saturday Magazine, and think this a good opportunity to answer your last kind letter. The difficulty which occurs to me in your Sermon project, is, how to make the work sufficiently systematic, or sufficiently particular. I mean this, a real sermon has very often no sort of connexion with last week's predecessor, or next week's successor; but then it is appropriate either to something in the service of the day, or else to something in the circumstances of the hearers, which makes it fitting for that especial season. And if it be nothing of any of these, but a mere sermon which might as well be preached on any other day, and in any other place as when and where it is actually preached, then I hold it to be, with rare exceptions, a very dull thing, and a very useless one. Now, in a monthly *publication* of Sermons, you lose all the advantages of local and personal applicability:—you have only the applicability of time, or of matter; that is, your month's sermons may be written on the lessons for the month, or the part of Scripture then read, or on the season of the year, whether natural or ecclesiastical; or else they may form successive parts of one great whole, to be completed in any given time, and to be announced in the first of the series. But if you publish a mere collection of miscellaneous sermons, I think that you will be wasting your labour.

Now then practically to the point. Fix on your plan, whether your arrangements be of time or of matter, or of both ; and let me know what part you would like me to take : *e.g.* whether sermons or any given book of Scripture, or on the Lessons for the Sundays in Advent, or in Lent, or at any other given period :—or sermons for Spring or Winter, &c., adapted either to an agricultural or manufacturing population ; or, if you like the arrangement of matter, give me any subject that you choose, whether of evidence, history, or exhortation upon doctrine, and I will do my best for you : but I cannot write sermons in the abstract. I like to have my own portion of any work to be kept to myself, and you would not thank me for copying out for you some of my old sermons out of my paper case.

I am sorry for what you say about my not writing anything *startling* ; because it shows how long we have been absent from one another, and that you are beginning to judge me in part upon the reports of others.   There are some people whom I must *startle*, if I am to do any good : and so you think too, I am sure.   But to startle the majority of good and sensible men, or to startle so as to disgust at once a majority of any sort, are things which I most earnestly should wish to avoid. At the same time, I do strongly object, on principle, to the use of that glozing, unnatural, and silly language, (for so it is in us now,) which men use one after another, till it becomes as worn as one of the old shillings. . . . .

I wish your Saturday Magazine all success ; I do not quite like the introductory article,—but I think it improves as it goes along.   The print of the departure of the Israelites was a good notion, and well executed ; and I like some of your poetry.   I could only do you good by sending you something very radical ; for you will have enough of what is right and proper.   But seriously, if I can persuade the Penny Magazine to receive things more in your tone, I think I·shall do more good than by writing for you—if, as I fear, I cannot do both. In fact, I have for some time past done neither, and I know not how or when I can mend.

XLVIII. TO THE ARCHBISHOP OF DUBLIN.

Rugby, September 6, 1832.

. . . . . Have you heard that the Useful Knowledge Society have resolved to publish a Bible, and asked —— to be editor? Hâc tamen lege, that, where doctrine is introduced, the opinions of the different sects of Christians should be fairly stated. Now Evans's Dictionary of all Religions is a useful book, but I do not want exactly to see it made a rider upon the Scriptures. We want something better than this plan. . . . . . I told —— that I must write to you before I gave him any promise of assistance. O! for your Bible plan, or, at least, for the sanction of your name: I think I see the possibility of a true comprehensive Christian Commentary, keeping back none of the counsel of God, lowering no truth, chilling no lofty or spiritual sentiment, yet neither silly, fanatical, nor sectarian. Your book on Romanism shows how this may be done, and it applies to all sects alike. They are not all error, nor we all truth ; *e.g.* the Quakers reject the communion of the Lord's Supper, thereby losing a great means of grace ; but are they not tempted to do so by the superstitions which other Christians have heaped upon the institution, and is there not some taint of these in the exhortation even in our own Communion Service ? And with regard to the greatest truths of all, you know how Pelagianism and Calvinism have encouraged each other, and how the Athanasian Creed, at this day, confirms and aggravates the evils of Unitarianism. I heard some time since, as a matter of fact, that, in the United States, where the Episcopal Church has expelled this creed, the character of Unitarianism is very different from what it is in England, and is returning towards high Arianism, just as here it has gone a downward course to the very verge of utter unbelief. I know how much you have on your hands and on your mind ; I, too, have my hobbies, but I know of nothing more urgent than to circulate such an edition of the Scriptures, as might labour, with God's help, to give their very express image without human addition or omission, striving to state clearly what is God's will with regard to us now ; for this seems to me to be one great use of a commentary, to make people understand where God spoke to their fathers, and where He speaks to them ; or rather—since in all He speaks to them, though not after the same manner—to teach them to distinguish where they are to follow the letter and where the spirit.

I have promised to send Tyler some sermons for his Magazine, though the abstract idea of a sermon is rather a puzzle to my faculties, accustomed as they are to cling to things in the concrete. But I am vexed to find how much of hopeless bigotry lingers in minds, οἷς ἥκιστα ἔχρη. I am sure old —— is personally cooled towards me, by the Essay attached to the Sermons, and the Sheffield *Courant* Letters. And another very old and dear friend wrote to me about my grievous errors and yours, praying "that I may be delivered from such false doctrines, and restrained from promulgating them." These men have the advantage over us, λέγω κατ' ἄνθρωπον, which the Catholics had over the Protestants : they taxed them with damnable heresy, and pronounced their salvation impossible ; the Protestants in return only charged them with error and superstition, till some of the hotter sort, impatient of such an unequal rejoinder, bethought themselves of retorting with the charge of damnable idolatry. But still I think that we have the best of it, in not letting what we firmly believe to be error and ignorance shake our sense of that mightier bond of union, which exists between all those who love the Lord Jesus Christ in sincerity ; perhaps I should say, in not letting our sense of the magnitude of the error lead us to question the sincerity of the love.

I must conclude with a more delightful subject—my most dear and blessed sister.* I never saw a more perfect instance of the spirit of power and of love, and of a sound mind ; intense love, almost to the annihilation of selfishness—a daily martyrdom for twenty years, during which she adhered to her early-formed resolution of never talking about herself; thoughtful about the very pins and ribands of my wife's dress, about the making of a doll's cap for a child,—but of herself, save only as regarded her ripening in all goodness, wholly thoughtless, enjoying everything lovely, graceful, beautiful, high-minded, whether in God's works or man's, with the keenest relish ; inheriting the earth to the very fulness of the promise, though never leaving her crib, nor changing her posture ; and preserved through the very valley of the shadow of death, from all fear or impatience, or from every cloud of impaired reason, which

---

* Susannah Arnold died at Laleham, August 20, 1832, after a complaint in the spine of twenty years' duration.

might mar the beauty of Christ's Spirit's glorious work.   May God grant that I might come but within one hundred degrees of her place in glory.   God bless you all.

XLIX.   TO J. T. COLERIDGE, ESQ.

Rugby, September 17, 1832.

. . . . . Much has happened since April, but nothing to me of so much interest as the death of my dear sister Susannah, after twenty-one years of suffering.   We were called up hastily to Laleham in June, hardly expecting then to find her alive ; but she rallied again and we went down with all our family to the Lakes for the holidays, intending to return to Laleham for a short time before the end of the vacation.   But the accounts became worse, and we went up to her, leaving the children at the Lakes, towards the end of July.   We spent more than a fortnight at Laleham, and returned to Rugby on the 18th of August, expecting, or at least not despairing of seeing her again in the winter.   On the 23rd we heard from Mrs. Buckland, to say that all was over ; she had died on the night of the 21st, so suddenly that the Bucklands could not be called from the next house in time.   The last months, I may say indeed the last twenty years of her life, had been a constant preparation, and she was only spared the nervous fear which none probably can wholly overcome, of expecting the approach of death within a definite time.   I never saw nor ever heard of a more complete triumph over selfishness, a more glorious daily re-newing of soul and spirit amidst the decays and sufferings of the body, than was displayed throughout her twenty years' martyrdom.   My poor aunt, well comparatively speaking in body, but decayed sadly in her mind, still lives in the same house, close to the Bucklands ; the only remaining survivor of what I call the family of my childhood.   I attach a very peculiar value to the common articles of furniture, the mere pictures, and china, and books, and candlesticks, &c., which I have seen grouped together in my infancy, and whilst my aunt still keeps them, it seems to me as if my father's house were not quite broken up.

You may have heard, perhaps, that great as is the loss of this dear sister, I was threatened with one still heavier in May last.   My wife was seized with a most virulent sore throat,

which brought on a premature confinement, and for some time
my distress was greater than it has been since her dangerous
illness in 1821. But she was mercifully recovered, not however
without the loss of our little baby, a beautiful little girl, who
just lived for seven days, and then drooped away and died of
no other disorder than her premature birth. We had nothing
but illness in our house during the whole spring ; wife, children,
servants, all were laid up one after the other, and for some time
I never got up in the morning without hearing of some new
case, either amongst my own family or amongst the boys.
Then came the cholera at Newbold : and I thought that, beat
as we were by such a succession of illnesses, we were in no
condition to encounter this new trouble ; and therefore, with
the advice of our medical men, I hastily dispersed the school.
We went down bodily to the Lakes, and took possession of
Brathay Hall, a large house and large domain, just on the head
of Winandermere. It was like Tinian to Anson's crew ; never
was there such a renewal of strength and spirits as our children
experienced from their six weeks' sojourn in this Paradise.
And for their mamma and papa, the month that we spent there
was not less delightful. Our intimacy with the Wordsworths
was cemented, and scenery and society together made the time
a period of enjoyment, which it seemed almost wholesome for
us not to have longer continued, μὴ νοστοῖο λαθώμεθα.

And now we are all at work again, the school very full, very
healthy, and I think in a most beautiful temper ; the Sixth
Form working μάλιστα κατ' εὐχὴν, and all things at present
promising. I am quite well, and enjoying my work exceedingly. May I only remember that, after all, the true work is to
have a daily living faith in Him whom God sent. Send me a
letter to tell me fully about you and yours ; it is sad that we can
never meet, but we must write oftener. Business ought not so
to master us as not to leave time for a better business, and one
which I trust will last longer, for I love to think that Christian
friendships may be part of the business of eternity. God ever
bless you.

CHAPTER VII.

HIS alarm about the state of the poor naturally subsided with the tranquillization of the disturbances amongst the rural population, but was succeeded by an alarm almost as great, lest the political agitation which, in 1832, took the form of the cry for Church Reform, should end in destroying what, with all its defects, seemed to him the greatest instrument of social and moral good existing in the country. It was this strong conviction, which, in 1833, originated his pamphlet on "the Principles of Church Reform." "I hung back," he said, "as long as I could, till the want was so urgent that I sat down to write, because I could not help it." But with him preservation was only another word for reform ; and here the reform proposed was great in proportion as he thought the stake at issue was dear, and the danger formidable. "Most earnestly do I wish to see the Establishment reformed," was the closing sentence of his Postscript, " at once, for the sake of its greater security, and its greater perfection : but, whether reformed or not, may God in his mercy save us from the calamity of seeing it destroyed !" As much of the misunderstanding of his character arose from a partial knowledge of this pamphlet, and of his object in writing it, it may be as well to give in his own words, the answer which he made to a friend, in 1840, to a general charge of indiscretion brought against him:

It seems to me that the charge of "Indiscretion," apart of course from the truth or error of the opinions expressed, belongs only to my Church Reform pamphlet. Now, I am quite ready to allow, that to publish such a pamphlet in 1840, or indeed at any period since 1834, would have been the height of indiscretion. But I wrote that pamphlet in 1833, when most men—myself among the number—had an exaggerated impression of the strength of the movement party, and of the changes which it was likely to effect. My pamphlet was written on the supposition—not implied, but expressed repeatedly—that the Church Establishment was in extreme danger; and therefore I proposed remedies, which, although I do still sincerely believe them to be in themselves right and good, yet would be manifestly chimerical, and to advise them might well be called indiscreet, had not the danger and alarm, as I supposed, been imminent. I mistook, undoubtedly, both the strength and intenseness of the movement, and the weakness of the party opposed to it; but I do not think that I was singular in my error—many persisted in it; Lord Stanley, for example, even in 1834 and the subsequent years—many even hold it still, when experience has proved its fallacy. But the startling nature of my proposals, which I suppose constitutes what is called their indiscretion, is to be judged by the state of things in 1832–33, and not by that of times present. Jephson finds that his patients will adopt a very strict diet, when they believe themselves to be in danger; but he would be very indiscreet if he prescribed it to a man who felt no symptoms of indisposition, for the man would certainly laugh at him, although perhaps the diet would do him great good, if he could be induced to adopt it.

The plan of the pamphlet itself is threefold; a defence of the national Establishment, a statement of the extreme danger to which it was exposed, and a proposal of what seemed to him the only means of averting this danger :—first, by a design for comprehending the Dissenters within the pale of the Establishment, without compromise of principle on either side ; secondly, by various details intended to increase its actual efficiency. The sensation created by the appearance of this pamphlet was considerable.   Within six months of its publication it passed through four editions.   It was quoted with approbation and condemnation by men of the most opposite parties, though with far more of condemnation than of approbation.   Dissenters objected to its attacks on what he conceived to be their sectarian narrowness, —the Clergy of the Establishment to its supposed latitudinarianism :—its advocacy of large reforms repelled the sympathy of many Conservatives—its advocacy of the importance of religious institutions repelled the sympathy of many Liberals.

Yet still it was impossible not to see, that it stood apart from all the rest of the publications for and against Church Reform, then issuing in such numbers from the press.   There were many, both at the time and since, who, whilst they objected to its details, yet believed its statement of general principles to be true, and only to be deprecated because the time was not yet come for their application.   There were many again, who, whilst they objected to its general principles, yet admired the beauty of particular passages, or the wisdom of some of the details.   Such were the statement of the advantages of a national and of a Christian Establishment,—his defence of the Bishops' seats in Parliament, and of the high duties of the Legislature.   Such, again, were the suggestions of a multiplication of Bishoprics, the creation of suffragan or subordinate Bishops—the revival of an inferior order of ministers or deacons in the Establishment—the use of churches on week days—the want of greater variety in our forms of worship than is afforded

by the ordinary course of morning and evening prayer—
all of them points which, being then proposed nearly for
the first time, have since received the sanction of a large
part of public opinion, if not of public practice.

One point of detail, so little connected with his general
views as not to be worth mentioning on its own account,
yet deserves to be recorded, as a curious instance of the
disproportionate attention, which may sometimes be
attracted to one unimportant passage ; namely, the suggestion that if Dissenters were comprehended within the
Establishment, the use of different forms of worship at
different hours of the Sunday in the parish church, might
tend to unite the worshippers more closely to the Church
of their fathers and to one another. This suggestion,
torn from the context and represented in language which
it is not necessary here to specify, is the one sole idea,
which many have conceived of the whole pamphlet,
which many also have conceived of his whole theological
teaching, which not a few have conceived even of his
whole character. Yet this suggestion is a mere detail,
only recommended conditionally, a detail occupying two
pages in a pamphlet of eighty-eight ; a detail, indeed,
which in other countries has been adopted without
difficulty amongst Protestants, Greeks, and Roman
Catholics, and which, in principle at least, has since been
sanctioned, in the alternate use in one instance of the
Prussian and English Liturgies, by the Archbishop of
Canterbury and the Bishop of London ;—but a detail
on which he himself laid no stress either then or afterwards, of which no mention occurs again in any one of
his writings, and of which, in common with all the other
details in the pamphlet, he expressly declared that he
was far from proposing anything with " equal confidence to that with which he maintained the principles
themselves ;", and that " he was not anxious about any

particular measure which he may have ventured to recommend, if anything could be suggested by others, which would effect the same great object of comprehension more completely." (Preface to Principles of Church Reform, p. iv.)

But, independently of the actual matter of the pamphlet, its publication was the signal for the general explosion of the large amount of apprehension or suspicion, which had been in so many minds contracted against him since he became known to the public—amongst ordinary men, from his Pamphlet on the Roman Catholic claims—amongst more thinking men, from his Essay on the Interpretation of Scripture—amongst men in general, from the union of undefined fear and dislike which is almost sure to be inspired by the unwelcome presence of a man who has resolution to propose, earnestness to attempt, and energy to effect, any great change either in public opinion or in existing institutions. The storm, which had thus been gathering for some time past, now burst upon him,—beginning in theological and political opposition, but gradually including within its sweep every topic, personal or professional, which could expose him to obloquy,—and continued to rage for the next four years of his life. The neighbouring county paper maintained an almost weekly attack upon him ; the more extreme of the London Conservative newspapers echoed these attacks with additions of their own ; the official dinner which usually accompanied the Easter speeches at Rugby was, on one occasion, turned into a scene of uproar by the endeavour to introduce into it political toasts ; in the University pulpit at Oxford he was denounced almost by name ; every incautious act or word in the management of the school, almost every sickness amongst the boys, was eagerly used as a handle against him. Charges which, in ordinary cases, would have passed by unnoticed, fell with double force on a man already marked out for public odium ; persons, who naturally would have been the last to suspect him, took up and repeated almost involuntarily the invectives which they heard reverberated around them in all directions ; the opponents of any new system of education were ready to assail every change which he had introduced ; the opponents of the old discipline of public schools were ready to assail every support which he gave to it; the general sale of his Sermons was almost stopped ; even his personal acquaintance began to look upon him with alarm, some dropped their intercourse with him altogether, hardly any were able fully to sympathize with him, and almost all remonstrated.

He was himself startled, but not moved by this continued outcry. It was indeed "nearly the worst pain which he had ever felt, to see the impression which either his writings, or his supposed opinions, produced on those whom he most dearly valued ;" it was a " trying thing to one who held his own opinions as strongly as he did, to be taxed continually with indifference to truth ;" and at times even his vigorous health and spirits seemed to fail under the sense of the estrangement of friends, or yet more, under his aversion to the approbation of some who were induced by the clamour against him to claim him as their own ally. But the public attacks upon himself he treated with indifference. Those which related to the school he was in one or two instances at their outset induced to notice; but he soon formed a determination, which he maintained till they died away altogether, never to offer any reply, or even explanation, except to his own personal friends. " My resolution is fixed," he said, "to let them alone, and on no account to condescend to answer them in the newspapers. All that is wanted is to inspire firmness into the minds of those engaged in the conduct of the school, lest their own confidence should be impaired by a succession of attacks, which I suppose is unparalleled in the experience of schools." Nor was he turned in the slightest degree from his principles. Knowing, from the example of those who presided over other schools, that, had he been on the opposite side of the questions at issue, he might have taken a far more active part in public matters without provoking any censure, and conscious that his exertions in the school were as efficient as ever, he felt it due alike to himself, his principles, and his position, never to concede that he had acted inconsistently with the duties of his situation ; and therefore in the critical election of the winter of 1834, when the outcry against him was at its height, he did not shrink from coming up from Westmoreland to Warwickshire to vote for the Liberal candidate, foreseeing, as he must have done, the burst of indignation which followed.

And, whilst the clamour against his pamphlet may have increased his original diffidence in the practicability of its details, it only drove him to a more determinate examination and development of its principles, which from this time forward assumed that coherent form which was the basis of all his future writings. What he now conceived and expressed in a systematic shape, had indeed always floated before him in a ruder and more practical form, and in his later life it received various enlargements and modifications. But in substance, his opinions, which up to this time had been forming, were, after it, formed ; he had now reached that period of life after which any change of view is proverbially difficult ; he had now arrived at that stage in the progress of his mind, to which all his previous inquiries had contributed, and from which all his subsequent inquiries naturally resulted. His views of national education became fixed

in the principles, which he expressed in his favourite
watch-words at this time, " Christianity without Sectarianism," and " Comprehension without Compromise ;" and
which he developed at some length in an (unpublished)
" Letter on the Admission of Dissenters to the Universities," written in 1834. His long-cherished views
of the identity of Church and State, he now first unfolded
in his Postscript to the pamphlet on " Church Reform,"
and in the first of his fragments on that subject, written
in 1834–35. Against what he conceived to be the profane
and secular view of the State, he protested in the Preface
to his third volume of Thucydides, and against the
practical measure of admitting Jews to a share in the
supreme legislature, he was at this time more than once
on the point of petitioning, in his own sole name.
Against what he conceived to be the ceremonial view
of the Church, and the technical and formal view of
Christian Theology, he protested in the Preface and
First Appendix to his third volume of Sermons ; whilst
against the then incipient school of Oxford Divinity, he
was anxious to circulate tracts vindicating the King's
Supremacy, and tracing in its opinions the Judaizing
principles which prevailed in the apostolical age. And
he still " dreamt of something like a Magazine for the
poor ; feeling sure from the abuse lavished upon him,
that a man of no party, as he has no chance of being
listened to by the half-informed, is the very person who
is wanted to speak to the honest uninformed."

From the fermentation against him, of which the
Midland Counties were the focus, he turned with a new
and increasing delight to his place in Westmoreland, now
doubly endeared to him as his natural home, by its contrast with the atmosphere of excitement with which he
was surrounded in the neighbourhood of Rugby. His
more strictly professional pursuits also went on undis-

turbed ; the last and best volume of his edition of Thucydides appeared in 1835, and in 1833 he resumed his Roman History, which he had long laid aside. It might seem strange that he should undertake a work of such magnitude, at a time when his chief interest was more than ever fixed on the great questions of political and theological philosophy. His love for ancient history was doubtless in itself a great inducement to continue his connexion with it after his completion of the edition of Thucydides. But besides, and perhaps even more than this, was the strong impression that on those subjects, which he himself had most at heart, it was impossible for him to bear up against the tide of misunderstanding and prejudice with which he was met, and that all hope for the present of direct influence over his countrymen was cut off. His only choice, therefore, lay in devoting himself to some work, which, whilst it was more or less connected with his professional pursuits, would afford him in the past a refuge from the excitement and confusion of the present. What Fox How was to Rugby, that the Roman History was to the painful and conflicting thoughts roused by his writings on political and theological subjects.

But besides the refreshment of Westmoreland scenery and of ancient greatness, he must have derived a yet deeper comfort from his increasing influence on the school. Greater as it probably was at a later period over the school generally, yet over individual boys it never was so great as at the period when the clamour to which he was exposed from without had reached its highest pitch. Then, when the institution seemed most likely to suffer from the unexampled vehemence with which it was assailed through him, began a series of the greatest successes at both Universities which it had ever known ;

then when he was most accused of misgovernment of the place, he laid that firm hold on the esteem and affections of the elder boys, which he never afterwards lost. Then, more than at any other time, when his old friends and acquaintance were falling back from him in alarm, he saw those growing up under his charge of whom it may be truly said, that they would have been willing to die for his sake.

Here, again, the course of his sermons in the third volume gives us a faithful transcript of his feelings ; whilst his increased confidence in the school appears throughout in the increased affection of their tone, the general subjects which he then chose for publication, indicate no less the points forced upon him by the controversy of the last two years,—the evils of sectarianism, —the necessity of asserting the authority of " Law, which Jacobinism and Fanaticism are alike combining to destroy "—Christianity, as being the sovereign science of life in all its branches, and especially in its aspect of presenting emphatically the Revelation of God in Christ. And in other parts, it is impossible to mistake the deep personal experience with which he spoke of the pain of severance from sympathy and of the evil of party spirit ; of " the reproach and suspicion of cold friendship and zealous enmity," which is the portion of those who strive to follow no party but Christ's—of the prospect that if " we oppose any prevailing opinion or habit of the day, the fruits of a life's labour, as far as earth is concerned, are presently sacrificed," and " we are reviled instead of respected," and " every word and action of our lives misrepresented and condemned,"—of the manner in which " the blessed Apostle, St. Paul, whose name is now loved and reverenced from one end of the Church of Christ to the other, was treated by his fellow-

Christians at Rome, as no better than a latitudinarian and a heretic."*

L.   TO REV. J. HEARN.

Rydal, January 1, 1833.

. . . . . New Year's Day is in this part of the country regarded as a great festival, and we have had prayers this morning, even in our village chapel at Rydal.   May God bless us in all our doings in the year that is now begun, and make us increase more and more in the knowledge and love of Himself and of His Son; that it may be blessed to us, whether we live to see the end of it on earth or no.

I owe you very much for the great kindness of your letters, and thank you earnestly for your prayers.   Mine is a busy life, so busy that I have great need of not losing my intervals of sacred rest; so taken up in teaching others, that I have need of especial prayer and labour, lest I live with my own spirit untaught in the wisdom of God. . . . . It grieves me more than I can say, to find so much intolerance; by which I mean over-estimating our points of difference, and under-estimating our points of agreement.   I am by no means indifferent to truth and error, and hold my own opinions as decidedly as any man; which of course implies a conviction that the opposite opinions are erroneous.   In many cases, I think them not only erroneous, but mischievous; still they exist in men, whom I know to be thoroughly in earnest, fearing God and loving Christ, and it seems to me to be a waste of time, which we can ill afford, and a sort of quarrel " by the way," which our Christian vow of enmity against moral evil makes utterly unseasonable, when Christians suspend their great business and loosen the bond of their union with each other by venting fruitless regrets and complaints against one another's errors, instead of labouring to lessen one another's sins.   For coldness of spirit and negligence of our duty, and growing worldliness, are things which we should thank our friends for warning us against; but when they quarrel with our opinions, which we conscientiously hold, it merely provokes us to justify ourselves, and to insist that we are right and they wrong.

We arrived here on Saturday, and on Sunday night there

* Sermons, vol. iii. pp. 263, 350, 363.

fell a deep snow, which is now however melting; otherwise it would do more than anything else to spoil this unspoilable country. We are living in a little nook under one of the mountains, as snug and sheltered as can be, and I have got plenty of work to do within doors, let the snow last as long as it will.

LI. TO W. K. HAMILTON, ESQ.

Rydal, January 15, 1833.

[After speaking of his going to Rome.] It stirs up many thoughts to fancy you at Rome. I never saw any place which so interested me, and next to it, but, longissimo intervallo, Venice—then of the towns of Italy, Genoa—and then Pisa and Verona. I cannot care for Florence or for Milan or for Turin. . . . . . For me this country contains all that I wish or want, and no travelling, even in Italy, could give me the delight of thus living amidst the mountains, and seeing and loving them in all their moods and in all mine. I have been writing on Church Reform, and urging an union with the Dissenters as the only thing that can procure to us the blessing of an established Christianity; for the Dissenters are strong enough to turn the scale either for an establishment or against one; and at present they are leagued with the antichristian party against one, and will destroy it utterly if they are not taken into the camp in the defence of it. And if we sacrifice that phantom Uniformity, which has been our curse ever since the Reformation, I am fully persuaded that an union might be effected without difficulty. But God knows what will come to pass, and none besides, for we all seem groping about in the dark together. I trust, however, that we shall be spared the worst evil of all, war.

LII. TO THE ARCHBISHOP OF DUBLIN.

Rydal, January 17, 1833.

. . . . . As my pamphlet will probably reach you next week, I wished you to hear something from me on the subject beforehand. My reasons for writing it were chiefly because the reform proposed by Lord Henley and others seemed to me not only insufficient, but of a wrong kind; and because I have heard the American doctrine of every man paying his minister as he would his lawyer, advanced and supported in high quarters, where it sounded alarming. I was also struck by the great vehemence displayed by the Dissenters at the late elections, and by the refusal to pay Church-rates at Birmingham. Nothing, as it seems to me, can save the Church, but an union with the Dissenters; now they are leagued with the antichristian party, and no merely internal reforms in the administration of the actual system will, I think, or can satisfy them. Further, Lord Henley's notion about a convocation, and Bishops not sitting in Parliament, and laymen not meddling with Church doctrine, seemed to me so dangerous a compound of the worst errors of Popery and Evangelicalism combined, and one so suited to the interest of the Devil and his numerous party, that I was very desirous of protesting against it. However, the pamphlet will tell its own story, and I think it can do no harm, even if it does no good.

LIII. TO THE SAME.

February 1, 1833.

. . . . . As for my coming down into Westmoreland, I may almost say that it is to satisfy a physical want in my nature, which craves after the enjoyment of nature, and for nine months in the year can find nothing to satisfy it. I agree with old Keble,* that one does not need mountains and lakes for this; the Thames at Laleham—Bagley Wood, and Shotover at Oxford were quite enough for it. I only know of five counties in England which cannot supply it; and I am unluckily perched down in one of them. These five are Warwick, Northampton, Huntingdon, Cambridge, and Bedford. I should add, perhaps, Rutland, and you cannot name a seventh; for Suffolk, which is otherwise just as bad, has its bit of sea coast. But Halesworth, so far as I remember it, would be just as bad as Rugby. We have no hills—no plains—not a single wood, and but one single copse: no heath—no down— no rock—no river—no clear stream—scarcely any flowers, for the lias is particularly poor in them—nothing but one endless monotony of inclosed fields and hedgerow trees. This is to me a daily privation; it robs me of what is naturally my anti-attrition; and as I grow older, I begin to feel it. My constitution is sound, but not strong; and I feel any little pressure

---

* Christian Year, First Sunday after Epiphany.

or annoyance more than I used to do ; and the positive dulness of the country about Rugby makes it to me a mere working place ; I cannot expatiate there even in my walks. So, in the holidays, I have an absolute craving for the enjoyment of nature, and this country suits me better than anything else, because we can be altogether, because we can enjoy the society, and because I can do something in the way of work besides. . . . .

Two things press upon me unabatedly—my wish for a bible, such as I have spoken of before ; and my wish for something systematic for the instruction of the poor. In my particular case, undoubtedly, the stamp-duties are an evil; for I still think, that a newspaper alone can help to cure an evil which newspapers have done and are doing ; the events of the day are a definite subject to which instruction can be attached in the best possible manner ; the Penny and Saturday Magazines are all ramble-scramble. I think often of a Warwickshire Magazine, to appear monthly, and so escape the stamp-duties, whilst events at a month's end are still fresh enough to interest. We ought to have, in Birmingham and Coventry, good and able men enough, and with sufficient variety of knowledge for such a work. But between the want of will and the want of power, the ten who were vainly sought to save Sodom, will be as vainly sought for now.

LIV.   TO REV. J. TUCKER.

(On his leaving England for India, as a Missionary.)

February, 1833.

[After speaking of the differences of tastes and habits which had interfered with their having common subjects of interest.] . . . . . It is my joy to think that there will be a day when these things will all vanish in the intense consciousness of what we both have in common. I owe you much more than I can well pay, indeed, for your influence on my mind and character in early life. The freshness of our Oxford life is continually present with me, and especially of the latter part of it. How well I recollect when you and Cornish did duty for your first time at Begbrooke and Yarnton, and when we had one of our last *skirmishes* together in a walk to Garsington in March, 1819. All that period was working for me constant good, and how delightful is it to have our University recollec-

tions so free from the fever of intellectual competition or
parties or jealousies of any kind whatever. I love also to
think of our happy meeting in later life, when Cornish and I,
with our wives and children, were with you at Malling, in 1823.
. . . . . Meantime, in a temporal point of view, you are going
from what bids fair, I fear, to deserve the name of a City
of Destruction. The state of Europe is indeed fearful; and
that of England, I verily think, worst of all. What is coming,
none can foresee, but every symptom is alarming; above all,
the extraordinary dearth of men professing to act in the fear of
God, and not being fanatics; as parties, the High Churchmen,
the Evangelicals, and the Dissenters, seem to me almost equally
bad, and how many good men can be found who do not belong
to one of them?

Your godson is now turned of ten years old, and I think of
keeping him at home for some time to familiarize him with
home feelings. . . . . I am sure that we shall have your prayers
for his bringing forth fruit unto life eternal. . . . . And
now farewell, my dear friend; may God be with you always
through Jesus Christ, and may He bless all your works to his
glory and your own salvation. You will carry with you, as
long as you live, my most affectionate and grateful remembrances, and my earnest wishes for all good to you, temporal
and spiritual.

LV.   TO AN OLD PUPIL AT OXFORD. (A.)*

February 25, 1833.

It always grieves me to hear that a man does not like
Oxford. I was so happy there myself, and above all so happy
in my friends, that its associations to my mind are purely
delightful. But, of course, in this respect, everything depends
upon the society you fall into. If this be uncongenial, the
place can have no other attractions than those of a town full of
good libraries.

. . . . . The more we are destitute of opportunities for
indulging our feelings, as is the case when we live in uncongenial society, the more we are apt to crisp and harden our
outward manner to save our real feelings from exposure. Thus
I believe that some of the most delicate-minded men get to

-----

* The letters of the alphabet thus affixed are intended to distinguish between
the different pupils so addressed.

appear actually coarse from their unsuccessful efforts to mask their real nature. And I have known men disagreeably forward from their shyness. But I doubt whether a man does not suffer from a habit of self-constraint, and whether his feelings do not become really, as well as apparently, chilled. It is an immense blessing to be perfectly callous to ridicule; or, which comes to the same thing, to be conscious thoroughly that what we have in us of noble and delicate is not ridiculous to any but fools, and that, if fools will laugh, wise men will do well to let them.

I shall really be very glad to hear from you at any time, and I will write to the best of my power on any subject on which you want to know my opinion. As for anything more, I believe that the one great lesson for us all is, that we should daily pray for an "increase of faith." There is enough of iniquity abounding to make our love in danger of waxing cold; it is well said, therefore, "Let not your heart be troubled: ye believe in God, believe also in *Me.*" By which I understand that it is not so much general notions of Providence which are our best support, but a sense of the personal interest, if I may so speak, taken in our welfare by Him who died for us and rose again. May his Spirit strengthen us to do his will, and to bear it, in power, in love, and in wisdom. God bless you.

LVI. TO THE REV. DR. HAWKINS.

Rugby, March 5, 1833.

[After speaking of a parcel sent to him.] I will not conceal, however, that my motive in writing to you immediately is to notice what you say of my pamphlet on Church Reform. I did not send it you for two reasons; first, because I feared that you would not like it; secondly, because a pamphlet in general is not worth the carriage. And I should be ashamed of myself if I were annoyed by your expressing your total disagreement with its principles or with its conclusions. But I do protest most strongly against your charge of writing "with haste and without consideration;" of writing "on subjects which I have not studied and do not understand," and "which are not within my proper province." You cannot possibly know that I wrote in haste, or that I have not studied the question; and I think, however much I might differ from any opinion of yours, I should scarcely venture to say that you had written on what you did not understand. I regret exceedingly the use of this kind of language in Oxford (for —— wrote to me exactly in the same strain,) because it seems to me to indicate a temper, not the best suited either to the state of knowledge or of feeling in other parts of the kingdom. It so happens that the subject of conformity, of communion, of the relations of Church and State, of Church Government, &c., is one which I have studied more than any other which I could name. I have read very largely about it, and thought about it habitually for several years, and I must say, that, sixteen or seventeen years ago, I had read enough of what were called orthodox books upon such matters, to be satisfied of their shallowness and confusion. I do not quarrel with you for coming to a different conclusion, but I do utterly deny that you are entitled to tax me with not being just as qualified as yourself to form a conclusion. I do not know that it gives me much pain, when my friends write what I do not like; for so long as I believe them to be honest, I do not think that they will be the worse for it; but assuredly my convictions of the utter falsehood and mischievous tendency of their opinions are quite as strong as theirs can be of mine; though I do not expect to convert them to my own views, for many reasons. As to the pamphlet, I am now writing a Post-script for the fourth edition of it, with some quotations in justi-fication of some of my positions. [After mentioning a pamphlet by a person of junior standing to himself.] If any respectable man of my own age chooses to attack my principles, I am per-fectly ready to meet him, and he shall see at any rate whether I have studied the question or no. I wish that I knew as much about Thucydides, which you think that I do understand.

I hope that I have expressed myself clearly. I complain merely of the charge of writing hastily on a subject which I have not studied. As a matter of fact, it is most opposite to the truth. But if you say that you think I have studied it to very bad purpose, and am all wrong about it, I have only to say, that I think differently; but I should not in the least complain of your giving me your own opinion in the plainest terms that you chose.

LVII. TO THE SAME.

Rugby, March 10, 1833.

I thank you entirely for your last letter; it is at once kind and manly, and I much value your notice of particular points in the pamphlet which you think wrong. It is very true that it was *written* hastily, *i.e.* penned, for the time was short ; but it is no less true that the matter of it, as far as its general principles are concerned, had been thought over in my mind again and again. In fact, my difficulty was how to write sufficiently briefly, for I have matter enough to fill a volume ; and some of the propositions, which I have heard objected to, as thrown out at random, are to my own mind the results of a very full consideration of the case ; although I have contented myself with putting down the conclusion and omitting the premises. [After answering a question of history.] I fear, indeed, that our differences of opinion on many points of which I have written must be exceedingly wide. I am conscious that I have a great deal to learn ; and, if I live ten years more, I hope I shall be wiser than I am now. Still I am not a boy, nor do I believe that any one of my friends has arrived at his opinions with more deliberation and deeper thought than I have at mine. And you should remember, that if many of my notions indicate in your judgment an imperfect acquaintance with the subject, this is exactly the impression which the opposite notions leave on my mind ; and, as I know it to be quite possible that a conclusion, which seems to me mere folly and ignorance, may really rest on some proof, of which I am wholly ignorant, and which to the writer's mind may have been so familiar from long habit as to seem quite superfluous to be stated—so it is equally possible, that what appears folly or ignorance to you, may also be justified by a view of the question which has escaped your notice, and which I may happen to have hit upon.

Undoubtedly I should think it wrong to write on any subject, and much more such a subject as the Church, without having considered it. It can hardly be an *honest* opinion if it be expressed confidently, without a consciousness of having sufficient reason for it. And though on subjects within the reach of our faculties, *sufficient* consideration, in the strict sense, must preclude error, (for all error must arise either from some premises being unknown, or from some faulty conclusion being derived from those which we do know,) yet of course for our moral justification, it is sufficient that we have considered it as well as we could, and so, that we seem to have a competent understanding of it compared with other men—to be able to communicate some truth to others, while we receive truths from them in return.

But my main object in writing was to thank you for your letter, and to assure you that my feeling of anger is quite subsided, if anger it could be called. Yet I think I had a right to complain of the tone of decided condemnation which ran through your first letter, assuming that I had written without reflection and without study, because my notions were different from yours; and I think that, had I applied similar expressions to any work of yours, you would have been annoyed as much as I was, and have thought that I had judged you rather unfairly. But enough of this; and I will only hope that my next work, if ever I live to write another, may please you better.

LVIII.   TO WM. SMITH, ESQ., FORMERLY M.P. FOR NORWICH.

(In answer to a letter on the subject of his pamphlet, particularly objecting to his making it essential to those included in his scheme of comprehension, that they should address Christ as an object of worship.)

Rugby, March 9, 1833.

I trust you will not ascribe it to neglect that I have not returned an earlier answer to your letter. My time has been very much occupied, and I did not wish to write, till I could command leisure to write as fully as the purport and tone of your letter required.

I cannot be mistaken, I think, in concluding that I have the honour of addressing Mr. Smith who was so long the Member for Norwich, and whose name must be perfectly familiar to any one who has been accustomed to follow the proceedings of Parliament.

The passage in my pamphlet to which you allude is expressly limited to the case of " the Unitarians preserving exactly their present character;" that is, as appears by a comparison with what follows (p. 36), their including many who " call themselves Unitarians, because the name of unbeliever is not yet thought creditable." And these persons are expressly distinguished from those other Unitarians whom I speak of " as really Christians." In giving or withholding the title of Christian, I was much more influenced by the spirit and temper of the parties alluded to than by their doctrinal opinions. For instance, my dislike to the works of the late Mr. Belsham arises more from what appears to me their totally unchristian tone, meaning particularly their want of that devotion, reverence, love of holiness, and dread of sin, which breathes through the Apostolical writings, than from the mere opinions contained in them, utterly erroneous as I believe them to be. And this was my reason for laying particular stress on the worship of Christ; because it appears to me that the feelings with which we regard Him are of much greater importance, than such metaphysical questions as those between Hamoousians and Hamoiousians, or even than the question of His humanity or proper divinity.

My great objection to Unitarianism in its present form in England, where it is professed sincerely, is that it makes Christ virtually dead. Our relation to Him is past instead of present; and the result is notorious, that instead of doing everything in the name of the Lord Jesus, the language of Unitarians loses this peculiarly Christian character, and assimilates to that of mere Deists; "Providence," the "Supreme Being," and other such expressions taking the place of "God, the Father of our Lord Jesus Christ," "the Lord," &c., which other Christians, like the Apostles, have found at once most natural to them, and most delightful. For my own part, considering one great object of God's revealing himself in the Person of Christ to be the furnishing us with an object of worship which we could at once love and understand; or, in other words, the supplying safely and wholesomely that want in human nature, which has shown itself in false religions, in "making gods after our own devices," it does seem to me to be forfeiting the peculiar benefits thus offered, if we persist in attempting to approach to God in His own incomprehensible essence, which as no man hath seen or can see, so no man can conceive it. And, while I am most ready to allow the provoking and most ill-judged language in which the truth, as I hold it to be, respecting God has been expressed by Trinitarians, so, on the other hand, I am inclined to think that Unitarians have deceived themselves by fancying that they could understand the notion of one God any better than that of God in Christ; whereas, it seems to me, that it is only of God in Christ that I can in my present state of being conceive anything at all. To know God the Father, that is, God as He is in Himself, in His to us incomprehensible essence, seems the great and most blessed promise reserved for us when this mortal shall have put on immortality.

You will forgive me for writing in this language; but I could not otherwise well express what it was, which I consider such a departure from the spirit of Christianity in modern Unitarianism.

Will you forgive me also for expressing my belief and fervent hope, that if we could get rid of the Athanasian Creed, and of some other instances of what I would call the technical language of Trinitarianism, many good Unitarians would have a stumbling-block removed out of their path, and would join their fellow Christians in bowing the knee to Him who is Lord both of the dead and the living.

But whatever they may think of His nature, I never meant to deny the name of Christian to those who truly love and fear Him, and though I think it is the tendency of Unitarianism to lessen this love and fear, yet I doubt not that many Unitarians feel it notwithstanding, and then *He* is their Saviour, and they are *His* people.

LIX.   TO THE CHEVALIER BUNSEN.

Rugby, May 6, 1833.

I thank you most heartily for two most delightful letters. They both make me feel more ardently the wish that I could see you once again, and talk over instead of write the many important subjects which interest us both, and not us only, but all the world. . . . .

First, as to our politics. I detest as cordially as you can do the party of the "Movement," both in France and England. I detest Jacobinism in its root and in its branches, with all that godless Utilitarianism which is its favourite aspect at this moment in England. Nothing within my knowledge is more utterly wicked than the party of . . . . . men, who, fairly and literally, as I fear, blaspheme not the Son of Man, but the Spirit of God ; they hate Christ, because He is of heaven and they are of evil.

For the more vulgar form of our popular party, the total ignorance of, and indifference to, all principle ; the mere money-getting and money-saving selfishness which cries aloud for *cheap* government, making as it were, αὐτὸ τ' ἀγαθὸν to consist in cheapness—my feeling is one of extreme contempt and disgust. My only difference from you, so far as I see, regards our anti-reformers, or rather the Tory party in general in England. Now, undoubtedly, some of the very best and wisest men in the country have on the Reform question joined this party, but they are as Falkland was at Oxford—had their party triumphed they would have been the first to lament the victory; for, not they would have influenced the measures carried into effect—but the worst and more selfish part of our aristocracy, with the coarsest and most profligate of their dependents, men like the Hortensii, and Lentuli, and Claudii of the Roman Civil wars, who thwarted Pompey, insulted Cicero, and ground down the provinces with their insolence and tyranny ; men so hateful and so contemptible, that I verily believe that the victory of Cæsar, nay even of Augustus, was a less evil to the human race than would have resulted from the triumph of the aristocracy.

And, as I feel that, of the two besetting sins of human nature, selfish neglect and selfish agitation, the former is the more common, and has in the long run done far more harm than the latter, although the outbreaks of the latter, while they last, are of a far more atrocious character ; so I have in a manner avowed to myself, and prayed that with God's blessing, no excesses of popular wickedness, though I should be myself, as I expect, the victim of them, no temporary evils produced by revolution, shall ever make me forget the wickedness of Toryism,—of that spirit which crucified Christ Himself, which has throughout the long experience of all history continually thwarted the cause of God and goodness, and has gone on abusing its opportunities, and heaping up wrath, by a long series of selfish neglect, against the day of wrath and judgment.

Again, I feel that while I agree with you wholly and most heartily in my abhorrence of the spirit of 1789, of the American war, of the French Economistes, and of the English Whigs of the latter part of the seventeenth century and beginning of the eighteenth, yet I have always been unable to sympathize with what you call "the historical liberty" which grew out of the system of the Middle Ages. For not to speak of the unhappy extinction of that liberty in many countries of Europe, even in England it showed itself to have been more the child of accident than of principle ; and throughout the momentous period of the eighteenth century, this character of it was fatally developed. For, not ascending to general principles, it foresaw not the evil, till it became too mature to be remedied, and the state of the poor and that of the Church are melancholy proofs of the folly of what is called "letting well alone ;" which, not watching for symptoms, nor endeavouring to meet the coming danger, allows the fuel of disease to accumulate in the unhealthy body, till, at last, the sickness strikes it with the suddenness and malignity of an incurable pestilence. But, when the cup is nearly full, and revolutions are abroad, it is a sign infallible that the old state of things is ready to vanish away. Its race is run, and no human power can preserve it. But, by attempting to preserve it, you derange the process of the new birth which must succeed it; and whilst the old perishes in spite of your efforts, you get a monstrous and mis-shapen creature in its place; when, had the birth been quietly effected, its proportions might have been better, and its inward constitution sounder and less irritable.

What our birth in England is likely to end in, is indeed a hard question. I believe that our only chance is in the stability of the present ministers. I am well aware of their faults; but still they keep out the Tories and the Radicals, the Red Jacobins of 1794 and the White Jacobins of 1795, or of Naples in 1799,—alike detestable. I do not think that you can fully judge of what the ascendancy of the Tories is; it is not the Duke of Wellington or Sir R. Peel who would do harm, but the base party that they would bring in in their train . . . . and all the tribe of selfish and ignorant lords and country squires and clergymen, who would irritate the feeling of the people to madness.

. . . . . If you see my pamphlet and Postscript, you will see that I have kept clear of the mere secular questions of tithes and pluralities, and have argued for a comprehension on higher grounds. I dislike Articles, because they represent truth untruly, that is, in an unedifying manner, and thus robbed of its living truth, whilst it retains its mere literal form; whereas the same truth, embodied in prayers, or confessions, or even in catechisms, becomes more Christian, just in proportion as it is less theological. But I fear that our reforms, instead of labouring to unite the Dissenters with the Church, will confirm their separate existence by relieving them from all which they now complain of as a burden. And continuing distinct from the Church, will they not labour to effect its overthrow, till they bring us quite to the American platform?

LX.   TO THE ARCHBISHOP OF DUBLIN.

Rugby, May 21, 1833.

. . . . . . It is painful to think that these exaggerations, in too many instances, cannot be innocent; in Oxford there is an absolute ἐργαστήριον ψευδῶν, whose activity is surprising. . . . . . I do hope that we shall see you all next month. When I am not so strong as usual, I feel the vexation of the school more than I could wish to do. . . . . And I have also been annoyed at the feeling excited in some of my old friends by my pamphlet, and by the constant and persevering falsehoods which are circulated concerning my opinions and my practice.

. . . . . Thucydides creeps on slowly, and nothing else, save my school work, gets on at all. I do confess, that I feel now more anxious than I used to do to get time to write, and especially to write history. But this will not be.

LXI. TO REV. J. HEARN.

Rugby, May 29, 1833.

. . . . . I do not know whether you have ever felt the intense difficulty of expressing in any other language the impression, which the Scripture statement of any great doctrine has left on your own mind.* It has grieved me much to find that some of my own friends, whilst they acquit me of any such intention, consider the tendency of my Church Reform plan as latitudinarian in point of doctrine. Now my belief is, that it would have precisely the contrary effect, and would tend ultimately to a much greater unity and strictness in true doctrine; that is to say, in those views of God's dealings and dispositions towards us, and of our consequent duties towards Him, which constitute, I imagine, the essence of the Gospel Revelation. Now, what I want is, to abstract from what is commonly called doctrine everything which is not of this kind; and secondly, for what is of this kind, to present it only so far forth as it is so, dropping all deductions which we conceive

---

* He often expressed this feeling with regard to the truths of Revelation. "They are placed before us in Scripture," he said, "as very vivid images are sometimes presented to us in dreams. It is like that point in Mousehold Heath," (in the neighbourhood of Norwich, where he had just been), "where, when we stood in one particular spot, all human habitations were shut out from our view—but by a single step we came again within sight of them, and lost the image of perfect solitude. So it is in the Scriptural statements of the Atonement—as long as we can place ourselves exactly in their point of view, and catch it as it is presented to us in this dream-like fashion, none of the false views which so often beset it can come across us: the highest act of love is the sacrifice of self—the highest act of God's infinite love to man was in the Redemption—but from the ineffable mystery which hangs over the Godhead, God could not be said to sacrifice Himself; —and therefore He sacrificed His only Son—that object which was so near and so dear to Him, that nothing could be nearer and dearer."—Compare Serm. on Rom. v. 7, in vol. vi. So again in a conversation in 1842, with regard to the controversy on Justification.

may be drawn from it, regarded as a naked truth, but which cannot be drawn from it, when regarded as a Divine practical lesson.

For instance, it is common to derive from our Lord's words to Nicodemus, " Except a man be born of water," &c., an universal proposition, " No being can be saved ordinarily without baptism;" and then to prove the fitness of baptizing infants, for this reason, as necessary, out of charity to them ; whereas our Lord's words are surely only for those who can understand them.   Take any person with the use of his faculties, and therefore the consciousness of sin in his own heart, and say to him, that " Except he be born again," &c., and then you apply Christ's word in its true meaning, to arouse men's consciences, and make them see that their evil and corrupt nature can of itself end only in evil.   But when we apply it universally as an abstract truth, and form conclusions from it, those conclusions are frequently either uncharitable or superstitious, or both.   It was uncharitable when men argued, though correctly enough as to logic, that, if no man could be saved without baptism, all the heathen must have perished ; and it was uncharitable and superstitious too, to argue, as Cranmer, that unbaptized infants must perish ; but that, if baptized, they were instantly safe. Now, I hold it to be a most certain rule of interpreting Scripture, that it never speaks *of* persons, when there is a physical impossibility of its speaking *to* them ; but as soon as the mind opens and understands the word, then the word belongs to it, and then the truth is his in all its fulness ; that " Except he be born again, he cannot see the kingdom of God."   So the heathen who died before the word was spoken, and in whose land it has never been preached, are dead to the word—it concerns not them at all ; but the moment it can reach them, then it is theirs and for them ; and we are bound to spread it, not from general considerations of their fate without it, but because Christ has commanded us to spread it, and because we see that Christianity has the promise of both worlds, raising men's nature, and fitting them for communion with God hereafter,— revealing Him in His Son.   Now, apply this rule to all the Scriptures, and ask at every passage, not " What follows from this as a general truth ?"—but " What is the exact lesson or impression which it was intended to convey?—what faults was it designed to correct ?—what good feelings to encourage ?" Our Lord says, " God is a Spirit :" now if we make conclusions from this metaphysically, we may, for aught I know, run into all kinds of extravagance, because we neither know what God is, nor what Spirit is : but if we take our Lord's conclusion, " Therefore we should worship Him in spirit and in truth ; " *i.e.* not with outward forms, and still less, with evil passions and practices,—then it is full of truth, and wisdom, and goodness. I have filled my paper, and yet perhaps have not fully developed my meaning ; but you will connect it perhaps with my dislike of Articles, because there truth is always expressed abstractedly and theoretically, and my preference of a Liturgy as a bond of union, because there it assumes a practical shape, as it is meant in Scripture to be taken.

LXII.   TO HIS SISTER, THE COUNTESS OF CAVAN.

(In answer to a question on Dr. Whately's " Thoughts on the Sabbath.")

Rugby, June 11, 1833.

. . . . . My own notions about the matter would take up rather too much room, I fear, to come in at the end of my paper.   But my conclusion is, that while St. Paul on the one hand, would have been utterly shocked, could he have foreseen that eighteen hundred years after Christianity had been in the world, such an institution as the Sabbath would have been still needed ; yet, seeing that it is still needed, the obligation of the old commandment is still binding in the spirit of it : that is, that we should use one day in seven, as a sort of especial reminder of our duties, and a relieving ourselves from the over-pressure of worldly things, which daily life brings with it.   But our Sunday is the beginning of the week, not the end —a day of preparation and strengthening for the week to come, and not of rest for the past ; and in *this* sense the old Christians kept it, because it was the day on which God *began* his work of creation ; so little did they think that they had anything to do with the old Jewish Sabbath.   You will see, also, by our common Catechism, that " the duty towards God," which is expressly given as a summary of the four first commandments to us, as *Christians*, says not one word about the Sabbath, but simply about loving God, worshipping him, and serving him truly *all the days* of our life.   It is not that we may pick and choose what commandments we like to obey, but as all the commandments have no force upon us *as such*—that is, as positive and literal commands addressed to ourselves—it is only a question how far each commandment is applicable to us—that is, how far we are in the same circumstances with those to whom it was given. Now, in respect to the great moral commands of worshipping and honouring God, honouring parents, abstaining from murder, &c.,—as these are equally applicable to all times and all states of society, they are equally binding upon all men, not as having been some of the commandments given to the Jews, but as being part of God's eternal and universal law, for all his reasonable creatures to obey. And here, no doubt, there is a serious responsibility for every one to determine how far what he reads in the Bible concerns himself; and no doubt, also, that if a man chooses to cheat his conscience in such a matter he might do it easily; but the responsibility is one which we cannot get rid of, because we see that parts of the Bible are not addressed directly to us; and thus we must decide what is addressed to us and what is not; and if we decide dishonestly, for the sake of indulging any evil inclination, we do but double our guilt.*

LXIII.   TO MR. SERJEANT COLERIDGE.

Rugby, June 12, 1833.

. . . . . Our Westmoreland house is rising from its foundations, and I hope, rearing itself tolerably " in auras æthereas." It looks right into the bosom of Fairfield,—a noble mountain, which sends down two long arms into the valley, and keeps the clouds reposing between them, while he looks

* The principle here laid down, is given more at length in the Essay on the Right Interpretation of Scripture, at the end of the second volume of his Sermons ; and also in the Sermon on the Lord's Day, in the third volume. It may be well to insert in this place a letter to Mr. Justice Coleridge, in 1830, relating to a libel in a newspaper, charging him with violation of the observance of Sunday.

" Surely I can deny the charge stoutly and in toto ; for, although I think that the whole law is done away with, so far as it is the law given on Mount Sinai ; yet so far as it is the Law of the Spirit, I hold it to be all binding ; and believing that our need of a Lord's day is as great as ever it was, and that therefore its observance is God's will, and is likely, so far as we see, to be so to the end of time, I should think it most mischievous to weaken the respect paid to it. I believe all that I have ever published about it is to be found at the end of my twentieth Sermon [of the first volume]; and as for my practice, I am busy every Sunday from morning till evening, in lecturing the boys, or preaching to them, or writing sermons for them. One feels ashamed to mention such things, but the fact is, that I have doubled my own work on Sunday, to give the boys more religious instruction ; and that I can, I hope, deny the charge of the libel in as strong terms as you would wish."

down on them composedly with his quiet brow; and the Rotha, " purior electro," winds round our fields, just under the house.   Behind we run up to the top of Loughrigg, and we have a mountain pasture, in a basin on the summit of the ridge, the very image of those " Saltus " on Cithæron, where Œdipus was found by the Corinthian shepherd.   The Wordsworths' friendship, for so I may call it, is certainly one of the greatest delights of Fox How,—the name of my χώριον,—and their kindness in arranging everything in our absence has been very great.   Meantime, till our own house is ready, which cannot be till next summer, we have taken a furnished house at the head of Grasmere, on a little shoulder of the mountain of Silver How, between the lake on one side, and Easedale, the most delicious of vales, on the other.

LXIV.   TO A PUPIL.

(Who had written, with much anxiety, to know whether he had offended him,
as he thought his manner changed towards him.)

Grasmere, July 15, 1833.

. . . . . The other part of your letter at once gratified and pained me.   I was not aware of anything in my manner to you that could imply disapprobation ; and certainly it was not intended to do so.   Yet it is true that I had observed, with some pain, what seemed to me indications of a want of enthusiasm, in the good sense of the word, of a moral sense and feeling corresponding to what I knew was your intellectual activity.   I did not observe anything amounting to a sneering spirit ; but there seemed to me a coldness on religious matters, which made me fear lest it should change to sneering, as your understanding became more vigorous : for this is the natural fault of the undue predominance of the mere intellect, unaccompanied by a corresponding growth and liveliness of the moral affections, particularly that of admiration and love of moral excellence, just as superstition arises, where it is honest, from the undue predominance of the affections, without the strengthening power of the intellect advancing in proportion. This was the whole amount of my feeling with respect to you, and which has nothing to do with your conduct in school matters.   I should have taken an opportunity of speaking to you about the state of your mind, had you not led me now to mention it. Possibly my impression may be wrong, and indeed it has been created by very trifling circumstances ; but I am always keenly alive on this point to the slightest indications, because it is the besetting danger of an active mind—a much more serious one, I think, than the temptation to mere personal vanity.

I must again say, most expressly, that I observed nothing more than an apparent want of lively moral susceptibility. Your answers on religious subjects were always serious and sensible, and seemed to me quite sincere ; I only feared that they proceeded, perhaps too exclusively, from an intellectual perception of truth, without a sufficient love and admiration for goodness. I hold the lines " nil admirari," &c., to be as utterly false as any moral sentiment ever uttered. Intense admiration is necessary to our highest perfection, and we have an object in the Gospel, for which it may be felt to the utmost, without any fear lest the most critical intellect should tax us justly with unworthy idolatry. But I am as little inclined as any one to make an idol out of any human virtue or human wisdom.

LXV.   TO W. W. HULL, ESQ.

Rugby, June 24, 1833.

An ordinary letter written to me when yours was, would have been answered some time since, but I do not like to write to you when I have no leisure to write at length. Most truly do I thank you, both for your affectionate recollection of my birthday, and for coupling it in your mind with the 4th of April.* May my second birthday be as blessed to me, as the 20th of August, I doubt not, has been to her. . . . . All writings which state the truth, must contain things which, taken nakedly and without their balancing truths, may serve the purposes of either party, because no party is altogether wrong. But I have no reason to think that my Church Reform pamphlet has served the purposes of the antichristian party in any way, it being hardly possible to extract a passage which they would like. The High Church party are offended enough, and so are the Unitarians, but I do not see that either make a cat's paw of me. . . . . The Bishop confirms here on Saturday, and I have had and have still a great deal to do in examining

* Alluding to his sister's birthday and death.

the boys for it. Indeed, the work is full heavy just now, but the fry are learning cricket, and we play nice matches sometimes to my great refreshment. . . . . God bless you and yours.

LXVI. TO REV. AUGUSTUS HARE.

(In answer to objections to his pamphlet.)

Grasmere, August 3, 1833.

. . . . . And now I feel that to reply to your letter as I could wish, would require a volume. You will say, Why was not the volume published before, or with the pamphlet? To which I answer that, first, it would probably not have been read, and secondly, I was not prepared to find men so startled at principles, which have long appeared to me to follow necessarily from a careful study of the New Testament. Be assured, however, that, whether mistakenly or not, I fully believe that such a plan as I have proposed, taken altogether, would lead to a more complete representation of Scripture truth in our forms of worship and preaching than we have ever yet attained to ; not, certainly, if we were only to cut away articles, and alter the Liturgy—then the effect would be latitudinarian—but if, whilst relaxing the theoretical bond, we were to tighten the practical one by amending the government and constitution of the Church, then I do believe that the fruit would be Christian union, by which I certainly do not mean an agreement in believing nothing, or as little as we can. Meantime, I wish to remind you that one of St. Paul's favourite notions of heresy is, "a doting about strifes of words." One side may be right in such a strife, and the other wrong, but both are heretical as to Christianity, because they lead men's minds away from the love of God and of Christ, to questions essentially tempting to the intellect, and which tend to no profit towards godliness. And again, I think* you will find that all the "false doctrines,"

---

* This is illustrated by his language in conversation on another subject. "Excommunication ought to be the expression of the public opinion of Christian society ; and the line of offences to be censured seems to me very much marked out by the distinction between sins against the Son of Man, and sins against the Holy Ghost. Obscene publications are of the latter character, and are actually under the ban of Christian public opinion ; and in proportion as the Church became more perfect, errors of opinion and unbelief, which are now only sins against the Son of Man, would then become sins against the Holy Ghost, because then the outward profession of Christianity would have become identical with moral goodness."

spoken of by the Apostles, are doctrines of sheer wickedness; that their counterpart in modern times is to be found in the Anabaptists of Munster, or the Fifth Monarchy Men, or in mere secular High Churchmen, or hypocritical Evangelicals—in those who make Christianity minister to lust, or to covetousness, or to ambition; not in those who interpret Scripture to the best of their conscience and ability, be their interpretation ever so erroneous.

LXVII.　TO REV. G. CORNISH.

Allan Bank, Grasmere, August 18, 1833.

. . . . . I have had a good deal of worry from . . . . . the party spirit of the neighbourhood, who in the first place have no notion of what my opinions are, and in the next place cannot believe that I do not teach the boys Junius and the Edinburgh Review, at the least, if not Cobbett and *The Examiner.* But this is an evil which flesh is heir to, if flesh, at least, will write as I have done. I am sorry that you do not like the pamphlet, for I am myself daily more and more convinced of its truth. I will not answer for its practicability; when the patient is at his last gasp, the dose may come too late, but still it is his only chance; he may die of the doctor; he must die of the disease. I fear that nothing can save us from falling into the American system, which will well show us the inherent evil of our Protestantism, each man quarrelling with his neighbour for a word, and all discarding so much of the beauty and solemnity, and *visible* power of the Gospel, that in common minds, where its spiritual power is not very great, the result is like the savourless salt, the vilest thing in the world. I would join with all those who love Christ and pray to Him; who regard him not as dead, but as living. [This part of the letter has been accidentally torn away; the substance of it seems to have been the same as that of Letters LVIII. and LXVI.] . . . . . Make the [Church a] living and active society, like that of the first Christians [and then], differences of opinion will either cease or will signify nothing. [Look] through the Epistles, and you will find nothing there condemned as [heresy] but what was mere wickedness; if you consider the real nature and connexion of the tenets condemned. For such differences of opinion as exist amongst Christians now, the 14th chapter of the Romans is the applicable lesson—not such passages as Titus iii. 10, or

2 John 10, 11, or Jude 3, (that much abused verse !) or 19
or 23. There is one anathema, which is indeed holy and just,
and most profitable for ourselves as well as for others (1 Corinth.
xvi. 22,) but this is not the anathema of a fond theology . . . .
Lo ! I have written you almost another pamphlet, instead of
telling you of my wife and the fry, who for more than five weeks
have been revelling amongst the mountains. But as far as
scenery goes, I would rather have heath and blue hills all the
year, than mountains for three months, and Warwickshire for
nine, with no hills, either blue or brown, no heath, no woods,
no clear streams, no wide plains for lights and shades to play
over, nay, no banks for flowers to grow upon, but one monotonous undulation of green fields and hedges, and very fat
cattle. But we have each our own work, and our own enjoyments, and I am sure that I have more than I can ever be
sufficiently thankful for.

LXVIII.   TO REV. JULIUS HARE.

Rugby, October 7, 1833.

. . . . . In Italy you met Bunsen, and can now sympathize with the all but idolatry with which I regard him. So
beautifully good, so wise, and so noble-minded ! I do not
believe that any man can have a deeper interest in Rome than
I have, yet I envy you nothing so much in your last winter's
stay there, as your continued intercourse with Bunsen. It is
since I saw you that I have been devouring with the most intense admiration the third volume of Niebuhr. The clearness
and comprehensiveness of all his military details is a new
feature in that wonderful mind, and how inimitably beautiful is that brief account of Terni. You will not, I trust, misinterpret, when I say that this third volume set me at work again
in earnest, on the Roman History, last summer. As to any
man's being a fit continuator of Niebuhr, that is absurd ; but I
have at least the qualification of an unbounded veneration for
what he has done, and, as my name is mentioned in his book,
I should like to try to embody, in a continuation of the Roman
History, the thoughts and notions which I have learnt from
him. Perhaps I may trouble you with a letter on this subject,
asking, as I have often done before, for information.*

* This alludes to a plan he   own Roman History with the Punic
at first entertained of beginning his   wars.

LXIX. TO MR. SERJEANT COLERIDGE.

Rugby, October 23, 1833.

I love your letters dearly, and thank you for them greatly ; your last was a great treat, though I may seem not to have shown my sense of it by answering it so leisurely. First of all, you will be glad to hear of the birth of my eighth living child, a little girl, to whom we mean to give an unreasonable number of names, Frances Bunsen Trevenen Whately ; the second after my valued friend, the Prussian Minister at Rome, of whom, as I know not whether I shall ever see him again, I wished to have a daily present recollection in the person of one of my children. I wish I could show you his two letters, one to me on the political state of Europe, and one to Dr. Nott on the perfect notion of a Christian Liturgy. I am sure that you would love and admire with me, the extraordinary combination of piety and wisdom and profound knowledge and large experience which breathes through every line of both.

. . . . . I go all lengths with you in deprecating any increase of political excitement, anything that shall tend to make politics enter into a man's daily thoughts and daily practice. When I first projected *The Englishman's Register*, I wrote to my nephew my sentiments about it in full; a letter which I keep, and may one day find it convenient to publish as my confession of faith ; in this letter I protested strongly against making the *Register* exclusively political, and entered at large into my reasons for doing so. Undoubtedly I fear that the Government lend an ear too readily to the Utilitarians and others of that coarse and hard stamp, whose influence can be nothing but evil. In church matters they have got Whately, and a signal blessing it is that they have him and listen to him ; a man so good and so great that no folly or wickedness of the most vile of factions will move him from his own purposes, or provoke him in disgust to forsake the defence of the Temple. . . . . .

I cannot say how I am annoyed, both on public and private grounds, by these extravagances [at Oxford ;] on private grounds, from the gross breaches of charity to which they lead good men ; and on public, because if these things do produce any effect on the clergy, the evil consequences to the nation are not to be calculated ; for what is to become of the Church, if the clergy begin to exhibit an aggravation of the worst superstitions of the Roman Catholics, only stripped of that consistency, which stamps even the errors of the Romish system with something of a character of greatness. It seems presumption in me to press any point upon your consideration, seeing in how many things I have learned to think from you. But it has always seemed to me that an extreme fondness for our "dear mother the panther"* is a snare, to which the noblest minds are most liable. It seems to me that all, absolutely all, of our religious affections and veneration should go to Christ Himself, and that Protestantism, Catholicism, and every other name, which expresses Christianity and some differentia or proprium besides, is so far an evil, and, when made an object of attachment, leads to superstition and error. Then, descending from religious grounds to human, I think that one's natural and patriotic sympathies can hardly be too strong; but, historically, the Church of England is surely of a motley complexion, with much of good about it, and much of evil, no more a fit subject for enthusiastic admiration than for violent obloquy. I honour and sympathize entirely with the feelings entertained; I only think that they might all of them select a worthier object; that, whether they be pious and devout, or patriotic, or romantic, or of whatever class soever, there is for each and all of these a true object on which they may fasten without danger and with infinite benefit; for surely the feeling of entire love and admiration is one, which we cannot safely part with, and there are provided, by God's goodness, worthy and perfect objects of it; but these can never be human institutions, which, being necessarily full of imperfection, require to be viewed with an impartial judgment, not idolized by an uncritical affection. And that common metaphor about our "Mother the Church" is unscriptural and mischievous, because the feelings of entire filial reverence and love which we owe to a parent, we do not owe to our fellow Christians; we owe them brotherly love, meekness, readiness to bear, &c., but not filial reverence, "to them I give place by subjection, no not for an hour." Now, if I were a Utilitarian, I should not care for what I think a misapplication of the noblest feelings; for then I should not care for the danger to which this misapplication exposes the feelings themselves; but as it is, I dread to see the evils of the Reformation of the sixteenth century repeated over again; superstition provoking profaneness, and ignorance and

* Dryden's Hind and Panther.

violence on one side leading to equal ignorance and violence on the other, to the equal injury of both truth and love. I should feel greatly obliged to you if you could tell me anything that seems to you a flaw in the reasoning of those pages of the Postscript of my pamphlet which speak of Episcopacy, and of what is commonly called the " alliance between Church and State." In the last point I am far more orthodox, according to the standard of our reformers, than either the Toleration* men or the High Church men, but those notions are now out of fashion, and what between religious bigotry and civil licentiousness, all, I suppose, will go. But I will have compassion on your patience.

It was delightful to hear of you and yours in Devonshire. I wish they would put you on a commission of some sort or other that might take you into Westmoreland some summer or winter. When our house is quite finished, do you not think that the temptation will be great to me to go and live there, and return to my old Laleham way of life on the Rotha, instead of on the Thames? But independent of more worldly considerations, my great experiment here is in much too interesting a situation to abandon lightly. You will be amused when I tell you that I am becoming more and more a convert to the advantages of Latin and Greek verse, and more suspicious of the mere *fact* system, that would cram with knowledge of particular things, and call it information. My own lessons with the Sixth Form are directed now to the best of my power to the furnishing rules or formulæ for them to work with, *e.g.* rules to be observed in translation, principles of taste as to the choice of English words, as to the keeping or varying idioms and metaphors, &c. ; or in history, rules of evidence or general forms for the dissection of campaigns, or the estimating the importance of wars, revolutions, &c. This, together with the opening as it were the sources of knowledge, by telling them where they can find such and such things, and giving them a notion of criticism, not to swallow things whole, as the scholars of an earlier period too often did—is what I am labouring at, much more than at giving information. And the composition is mending decidedly; though speaking to an Etonian, I am well aware that our amended state would be with you a very degenerate one. But we are looking up certainly, and pains

---

* "I should like," he said, "to see the Toleration Act and the Act of Uniformity burnt side by side."

are taking in the lower Forms, of which we shall I think soon
see the fruit. . . . .

I am getting on with Thucydides myself, and am nearly in
the middle of the seventh book ; at Allan Bank in the summer
I worked on the Roman History, and hope to do so again in
the winter. It is very inspiring to write with such a view
before one's eyes as that from our drawing-room at Allan
Bank, where the trees of the shrubbery gradually run up into
the trees of the cliff, and the mountain side, with its infinite
variety of rocky peaks and points on which the cattle expatiate,
rises over the tops of the trees. Trevenen Penrose and his
wife were with us for nearly a month in Westmoreland, and
enjoyed the country as much as we did. He is labouring
most admirably and effectually at Coleby. I saw Southey once
at Keswick, and had a very friendly interview: he asked me
to go over and stay with him for a day or two in the winter,
which I think I should like much. His cousin, Herbert Hill,
is now the tutor to my own boys. He lives in Rugby, and the
boys go to him every day to their great benefit. He is a
Fellow of New College, and it rejoices me to talk over Winchester recollections together. Your little goddaughter is my
pupil twice a week in Delectus. . . . . Her elder sister is my
pupil three times a week in Virgil, and once in the Greek Testament, and promises to do very well in both. I have yet a
great many things to say, but I will not keep my letter ; how
glad I should be if you could ever come down to us for even a
single Sunday, but I suppose I must not ask it.

LXX. TO JACOB ABBOTT.

(Author of The Young Christian, &c.)

Rugby, November 1, 1833.

Although I have not the honour of being personally known
to you, yet my great admiration of your little book, The
Young Christian, and the circumstance of my being engaged,
like yourself, in the work of education, induce me to hope that
you will forgive the liberty I am taking in now addressing you.
A third consideration weighs with me, and in this I feel sure
that you will sympathize ; that it is desirable on every occasion
to enlarge the friendly communication of our country with
yours. The publication of a work like yours in America was

far more delightful to me than its publication in England could have been. Nothing can be more important to the future welfare of mankind than that God's people, serving Him in power and in love, and in a sound mind, should deeply influence the national character of the United States, which in many parts of the Union is undoubtedly exposed to influences of a very different description, owing to circumstances apparently beyond the control of human power and wisdom.

I request your acceptance of a volume of Sermons, most of which, as you will see, were addressed to boys or very young men, and which therefore coincide in intention with your own admirable book.* And at the same time I venture to send you a little work of mine on a different subject, for no other reason, I believe, than the pleasure of submitting my views upon a great question to the judgment of a mind furnished morally and intellectually as yours must be.

I have been for five years head of this school. [After describing the manner of its foundation and growth.] You may imagine then that I am engaged in a great and anxious labour, and must have considerable experience of the difficulty of turning the young mind to know and love God in Christ.

I have understood that Unitarianism is becoming very prevalent in Boston, and I am anxious to know what the complexion of Unitarianism amongst you is. I mean whether it is Arian or Socinian, and whether its disciples are for the most part men of hard minds and indifferent to religion, or whether they are zealous in the service of Christ, according to their own notions of his claims upon their gratitude and love. It has long been my firm belief that a great proportion of Unitarianism might be cured by a wiser and more charitable treatment on the part of their adversaries, if these would but consider what is the main thing in the Gospel, and that even truth is not always to be insisted upon, if by forcing it upon the reception of those who are not prepared for it, they are thereby tempted to renounce what is not only true but essential—a character which assuredly does not belong to all true propositions, whether about things human or things divine.

---

* His opinion of the Corner-stone is given in a note to the second Appendix of his third volume of Sermons, p. 440.

LXXI. TO THE ARCHBISHOP OF DUBLIN.

Rugby, November 8, 1833.

. . . . . Would any good be likely to come of it, if I were one day to send you a specimen of such corrections in our authorized version of the Scriptures, such as seem to me desirable, and such as could shock no one? I have had, and am having daily, so much practice in translation, and am taking so much pains to make the boys vary their language and their phraseology, according to the age and style of the writer whom they are translating, that I think I may be trusted for introducing no words or idiom unsuited to the general style of the present translation, nothing to lessen the purity of its Saxon, or to betray a modern interpolation. My object would be to alter in the very language, as far as I could guess it, which the translators themselves would have used, had they only had our present knowledge of Greek. I think also that the results of modern criticism should so far be noticed, as that some little clauses, omitted in all the best MSS., should be printed in italics, and important various readings of equal or better authority than the received text, should be noticed in the margin. Above all, it is most important that the division into chapters should be mended, especially as regards the public reading in the Church, and that the choice of lessons from the Old Testament should be improved, which really could hardly have been worse, unless it had been done on purpose.

It is almost inconceivable to me that you should misunderstand any book that you read : and, if such a thing does happen, I am afraid that it must be the writer's fault. But I cannot remember that I have altered my opinions since my pamphlet (on the Catholic claims), nor do I see anything there inconsistent with my doctrine (of Church and State) in the Postscript to the pamphlet on Church Reform. I always grounded the right to emancipation on the principle that Ireland was a distinct nation, entitled to govern itself. I know full well that my principles would lead to the establishment of the Roman Catholic religion in three-fourths of Ireland ; but this conclusion was not wanted then, and the right to emancipation followed à fortiori from the right to govern themselves as a nation, without entering upon the question of the Establishment. Those who think that Catholicism is idolatry ought, on their own principles, to move heaven and earth for the repeal of the Union, and to let O'Connell rule his Kelts their own way. I think that a Catholic is a member of Christ's Church just as much as I am; and I could well endure one form of that Church in Ireland, and another in England. And if you look (it is to be found in the second volume of Voltaire's Siècle de Louis XIV.) for the four Articles resolved on by the Gallican Church in the middle of the seventeenth century, you will see a precedent and a means pointed out, whereby every Roman Catholic national Church may be led to reform itself; and I only hope that when they do they will reform themselves so far as to be thorough Christians, and avoid, as they would a dog or a viper, the errors which marred the Protestant Reformation of the sixteenth century, destroying things most noble and most purifying, as well as things superstitious and hurtful.

[After speaking of a reported calumny against himself in Oxford.] I will trust no man when he turns fanatic; and really these High Churchmen are far more fanatical and much more foolish than Irving himself. Irving appealed to the gifts of tongues and of healing, which he alleged to exist in his congregation, as proofs that the Holy Spirit was with them; but the High Churchmen abandon reason and impute motives, and claim to be Christ's only Church,—and where are the "signs of an apostle" to be seen among them, or where do they pretend to show them?

LXXII. TO W. W. HULL, ESQ.

Rugby, February 24, 1834.

. . . . . . I have, as usual, many things on hand, or rather in meditation; but time fails me sadly, and my physical constitution seems to require more sleep than it did, which abridges my time still more. Yet I was never better or stronger than I was in Westmoreland during the winter, or indeed than I am now. But I feel, more and more, that, though my constitution is perfectly sound, yet it is not strong; and my nervous system would soon wear me out if I lived in a state of much excitement. Body and mind alike seem to repose greedily in delicious quiet without dulness, which we enjoy in Westmoreland.

It is easier to speak of body and mind than of that which is more worth than either. I doubt whether we have enough of Christian Confession amongst us;* the superstition of Popery

------

* See Sermons, vol. iii. p. 313.

in this, as in other matters, doubly injured the good which it corrupted ; first by corrupting it, and then, " traitor like, by betraying it to the axe " of too hasty reformation.   Yet surely one object of the Christian Church was to enable us to aid in bearing one another's burthens ; not to enable a minister to pretend to bear those of all his neighbours. One is so hindered from *speaking* of one's spiritual state, that one is led even to *think* of it less frequently than is wholesome.   I am learning to think more and more how unbelief is at the bottom of all our evil ; how our one prayer should be " Increase our faith." And we do fearfully live, as it were, out of God's atmosphere ; we do not keep that continual consciousness of His reality which I conceive we ought to have, and which should make him more manifest to our souls than the Shechinah was to the eyes of the Israelites.   I have many fresh sermons ; and my wife wants another volume printed ; but I do not think there would be enough of systematic matter to make a volume, and mere specimens of my general preaching I have given already.   I trust you will come next week ; life is too uncertain to admit of passing over opportunities.   You have heard, probably, that Augustus Hare is likely soon to follow poor Lowe, and to lay his bones in Rome ; he is far gone, they say, in a consumption. May God bless you, my dear Hull, in Jesus Christ, both you and yours for ever.

LXXIII.   TO REV. F. C. BLACKSTONE.

Rugby, February 26, 1834.

. . . . . I often think what may be your views of the various aspects of things in general—to what notions you are more and more becoming wedded ; for, though I think that men, who are lovers of truth, become less and less attached to any mere party as they advance in life, and certainly become, in the best sense of the word, more tolerant, yet their views also acquire greater range and consistency, and what they once saw as scattered truths, they learn to combine with one another, so as to make each throw light on the other ; so that their principles become more fixed, while their likings or dislikings of particular persons or parties become more moderate. . . . .

Our residence in Westmoreland attaches us all to it more and more ; the refreshment which it affords me is wonderful ; and it is especially so in the winter, when the country is quieter, and actually, as I think, more beautiful than in summer. I was often reminded, as I used to come home to Grasmere of an evening, and seemed to be quite shut in by the surrounding mountains, of the comparison of the hills standing about Jerusalem, with God standing about his people. The impression which the mountains gave me, was never one of bleakness or wildness, but of a sort of paternal shelter and protection to the valley; and in those violent storms, which were so frequent this winter, our house lay snug beneath its cliff, and felt comparatively nothing of the wind. We had no snow in the valleys, but frequently a thick powdering on the higher mountains while all below was green and warm. The School goes on very fairly; with its natural proportion of interest and of annoyance. I am daily more and more struck with the very low average of intellectual power, and of the difficulty of meeting those various temptations, both intellectual and moral, which stand in boys' way; a school shows as undisguisedly as any place the corruption of human nature, and the monstrous advantage with which evil starts, if I may so speak, in its contest with good.

LXXIV. TO REV. JULIUS HARE.

(On the death of his brother, Augustus Hare.)

Rugby, March 10, 1834.

I will not trouble you with many words; but it seemed unnatural to me not to write, after the account from Rome, which Arthur Stanley this morning communicated to me. I do not attempt to condole, or to say anything further, than that, having known your brother for more than twenty-five years, and having experienced unvaried kindness from him since I first knew him, I hope that I can in some degree appreciate what you have lost. Of all men whom I ever knew, he was one of whom Bunsen most strongly reminded me, so that he seemed like Bunsen in England, as Bunsen had seemed like him in Italy. God grant that I may try to resemble them both in all the nobleness and beauty of their goodness.

LXXV.   TO REV. DR. HAWKINS.

(With regard to tracts which he had intended to circulate in opposition to the early numbers of the Tracts for the Times.)

Rugby, April 14, 1834.

The concluding part of your letter is a very good reason for my not asking you to trouble yourself any further about my papers. If the Tracts in question are not much circulated, then, of course, it would be a pity to make them known by answering them; but this is a matter of fact which I know not how to ascertain. They are strenuously puffed by the British Magazine, and strenuously circulated amongst the clergy; of course I do not suppose that any living man out of the clergy is in the slightest danger of being influenced by them, except so far as they may lead him to despise the clergy for countenancing them.

You do not seem to me to apprehend the drift of these Tracts, nor the point of comparison between these and St. Paul's adversaries. If they merely broached one opinion and I combated it, it might be doubted which of us most disturbed the peace of the Church. But they are not defending the lawfulness or expediency of Episcopacy, which certainly I am very far from doubting, but its *necessity*; a doctrine in ordinary times gratuitous, and at the same time harmless, save as a folly. But now the object is to provoke the clergy to resist the Government Church Reforms, and if, for so resisting, they get turned out of their livings, to maintain that they are the true clergy, and their successors schismatics; above all, if the Bishops were deprived, as in King William's time, to deny the authority of the Bishops who may succeed them, though appointed according to the law of the land. All this is essentially schismatical and anarchical: in Elizabeth's time it would have been reckoned treasonable; and in answering it, I am not attacking Episcopacy, or the present constitution of the English Church, but simply defending the common peace and order of the Church against a new outbreak of Puritanism, which will endure nothing but its own platform.

Now, to insist on the necessity of Episcopacy is exactly like insisting on the necessity of circumcision; both are and were lawful, but to insist on either as *necessary*, is unchristian, and binding the Church with a yoke of carnal ordinances; and the reason why circumcision, although expressly commanded once, was declared not binding upon Christians, is much stronger against the binding nature of Episcopacy, which never was commanded at all; the reason being, that all forms of government and ritual are in the Christian Church indifferent, and to be decided by the Church itself, pro temporum et locorum ratione. "the Church" not being the clergy, but the congregation of Christians.

If you will refer me to any book which contains what you think the truth, put sensibly, on the subject of the Apostolical Succession, I shall really be greatly obliged to you to mention it. I went over the matter again in the holidays with Warburton and Hooker; and the result was a complete confirmation of the views which I have entertained for years, and a more complete appreciation of the confusions on which the High Church doctrine rests, and of the causes which have led to its growth at different times.

By the way, I never accused Keble or Newman of saying that to belong to a true Church would save a bad man ! but of what is equally unchristian, that a good man was not safe unless he belonged to an Episcopal Church; which is exactly not allowing God's seal without it be countersigned by one of their own forging. Nor did I say they were bad men, but much the contrary; though I think that their doctrine, which they believe, I doubt not, to be true, is in itself schismatical, profane, and unchristian. And I think it highly important that the evils of the doctrine should be shown in the strongest terms; but no word of mine has impeached the sincerity or general character of the men; and, in this respect, I will carefully avoid every expression that may be thought uncharitable.

LXXVI.   TO W. W. HULL, ESQ.

Rugby, April 30, 1834.

. . . . . . I have indeed written a large part of a volume on Church and State, but it had better be broken up into smaller portions, to be published at first separately, though afterwards it may be altogether.   My outline of the whole question is this:—
I. That the State, being the only power sovereign over human life, has for its legitimate object the happiness of its people— their highest happiness, not physical only, but intellectual and moral; in short, the highest happiness of which it has a con-

ception.　This was held, I believe, nearly unanimously, till the eighteenth century.　Warburton, the Utilitarians, and I fear Whately,* maintain, on the contrary, that the State's only object is "the conservation of body and goods."　They thus play, though unintentionally, into the hands of the upholders of ecclesiastical power, by destroying the highest duty and prerogative of the Commonwealth.　II.　Ecclesiastical officers may be regarded in two lights only, as sovereigns, or independent; if they are *priests*, or if they are *rulers*.　A. *Priests* are independent, as deriving either from supposed holiness of race or person, or from their exclusive knowledge of the Divine Will, a title to execute certain functions, which none but themselves can perform; and therefore these functions, being of prime necessity, enable them to treat with the State, not as members or subjects of it, but as foreigners conferring on it a benefit, and selling this on their own terms.　B. *Rulers*, of course, are independent and sovereign, ipsâ vi termini.　III. But the ecclesiastical officers of Christianity, are by God's appointment neither priests nor rulers.　A.　Not *Priests*, for there is one only Priest, and all the rest are brethren; none has any holiness of person or race more than another, none has any exclusive possession of divine knowledge.　B.　Not *Rulers*, for Christianity not being a θρήσκεια or ritual service, but extending to every part of human life, the rules of Christians, quà Christians, must rule them in all matters of principle and practice; and, if this power be given to Bishops, Priests, and Deacons, by divine appointment, Innocent the Third was right, and every Christian country should be like Paraguay. You shall have the rest by-and-by; meantime, I send you up a paper about the Universities.　If you like it, sign it, and try to get others to do so; if you do not, burn it.

LXXVII.　TO REV. JULIUS HARE.

Rugby, May 12, 1834.

. . . . . . I would admit Unitarians, like all other Christians, if the University system were restored, and they might have halls of their own.　Nay, I would admit them at the colleges if they would attend chapel and the Divinity Lectures, which

* The views of Archbishop Whately set forth in the fourth and fifth volumes on this subject were afterwards fully of his essays.

some of them, I think, would do.   But everything seems to me
falling into confusion between two parties, whose ignorance
and badness I believe I shrink from with the most perfect
impartiality of dislike.   I must petition against the Jew Bill,
and wish that you or some man like you would expose that
low Jacobinical notion of citizenship, that a man acquires a
right to it by the accident of his being littered inter quatuor
maria, or because he pays taxes.*   I wish I had the knowledge
and the time to state fully the ancient system of πάροικοι, μέτοικοι,
&c., and the principle on which it rested ; that different races
have different νόμιμα, and that an indiscriminate mixture breeds
a perfect "colluvio omnium rerum."   Now Christianity gives
us that bond perfectly, which race in the ancient world gave
illiberally and narrowly, for it gives a common standard of
νόμιμα, without observing distinctions, which are, in fact, better
blended.

[This letter, as well as the preceding, alludes to the subjoined Declaration, circulated by him for signature.]

"The undersigned members of the universities of Oxford
and Cambridge, many of them being engaged in education,
entertaining a strong sense of the peculiar benefits to be
derived from studying at the Universities, cannot but consider
it as a national evil, that these benefits should be inaccessible
to a large proportion of their countrymen.

"While they feel most strongly that the foundation of all
education must be laid in the great truths of Christianity, and
would on no account consent to omit these, or to teach them
imperfectly, yet they cannot but acknowledge, that these truths
are believed and valued by the great majority of Dissenters
no less than by the Church of England ; and that every essential point of Christian instruction may be communicated
without touching on those particular questions on which the
Church and the mass of Dissenters are at issue.

"And, while they are not prepared to admit such Dissenters as differ from the Church of England on the most

* Extract from a letter to Mr. Serjeant Coleridge. "The correlative to
taxation, in my opinion, is not citizenship but protection. Taxation may
imply representation quoad hoc, and
I should have no objection to let the
Jews tax themselves in a Jewish House
of Assembly, like a colony or like the
clergy of old ; but to confound the
right of taxing oneself with the right
of general legislation, is one of the
Jacobinical confusions of later days,
arising from those low Warburtonian
notions of the ends of political society."
See also Preface to his Edition of
Thucydides, vol. iii. p. xv., now published in Miscellaneous Works.

essential points of Christian truth, such as the modern Unitarians of Great Britain, they are of opinion, that all other Dissenters may be admitted into the Universities, and allowed to take degrees there with great benefit to the country, and to the probable advancement of Christian truth and Christian charity amongst members of all persuasions."

LXXVIII.   *TO H. BALSTON, ESQ.*

Rugby, May 19, 1834.

. . . . . I am very glad that you continue to practise composition, but above all I would advise you to make an abstract of one or two standard works. One, I should say, in philosophy;—the other in history. I would not be in a hurry to finish them, but keep them constantly going,—with one page always clear for Notes. The abstract itself practises you in condensing and giving in your own words what another man has said; a habit of great value, as it forces one to think about it, which extracting merely does not. It further gives a brevity and simplicity to your language, two of the greatest merits which style can have, and the notes give you an opportunity of a great deal of original composition, besides a constant place to which to refer anything that you may read in other books; for having such an abstract on hand, you will be often thinking when reading other books, of what there may be in them which will bear upon your abstract.

The latter part of your letter I very heartily thank you for: it is a great over-payment of any exertions of mine when what it would be a breach of duty in me to omit is received so kindly and gratefully. At the same time I have always thought that it was quite impossible in my situation to avoid feeling a strong personal interest in most of those whom I have had to do with, independently of professional duty.

I shall be always glad to see you or to hear from you.

LXXIX.   TO W. EMPSON, ESQ.

Rugby, June 11, 1834.

. . . . . The political matters on which you touch, are to me of such intense interest, that I think they would kill me if I

---

* For the sake of convenience, an asterisk has been prefixed to the names of those correspondents who had been his pupils at Rugby.

lived more in the midst of them ; unless, as was said to be the case with the Cholera, they would be less disturbing when near than when at a distance. I grieve most deeply at this ill-timed schism in the Ministry, and as men who have no familiarity with the practice of politics, may yet fancy that they understand their principles, so it seems to me that both Lord Grey and the seceders are wrong. We are suffering here, as in a thousand other instances, from that accursed division between Christians, of which I think the very Arch-fiend must be κατ' ἐξόχην the author. The good Protestants and bad Christians have talked nonsense, and worse than nonsense, so long about Popery, and the Beast, and Antichrist, and Babylon,* that the simple, just, and Christian measure of establishing the Roman Catholic Church in three-fifths of Ireland seems renounced by common consent. The Protestant clergy ought not to have their present revenues in Ireland—so far I agree with Lord Grey—but not on a low economical view of their pay being over-proportioned to their work; but because Church property is one of the most sacred trusts, of which the sovereign power in the Church (*i.e.* the King and Parliament, not the Bishops and Clergy) is appointed by God trustee. It is a property set apart for the advancement of direct Christian purposes : first, by furnishing religious instruction and comfort to the grown-up part of the population ; next, by furnishing the same to the young in the shape of religious education. Now, the Christian people of Ireland, *i.e.*, in my sense of the word, the Church of Ireland, have a right to have the full benefit of their Church property, which now they cannot have, because Protestant clergymen they will not listen to. I think, then, that it ought to furnish them with Catholic clergymen, and the general local separation of the Catholic and Protestant districts

---

* " The Babylon of the Revelation is chiefly taken from the Babylon of the Old Testament, which it resembles in pride of power, whilst the images of wealth are from Tyre. Pagan Rome, no doubt, was the immediate object—as it is said, 'the city on the seven hills,'—then answering in power and wealth to the city here described. But in the higher sense it is the word—ὁ κόσμος ; and wherever a worldly spirit prevails, there, in some sense, is Babylon. Thus, Rev. xviii. 4 is another mode of expressing Rom. xii. 2, and Rev. xviii. 24, of 1 John iii. 13, John xv. 19."—Note on Rev. xviii. " The great secret," he said, " of interpreting the Revelation is, to trace the images back to their first appearance in the Old Testament Prophets. What to me is a decisive proof of the falsehood of the usual commentaries on the Apocalypse is, that the history which they present of the Middle Ages, and of Europe generally, is such as no one in his senses fairly reading that history would find there."

would render this as easy to effect in Ireland as it was in Switzerland, where, after their bloody religious wars of the sixteenth century, certain parishes in some of the Cantons, where the religions were intermixed, were declared Protestant and others Catholic; and if a man turned Catholic in a Protestant parish, he was to migrate to a Catholic parish, and vice versâ. If this cannot be done yet, then religious grammar-schools, Catholic and Protestant, such as were founded in England so numerously after the Reformation, would be the next best thing; but whilst Ireland continues in its present low state of knowledge and religion, I cannot think that one penny of its Church property ought to be applied to the merely physical or ordinary objects of government. I have one great principle which I never lose sight of: to insist strongly on the difference between Christian and non-Christian, and to sink into nothing the differences between Christian and Christian. I am sure that this is in the spirit of the Scriptures: I think it is also most philosophical and liberal; but all the world quarrels either with one-half of my principle or with the other, whereas I think they stand and fall together. I know not whether Mr. Spring Rice takes a strong interest in questions concerning education, but I am very anxious—the more so because of the confusions prevailing about the nature of the Universities—that the Universities should be restored, that is, that the usurpations of the heads of the colleges should be put down, according to those excellent articles of Sir W. Hamilton's, which appeared in The Edinburgh Review some time since. I think that this is even more important than the admission of the Dissenters. And, also, if ever the question of National education comes definitely before the government, I am very desirous of their not " centralizing " too much, but availing themselves of the existing machinery, which might be done to a great extent, with very little expense, and none of that interference with private institutions, or even with foundations, of which there is so great, and I think in some respects, a reasonable fear. But I will conclude and release you.

LXXX.   TO REV. DR. LONGLEY.

Rugby, June 25, 1834.

Though sorry that you did not concur with my views, yet I was not much surprised, being long since used to find myself in a minority on those matters. Yet I do not see how any man can avoid the impression that Dissent cannot exist much longer in this country as it does now ; either it must be comprehended within the Church, or it will cease in another way, by there being no Establishment left to dissent from. And as I think that men will never be wise and good enough for the first, so I see everything tending towards the second ; and this fancied reaction in favour of the High Church party seems to me the merest illusion of the world ; it is like that phantom which Minerva sent to Hector to tempt him to his fate, by making him believe that Deiphobus was at hand to help him.

Meantime our little commonwealth here goes on very quietly, and I think satisfactorily. I have happily more power than Lord Grey's government, and neither Radicals to call for more nor Tories to call for less, and so I can reform or forbear at my own discretion. . . . I find Westmoreland very convenient in giving me an opportunity of having some of the Sixth Form with me in the holidays ; not to read, of course, but to refresh their health when they get knocked up by the work, and to show them mountains and dales ; a great point in education, and a great desideratum to those who only know the central or southern counties of England. I must ask your congratulations on having finished Thucydides, of which the last volume will appear, I hope, in October. I have just completed the eighth book, and hope now to set vigorously to work about the Roman History.

LXXXI. TO THE ARCHBISHOP OF DUBLIN.

Rugby, July 2, 1834.

I must write to thank you for your Charge, which delighted me. . . . . It is delightful to read a Charge without any folly in it, and written so heartily in the spirit of a Christian Episcopacy, for which I have always had a great respect, though not exactly after the fashion of Keble and Newman. I trust, if it please God, that we shall meet this summer ; and it is truly kind in you to try to make your arrangements suit ours. . . . . I shall bring over to you my beginning of The State and the Church, which I shall like to talk over with you. . . . . The other day —— slept at our house, and fairly asked me for my opinion about the connexion of Church and State, which I gave him at some length ; and I found, as indeed he confessed, that the subject was one on which his ideas were all at sea ; and he expressed a great earnestness that something should be written on the subject before the next session of Parliament. He did not know (and I think it is a common complaint) the statutes passed about the Church in Henry the Eighth's and Edward the Sixth's reigns, and which are still the ἀρχαί of its constitution ; if that may be said to have a constitution which never was constituted, but was left as avowedly un-finished as Cologne Cathedral, where they left a crane standing on one of the half-built towers three hundred years ago, and have renewed the crane from time to time, as it wore out, as a sign not only that the building was incomplete, but that the friends of the Church hoped to finish the work whenever they could. Had it been in England the crane would have been speedily destroyed, and the friends of the Church would have said that the Church was finished perfectly already, and that none but its enemies would dare to suggest that it wanted anything to complete its symmetry and usefulness.

I have been writing two sermons on the evidences—1st, of Natural Religion, and, 2nd, of Christianity, intended for the use of those of my boys who are now leaving us for college. I mean, if I live, to preach a third next Sunday on the differ-ences between Christians and Christians, which, as our two examiners will hear it, both of whom have published pamphlets against Dissenters, will not, I suspect, be very agreeable to them. We are all very well, and rather desire our mountains, though all things have gone on very pleasantly so far ; but the half year is a long one certainly. Do you know that we have got a sort of Mechanics' or Tradesmen's Institution in Rugby ; where I have been lecturing twice upon History, and drawing two great charts, and colouring them to illustrate my lecture. I drew one chart of the History of England and France for the last 350 years, colouring red the periods of the wars of each country, black the periods of civil war, and a bright yellow line at the side, to show the periods of constitutional government, with patches of brown to indicate seasons of great distress, &c. I have some thoughts of having them lithographed for general use. . . . . .

LXXXII. TO A PERSON WHO HAD ONCE BEEN HIS LANDLORD,

*And was ill of a painful disorder, but refused to see the clergyman of the parish,
or allow his friends to address him on religious subjects.*

I was very sorry to see you in such a state of suffering, and
to hear from your friends that you were so generally. I do
not know that I have any title to write to you ; but you once
let me speak to you, when I was your tenant, upon a subject
on which I took it very kind that you heard me patiently, and
trusting to that, I am venturing to write to you again.

I have myself been blessed with very constant health ; yet
I have been led to think from time to time what would be my
greatest support and comfort, if it should please God to visit
me either with a very painful or a very dangerous illness ; and
I have always thought that in both nothing would do me so
much good, as to read over and over again the account of the
sufferings and death of Christ, as given in the different Gospels.
For, if it be a painful complaint, we shall find that, in mere
pain, He suffered most severely and in a great variety of ways;
and, if it be a dangerous complaint, then we shall see that
Christ suffered very greatly from the fear of death, and was very
sorely troubled in His mind up to the very time almost of His
actually dying. And one great reason why He bore all this,
was that we might be supported and comforted when we have
to bear the same.

But when I have thought how this would comfort me, it is
very true that one cannot help thinking of the great difference
between Christ and oneself—that he was so good, and that we
are so full of faults and bad passions of one kind or another.
So that if He feared death, we must have very much greater
reason to fear it ; and so indeed we have were it not for Him.
But He bore all His sufferings, that God might receive us after
our death, as surely as He received Christ himself. And surely
it is a comfort above all comfort, that we are not only suffering
no more than Christ suffered, but that we shall be happy after
our sufferings are over, as truly as He is happy.

Dear Mr. ——, there is nothing in the world which hinders
you or me from having this comfort, but the badness and hard-
ness of our hearts, which will not let us open ourselves heartily
to God's love towards us. He desires to love us and to keep
us, but we shut up ourselves from Him, and keep ourselves in
fear and misery, because we will not receive His goodness.

Oh ! how heartily we should pray for one another, and for ourselves, that God would teach us to love Him, and be thankful to Him, as He loves us. We cannot, indeed, love God, if we keep any evil or angry passion within us. If we do not forgive all who may have wronged or affronted us, God has declared most solemnly that He will not forgive us. There is no concealing this, or getting away from it. If we cannot forgive we cannot be forgiven. But when I think of God's willingness to forgive me every day—though every day I offend Him many times over—it makes me more disposed than anything else in the world to forgive those who have offended me : and this, I think, is natural; unless our hearts are more hard, than with our faults they commonly are. If you think me taking a liberty in writing this, I can only beg you to remember, that as I hope Christ will save me, so He bids me try to bring my neighbours to Him also ; and especially those whom I have known, and from whom I have received kindness. May Christ save us both, and turn our hearts to love Him and our neighbours, even as He has loved us, and has died for us.

LXXXIII.   TO HIS AUNT, MRS. FRANCIS DELAFIELD.

(On her 77th birthday.)

Rugby, September 10, 1834.

This is your birthday, on which I have thought of you, and loved you, for as many years past as I can remember. No 10th of September will ever pass without my thinking of you and loving you. I pray that God will keep you, through Jesus Christ, with all blessing, under every trial which your age may bring upon you ; and if, through Christ, we meet together after the Resurrection, there will then be nothing of old or young— of healthy or sickly—of clear memory or of confused—but we shall be all one in Christ Jesus.

LXXXIV.   TO CHEVALIER BUNSEN.

Rugby, September 29, 1834.

. . . . . Your encouragement of my Roman History is the most cheering thing I have ever had to excite me to work upon it. I am working a little on the materials, and have got Orelli's Inscriptiones, and Haubold's Monumenta Legalia, which seem both very useful works. But I am stopped at every turn by my ignorance; for instance, what is known of the Illyrians, the great people that were spread from the borders of Greece to the Danube?—what were their race and language? —and what is known of all their country at this moment? I imagine that even the Austrian provinces of Dalmatia are imperfectly known? and who has explored the details of Mœsia? It seems to me that a Roman History should embrace the history of every people with whom the Romans were successively concerned; not so as to go into all the details, which are generally worthless, but yet so as to give something of a notion of the great changes, both physical and moral, which the different parts of the world have undergone. How earnestly one desires to present to one's mind a *peopled landscape* of Gaul, or Germany, or Britain, before Rome encountered them; to picture the freshness of the scenery, when all the earth's resources were as yet untouched, as well as the peculiar form of the human species in that particular country, its language, its habits, its institutions. And yet, these indulgences of our intellectual faculties match strangely with the fever of our times, and the pressure for life and death which is going on all around us. The disorders in our social state appear to me to continue unabated; and you know what trifles mere political grievances are, when compared with these. Education is wanted to improve the physical condition of the people, and yet their physical condition must be improved before they can be susceptible of education. I hear that the Roman Catholics are increasing fast amongst us: Lord Shrewsbury and other wealthy Catholics are devoting their whole incomes to the cause, while the tremendous influx of Irish labourers into Lancashire and the west of Scotland is tainting the whole population with a worse than barbarian element. You have heard also, I doubt not, of the Trades' Unions; a fearful engine of mischief, ready to riot or to assassinate, with all the wickedness that has in all ages and in all countries characterized associations not recognised by the law,—the ἑταιρίαι of Athens, the clubs of Paris; and I see no counteracting power. . . . . .

I shall look forward with the greatest interest to your Kirchen-und-Haus Buch; I never cease to feel the benefit which I have derived from your letter to Dr. Knott; the view there contained of Christian Worship, and of Christian Sacrifice as the consummation of that worship, is to my mind quite perfect. What would I give to see our Liturgy amended on that model ! But our Bishops cry, " Touch not, meddle not," till indeed it will be too late to do either. I have been much delighted with two American works which have had a large circulation in England ; The Young Christian, and The Corner Stone, by a New Englander, Jacob Abbott. They are very original and powerful, and the American illustrations, whether borrowed from the scenery or the manners of the people, are very striking. And I hear, both from India and the Mediterranean, the most delightful accounts of the zeal and resources of the American Missionaries, that none are doing so much in the cause of Christ as they are. They will take our place in the world, I think not unworthily, though with far less advantages in many respects, than those which we have so fatally wasted. It is a contrast most deeply humiliating to compare what we might have been with what we are, with almost Israel's privileges, and with all Israel's abuse of them. I could write on without limit, if my time were as unlimited as my inclinations ; it is vain to say what I would give to talk with you on a great many points, though your letters have done more than I should have thought possible towards enabling me in a manner to talk with you. I feel no doubt of our agree-ment ; indeed it would make me very unhappy to doubt it, for I am sure our principles are the same, and they ought to lead to the same conclusions. And so I think they do. God bless you, my dear friend ; I do trust to see you again ere very long.

LXXXV.   TO AN OLD PUPIL. (A.)

Rugby, October 29, 1834.

I thank you very much for your letter ; I need not tell you that it greatly interested me, at the same time that it also in some respects has pained me. I do grieve that you do not enjoy Oxford ; it is not, as you well know, that I admire the present tone of the majority of its members, or greatly respect their judgment, still there is much that is noble and good about the place, and you, I should have hoped, might have benefited by the good, and escaped the folly. If you have got your views for your course of life into a definite shape, so as to see your way clear before you, and this course is wholly at variance with the studies of a University, then there is nothing to be said, except that I am sorry and surprised, and should be very anxious to learn what your views are.   But if you look forward to any of what are called the learned professions, and wish still to carry on the studies of a well-educated man, depend upon it that you are in the right place where you are, and have greater means within your reach there, than you can readily obtain elsewhere.   University distinctions are a great starting-point in life; they introduce a man well, nay, they even add to his influence afterwards.   At this moment, when I write what is against the common opinion of people at Oxford, they would be too happy to say, that I objected to their system, because I had not tried it, or had not succeeded in it.   Consider that a young man has no means of becoming independent of the society about him.   If you wish to exercise influence hereafter, begin by distinguishing yourself in the regular way, not by seeming to prefer a separate way of your own.   It is not the natural order of things, nor, I think, the sound one.   I knew a man at Oxford sixteen years ago, very clever, but one who railed against the place and its institutions, and would not read for a class.   And this man, I am told, is now a zealous Conservative, and writes in the British Magazine.

As to your disappointment in society, I really am afraid to touch on the subject without clearer knowledge.   But you should, I am sure, make an effort to speak *out*, as I am really grateful for your having *written out* to me.   Reserve and fear of committing oneself are, beyond a certain point, positive evils; a man had better expose himself half a dozen times than be shut up always; and, after all, it is not exposing yourself, for no one can help valuing and loving what seems an abandonment to feelings of sympathy, especially when from the character of him who thus opens his heart, the effort is known to be considerable.   I am afraid that I may be writing at random; only believe me that I feel very deeply interested about you, and perhaps have more sympathy with your case than many a younger man; for the circumstances of my life have kept me young in feelings, and the period of twenty years ago is as vividly present to my mind, as though it were a thing of yesterday.

LXXXVI.   TO T. F. ELLIS, ESQ.

Rugby, November 21, 1834.

I was very glad to see your handwriting once again, and shall be very ready to answer your question to the best of my power, although I am well aware of its difficulty. It so happens that I have said something on this very subject in the introduction to the new volume of my sermons, which is just published, so that it has been much in my thoughts lately, though I am afraid it is easier here, as in other things, to point out what is of no use, than to recommend what is.

The preparation for ordination, so far as passing the Bishop's examination is concerned, must vary according to the notions of the different Bishops, some requiring one thing and some another. I like no book on the Articles altogether, but Hey's Divinity Lectures at Cambridge seem to me the best and fairest of any that I know of.

But with regard to the much higher question, "What line of study is to be recommended for a Clergyman?" my own notions are very decided, though I am afraid they are somewhat singular. A clergyman's profession is the knowledge and practice of Christianity, with no more particular profession to distract his attention from it. While all men, therefore, should study the Scriptures, he should study them thoroughly : because from them only is the knowledge of Christianity to be obtained. And they are to be studied with the help of philological works and antiquarian, not of dogmatical theology. But then for the application of the Scriptures, for preaching, &c., a man requires, first, the general cultivation of his mind, by constantly reading the works of the very greatest writers, philosophers, orators, and poets ; and, next, an understanding of the actual state of society—of our own and of general history, as affecting and explaining the existing differences amongst us, both social and religious—and of political economy, as teaching him how to deal with the poor, and how to remove many of the natural delusions which embitter their minds against the actual frame of society. Further, I should advise a constant use of the biography of good men ; then inward feelings, prayers, &c., and of devotional and practical works, like Taylor's Holy Living, Doddridge's Rise and Progress of Religion in the Soul, &c. &c. About Ecclesiastical History, there is a great difficulty. I do not know Waddington's book well, but the common histories, Mosheim, Milner, Dupin, &c., are all bad ; so is Fleury, except the Dissertations prefixed to several of his volumes, and which ought to be published separately. For our own Church again, the truth lies in a well ; Strype, with all his accuracy, is so weak and so totally destitute of all sound views of government, that it is positively injurious to a man's understanding to be long engaged in so bad an atmosphere. Burnet is much better in every way, yet he is not a great man ; and I suppose that the Catholic and Puritan writers are as bad or worse. As commentators on the Scriptures, I should recommend Lightfoot and Grotius ; the former, from his great Rabbinical learning, is often a most admirable illustrator of allusions and obscure passages in both the Old and New Testament ; the latter, alike learned and able and honest, is always worth reading. But I like Pole's Synopsis Criticorum altogether, and the fairness of the collection is admirable. For Hebrew, Gesenius's Lexicon and Stuart's Grammar are recommended to me, but I cannot judge of them myself. Schleusner's well-known Lexicons for the Septuagint and New Testament are exceedingly valuable as an index verborum, but his interpretations are not to be relied on, and he did not belong to the really great school of German philology. . . . . .

LXXXVII.	*TO H. HIGHTON, ESQ.

Rugby, November 26, 1834.

I have not time to send you a regular letter in answer, but you wish to hear my opinion about the Rugby Magazine before Lake leaves Oxford. I told him that what I wanted to know was, in whose hands the conduct of the work would be placed. Everything depends on this; and as, on the one hand, if the editors are discreet and inexorable in rejecting trash, I should be delighted to have such a work established ; so, on the other hand, if they do admit trash, or worse still, anything like local or personal scandal or gossip, the Magazine would be a serious disgrace to us all. And I think men owe it to the name of a school not to risk it lightly, as of course a Magazine called by the name of Rugby would risk it. Again, I should most deprecate it, if it were political, for many reasons which you can easily conceive yourself. I do not wish to encourage the false notion of my making or trying to make the school political. This would be done were the Magazine liberal : if otherwise, I should regret it on other grounds. If the editors are good, and the plan well laid down and steadily kept to, I shall think the Magazine a most excellent thing, both for the credit of the school, and for its real benefit. Only remember that the result of such an attempt cannot be neutral ; it must either do us great good or great harm.

LXXXVIII.   TO REV. J. HEARN.

Fox How, December 31, 1834.

. . . . . It delights me to find that so good a man as Mr. H. thinks very well of the New Poor Law, and anticipates very favourable results from it, but I cannot think that this or any other single measure can do much towards the cure of evils so complicated.   I groan over the divisions of the Church, of all our evils I think the greatest—of Christ's Church I mean—that men should call themselves Roman Catholics, Church of England men, Baptists, Quakers, all sorts of appellations, forgetting that only glorious name of CHRISTIAN, which is common to all, and a true bond of union.   I begin now to think that things must be worse before they are better, and that nothing but some great pressure from without will make Christians cast away their idols of Sectarianism—the worst and most mischievous by which Christ's Church has ever been plagued.

LXXXIX.   TO MR. JUSTICE COLERIDGE.

Fox How, January 24, 1835.

I do not know when I have been so much delighted as by a paragraph in *The Globe* of this morning, which announced your elevation to the Bench.   Your late letters, while they in some measure prepared me for it, have made me still more rejoice in it, because they told me how acceptable it would be to yourself.   I do heartily and entirely rejoice at it, on public grounds no less than on private ; as an appointment honourable to the Government, beneficial to the public service, and honourable and desirable for yourself ; and I have some selfish pleasure about it also, inasmuch as I hope that I shall have some better chance of seeing you now than I have had hitherto, either in Warwickshire or in Westmoreland.   For myself, when I am here in this perfection of beauty, with the place just coming into shape, and the young plantations naturally leading one to anticipate the future, I am inclined to feel nothing but joy that the late change of Government has destroyed all chance of my being ever called away from Westmoreland.   At least I can say this, that I should only have valued a Bishopric as giving me some prospect of effecting that Church Reform which I so earnestly long for—the commencement of an union with all

Christians, and of a true *Church* government as distinguished from a *Clergy* government, or from none at all. For this I would sacrifice anything; but as for a Bishopric on the actual system, and with no chance of mending it, it would only make me feel more strongly than I do at present the ἐχθίστην ὀδύνην πολλὰ φρονέοντα, μηδενὸς κρατέειν.

Wordsworth is very well; postponing his new volume of poems till the political ferment is somewhat abated. "At ille labitur et labetur," so far as I can foresee, notwithstanding what the Tories have gained at the late elections.

Have you seen your uncle's Letters on Inspiration, which I believe are to be published? They are well fitted to break ground in the approaches to that momentous question which involves in it so great a shock to existing notions; the greatest probably that has ever been given since the discovery of the falsehood of the doctrine of the Pope's infallibility. Yet it must come, and will end, in spite of the fears and clamours of the weak and bigoted, in the higher exalting and more sure establishing of Christian truth.

XC. TO REV. JULIUS HARE.

Fox How, January 26, 1835.

I cordially enter into your views about a Theological Review, and I think the only difficulty would be to find an Editor; I do not think that Whately would have time to write, but I can ask him; and undoubtedly he would approve of the scheme. Hampden occurs to me as a more likely man to join such a thing than Pusey, and I think I know one or two of the younger Masters of Arts who would be very useful. My notion of the main objects of the work would be this: 1st. To give really fair accounts and analyses of the works of the early Christian writers; giving also, as far as possible, a correct view of the critical questions relating to them, as to their genuineness, and the more or less corrupted state of the text. 2nd. To make some beginnings of Biblical Criticism, which, as far as relates to the Old Testament, is in England almost non-existent. 3rd. To illustrate in a really impartial spirit, with no object but the advancement of the Church of Christ, and the welfare of the Commonwealth of England, the rise and progress of Dissent; to show what Christ's Church and this nation have owed to the Establishment and to the Dissenters; and, on the other hand, what injury they have received from each; with a view of promoting a real union between them. These are matters particular, but all bearing upon the great philosophical and Christian truth, which seems to me the very truth of truths, that Christian unity and the perfection of Christ's Church are independent of theological Articles of opinion; consisting in a certain moral state and moral and religious affections, which have existed in good Christians of all ages and all communions, along with an infinitely-varying proportion of truth and error; that thus Christ's Church has stood on a rock and never failed; yet has always been marred with much of intellectual error, and also of practical resulting from the intellectual; that to talk of Popery as the great Apostacy, and to look for Christ's Church only amongst the remnant of the Vaudois, is as absurd as to look to what is called the Primitive Church or the Fathers for pure models of faith in the sense of opinion or of government; that Ignatius and Innocent III. are to be held as men of the same stamp,—zealous and earnest Christians both of them, but both of them overbearing and fond of power; the one advancing the power of Bishops, the other that of the Pope, with equal honesty,—it may be, for their respective times, with equal benefit,—but with as little claim the one as the other to be an authority for Christians, and with equally little impartial perception of universal truth. But then for the Editor; if he must live in London or in the Universities, I cannot think of the man. . . . .

XCI. TO REV. DR. LONGLEY.

Fox How, January 28, 1835.

I suppose, as you have an Easter vacation, that you have by this time returned or are returning to Harrow. Next week we shall be also beginning work at Rugby, with the prospect of one-and-twenty weeks before us;—too long a period, I think, either for boys or masters. In the mean time we have been here for nearly six weeks, enjoying ourselves as much as possible, though we have had much more snow, I imagine, than you have had in the south. But we have had a large and cheerful party within doors, and sufficient variety of weather to allow of a great deal of enjoyment of scenery; besides the perpetual beauty and interest of this particular place and the delight of watching the progress of all our improvements. We have done, however, at last, with workmen, and have now only to wait for Nature's work in bringing on our shrubs and trees to their maturity; though many people tell me that every additional tree will rather injure the beauty of this place than improve it.

I have tried the experiment which I mentioned to you about the Fifth Form with some modifications. I have not given the Fifth the power of fagging, but by reducing their number to about three or four-and-twenty, we have made them much more respectable both in conduct and scholarship, and more like boys at the head of the school. I do not think that we have at present a large proportion of clever boys at Rugby, and there are many great evils which I have to contend with, more than are generally known. I think, also, that we are now beginning to outlive that desire of novelty which made so many people send their sons to Rugby when I first went there. I knew that that feeling would ebb, and therefore got the school limited; or else as the flood would have risen higher, so its ebb would have been more marked; but, as it was, the limit was set too high, and I do not think that we shall keep up to it, especially as other foundation schools are every day becoming reformed, and therefore entering into competition with us. But I say this without the least uneasiness, for the school is really mending in itself; and its credit at the Universities increasing rather than falling off; and, so long as this is the case, I shall be perfectly satisfied: if we were really to go down in efficiency, either from my fault, or from faults which I could not remedy, I should soon establish myself at Fox How.

I wrote to Hawtrey to congratulate him on his appointment, and I took that opportunity to ask him what he thought of the expediency of getting up good grammars, both Latin and Greek, which, being used in all or most of the great public schools, would so become, in fact, the national grammars. I should propose to adopt something of the plan followed by our Translators of the Bible; *i.e.* that a certain portion of each grammar should be assigned to the master or masters of each of the great schools: *e.g.* the accidence to one, syntax to another, prosody to a third; or probably with greater subdivisions; that then the parts so drawn up should be submitted to the revision of the other schools, and the whole thus brought into shape. Hawtrey exclaims strongly against the faults of the Eton grammars, and I am not satisfied with Matthiæ, which seems to me too difficult, and almost impossible to be learnt by heart. Hawtrey said he would write to me again, when he found himself more settled, and I have not heard from him since. I should like to know what your sentiments are about it; it would be μάλιστα κατ' εὐχὴν to have a common grammar jointly concocted; but if I cannot get other men to join me, I think we must try our hands on one for our own use at Rugby; I shall not, however, think of this till all hope of something better* is out of the question.

It seems to me that we have not enough of co-operation in our system of public education, including both the great schools and Universities. I do not like the centralizing plan of compulsory uniformity under the government; but I do not see why we should all be acting without the least reference to one another. Something of this kind is wanted, particularly I think with regard to expulsion. Under actual circumstances it is often no penalty at all in reality, while it is considered ignorantly to be the excess of severity and the ruin of a boy's prospects. And until the Universities have an examination upon admission as a University, not a college regulation, the standard of the college lecture-rooms will be so low, that a young man going from the top of a public school will be nearly losing his time, and tempted to go back in his scholarship by attending them. This is an old grievance at Oxford, as I can bear witness, when I myself was an under-graduate just come from Winchester.

XCII. TO REV. F. C. BLACKSTONE.

Fox How, January 29, 1835.

We have now been here nearly six weeks, enjoying this country to the full, in spite of the snow, of which we have had more than our usual portion. Now, however, it is all gone, and the spring lights and gentle airs of the last few days have made the beauty of the scenery at its very highest. We have so large a party in the house, that we are very independent of any other society; my wife's two sisters and one of my nieces, besides one of our Sixth Form at Rugby, in addition to our own children. I was much annoyed at being called away into Warwickshire to vote at the election,—a long and hurried and expensive journey, with no very great interest in the contest: only as having a vote, I thought it right to go, and deliver my

---

* The necessity for such a plan was eventually obviated by his adoption of the Rev. C. Wordsworth's Greek Grammar.

testimony. We were at one time likely to have a contest in Westmoreland, but that blew over. I wish that in thinking of you with a pupil, I could think of you as enjoying the employment, whereas I am afraid you will feel it to be a burden. It is, perhaps, too exclusively my business at Rugby; at least I fancy that I should be glad to have a little more time for other things; but I have not yet learnt to alter my feelings of intense interest in the occupation. I feel, perhaps, the more interest in it, because I seem to find it more and more hopeless to get men to think and inquire freely and fairly, after they have once taken their side in life. The only hope is with the young, if by any means they can be led to think for themselves without following a party, and to love what is good and true, let them find it where they will. . . . .

The Church question remains more uncertain than ever; we have got a respite, I trust, from the Jew Bill for some time; but in other matters, I fear, Reform, according to my views, is as far off as ever; I care not in the least about the pluralities and equalizing revenues; let us have a real Chucrh Government and not a pretended one; and this government vested in the Church, and not in the clergy, and we may have hopes yet. But I dread above all things the notion either of *the* Convocation or of any convocation, in which the Laity had not at least an equal voice. As for the Irish Church, that I think will baffle any man's wits to settle as it should be settled.

XCIII. TO CHEVALIER BUNSEN.

Rugby, February 10, 1835.

I know not how adequately to answer your last delightful and most kind letter, so interesting to me in all its parts, so full of matter for the expression of so many thoughts and so many feelings. I think you can hardly tell how I prize such true sympathy of heart and mind as I am sure to find in your letters; because I hope and believe that it is not so rare to you as it is to me. . . . . I find in you that exact combination of tastes, which I have in myself, for philological, historical, and philosophical pursuits, centering in moral and spiritual truths; the exact Greek πολιτική, if we understand, with St. Paul, where the ἄστυ of our πολιτεία is to be sought for. Your Hymn Book reached me before the holidays, and I fed upon it with unceasing delight in Westmoreland. It is, indeed, a treasure; and how I delighted in recognising the principles of the Letter to Dr. Knott in the first Appendix to the volume. As to the Hymns, I have not yet read a single one which I have not thought good. I should like to know some of your favourites; for myself, I am especially fond of the Hymn 24, Seele, du musst munter werden, &c.; of 697, Der Mond ist aufgegangen; of 824, O liebe Seele, konntst du werden; of 622, Erhebt euch frohe Jubellieder; of 839, O Ewigkeit! O Ewigkeit! and of 933 and 934. I have tried to translate some of them, but have been sadly disappointed with my own attempts. But I must give you one or two stanzas of the Morning Hymn, as a token of my love to it, and to show you also, for your satisfaction, how much our language is inferior to yours in flexibility and power, by having lost so much of its native character, and become such a jumble of French and Latin exotics with the original Saxon. . . . . I shall send you, almost immediately, the third volume of Thucydides, and the third volume of Sermons. The Appendix to the latter is directed against an error which is deeply mischievous in our Church, by presenting so great an obstacle to Christian union, as well as to Christian Church Reform. Still, as in Catholic countries, "the Church," with us, means, in many persons' mouths, and constantly in Parliament, only "the clergy;" and this feeling operates, of course, both to produce superstition and profaneness—in both respects exactly opposed to Christianity. Church Reform, in any high sense of the word, we shall not have; the High Church party idolize things as they are; the Evangelicals idolize the early Reformers; their notion at the best would be to carry into full effect the intentions of Cranmer and Ridley; neither party are prepared to acknowledge that there is much more to be done than this; and that Popery and narrow dogmatical intolerance tainted the Church as early as the days of Ignatius; while, on the other hand, Christ's true Church lived through the worst of times, and is not to be confined to the small congregations of the Vaudois. The state of parties in England, and that ignorance of and indifference to general principles, which is so characteristic of Englishmen, is enough to break one's heart. I do not think that you do justice to the late government; you must compare them not with the government of a perfect Commonwealth, but with that worse than "Fæx Romuli," the Tory system that preceded them, and which is now threatening us again under a new aspect. . . . . It strikes me that a noble work might be written on the Philosophy of Parties and Revolutions, showing what are the essential points of division in all civil contests, and what are but accidents. For the want of this, history as a collection of facts is of no use at all to many persons; they mistake essential resemblances, and dwell upon accidental differences, especially when those accidental differences are in themselves matters of great importance, such as differences in religion, or, more or less, of civil liberty and equality. Whereas it seems to me that the real parties in human nature are the Conservatives and the Advancers; those who look to the past or present, and those who look to the future, whether knowingly and deliberately, or by an instinct of their nature, indolent in one case and restless in the other, which they themselves do not analyze. Thus Conservatism may sometimes be ultra democracy (see Cleon's speech in Thucydides, III.), sometimes aristocracy, as in the civil wars of Rome, or in the English constitution now; and the Advance may sometimes be despotism, sometimes aristocracy, but always keeping its essential character of advance, of taking off bonds, removing prejudices, altering what is existing. The Advance in its perfect form is Christianity, and in a corrupted world must always be the true principle, although it has in many instances been so clogged with evil of various kinds, that the Conservative principle, although essentially false since man fell into sin, has yet commended itself to good men while they looked on the history of mankind only partially, and did not consider it as a whole.*

. . . . . How you astonish and shame me by what you are yourself continually effecting and proposing to effect amidst all your official and domestic engagements. I do not know how you can contrive it, or how your strength and spirits can sup-

---

* "Cobbett is an anti-advance man to the back-bone, he is sometimes Jacobin, sometimes Conservative, but never Liberal; and the same may be said of most of the party writers on both sides, of which there is a good proof in their joint abuse of the French government, which is, I think, the most truly liberal and 'advancing' that exists in Europe, next perhaps to the Prussian, which is one of the most advancing ever known."—Extract from a Letter to Mr. Justice Coleridge in the same year.

The doctrine alluded to in these Letters was one to which he often recurred, and which he believed to be peculiarly applicable to modern Europe. "A volume," he said, "might be written on those words of Harrington, 'that we are living in the dregs of the Gothic empire.' It is that the *beginnings* of things are bad—and when they have not been altered, you may safely say that they want altering. But then comes the question whether our fate is not fixed, and whether you could not as well make the muscles and sinews of a full-grown man perform the feats of an Indian juggler; great changes require great docility, and you can only expect that from perfect knowledge or perfect ignorance."

port it.   O how heartily do I sympathize in your feeling as to
the union of philological, historical, and philosophical research,
all to minister to divine truth ; and how gladly would I devote
my time and powers to such pursuits, did I not feel as much
another thing in your letter, that we should abide in that
calling which God has set before us.   And it is delightful, if at
any time I may hope to send out into the world any young
man willing and trained to do Christ's work, rich in the combined and indivisible love of truth and of goodness.

 . . . . . It is one of my most delightful prospects to bring.
my two elder boys, and I hope their dear mother also, to see
you and Mrs. Bunsen, whether it be at Rome or at Berlin.   I
only wait for the boys being old enough to derive some lasting
benefit from what they would see and hear on the Continent.
They are too young now, for the eldest is but just twelve years
old—the second just eleven.   Your little namesake is the
smallest creature of her age that I ever saw—a mere doll walking about the room—but full of life and intelligence—and the
merriest of the merry.

I have been trying to begin Hebrew, but am discouraged
by my notions of the uncertainty of the best knowledge hitherto
gained about it.   Do you think it possible to understand
Hebrew well, that is, as we understand Greek, where the
language is more precise and more clear than even our own
could be ?   Conceive the luminous clearness of Demosthenes,
owing to his perfect use of an almost perfect language, and our
complete understanding of it ; but the interpretation of the
Hebrew Prophets* seems to me, judging from the different
Commentaries, to be almost guess-work ; and I doubt whether
it can ever be otherwise.   Then the criticism of the Old Testament, the dates of the several books, their origin, &c., all
seem to me undecided, and what Wolf and Niebuhr have done
for Greece and Rome seems sadly wanted for Judæa.

XCIV.   *TO C. J. VAUGHAN, ESQ.

Rugby, February 25, 1835.

You must not think that I had forgotten you, though your
kind letter has remained so long unanswered.   I was always

---

* This opinion was greatly modified by his later study of the Prophets.
The general coincidence of two men
so different as Lowth and Gesenius in
their interpretation of Isaiah, he used
to instance as a satisfactory proof that
the meaning of the Hebrew Scriptures
could be really ascertained.

conscious of my debt to you, and resolved to pay it; but though I write letters of business at any time, yet it is not so with letters to friends, which I neither like to leave unfinished in the middle, nor, to say the truth, do I always feel equal to writing them, for they require a greater freshness and abstractedness of mind from other matters than I am always able to command. I have been greatly delighted with all I have heard of you since you have been at Cambridge; it is vexatious to me, however, that from want of familiarity with the system, I cannot bring your life and pursuits there so vividly before my mind, as I can those of an undergraduate in Oxford; otherwise, to say nothing of my personal interest for individuals, I think that I am as much concerned about one university as the other. Lake will have told you, I dare say, all our vacation news, and probably all that has happened worth relating since our return to Rugby. In fact, news of all sorts you will be sure to hear from your other correspondents earlier and more fully than from me.

I was obliged to you for a hint in your letter to Price, about our reading more Greek poetry, and accordingly we have begun the Harrow Musa Græca, and are doing some Pindar. You may be sure that I wish to consult the line of reading at both Universities, so far as this can be done without a system of direct cramming, or without sacrificing something, which I may believe to be of paramount importance. Aristophanes, however, I had purposely left for Lee to do with the Fifth Form, as it is a book which he had studied well, and can do much better than I can.

I am doing nothing, but thinking of many things. I forget whether you learnt any German here, but I think it would be well worth your while to learn it without loss of time. Every additional language gained, is like an additional power, none more so than German. I have been revelling in my friend Bunsen's collection of hymns, and have lately got a periodical work on Divinity, published by some of the best German Divines, Theologische Studien und Kritiken. I mention these, because they are both so utterly unlike what is called Rationalism, and at the same time so unlike our High Church or Evangelical writings; they seem to me to be a most pure transcript of the New Testament, combining in a most extraordinary degree the spirit of love with the spirit of wisdom.

It is a very hard thing, I suppose, to read at once passionately and critically, by no means to be cold, captious, sneering, or scoffing; to admire greatness and goodness with an intense love and veneration, yet to judge all things; to be the slave neither of names nor of parties, and to sacrifice even the most beautiful associations for the sake of truth. I would say, as a good general rule, never read the works of any ordinary man, except on scientific matters, or when they contain simple matters of fact. Even on matters of fact, silly and ignorant men, however honest and industrious in their particular subject, require to be read with constant watchfulness and suspicion; whereas great men are always instructive, even amidst much of error on particular points. In general, however, I hold it to be certain, that the truth is to be found in the great men, and the error in the little ones.

XCV.   *TO A. P. STANLEY, ESQ.

Rugby, March 4, 1835.

. . . . . I am delighted that you like Oxford, nor am I the least afraid of your liking it too much. It does not follow because one admires and loves the surpassing beauty of the place and its associations, or because one forms in it the most valuable and most delightful friendships, that therefore one is to uphold its foolishness, and to try to perpetuate its faults. My love for any place, or person, or institution, is exactly the measure of my desire to reform them; a doctrine which seems to me as natural now, as it seemed strange when I was a child, when I could not make out, how, if my mother loved me more than strange children, she should find fault with me and not with them. But I do not think this ought to be a difficulty to any one who is more than six years old. I suppose that the reading necessary for the schools is now so great, that you can scarcely have time for anything else. Your German will be kept up naturally enough in your mere classical reading, and ancient history and philosophy will be constantly recalling modern events and parties to your mind, and improving in fact, in the best way, your familiarity with and understanding of them. But I hope that you will be at Oxford long enough to have one year at least of reading directly on the Middle Ages or modern times, and of revelling in the stores of the Oxford libraries. I have never lost the benefit of what I enjoyed in this respect, though I have often cause to regret that it is no longer within my reach.

I do not know why my Thucydides is not out; I sent off the last corrected sheet three weeks ago. I am amused with thinking of what will be said of the latter part of the Preface, which is very conservative, insomuch that I am rather afraid of being suspected of ratting; a suspicion which, notwithstanding, would be quite unfounded, as you will probably believe without any more solemn assurance on my part. Nor do I feel that I am in any greater danger of becoming a Radical, if by that term be meant one who follows *popular* principles, as opposed to or distinct from *liberal* ones. But liberal principles are more or less popular, and more or less aristocratical, according to circumstances, and thus in the application of precisely the same principles which I held two years ago, and ten years ago, I should write and act as to particular persons and parties somewhat differently. . . In other words, the late extraordinary revolution has shown the enormous strength of the aristocracy and of the corrupt and low Tory party; one sees clearly what hard blows they will not only stand, but require, and that the fear of depressing them too much is chimerical. A deeper fear is behind: that like the vermin on the jacket in Sylla's apologue, they will stick so tight to the form of the constitution, that the constitution itself will at last be thrown into the fire, and a military monarchy succeed. . . . . But of one thing I am clear, that if ever this constitution be destroyed, it will be only when it ought to be destroyed; when evils long neglected, and good long omitted, will have brought things to such a state, that the constitution must fall to save the commonwealth, and the Church of England perish for the sake of the Church of Christ. Search and look whether you can find that any constitution was ever destroyed from within by factions or discontent, without its destruction having been, either just penally, or necessary, because it could not any longer answer its proper purposes. And this ripeness for destruction is the sure consequence of Toryism and Conservatism, or of that base system which joins the hand of a Reformer to the heart of a Tory, reforms not upon principle, but upon clamour; and therefore both changes amiss, and preserves amiss, alike blind and low-principled in what it gives and what it withholds. And therefore I would oppose to the utmost any government predominantly Tory, much more one exclusively Tory, and most of all a government, at once exclusively Tory in heart, and in word and action simulating reform. Conceive the Duke of Ormond, and Bolingbroke, and Atterbury, and Sir W. Wyndham, intrusted with the administration of the Act of Settlement. So have I filled my paper; but it is idle to write upon things of this kind, as no letter will hold all that is to be said, much less answer objections on the other side.   Write to me when you can, and tell me about yourself fully.*

XCVI.   TO THE ARCHBISHOP OF DUBLIN.

Rugby, March 22, 1835.

. . . . . I have been thinking of what you say as to a book on the origin of Civilization, and considering whether I could furnish anything towards it.   But history, I think, can furnish little to the purpose, because all history properly so called belongs to an age of at least partial civilization; and the poetical or mythical traditions, which refer to the origin of this civilization, cannot be made use of to prove anything, till their character has undergone a more complete analysis.   I believe with you that *savages* could never civilize themselves, but *barbarians* I think might; and there are some races, *e.g.* the Keltic, the Teutonic, and the Hellenic, that we cannot trace back to a savage state, nor does it appear that they ever were savages.   With regard to such races as have been found in a savage state, if it be admitted that all mankind are originally one race, then I should say that they must have degenerated; but, if the physiological question be not settled yet, and there is any reason to suppose that the New Hollander and the Greek never had one common ancestor, then you would have the races of mankind divided into those improvable by themselves, and those improvable only by others; the first created originally with such means in their possession, that out of these they could work indefinitely their own improvement, the $\pi o \hat{v}\ \sigma \tau \hat{\omega}$ being in a manner given to them; the second without the $\pi o \hat{v}\ \sigma \tau \hat{\omega}$, and intended to receive it in time, through the instrumentality of their fellow-creatures.   And this would be sufficiently analogous to the course of Providence in other known cases, *e.g.* the communicating all religious knowledge to mankind through the Jewish people, and all intellectual civilization through the Greeks; no people having ever yet possessed that

---

* The latter part of this letter was occasioned by a regret expressed at his vote in the Warwickshire election. For the distinction between "Liberal and Popular principles," see his article in the Quarterly Journal of Education, vol. ix. p. 281.

activity of mind and that power of reflection and questioning of things, which are the marks of intellectual advancement, without having derived them mediately or immediately from Greece. I had occasion in the winter to observe this in a Jew, of whom I took a few lessons in Hebrew, and who was learned in the writings of the Rabbis, but totally ignorant of all the literature of the West, ancient and modern. He was consequently just like a child,—his mind being entirely without the habit of criticism or analysis, whether as applied to words or to things; wholly ignorant, for instance, of the analysis of language, whether grammatical or logical; or of the analysis of a narrative of facts, according to any rules of probability external or internal. I never so felt the debt which the human race owes to Pythagoras, or whoever it was that was the first founder of Greek philosophy.

. . . . . The interest of present questions, involving as they do great and eternal principles, hinders me from fixing contentedly upon a work of past history; while the hopelessness of persuading men, and the inevitable odium which attends anything written on the topics of the day, hinder me on the other hand from writing much about the present. How great this odium is, I really could have hardly conceived, even with all my former experience. [The rest of the letter is lost.]

XCVII. TO AN OLD PUPIL. (A.)

Rugby, March 30, 1835.

Just as I have begun to write, the clock has struck five, which you know announces the end of Fourth lesson, so that I fear I shall not make much progress now; I shall let the Sixth Form, however, have the pleasure of contemplating a very beautiful passage out of Coleridge for a few minutes longer, while I write on a few lines to you. It gave me great pleasure to find that you enjoy ——'s society so much, and I hope that it makes Oxford seem at any rate more endurable to you. I was very much interested by your story of ——'s comment upon a little burst of yours about Switzerland. I suppose that Pococuranteism (excuse the word) is much the order of the day amongst young men. I observe symptoms of it here, and am always dreading its ascendancy, though we have some who struggle nobly against it. I believe that "Nil admirari" in this sense is the Devil's favourite text; and he could not choose a better to introduce his pupils into the more esoteric parts of his doctrine.   And therefore I have always looked upon a man infected with this disorder of anti-romance, as on one who has lost the finest part of his nature, and his best protection against everything low and foolish.   Such a man may well call me mad, but his party are not yet strong enough to get me fairly shut up,—and till they are, I shall take the liberty of insisting that their tail is the longest, and the more boldly I assume this, the more readily will the world believe me.   I have lived now for many years,—indeed, since I was a very young man,—in a very entire indifference as to the opinion of people, unless I have reason to think them good and wise ; and I wish that some of my friends would share this indifference, at least as far as I am concerned.   The only thing which gives me the slightest concern in the attacks which have been lately made on me, is the idea of their in any degree disturbing my friends.   I am afraid that —— is not as indifferent as I could wish, either to the attacks in newspapers, or to the gossip of Oxford about Rugby, of which last I have now had some years' experience, and I should pay it a very undeserved compliment, if I were to set any higher value on it than I do on my friend Theodore Hook and his correspondents in *John Bull.*   It is a mere idleness to attend to this sort of talking, and as to trying to act so as to avoid its attacks,—a man would have enough to do, and would lead a strange life, if he were to be shaping his conduct to propitiate gossip.   I hold it also equally vain to attempt to explain or to contradict any reports that may be in circulation ; in order to do so, it would be necessary to write a weekly despatch at the least ; and even then it would do little good, while it would greatly encourage the utterers of scandal, as it would show that their attacks were thought worth noticing. . . . . .   You will be glad to hear that the English Essays are again very good, and so I think are some of the Latin Essays ; the verse we have not yet received.   On the other hand, there is constantly sufficient occasion to remember our humanity, without any slave to prompt us.

XCVIII. TO SIR THOMAS SABINE PASLEY, BART.

(In answer to a question about Public and Private Schools.)

Rugby, April 15, 1835.

. . . . . The difficulties of education stare me in the face whenever I look at my own four boys. I think by-and-by that I shall put them into the school here, but I shall do it with trembling. Experience seems to point out no one plan of education as decidedly the best; it only says, I think, that public education is the best where it answers. But then the question is, will it answer with one's own boy? and if it fails, is not the failure complete? It becomes a question of particulars : a very good private tutor would tempt me to try private education, or a very good public school, with connexions amongst the boys at it, might induce me to venture upon public. Still there is much chance in the matter: for a school may change its character greatly, even with the same master, by the prevalence of a good or bad set of boys ; and this no caution can guard against. But I should certainly advise anything rather than a private school of above thirty boys. Large private schools, I think, are the worst possible system : the choice lies between public schools, and an education whose character may be strictly private and domestic. This, I fear, is but an unsatisfactory opinion ; but I shall be most happy to give you all the advice that I can upon any particular case that you may have to propose, when I have the pleasure of seeing you in Westmoreland. We are just going to embark on our time of gaiety, or rather, I may say, of bustle ; for we shall not dine alone again for the next fortnight. I am going southwards instead of northwards, to my old home at Laleham, which I can reach in twelve hours instead of twenty-four. You may imagine that we often think of Fox How, and I sighed to see the wood anemones on the rock, when on Tuesday I went with all the children, except Fan, to the only place within four miles of us, where there is a little copse and wood flowers.

———— •

XCIX. † TO H. STRICKLAND, ESQ.

Rugby, May 18, 1835.

I congratulate you on your prospects of exploring Asia Minor, and I should be most happy to give you any assistance

in my power towards furthering your objects. You know, I
dare say, a map of Asia Minor published a few years since, by
Colonel Leake, and showing all that was then known of that
country. The Geographical Society will give you all information which you may need as to more recent journeys; but I
imagine little has been done of any account. What *is to be done*,
may be divided naturally into two heads, physical research,
and moral, in the widest sense of the term. As to the former,
you can need no suggestions from me. I am curious to know
about the geology—whether the salt lakes of the interior belong
to the red marl formation, and whether there are any traces of
coal. With regard to the botany, every observation, I suppose,
will be valuable—what trees and shrubs appear to be the weeds
of the soil; and whether there is any.appearance or tradition
that these have changed within historical memory; whether
there are any traces of destroyed forests, and whether the sands
have encroached or are encroaching on the available soil, either
in the valleys or elsewhere. Again, all meteorological observations will be precious :—variations of temperature at different
levels or distances from the sea; suddenness of changes of
temperature; prevailing winds, quantity of rain that falls, &c.
All facts that may throw any light upon the phenomena of
malaria are highly important; and I think it is worth while to
bear in mind the possible, if not probable, connexion between
epidemic disorders and the outbreak of volcanic agency and
electrical phenomena. The return of crops—how many fold
the seed yields in average seasons—is also, I think, a fact always
worth getting at.

Now for matters relating to man. Asia Minor has little
historical interest, except as to its coasts : you will not find any
places of note, but you may find inscriptions, and of course
coins, which may be valuable. The point for inquiry, as far
as it may be possible, seems to me to be the languages and
dialects of the country. The existence of the Basque language,
as well as of the Breton and Welsh, shows how aboriginal dialects will linger on through successive conquests in remote districts. Turkish can hardly be the universal language or, if it
is, it must be more or less corrupting with a foreign intermixture; and then, any of these corrupting words may be very
curious, as relics of the original languages; and Phrygian, we
know, had, even amongst the Greeks, a character of high
antiquity. If you find any unexplored libraries, look out for
palimpsests : in these lies our only chance of recovering any-

thing of great value; and though you will not have time to spell them out, yet a cursory glance may give you some hints as to what they are, and may enable you to direct the inquiries of others. All old or actual lines of road are worth attending to, and, of course, all statistical information. If possible, I would take a Strabo with me, and an Herodotus; also, if you go to Trebizond, the Anabasis. I should like ·to explore the valley of the Halys, which, I suppose, must be one of the finest parts of the whole country; but the greatest part of it, I imagine, will be sadly tiresome.

C. TO MR. JUSTICE COLERIDGE.

Rugby, May 20, 1835.

I have just been setting my boys a passage out of your edition of Blackstone, to translate into Latin prose, and while they are doing it, I will begin a letter to you. I have had un-mixed satisfaction in all I have heard said of you since your elevation. So entirely do I rejoice in it, both publicly and privately, that I could almost forgive Sir R. Peel's ministry their five months of office for the sake of that one good deed. I do hope I shall see you ere long, for I yearn sadly after my old friends. . . . . I live alone, so far as men friends are concerned, and am obliged more and more to act and think by myself and for myself. It was therefore very delightful to me to get your little bit of counsel touching the delay of my book, and I am gladly complying with it. But I have read more about it, and for a longer period than perhaps you are aware of; and in history, after having reached a certain point of knowledge, the after progress increases in a very rapid ratio, because the particular facts group under their general principle, and gain a clearness and instructiveness from the comparison with other analogous facts, which in their solitary state they could not have.

Your uncle said, many years ago, that, "it could not be wondered at if good men were slow to join Mr. Pitt's party, seeing that it dealt in such atrocious personal calumnies." I think I have had within the last three or four months ample reason to repeat his observation. Had you not been on the Bench, I should have consulted you as to the expediency of noticing some of them legally; and now, as far as you can

with propriety, I should much like to hear what you would
say.   The attacks go on weekly, charging me with corrupting the boys' religious principles, and intending, if they can,
to injure me in my trade.   I am assured that many copies
of the paper in which most of these libels appear, are sent
gratuitously to persons in Ireland, who have been supposed
likely to send their sons here ; and the same tone of abuse was
followed for some weeks in the *John Bull.*   I think that this
spirit of libel is peculiar to the Tories, from L'Estrange and
Swift downwards : just ask yourself, if you have known any Tory
not more engaged in public life than I am, and having given as
little ground for attack by personalities on my part, who was
abused by the Liberal papers as I have been by the Tories.
I often think of the rancorous abuse which the same party
heaped upon Burnet, and how that Exposition of the Articles,
which Bishops and Divinity Professors and Tutors now recommend, was censured by the Lower House of Convocation as
latitudinarian.   δέχομαι τὸν o'ἰωνον.

. . . . . I hope you saw Wordsworth when he was in London,
and that you enjoy his new volume.   I have been reading a
good deal of Pindar and of Aristophanes lately—Pindar after
twenty years' interval, and how much more interesting he is to
the man than to the boy.   As for Homer, it is my weekly
feast to get better and better acquainted with him.   In English
I read scarcely anything, and I know not when I shall be able
to, do it.   We go on here very comfortably, and the school is
in a very satisfactory state.   I had the pleasure of seeing some
of the best of my Rugby pupils here at Easter, and one of the
best of my Laleham ones was here a little before.   It is the
great happiness of my profession to have these relations so
dear and so enduring.   I had intended to go to Oxford to-
day, to have voted in favour of the Declaration, instead of the
Subscription to the Articles, but I could not well manage it,
and it was of little consequence, as we were sure to be beaten.
It makes me half daft to think of Oxford and the London
University, as bad as one another in their opposite ways, and
perpetuating their badness by remaining distinct, instead of
mixing.

CI.   TO REV. DR. HAWKINS.

Rugby, May 27, 1835.

. . . . . I sincerely congratulate you on being honoured with the abuse of my friend *The Northampton Herald,* in company with Whately, Hampden, and myself; and perhaps I feel some malicious satisfaction that you should be thus in a manner forced into the boat with us, while you perhaps are thinking us not very desirable companions. It was found, I believe, at the Council of Trent, that the younger clergy were far more averse to reform than the older; just as the Juniores Patrum at Rome, were the hottest supporters of the abuses of the aristocracy; and so the Convocation has shown itself far more violent and obstinate against improvement than the Heads of Houses. It is a great evil—a national evil, I think, of very great magnitude; for the Charter must be, and ought to be, granted to the London University, if you will persist in keeping out Dissenters; and then there will be two party places, instead of one, to perpetuate narrow views, and disunion to our children's children. For it is vain to deny, that the Church of England clergy have politically been a party in the country, from Elizabeth's time downwards, and a party opposed to the cause, which in the main has been the cause of improvement. There have been at all times noble individual exceptions, and, for very considerable periods; in the reign of George the Second, and in the early part of George the Third's reign, for instance, the spirit of the body has been temperate and conciliatory; but in Charles the First and Second's reigns, and in the period following the Revolution, they deserved so ill of their country, that the Dissenters have at no time deserved worse; and, therefore, it will not do for the Church party to identify themselves with the nation, which they are not, nor with the constitution, which they did their best to hinder from ever coming into existence. I grant that the Dissenters are, politically speaking, nearly as bad, and as narrow-minded; but then they have more excuse, in belonging generally to a lower class in society, and not having been taught Aristotle and Thucydides. *June 1st.* I was interrupted, for which you will not be sorry, and I will not return to the subject. I was much obliged to you for your letter, and pamphlet; but though I approve of the proposed change, yet of course it does not touch the great question.

CII.   TO A PERSON DISTRESSED BY SCEPTICAL DOUBTS.

Rugby, June 21, 1835.

I have been very far from forgetting you, or my promise to write down something on the subject of our conversation, though I have some fears of doing more harm than good, by not meeting your case satisfactorily.   However, I shall venture, hoping that God may bless the attempt to your comfort and benefit.

The more I think of the matter the more I am satisfied that all speculations of the kind in question are to be repressed by the will, and if they haunt us, notwithstanding the efforts of our will, that then they are to be prayed against, and silently endured as a trial.   I mean speculations turning upon things wholly beyond our reach, and where the utmost conceivable result cannot be truth, but additional perplexity.   Such must be the question as to the origin and continued existence of moral evil; which is a question utterly out of our reach, as we know and can know nothing of the system of the universe, and which can never bring us to truth; because if we adopt one hypothesis as certain, and come to a conclusion upon one theory, we shall be met by difficulties quite as insuperable on the other side, which would oblige us in fairness to go over the process again, and to reject our new conclusion, as we had done our old one ; because in our total ignorance of the matter, there will always be difficulties in the way of any hypothesis which we cannot answer, and which will effectually preclude our ever arriving at a state of intellectual satisfaction, such as consists in having a clear view of a whole question from first to last, and seeing that the premises are true, the conclusion fairly drawn, and that all objections to either may be satisfactorily answered. This state, which alone I suppose deserves to be called knowledge, is one which, if we can ever attain it, is attainable only in matters merely human, and only within the range of our understanding and experience.   It is manifest that the sole difficulty in the subject of your perplexity is merely the origin of moral evil, and it is manifest also that this difficulty equally affects things actually existing around us.   Yet if the sight of wickedness in ourselves or others were to lead us to perplex ourselves as to its origin, instead of struggling against it and attempting to put an end to it, we know that we should be wrong, and that evil would thrive and multiply on such a system of conduct.

This would have been the language of a heathen Stoic or Academician, when an Epicurean beset him with the difficulty of accounting for evil without impugning the power or the goodness of the gods. And I think that this language was sound and practically convincing, quite enough so to show that the Epicurean objection sets one upon an error, because it leads to practical absurdity and wickedness. But I think that with us the authority of Christ puts things on a different footing. I know nothing about the origin of evil, but I believe that Christ did know; and as our common sense tells us, that we can strive against evil and sympathize in punishment here, although we cannot tell how there comes to be evil, so Christ tells us that we may continue these same feelings to the state beyond this life, although the origin of evil is still a secret to us. And I know Christ to have been so wise and so loving to men, that I am sure I may trust His word, and that what was entirely agreeable to His sense of justice and goodness, cannot, unless through my own defect, be otherwise than agreeable to mine.

Further, when I find Him repelling all questions of curiosity, and reproving in particular such as had a tendency to lead men away from their great business,—the doing good to themselves and others,—I am sure that if I stood before Him, and said to Him, "Lord, what can I do? for I cannot understand how God can allow any to be wicked, or why He should not destroy them, rather than let them exist to suffer;" that His mildest answer would be, "What is that to thee—follow thou me." But if He, who can read the heart, knew that there was in the doubt so expressed anything of an evil heart of unbelief—of unbelief that had grown out of carelessness and from my not having walked watchfully after Him, loving Him, and doing His will,—then I should expect that He would tell me, that this thought had come to me, because I neither knew Him nor His Father, but had neglected and been indifferent to both; and then I should be sure that He would give me no explanation or light at all, but would rather make the darkness thicker upon me, till I came before Him not with a speculative doubt, but with an earnest prayer for His mercy and His help, and with a desire to walk humbly before Him, and to do His will, and promote His Kingdom. This, I believe, is the only way to deal with those disturbances of mind which cannot lead to truth, but only to perplexity. Many persons, I am inclined to think, endure some of these to their dying day, well aware of their nature, and not sanctioning them by their will, but unable to shake them off, and enduring them as a real thorn in the flesh, as they would endure the far lighter trials of sickness or outward affliction. But they should be kept, I think, to ourselves, and not talked of even to our nearest friends, when we once understand their true nature. Talking about them gives them a sort of reality which otherwise they would not have; just like talking about our dreams. We should act and speak, and try to feel as if they had no existence, and then in most cases they do cease to exist after a time; when they do not, they are harmless to our spiritual nature, although I fully believe that they are the most grievous affliction with which human nature is visited.

Of course, what I have here said relates only to such questions as cannot possibly be so answered as to produce even entire intellectual satisfaction, much less moral advantage. I hold that Atheism and pure Scepticism are both systems of absurdity; which involves the condemnation of hypotheses leading to either of them as conclusions. For Atheism separates truth from goodness, and Scepticism destroys truth altogether; both of which are monstrosities, from which we should revolt as from a real madness. With my earnest hopes and prayers that you may be relieved from what I know to be the greatest of earthly trials, but with a no less earnest advice, that, if it does continue, you will treat it as a trial, and only cling the closer, as it were, to that perfect Saviour, in the entire love and truth of whose nature all doubt seems to melt away, and who, if kept steadily before our minds, is, I believe, most literally our Bread of Life, giving strength and peace to our weakness and distractions.

CIII. TO ONE OF THE SIXTH FORM, THREATENED WITH CONSUMPTION.

Fox How, July 31, 1835.

. . . . . I fear that you will have found your patience much tried by the return of pain in your side, and the lassitude produced by the heat; it must also be a great trial not to be able to bear reading. I can say but little of such a state from my own experience, but I have seen much of it, and have known how easy and even happy it has become, partly by time, but more from a better support, which I believe is never denied when it is honestly sought.   And I have always supposed that the first struggle in such a case would be the hardest; that is, the struggle in youth or middle age, of reconciling ourselves to the loss of the active powers of life, and to the necessity of serving God by suffering rather than by doing.   Afterwards, I should imagine the mind would feel a great peace in such a state, in the relief afforded from a great deal of temptation and responsibility, and the course of duty lying before it so plain and so simple.

CIV.   TO REV. F. C. BLACKSTONE.

Fox How, July 28, 1835.

. . . . Next week we probably shall return to Warwickshire, and I expect the unusual circumstance of being at Rugby for a fortnight in the holidays, a thing which in itself I shall be far from regretting, though I certainly am not anxious to hasten away from Westmoreland.   But I often look at the backs of my books with such a forlorn glance during the half-year—it being difficult then to read consecutively—that I rather hail the prospect of being able to employ a few mornings in some employment of my own.   The school will become more and more engrossing, and so it ought to be, for it is impossible ever to do enough in it.   Yet I think it essential that I should not give up my own reading, as I always find any addition of knowledge always to turn to account for the school in some way or other. I fear, however, that I am growing less active; and I find myself often more inclined to read to the children, or to amuse myself with some light book after my day's work at Rugby, than to enter on any regular employment.

My volume of Sermons connected with Prophecy is still waiting, but I hope that it may come out before the winter.   It is a great joy to me to think that it will not give offence to any one, but will at any rate, I trust, be considered as safe, and as far as it goes useful.   I have no pleasure in writing what is unacceptable, though I confess, that, the more I study any subject, the more it seems to me to require to be treated differently from the way in which it has been treated.   It is grievous to think how much has been written about things with such imperfect knowledge, or with such narrow views, as leaves the whole thing to be done again.   Not that I mean that it can be so done in our time, as to leave nothing for posterity :— on the contrary, we know how imperfect our own knowledge is, and how much requires yet to be learned.   Still in this generation an immense step has been made, both in knowledge and in large and critical views ; and this makes the writings of a former age so unsatisfactory.   In reading them I never can feel satisfied that we have got to the bottom of a question.

. . . . . I was very much delighted to have ——— staying at Rugby for nearly a week with us in the spring.   I had not had any talk with him since he was my pupil at Laleham.   I was struck with the recoil of his opinions towards Toryism, or, at any rate, half-Toryism—a result, which I have seen in other instances where the original anti-Tory feeling was what I call "popular" rather than "liberal," and took up the notion of liberty rather than of improvement.   I do not think that Liberty can well be the idol of a good and sensible mind after a certain age.   My abhorrence of Conservatism is not because it checks liberty—in an established democracy it would favour liberty ; but because it checks the growth of mankind in wisdom, goodness, and happiness, by striving to maintain institutions which are of necessity temporary, and thus never hindering change, but often depriving the change of half its value.

CV.   TO MR. JUSTICE COLERIDGE.

Rugby, July 1, 1835.

I thank you most heartily for *both* your affectionate letters. When I suspect you of unkindness, or feel offended with anything that you say or write to me, I must have cast off my nature indeed very sadly.   Be assured that there was nothing in your first letter which you could wish unwritten, nothing that was not written in the true spirit of friendship.   I was vexed only thus far, that I could not explain many points to you, which I think would have altered your judgment as to the facts of the case.

. . . . . My dear friend, I know and feel the many great faults of my life and practice ; and grieve more than I can say not to have more intercourse with those friends who used to reprove me, I think, to my great benefit—I am sure without ever giving me offence.   But I cannot allow that those opinions, which I earnestly believe, after many years' thought and study, to be entirely according to Christ's mind, and most tending to His glory, and the good of His Church, shall be summarily called heretical ; and it is something of a trial to be taxed with perverting my boys' religious principles, when I am labouring, though most imperfectly, to lead them to Christ in true and devoted faith ; and when I hold all the scholarship that ever man had, to be infinitely worthless in comparison with even a very humble degree of spiritual advancement. And I think that I have seen my work in some instances blessed ;—not, I trust, to make me proud of it, or think that I have anything to be satisfied with,—yet so far as to make it very painful to be looked upon as an enemy by those whose Master I would serve as heartily, and whom, if I dare say it, I love with as sincere an affection as they do.

God bless you, and thank you for all your kindness to me always.

CVI.   TO C. J. VAUGHAN, ESQ.

Rugby, September 9, 1835.

..... It is very hard to know what to say of Hatch as to his bodily health, because, though appearances are unfavourable, Dr. Jephson still speaks confidently of his recovery ; but it is not hard to know what to say of his mind, which I believe is quite what we could wish it to be. He always seemed to me a most guileless person when in health—guileless and living in the fear of God—in such circumstances sickness does but feed and purify the flame which was before burning strong and brightly. He will be delighted to hear from you, and would be interested by any Cambridge news that you could send him, for I think he must find himself often in want of amusement, and of something to vary the day. I am glad that you have made acquaintance with some of the good poor. I quite agree with you that it is most instructive to visit them, and I think that you are right in what you say of their more lively faith. We hold to earth and earthly things by so many more links of thoughts, if not of affection, that it is far harder to keep our view of heaven clear and strong ; when this life is so busy, and therefore so full of reality to us, another life seems by comparison unreal. This is our condition, and its peculiar temptations ; but we must endure *it*, and strive to overcome *them*, for I think we may not try to flee from it.

. . . . . I have begun the Phædo of Plato with the Sixth, which will be a great delight to me. There is an actual pleasure in contemplating so perfect a management of so perfect an instrument as is exhibited in Plato's language, even if the matter were as worthless as the words of Italian music; whereas the sense is only less admirable in many places than the language. I am still in distress for a Latin book, and wish that there were a cheap edition of Bacon's Instauratio Magna. I would use it, and make it useful in point of Latinity, by setting the fellows to correct the style where it is cumbrous or incorrect. As to Livy, the use of reading him is almost like that of the drunken Helot. It shows what history should *not be* in a very striking manner; and, though the value to us of much of ancient literature is greatly out of proportion to its intrinsic merit, yet the books of Livy, which we have, relate to a time so uninteresting, that it is hard even to extract a value from them by the most complete distillation ; so many gallons of vapid water scarcely hold in combination a particle of spirit.

CVII. TO CHEVALIER BUNSEN.

Rugby, September 21, 1835.

. . . . . I have been and am working at two main things, the Roman History and the nature and interpretation of Prophecy. For the first I have been working at Hannibal's passage of the Alps. How bad a geographer is Polybius, and how strange that he should be thought a good one ! Compare him with any man who is really a geographer, with Herodotus, with Napoleon—whose sketches of Italy, Egypt, and Syria, in his Memoirs, are to me unrivalled—or with Niebuhr, and how striking is the difference. The dulness of Polybius' fancy made it impossible for him to conceive or paint scenery clearly, and how can a man be a geographer without lively images of the formation and features of the country which he described. How different are the several Alpine valleys, and how could a few simple touches of the scenery which he seems actually to have visited, yet could neither understand nor feel it, have decided for ever the question of the route ! *Now* the account suits no valley well, and therefore it may be applied to many; but I believe the real line was by the Little St. Bernard, although I cannot trace those particular spots, which De Luc and Cramer fancy they could recognise. I thought so on the spot (*i.e.* that the spots could not be traced), when I crossed the Little St. Bernard, in 1825, with Polybius in my hand, and I think so still. How much we want a physical history of countries, tracing the changes which they have undergone, either by such violent revolutions as volcanic phenomena, or by the slower but not less complete change produced by ordinary causes ; such as alterations of climate occasioned by enclosing and draining ; alteration in the course of rivers, and in the level of their beds ; alteration in the animal and vegetable productions of the soil, and in the supply of metals and minerals ; noticing also the advance or retreat of the sea, and the origin and successive increase in the number and variation in the line of roads, together with the changes in the extent and character of the woodlands. How much might be done by *our* society at Rome if some of its attention were directed to these points: for instance, drainage and an alteration in the course of the waters have produced great changes in Tuscany; and there is also the interesting question as to the spread of malaria in the Maremme. . . . . . I read with the greatest interest all that you say about Hebrew and the Old Testament, and your researches into the chronology and composition of the books of the New. It is strange to see how much of ancient history consists apparently of patches put together from various quarters without any *redaction.** Is not this largely the case in the books of Samuel, Kings, and Chronicles ? For instance, are not chapters xxiv. and xxvi. of 1 Samuel, merely different versions of the same event, just as we have two accounts of the creation in the early chapters of Genesis? And must not chapters xvi. and xvii. of the same book be also from different sources, the account of David in the one being quite inconsistent with that in the other ? So, again, in 2 Chronicles xi. 20, and xiii. 2, there is a decided difference in the parentage of Abijah's mother, which is curious on any supposition. Do you agree with Schleiermacher in denying Paul to be the author of the Epistles to Timothy and Titus ? I own it seems to me that they are as certainly Paul's as the Epistle to the Romans ; nor can I understand the reason for any

---

* For his full view of the apparent discrepancies of Scripture, see Sermons, volume iv. 481, 491.

doubt about the matter. And yet Schleiermacher could not write anything, I should suppose, without some good reasons for it.*

CVIII.   *TO J. P. GELL, ESQ.

Rugby, September 30, 1835.

My situation here, if it has its anxieties, has also many great pleasures, amongst the highest of which are such letters as that which you have had the kindness to write to me. I value it indeed very greatly, and sincerely thank you for it. I had been often told that I should know you much more after you had left Rugby, than I had ever done before, and your letter encourages me to hope that it will be so. You will not think that it is a mere form of civil words, when I say we shall be very glad to see you here, if you can take us in your way to Cambridge, or in Westmoreland in the winter, if you do not start at the thought of a Christmas among the mountains. But I can assure you that you will find them most beautiful in their winter dress, and the valleys very humanized. I have just seen, but not read, the second number of the Rugby Magazine. I have an unmixed pleasure in its going on,—perhaps, just under actual circumstances, more than at some former time, because I think it is more wanted. We shall soon lose Lake and Simpkinson and the others, who go up this year to the University. There is always a melancholy feeling in seeing the last sheaf carried of a good harvest; for who knows what may be the crop of the next year? But this, happily for us, is, both in the natural and in the moral harvest, in the hands of Him who can make disappointment and scarcity do His work, no less than success and plenty.

---

* "One of the greatest of modern critics, Schleiermacher, doubted the genuineness of the Epistles to Timothy. This arose from his habit, which many Germans have (though Niebuhr and Bunsen are entirely free from it), of taking a one-sided view of such questions, and suffering small objections to prevail over greater confirmations. The difference of language is merely that some expressions are used such as we may well understand a man to get into the habit of using at one time of his life and not at another, and it is absurd to let these prevail over the strong internal evidence. The fact of Timothy being spoken of as young in both Epistles, has been made an objection to considering these Epistles as later in date than the others; but it is probable that Timothy was very young when he first became known to St. Paul—perhaps not more than sixteen or seventeen. St. Paul seems to have known his grandmother." [Note of a conversation in 1840.]

CIX.   *TO A. P. STANLEY, ESQ.

Rugby, October 7, 1835.

I am delighted to find that you are coming to Rugby; in fact, I was going to write to you to try whether we could not get you here either in your way to or from Oxford,—as I suppose that, even after all the length of the long vacation, you will be at liberty before us at Christmas.   Thank you for your congratulations on my little boy's birth : he grows so much and Fan so little, that I think he will soon overtake her ; though it will be well if ever he rivals her in quickness and liveliness.

I think it probable that about the time when his old companions are beginning their new course of earthly life at the Universities, Hatch will be entering upon the beginning of his eternal life.   He grows so much worse, that yesterday he was hardly expected to outlive the day.   I think myself that his trial will be somewhat longer ; but I believe that his work is over, and am no less persuaded that his rest in Christ is sure.

I shall be glad to talk over all things with you when we meet ; be sure that you cannot come here too often :—I never was less disposed than I am at this moment to let drop or to intermit my intercourse with my old pupils ; which is to me one of the freshest springs of my life.

CX.   TO AN OLD PUPIL. (D.)

Rugby, October 30, 1835.

. . . . . . I am a little disturbed by what you tell me of your health, and can readily understand that it makes you look at all things with a less cheerful eye than I could wish.   Besides, all great changes in life are solemn things, when we think of them, and have naturally their grave side as well as their merely happy one.   This is in itself only wholesome, but the grave side may be unduly darkened if we who look on it are ourselves out of tune.   I am glad that you have written again to Thomson : his report of you to me was very satisfactory, and I have great faith in his skill.   Remember, however, that exercise must not be wearisome, and especially not wearisome to the mind, if it is to be really beneficial. I never have regarded a regular walk along a road, talking the while on subjects of interest, as exercise in the true sense of the term. A skirmish over the country is a very different thing, and so is all that partakes of the character of play or sport.

. . . . . Believe me that it is a great pleasure to me to hear from you, and you must not think that any parts of your letters are unnoticed by me, or uninteresting, if I do not especially reply to them. I value very much the expression of your feelings, and I think have a very true sympathy with them.

CXI. TO MR. JUSTICE COLERIDGE.

Rugby, October 12, 1835.

. . . . Our visit to Westmoreland was short, for we returned home early in August, to be ready for my wife's confinement. But I could not have enjoyed three weeks more; for the first week we had so much rain that the Rotha flooded a part of our grass. Afterwards we had the most brilliant weather, which brought our flowers out in the greatest beauty; but the preceding rain kept us quite green, and the contrast was grievous in that respect when we came back to the brown fields of Warwickshire. But I cannot tell you how I enjoyed our fortnight at Rugby before the school opened. It quite reminded me of Oxford, when M—— and I used to sit out in the garden under the enormous elms of the School-field, which almost overhang the house, and saw the line of our battlemented roofs and the pinnacles and cross of our Chapel cutting the unclouded sky. And I had divers happy little matches at cricket with my own boys in the School-field—on the very cricket ground of the "eleven," that is, of the best players in the school, on which, when the school is assembled, no profane person may encroach. Then came my wife's happy confinement, before which we had had a very happy visit of a day from the whole family of Hulls, and which was succeeded by a no less happy visit from the whole family of Whatelys.

Have you seen our Rugby Magazine, of which the second number has just made its appearance? It is written wholly either by boys actually at the school, or by undergraduates within their first year. I delight in the spirit of it, and think there is much ability in many of the articles.   I think also that it is likely to do good to the school.

We have lost this year more than half of our Sixth Form, so that the influx of new elements has been rather disproportionately great; and unluckily the average of talent just in this part of the school is not high.   We have a very good promise below, but at present we shall have great difficulty in maintaining our ground; and then I always fear that, where the intellect is low, the animal part will predominate; and that moral evils will increase, as well as intellectual proficiency decline, under such a state of things.   At present I think that the boys seem very well disposed, and I trust that, in this far more important matter, we shall work through our time of less bright sunshine without material injury.   It would overpay me for far greater uneasiness and labour than I have ever had at Rugby, to see the feeling both towards the school and towards myself personally, with which some of our boys have been lately leaving us. One stayed with us in the house for his last week at Rugby, dreading the approach of the day which should take him to Oxford, although he was going up to a most delightful society of old friends; and, when he actually came to take leave, I really think that the parting was like that of a father and his son. And it is delightful to me to find how glad all the better boys are to come back here after they have left it, and how much they seem to enjoy staying with me; while a sure instinct keeps at a distance all whose recollections of the places are connected with no comfortable reflections.   Meantime I write nothing, and read barely enough to keep my mind in the state of a running stream, which I think it ought to be if it would form or feed other minds; for it is ill drinking out of a pond, whose stock of water is merely the remains of the long-past rains of the winter and spring, evaporating and diminishing with every successive day of drought.   We are reading now Plato's Phædo, which I suppose must be nearly the perfection of human language.   The admirable precision of the great Attic writers is to me very striking.   When you get a thorough knowledge of the language, they are clearer than I think an English writer can be, from the inferiority of his instrument.   I often think that I could have understood your Uncle better if he had written in Platonic Greek.   His Table Talk marks him, in my judgment, ... as a very great man indeed, whose equal I know not where to find in England.   It amused me to recognise, in your contributions to the book, divers

anecdotes which used to excite the open-mouthed admiration
of the C.C.C. Junior Common Room in the Easter and Act
Terms of 1811, after your Easter vacation spent with Mr. May
at Richmond. My paper is at an end, but not my matter.
Perhaps I may see you in the winter in town.

END OF VOL. I.